UNBIND

ELODIE HART

ALCHEMY PUBLISHING LTD

For all my readers who've embraced the Alchemy family...

THANK YOU!

It's not over yet...

xx

CONTENT ADVISORY

To start with, here's a weird reverse content advisory: I'd say this is the least spicy of the Alchemy books! So please consider yourself warned and do not come for me! It's still extremely spicy - and pretty kinky - by most people's standards, but it's a little slower burn than you're used to, simply because Adam has to earn Natalie's trust outside the bedroom before he can earn it in the bedroom.

Slow burn does not mean slow paced - no sir! The tension and intrigue is there from the first chapter!

So let's get to the content:

SEXUAL:

Corporal punishment of various types, restraints of various types, light BDSM, rough sex. He has sex with someone else on the page before they know each other properly. There is no OW / OM drama.

NON-SEXUAL:

On the page: type 1 diabetes rep and graphic descriptions of hypoglycaemic episodes

Off the page but discussed: death of a child, alcoholism, parental neglect, incarceration, serious assault and loss of an eye

1

NATALIE

I play with buttons like children play with toy cars or tiny, doll-house-sized dolls: driving them over the hills and valleys of textured brocade; spinning them on shiny silk to make them sparkle; lining them up on double-faced cashmere.

There are things we don't permit ourselves to do in adulthood, I think. Things we pretty much forget how to do. Most of us wouldn't remember how to indulge in childlike play even if we wanted to, and if we did remember, we'd probably feel too stupid to give it a go.

Of all the things I love about my chosen career as a fashion designer, it's the playing. Pairing and swapping buttons and fabrics and trims; wrapping lengths of weighty duchesse satin around my body in a poor approximation of draping; piling swatches and samples of utter gorgeousness on top of each other with no rhyme or reason until suddenly, a purely accidental combination will have me gasping and clutching my heart because it's all too perfect. It's all too *right*.

The members at Alchemy would think I was a few sandwiches short of a picnic if they heard me talk like that about something that should be grown-up and serious—because it doesn't get much more grown-up and serious than running a couture brand, even if it's technically demi-couture, and even if my position as Creative Director sounds far grander than the back-breaking reality of it.

Even then.

Because the people who frequent this club are sophisticated and successful and so world-weary that they've sought this place out to provide the particular—extreme—kind of dopamine hit that their seemingly fabulous careers and lifestyles just can't manage to provide.

It's a little weird, if you think about it. By day, I play with jewelled buttons and fabric swatches and, by night, I work as the host at a fabulous, swanky sex club whose fancy Play-room provides the backdrop for the kind of playing my brain couldn't compute, even if it tried.

Because when the rich, gorgeous people who frequent Alchemy play? Believe me, they *play*.

Alchemy has hosts in The Playroom—sexy, experienced, uninhibited people who are there to ensure the members have a great time. The female hosts wear white dresses, the guys form-fitting black.

I'm not that type of host.

Not on your life.

Instead, I stick firmly to the reception desk. When a member walks up those smart sandstone steps and passes through the glossy black door, I'm the first employee they see. It's my job to be glamorous and classy and respectful and professional, and I do it with pride.

I only have to meet someone once to remember their face. I greet our guests by name, I make small talk, and, most importantly, I set the tone. I'm as key to one's first impression of the Alchemy brand as are the dimly lit crystal chandeliers that line the lobby or the sensual, heady scent of the numerous Diptyque *Baies* candles burning on every surface.

I'm not here to sell sex, exactly. I'm here to kick off their experience of exclusivity. Luxury. Desire. I'm here to reassure every member that we've got them—that only the very best that money can buy lies beyond the double doors behind me.

It's something I revel in. When you've had some—albeit fleeting—knowledge of how lavish, how privileged life can be, and then it's been ripped from you, you never, ever stop trying to get it back. It's a drug injected early on, an addiction you can never un-feel. Most of life feels like a cruel joke: the life my family leads now; the unstoppable leeching of disappointment; the sense of loss.

So when it's near, I open myself to it like a sunflower to the sun, and I bask in it. In other words, it's never a hardship to hang out at Alchemy, to soak up that wealth and entitlement and luxury.

You'd think it would hurt, but it doesn't. On the contrary, it's wonderful. It's the comfort of a log fire when you're chilled to the literal bone. It's sustenance when your soul is starved.

Or so I find, anyway. As long as I don't dwell too much on what the beautiful people I greet do when they pass through those double doors and shed their finery and transform into the animals they actually are.

The reality of running a fashion brand is far from glamorous, especially when your brand is housed in an attic in Soho. It's a little too real. Gritty. Alchemy, on the other hand, is the very opposite. It's escape. It's an alternate reality. And when I'm here, I play my part.

If I run my brand in high street yoga pants most days, I host Alchemy's guests in outfits that are as close to couture as I can make them. Gen, Alchemy's COO and the person who hired me, gives me a clothing allowance that I suspect is way more generous than it should be. I've bought a couple of things from nice stores, but I spend most of the budget on raw materials—fabrics and rhinestones and the highest quality zips—and make my own outfits.

It's chilly out tonight, but the lobby is lovely and warm, and the deceptively scary doormen are really good about closing the front door quickly each time they let someone in. They're teddybears, really.

I'm in a black velvet catsuit tonight. The velvet is synthetic, but it has a decent stretch and fits me like a second skin. It's high-necked and sleeveless, cut away at the shoulders. The matching gloves come all the way to my armpits, leaving only my shoulders exposed.

Best of all, I've embellished the gloves, neckline, waist, and matching velvet headband with an intricate garland of silver thread and leaf-shaped crystals that catch the lights of the chandeliers whenever I move and bedazzle the walls of the lobby with dancing light.

I feel good. More critically, I don't feel out of place, and that matters to me. I want to do a good job for Gen, as well as for the guys—her lovely co-founders, Rafe, Zach, and Cal. I want to represent this amazing business they've built to the best of my ability, and I want to be able to hold my own with their members, no matter how different our realities are.

Most of all, I want to show my gratitude to Gen, who met me when I served her at a nearby restaurant, took a hell of a chance on me, and jacked my pay up to over double what I was making waiting tables.

So when she arrives at the club, her husband Anton and another guy trailing in behind her, I give her a smile that's bright and sincere in equal measure, because I adore this woman. The society pages say she landed the most eligible bachelor in London when she married the billionaire Anton Wolff, but for what it's worth, I think he got the best deal. She's simply amazing: warm, and gorgeous, and driven, and badass.

Tonight, she looks like a Hitchcock heroine, her platinum hair swept back and her makeup dewy and immaculate. At a time of year when the rest of us look like corpses, she's glowing, thanks to a recent trip to the Caribbean with Anton. She's in her favourite huge black faux-fur coat from Max Mara, and I instantly recognise the pattern of the gold sequins visible at her neck as belonging to Zuhair Murad's current Autumn/Winter collection.

I could live vicariously through this woman's wardrobe all day long.

The guys are laughing and joking behind her as they wait. Anton, too, looks tanned and well—he's older but ridiculously dashing—and the other guy has his back to me. He's seriously tall, taller even than Anton, with a head of dark curls.

'Evening, Nat,' Gen says, laying her evening bag on the lectern as I check her and Anton in on the iPad. 'How's tricks?'

'Good,' I tell her. 'It's busy in there.'

'Always happy to hear that,' she says, peering over the lectern to get a better look at my outfit. 'Is that a *catsuit*? Holy shit, it's incredible.'

'It is. Thanks.' I smile happily, because a sartorial seal of approval from Gen always makes me feel better. I take a step back and hold my arms out so she can see better. She sweeps her gaze over me approvingly.

'Stunning. Did you make it?'

'You know it.'

She shakes her head. 'Bloody amazing. You clever, clever girl. Don't be a stranger when you're running Dior, will you?'

I smile ruefully at her ridiculous suggestion as I look down at the iPad again. 'I wish. Just one guest tonight, is it?'

Members can sign in up to three guests each month. Their guests aren't party to the same rigorous background checks and interviews that the members undergo, but they have to electronically sign an NDA, an acknowledgment of the code of conduct here at Alchemy, and an understanding that failure to comply with said rules can jeopardise the membership of whoever is signing them in.

In other words, if you invite someone along, you'd better be damn sure they'll behave themselves (even if *good behaviour* at Alchemy means something quite different from its meaning at most other elegant London establishments).

'Yep, just one,' Gen says as I hand her the stylus and the iPad with the necessary paperwork loaded up. 'You should meet Adam, actually. He runs a few fashion brands.' She cranes her neck. 'Adam, darling? Come here. We need you to sign your life away before we unleash you on all those unsuspecting women.'

He turns, and steps in beside Gen at the lectern, and oh my God.

Oh my fucking God.

It's him.

2

NATALIE

Have you ever seen a celebrity in the flesh? I have, a few times. Mainly here. It's always surreal, seeing the flesh-and-blood version of what you're used to seeing as pixels. It can even be underwhelming. You know, when you can see up close just how much work they've had done, or when the guys are a good three or four inches shorter than their Instagram feed would have you believe.

This guy is anything but underwhelming as he towers above me, in front of me, his rich-guy cologne invading my nostrils and his very presence invading my nervous system.

Gen's voice cuts through the tangled blur of my emotions like a speedboat through a swamp. 'Nat? *Nat.* Are you okay? Are you crashing?'

I'm conscious, somewhere, of finding that mildly amusing, because, bless her, this isn't my blood glucose.

This is something far, far worse.

I manage to shake my head as I hold onto the edge of the lectern, keeping my eyes squeezed tightly shut. My hair falls over my face. I must look absolutely ridiculous, but it's far better than having to look at him. I know she means well, but the heat radiating from my skin is enough to reassure anyone that this isn't a hypoglycaemic episode.

My face is on fire, and my brain is being squeezed as if it's being clamped. This is a rush of blood to the head the like of which I don't think I've ever experienced, but I've never experienced *this*, either.

Coming face to face with the man who ruined my brother's life, that is.

The man I've hated, resented from afar for over twenty years.

The man I've stabbed in my fantasies, in my dreams, over and over and over until he's bloodied, lifeless pulp on the floor.

(Maybe that's taking it too far. After all, we're not all violent shits. Some of us are capable of normal levels of self-control.)

Adam Wright.

Standing right in front of me, about a foot away from me. So close I can smell him. Joking with Anton as he waits to, in Gen's own words, *unleash himself on all those unsuspecting women.*

Ugh ugh ugh.

'I'll call a doctor,' Anton says, his voice decisive, and it's enough to have me opening my eyes and training them fixedly on his face. In my peripheral vision, Adam hovers by the desk.

'No. I'm fine—I'm so sorry.'

'I think you should take a break,' Gen says kindly, coming around behind me and taking hold of my biceps.

'I'm absolutely fine, honestly,' I tell her now. 'I'm so sorry.'

I do what may just be the bravest, scariest thing I've ever done, and I look up, up, up to meet Adam's eyes. And for a second—for one despicable, traitorous second—I feel only appreciation. Because if Tom Ellis reminded us of anything in *Lucifer*, it's that Satan is in fact a fallen angel... and he looks every inch of the celestial being he once was.

But that appreciation dissolves a second later, because the way he's looking at me tells me he has no clue who I am. There's something on his offensively handsome face that on anyone else would look like genuine concern, and, if my instincts are right, some appreciation is working its dark magic on him, too.

But nothing else.

What must it be like to ruin a life—several lives—and just walk away? To show up at a place like Alchemy in a suit that costs more than I make in a year, idly wondering how many women to fuck and in which ways you'll violate them while a fellow human goes about his day with a life-altering injury?

I have no idea, and I don't want to know. I don't want a single insight into how the mind of a monster works. I don't want a second more exposure to his toxic energy.

'Are you okay?' he asks. 'Can I get you a glass of water?' His voice isn't overly posh, but it's modulated. The South London vowels are long gone, polished up as a part of whatever bullshit reinvention he's undertaken over these past two decades.

I can't actually speak, so I shake my head. I just hope that, even if the force of my glare in this moment isn't quite enough to transform into deadly laser beams, it's quite sufficient to telegraph my deep, deep contempt for him.

'Nat, this is our good friend, Adam,' Gen says softly, rubbing my arms through my long gloves. 'Anton can get him signed in. You're going to come and sit down for five minutes. Okay? I'll tell the guys outside to grab me if anyone else turns up.'

With that, she gently frogmarches me around the lectern and through the large doorway to Alchemy's beautiful meeting space. She ducks outside quickly to speak to the doormen and returns, closing the door behind us.

The room is dim at this hour, lit mainly by the street-lights outside and by the pink onyx vulva sculpture in one corner. It's the main clue that Alchemy isn't your average members' club.

I sit thankfully on the huge grey sofa. I'm an absolute tumult of emotions, sweat pricking along my spine under the velvet and heart racing as my adrenal system attempts to make sense of everything. I'm simultaneously mortified at how I've behaved in front of Gen and Anton and fucking furious that a guy like Adam Shithead Wright gets to walk around Mayfair as if he owns it, after the past he's had.

Gen lets her huge coat drop from her shoulders and sinks far more elegantly down on the sofa than I did. She's all gold now, and she's so beautiful. That dress is a work of art, and right now it's the anchor tethering me to sanity.

'Okay,' she says. 'Something's not right, and I'm not letting you out of here until you've told me exactly what's going on. I'm pretty sure I should be calling a doctor right now.'

'You don't need to call a doctor,' I mutter, resting my elbows on my knees and letting my head drop into my hands. 'It's not a crash, I promise.'

'Well, something's going on,' she presses in a voice that's genuinely kind but still reminds me why the most formidable businessman in this country obeys her every word. 'So why don't you explain it to me?'

I'm never like this with Gen. She makes me my most polished and sparkly. She's the kind of woman you stand up straighter around. So I would never be weird or sluggish or mute like I am now. At the same time, though, I can't bear that she doesn't know. That man has waltzed in here with her and Anton. He presumes to a friendship with two of the most upstanding, impressive people I know, and it honestly makes me sick.

So if she wants an explanation, that's what I'll give her.

Except I start crying the second I raise my head and see the worry on her beautiful face, and that's even more mortifying than my little episode out in the hallway, because I need to pull myself together right this second and get back out there and do the job Gen pays me to do.

'Holy crap.' She shimmies over on the sofa so she's sitting right next to me and puts her arm tightly around me. 'Please tell me what's the matter, sweetie. Has one of the members been rude to you, or made you feel unsafe?'

One of the members has made me feel very unsafe, but not in the way you think. I let out a shuddery breath. 'No, they haven't, but there's a problem with… that guy you brought.'

'Adam?'

'Yes.' Here goes. I watch her face. 'Do you know much about his past?'

She frowns. 'I know it was rough—I know he's overcome a lot to get where he is.'

I snort. I'm sorry, but for fuck's sake. It's no secret that Adam Wright has a past; he's milked it shamelessly as part of his "personal brand", which, from what I can tell, is heavy on redemption and equally heavy on bullshit. But clearly Gen's been drinking his Kool-Aid, because her eyebrows fly up at my very unprofessional snort. She's not pissed off, but she's surprised.

'Yeah, well, so have a lot of us. But some of us can't just "overcome" the things that happen to us.'

'I don't get it,' she says. 'Do you know him, or you're just not a fan?'

'You're friends with him,' I say.

'He's a mate of Anton's, yes, and I'm fond of him. But not as fond as I am of you, so spit it out.'

Fine. 'I know him,' I tell her. 'He doesn't know who I am, but he was at school with my brother.'

Gen presses her lips together like she already knows she won't like what's coming.

'Adam used to bully him,' I say, my voice shaking. 'Badly.'

'*Fuck.*'

The tears are flowing freely now, and I sniff hard and wetly as I drag the heel of my hand over my cheek. 'Yeah, fuck. And one day, he—Adam—beat Stephen to a pulp, and it was so bad he lost his left eye. They couldn't save it—they had to take the whole thing out.'

She reacts to this like all normal people do when they hear my story: with utter horror. She gasps loudly, covering her mouth with her hand, her eyes huge and appalled. 'Oh my *God*,' she says, voice muffled.

'Yeah.'

'Adam Wright did this.' It's not a question.

'Yep.'

'I can't believe it—I mean, I knew he'd done time for GBH, but I didn't know the exact details. Jesus, Nat, I'm so fucking sorry for bringing him here.'

GBH. *Grievous Bodily Harm.* So laughably inadequate for what that ruthless thug did to Stephen. 'It's not your fault,' I say feebly. She takes my hand and squeezes it, her other arm still around me, and honestly, it feels nice. Comforting. I think I might be in shock. Coming face to face with the man you've loved to hate all these years will do that to you.

'And your brother? What... is he okay?'

Our faces are close enough that, even in the dim light, I can see the unshed tears brimming in her big blue eyes. I nod. I assume she's asking for an overview. For a broad yes/no answer. She doesn't want or need to know about the years of physical and mental struggle Stephen went through after the attack. 'I mean, he lost the eye, obviously, but he's alive. He has a prosthetic one.'

She shudders and rubs my arm briskly. 'Good Lord above. That poor, poor guy. How utterly horrific.'

I stay silent, because it's hard to disagree with that.

'I can't believe I brought him here,' she says with a groan as she releases me from her embrace. 'Jesus fucking Christ. What are the fucking chances?'

I love that Gen looks like a supermodel and sounds for the most part like she's presenting *The Antiques Roadshow* but actually swears like a sailor. I've always found it a brilliant proof of her sincerity. There's no artifice for her. And right now, her F-bombs at the situation she's unknowingly put me in are little shows of solidarity. It's not just me who finds this coincidence—if you can call it that—beyond horrific.

'He's your friend.' I shrug weakly. 'You weren't to know.'

'Yeah,' she says, 'but he's also... Oh, fucking hell. *Shite.*'

Now it's her turn to drop her head to her hands.

'What?' I ask with growing alarm.

She looks up at me, what looks like conflict written all over her face. 'Nothing. *Hell.*' She inhales, nostrils flaring like she's bracing for something. 'Right. Here's what we'll do.

I'm going to put you in a cab home—no, don't argue. It's the least I can do. I'll get someone to cover for you. And I'm going to go and have a little chat with Mr Wright.'

3

ADAM

I'm used to women staring.

But not like *that*.

The staring happens a lot. It tends to take the form of recognition or desire or curiosity or intimidation—sometimes a mixture of all those. But I'll tell you now: that mysterious beauty back there, in a jewel-encrusted catsuit that I'd swear was high-end ready-to-wear if not actual couture, stared at me with nothing short of horror.

I don't get it. Disdain I can handle. Plenty of people are haters, plenty abhor it when others succeed, especially when they get there on their own merit. Deserved success? Ugh. That'll provoke the *Daily Mail* readers at every turn.

This wasn't that.

It was more like abject, horrified disbelief, and the force of it still rankles as I sign the bottom of each page, swiping as I go.

'Do you think she's all right?' I ask Anton as we head down the broad corridor. *In the head, I mean.* Maybe she's delusional.

'I don't know,' he says, pulling open one of the double

doors in front of us. 'Nat's a lovely girl. Always very professional, very friendly. She's diabetic, though, so that could
be it.'

I freeze, stopping in the doorframe, my entire body tens-
ing. 'Shit. Type 1?'

'I believe so, yeah.'

My body may be frozen, but my brain is in processing
overdrive, cataloging the clues she gave us back there,
analysing. Something was wrong, but it didn't *look* like she
was hypo. I run through the diagnostics. She didn't look
pale or wan—on the contrary, her face and neck were
flushed when she gazed up at me. No visible beads of sweat
on her forehead or upper lip. She was flustered, which is
worrying, but not overly panicky, and, when she finally got
her words out, she was lucid. No obviously jerky or
thrashing movements.

I exhale hard. You can't fuck around with this stuff.
Failing to spot a hypo episode within the correct window
can be catastrophic. 'Perhaps I should go back and see if I
can help,' I tell Anton. 'Maybe we should call an ambulance,
just in case.'

For fuck's sake, Gen even *asked* her if she was crashing in
front of me. How could I not have clicked? I twist my body
and watch as Gen says something to the doormen and
closes the front door before disappearing into a room off to
the left.

I'm in two minds. There's no reason not to check, except
for the very valid one that the look in that young woman's
eyes when she finally met my gaze was *not* one that
suggested she'd be happy to see me again so soon. I muddle
my bottom lip between my teeth, feeling uncharacteristi-
cally flustered and indecisive.

'Nah.' He gestures at the open door. 'Gen will have it in

hand, I promise. So, this is the main bar area. The Playroom is through there.'

Rationally, I know he's right. I stride through the doorway, urging myself to shake off my feeling of unease, reminding myself that my reaction is wholly down to my personal triggers and not based in any way on the facts of what just went down.

Before me is a beautiful, high-ceilinged room sporting what at a glance is an exquisite fit-out. The main sources of light are the small, silk-shaded lamps dotted on the low tables and the long bar, crafted from pink onyx and back-lit to perfection. I nod approvingly before following Anton's gesture to look to my right, where a security guard stands sentry in front of another set of double doors.

The space I've heard so much about.

The Playroom.

I'm very much looking forward to giving it a whirl—if I can pull myself the fuck together and shake off my unease.

'Nice place,' I tell Anton before turning my attention to the clientele. First impressions: well-heeled. Sophisticated. Some hot-as-fuck women.

Alchemy has been hyped up by what feels like everyone I know, but they haven't lied. My gut tells me Gen and Anton are onto a winner here.

I may have made my fortune in tech, but I diversify more and more these days. *Di-worse-ify,* as the consultants call it, as if the only consideration that matters is one's return on investment. The closer I get to forty, the closer to three billion my net worth climbs, the fewer fucks I find myself giving about ROIs. Rather—the fewer fucks I give about *financial* ROIs.

Question: what's the fastest way to make a small fortune?

Answer: start with a large fortune and invest in a fashion brand. That may be the case—the fashion industry's ability to destroy value is well documented—but the growing stable of luxury brands I've acquired and quietly nurtured gives me more pleasure than the tech startup, OfficeScape, that made me ten figures.

I don't need Freud to explain to me why luxury goods fill the particular void inside me, because I don't fucking care what Freud—or my therapist—thinks. I do it because I love it.

Luxury *experiences*, however, are a newer concern for me. That money-can't-buy offering is the next obvious step for me on my journey to build a premium portfolio that transcends sectors. And this joint venture with Alchemy might push the envelope in just the way I need on every front: personal and professional.

A new era, a new challenge, and serendipitous timing? It's too intriguing not to give due consideration to. When Anton mentioned it, my interest was immediately piqued. By my understanding, if he had his way, the JV his company has with Alchemy for the club's overseas pop-ups would only expand.

But he's no longer CEO of Wolff, and since the company's flotation last week on the London Stock Exchange, his Board has faced increased pressure to sever its ties with a sex club. It's a fucking joke, if you ask me. The JV is a tiny line item on Wolff's vast financial statements, but its mere existence has pissed off the many ethical and sustainable funds that are required, for indexing purposes, to hold a stake in one of the FTSE 100's biggest companies.

Long story short, Wolff needs to divest, and Anton, who's still the Non-Executive Chairman and far more involved than his new wife thinks he should be, suggested I take a gander before they formally look for a buyer.

So here I am.

I lounge at the bar with Anton, enjoying the quality of both the whiskey and the women. The former is in shorter supply than the latter, thanks to Alchemy's two-drink limit. But I'm not short of female attention, much to Anton's amusement.

I exchange some loaded glances across the room and politely fob off the three or four women who approach me as I chat with my friend, more distractedly than I'd like. There'll be time for hookups later, but I'm keen to get an update on that woman—Nat, I think—before I allow myself to fully relax or get stuck in.

Eventually, Gen shows up in the bar, her gold sequins rippling over her body and casting their light as she walks across the room. As with every other time I've met her, she looks fucking glorious. Unfortunately, she also looks fucking pissed off.

'You two.' She jerks her thumb over her shoulder. 'Grab a table and sit. *Now.* I'm getting a drink.'

I look at Anton, eyebrows raised. He murmurs something in Gen's ear and kisses her on the cheek before guiding me to a nearby empty table. 'You heard the lady.'

If I thought tonight might be an occasion on which the formidable Genevieve Wolff attempts to ingratiate herself with me on behalf of her club, clearly I was deluded. Anton and I sit and wait as sheepishly as two schoolboys who've just smashed a window might await their headmistress, but within a minute, she's joined us. She falls just short of slamming her champagne coupe down on the table and sits on the free bar stool.

'Is Nat okay?' Anton asks her, and she shakes her head.

'Honestly? No. No, she's not,' she says, glaring at me. I can feel the guilt, the defensiveness, instantly, even though I'm a grown man and completely innocent. After all these years, it's still an instinct.

Blame Adam.

It must be his fault.

'Why?' I ask. 'What's wrong? Was it her diabetes?'

She shakes her head impatiently, but nothing on God's green earth can prepare me for the next words to come out of her mouth.

'Does the name Stephen Bennett mean anything to you?'

Stephen Bennett.

His name may evoke an incident that happened two decades ago—over half a *lifetime* ago—but it's as fresh and as horrifying and as triggering tripping off Gen's scarlet lips as it was all those years ago.

Stephen Bennett belongs to a different lifetime and a different me, as does the unspeakable, inhuman thing I did to him. My fun, sexy evening at Alchemy belongs to the here and now. It belongs to the Adam Wright who's told himself a million times over that he's earned his place in this world.

But the mention of his name forms a bridge from this world to that, a portal that has me hurtling through time and space to a past I'd give anything to erase.

I whisper my *yes*.

Somehow, impossibly, I know what she's going to say next before she says it.

'Well, it seems Nat is his sister.'

4

ADAM

Contrition wears many faces, as does regret. They're both complex emotions, both weighty enough to behave in similar, cyclical ways to grief. I should know.

I have enough experience of all three.

I bow my head. I learnt in prison that the aggressor is capable of regretting the occurrence of a past trauma just as fully as his victim, and in myriad ways that are all as necessary to rehabilitation as they are painful to digest.

Over the past two decades, I've forged for myself an existence that allows me to endure my past, to make the only kind of fractured, imperfect peace with it that I'll ever make. Empathy has played a key role, even if it's been one of the toughest lessons of all.

There are people who...people who've helped on that front, let's say, people for whose compassion I've been indescribably, pathetically grateful, even if their roles belong in the shadows of my journey back to myself.

But the careful, ring-fenced form of empathy for Stephen Bennett that I've espoused over the past two decades threatens tonight to burst its banks and become a tidal wave that will fucking engulf me, and that's because someone who loves him, someone whose life I presumably shattered alongside Stephen's, is right here, in the same building as me, and *now* I understand what it was I saw in her beautiful eyes.

Staggering, unequivocal hatred.

My overwhelming instinct is to bury my face in my hands, to shield myself from the disgust, the disappointment, written across Gen's face.

But I don't.

I won't shy away from it.

I'll take it.

I'll own it all.

Because that, quite simply, is what I deserve.

'I see,' I say quietly, holding eye contact with her. I can't imagine the conversation she's just had, the things she's heard about me. She's watching my face to see how I'll react. There's no sign of spite; she's simply pissed off beyond belief on behalf of her employee, and so she should be.

'What am I missing here?' Anton barks, and I turn to him.

'Give me a sec and I'll explain. But first—is she okay? Nat, is that her name?'

'*Natalie* to you, and no, she's not okay,' Gen says, picking up her coupe and taking a healthy slug of champagne. I wait. 'She's extremely shocked and distressed, so I sent her home.'

My mind reels at what Natalie must think of me. I recall the fire in her eyes, the way she couldn't even bring herself to reply to my banal offer of a glass of water. No surprise there.

'I'm waiting,' Anton says in the voice of a man who is

most definitely unused to being on the fringes of a conversation.

I give Gen a little nod to show her I understand what she's telling me. 'I'm sorry,' I say. It's so fucking inadequate, but I swivel on my stool towards Anton nonetheless. Once again, this is my problem to own, to deal with, even if it makes my position as his and Gen's preferred buyer for Wolff's Alchemy stake untenable.

'The guy I assaulted,' I tell him, my voice as steady as if I was updating him on the weather. 'The one I served time for hurting.'

He nods. He knows my history well. I was in prison when we first met as part of an entrepreneurial programme he ran for young offenders. 'Nat's brother, I assume.'

'Yes.' I inhale sharply and continue, the sound of my voice dispassionately recounting my own crime surreal in my ears, surrounded as we are by Swiss watches and crystal chandeliers and expensive women. 'I got some of my mates to hold him down while I had at him. I beat him to a pulp, and he lost an eye and broke three ribs.'

Those were the headlines, rather than the full extent of his injuries. The prosecution made sure to spell each one out at my trial, to show colour photographs of every bruise and welt I'd inflicted, and of the back of his head, shaved so the medical staff who treated him could remove every last piece of gravel embedded in the back of his skull.

Anton sucks in a horrified breath and squeezes his eyes shut, as well he should. It's barbaric. Grotesque. Abhorrent. And though he knows I was sent down for GBH, he's never asked me for the specifics. When he opens his eyes, he looks at me, pausing before he speaks.

'Fuck, mate,' he says, and there's an element of censure,

of disappointment, there, naturally, but that's not all. There's also, I think, compassion, and space, and acceptance.

'I know.' I look down, tilting my tumbler so the amber liquid swirls enticingly around it, before forcing myself to meet his eye again. But he's looking at Gen—for guidance, I assume.

'We're not here to be judge and jury,' he says slowly. 'You've had that, you've served your time. You deserve to be judged on the man you are today, and I'm proud to call you a friend. I've *been* proud since the day we met.'

'Thank you.' There's an ache in my throat. Anton is intimately familiar with my past. He's mentored me for two decades now, since I was blessed enough to stumble into a business programme he was running for inmates when I was inside, and I value his friendship and support enormously. Still, there's a vast gulf between his being aware of my past crimes and our coming face to face with someone whose family I shattered when I inflicted those vicious injuries on her brother.

'I maintain that you're the right person to take over the JV,' he continues, looking at Gen again, 'but I really need to defer to my wife here. This is her company, Nat is her employee, and I'm unclear how we proceed in light of this… *revelation*, I suppose, for want of a better term.' He leans back defeatedly.

'Of course,' I say. I wouldn't expect anything else. I remind myself that this Alchemy thing is a tiny deal for me, a kind of potential pet project, more than anything else. A nice little bolt-on acquisition.

I'm no stranger to the sensation of doors being slammed in my face—both literally, in prison, and metaphorically, in business. So to be back here, essentially being judged on crimes I committed half a lifetime ago, should smart far less than it does.

Gen's surveying me through narrowed, thoughtful eyes. She's not being outright hostile, but she doesn't have the personal relationship with me that her husband does. She's firmly in Natalie's camp, I suspect, and rightly so.

She blows out a breath. 'Fucking hell,' she sighs. 'I honestly didn't see this coming. I've had no problem with you coming on board, Adam. Not until just now, at least. And the JV mainly concerns itself with our overseas pop-ups—and Manhattan, of course.'

Manhattan, which opens next month, will be the only permanent Alchemy outpost and has largely been funded through the joint venture. Post Gen and Anton's union, the JV expanded so that Wolff bought a stake in the entire group —a stake I'd assume in full if I came on board. That said, the management of this London club remains under the control of its executive team: Gen and her three co-founders.

'So you've got no actual jurisdiction here, really,' she continues. 'But I have to say, I'm reticent to bring on an investor who has such a particularly horrendous personal history with the family of a trusted employee.'

I wait, and so does Anton, because it sounds like she's working through her thought process aloud here. Sure enough, she keeps talking.

'I need to chat to the guys about this, and I'd want to talk to Nat again, when she's had some time to gather her wits.' Anton opens his mouth to speak, but she cuts him off. 'Don't worry, we'll get her to sign an NDA.'

He grins fondly at her. 'You read my mind.'

'I always do,' she retorts, but there's no missing the affection on her face when she looks at her husband.

'You'd run the acquisition past her?' I clarify, surprised. I understand I'm on dangerous ground here, but I can't see any circumstances when I'd allow a lowly host any say in my management affairs.

'I would,' Gen says. Her voice is neutral, but something in it tells me she wouldn't welcome being challenged on this. 'Nat is a loyal employee. She works incredibly hard, and I would never put her, or *any* of my team, in a position where I brought in someone at a management level who made them feel unsafe in their place of work, however unlikely *I* find the threat.'

Her words hit me like a blow to the stomach. Here was I thinking this was about a potential employee's deep dislike of me, but it's not.

It's about the fact that in Natalie's eyes I'm still a common thug—a violent, volatile entity.

And a danger to those around me.

5

ADAM

My first evening at Alchemy may have spiralled from the fantasies I was expecting into a reality far too grim for my liking, but I opt not to go home when I've wrapped up my uncomfortable chat with Gen and Anton.

The blood is coursing far too readily through my veins for that. My mind is far too uneasy, the phantom cold of long-gone steel handcuffs around my wrists too close to the surface to give me comfort.

There's only one thing for it tonight, and that's oblivion. The kind Alchemy promises, at least, as enticing as it is temporary. But it's what I need. It's the only way I'll slay those demons, alter my biochemistry.

Let's see if the women next door can provide the elixir this place promises. The sedative I crave.

I bid goodnight to my hosts and head through the heavy double doors that lead from the main bar to The Playroom.

My permitted double shot of whisky has done nothing to settle me.

But this just might.

I stand at the threshold of the large room and attempt to make sense of the instant sensory assault. The music was loud next door, but in here it's deafening, that same heady thump as the one that always hits your bloodstream when you walk into a nightclub. The one that screams *let's do this.*

Like a nightclub, the lighting is dim, complex. The enormous white pillars are up-lit in pink, as are the gauzy white drapes that hang between them. A woman twirls languorously onstage in a suspended hoop. It's busy, too busy for a clear view of the room, but I take in the patrons dancing in time to the house music while others fuck on sofas.

It's a clever setup, the music and drapes and lighting and even some dry ice conspiring to trick the mind somewhat, to confuse the senses as much as to delight them.

Forget the whisky.

This can be my drug of choice tonight.

Anton mentioned that the female hosts in here wear identical white dresses so they can be easily spotted. It won't be hard to find a woman—or women—to fuck, but this evening I want a professional. The fact of Alchemy being a sex club won't completely protect me from clinginess or hopefulness, of cards with phone numbers being slipped into my trouser pocket.

I have no tolerance for that kind of bullshit tonight, just as I have no tolerance for a woman who thinks she wants what I have to offer but who will, at the first strike of my palm, run for the hills.

I make my way through the crowd, pausing to appreciate the view of a stunning blonde laid out on a low couch while one guy eats her and another holds her hands above her head. Fuck, that's hot. Vanilla, but hot nonetheless, mainly because it's so carnal. So unapologetic.

And I am most definitely in an unapologetic mood tonight. I know with absolute certainty that the remorse and self-disgust my run-in with Natalie has triggered will haunt my dreams tonight and hit me with blunt force when I surface tomorrow morning. So for now, I need to sate myself, empty my body of this friction, this restless energy buzzing under my skin.

I need to do it without having to hold back.

Gen offered to make some introductions for me, but I've certainly never needed any help getting laid, and I'm not about to start asking for it now. I stride over to the pink-lit bar, my eyes on the back view of a willowy brunette. Short white dress. Endless, shapely legs. Sky-high heels. Long, dark hair that reminds me fleetingly of that girl Natalie's.

That's fucked-up, even by my standards: homing in on a woman who resembles, even slightly, the woman who quite justifiably made me feel less-than earlier. I wonder what my therapist would say. I tell myself it's less about reasserting my wounded authority than about showing her who's boss. After all, that's the despicable act of a cowardly bully, and I'm not that man anymore.

This is about restoration by proxy. About making amends. I'm imagining giving it to Natalie so hard that I'll obliterate any pain I've inadvertently caused her.

What a crock of shit. Apparently, even a man who's made self-awareness his entire personality for two decades can have staggering lapses.

When the woman at the bar turns around, she of course looks nothing like Natalie. She's very sexy—not that I'd expect anything less from this place—but there's something missing when I look at her. I decide I don't mind. I'm certainly not in the market for introspection this evening.

The genuine way her face lights up when she takes me

in is impossible to ignore. I'm sure she's good at her job, but no one's *that* good. Besides, I have enough datapoints from other women at other bars to accept, if not expect, this kind of reaction. If I were a better man, I'd surely take issue with having been granted an outward appearance that opens many more doors than my track record deserves.

'What's your name?' I ask her, leaning an elbow on the bar, and she smiles her seductive, practised smile at me.

'Rose. How about you?'

I shake my head smilingly. 'Oh, it's a lot more fun if I don't tell you. Don't you agree?'

'If that's how you want to play it, sure.'

'Being fucked, slow and deep, by an anonymous man? I'm pretty confident I can make that fun for you.'

'I have no doubt,' she manages, her voice breathy.

'You can call me *sir*. Are you free right now, Rose?'

'I certainly am, sir.'

She takes me in as she waits for me to elaborate. What a very good girl. I lay my cards on the table. I have no desire to pussyfoot around—not when there's no need.

'Are you comfortable with corporal punishment? Just spanking,' I add.

Her eyes widen. She really is very sexy, and that white dress is a second skin on her. Her nipples are two lovely peaks through the thin fabric, and I ache to pinch them.

'Yes, sir, of course.'

Excellent. 'Do you enjoy it, or do you merely tolerate it?'

She looks as though she finds me highly amusing. 'I promise you, if *you* spank me, I'll enjoy it. You definitely don't need to worry about that.' She accompanies her oath with a visual sweep of my body. I'm in my work clothes: black trousers and a white shirt, unbuttoned at the neck, tie loosened. She seems to like what she sees.

'Good,' I say, and I mean it.

These days, I only hurt people who enjoy it.

'Can you get us a private room?' I ask her.

I'm sure this circus can be fun in the right circumstances, but I don't need it tonight. My mind craves peace. I want to be able to control my environment as much as my emotions, my urges, my actions. I want enough quiet, enough calm, that when my hand meets the firm skin of her arse, that perfect *crack* will ring cleanly around the room. I want to hear every strangled noise she makes when I drive my dick into her from behind.

She trails her hand along the bar and lays it on top of mine.

'Come with me.'

6

ADAM

'U ndress,' I command, lounging against the closed door to the small but luxurious room. I fold my arms over my chest and watch as this attractive woman, whose name is almost certainly *not* Rose, obliges. She slips the thin straps off her shoulders and proceeds to shimmy sexily out of the dress. Her tits pop out first, luscious and pert, and then she's sliding it over her hips and down her legs to reveal that she is, in fact, naked underneath.

'Very nice. Do you have a safe word?'

'Daisy, sir.'

Going all in with the floral theme tonight, I see. 'Daisy. Got it. Say it if you need to, and I'll stop immediately. Are you wet?'

She gives a little laugh. 'You look like *that* and you've already told me what you're planning on doing to me—what do you think, *sir?*'

'Show me. Go deep.'

Slowly, deliberately, she slides her hand down over her stomach and between her legs, widening her stance. She holds my gaze as she finger fucks herself, and I smile inwardly. What a little star. She'll do very well for my purposes. Very well indeed.

'Let me taste.'

She steps out of the dress pooled around her heels and approaches, holding up the fingers that were just buried in her cunt. I snag her wrist and dip my head so I can suck on them, taste their sweet, slippery coating.

She wasn't lying.

'You taste just as sweet as your name, Rose. Are there restraints in here?'

'Of course, sir. Silk ties, ropes, cuffs, spreader bars...' She trails off.

Hmm. What to use? I cock my head, taking her in as I consider. Creamy skin, perky nipples that are a lovely shade of pinky red. An immaculate strip of dark hair down her pubic bone. I'd fucking love to put her on a spreader another time, but honestly, I just want to shoot my load inside her body. I don't have the emotional wherewithal to direct an entire scene tonight. I may come back another evening and spread her out for my enjoyment.

Assuming I don't find myself blacklisted here, that is.

'Grab me some rope,' I decide.

I bind her wrists efficiently together in front of her, my cock rock-hard and straining as I knot the rope and test the binding. Satisfied with my handiwork, I nod.

Now the fun begins.

She's not short, but even in her heels she's at least half a head shorter than me. I'm not about to indulge in any extended form of foreplay, but there's no harm in exploring my latest conquest a little, delaying my own gratification. She certainly looks alluring, standing there like a naughty Snow White, wearing nothing but a pair of heels and a length of rope, her bound arms pushing her tits together and her dark hair falling over creamy shoulders.

I run my palms up her arms, skating them over her shoulders and cupping her tits before I pinch both juicy little nipples hard. I suck in a breath through gritted teeth as I pinch, because the look on her face has me floored. She looks like she could come just from that. Her anguished moan tells me I'm not wrong.

I release them, and she visibly sags.

'Your skin is very soft,' I say, running my hands down the smooth satin of her back and cupping her arse. She has a lovely little arse. I raise a hand and give it a good slap to test it out. I don't rub it. I may take pity on her a bit later, but for now I want it to smart.

She lets out a surprised yelp, and I pause to see if she intends to fall at the first hurdle, but she shakes her head. She's all good.

'Stand still for me,' I tell her. 'Don't make a sound. I need to check that you really are a good girl.'

I allow myself a few minutes of exploration that's as dispassionate as it is leisurely, stroking my hands over her body, grabbing handfuls of her arse cheeks again, kneading her tits. I nudge her hands out of the way and slide a couple of fingers between her legs, over her already swollen clit and along velvety wetness until I reach her cunt. She widens her stance and lets out a shuddery breath as I slide them inside her, but, like the good girl she is, doesn't say a word.

Satisfied by what I find, I pull them out.

'I want you on the very end of the bed, elbows and knees, legs as open as you can get them, facing the head-board so I can fuck you standing. The heels can stay on.'

Oh, yes. This is precisely what I need. A beautiful woman arranged on a bed for me, naked and bound and spread open, primed to do my bidding. I take my time, stoking the flames of my anticipation as much as hers, padding about the room as I slip off my loafers, turn down the music using the dial on the wall, and locate the condoms and the lube. She's beautifully wet, but I'm big and I don't plan on being gentle.

I unzip my trousers and push down the waistband of my boxer briefs to free my poor, weeping cock from its prison and sheath it. A couple of generous pumps of the lube bottle and I'm slathering myself in it, the strokes of my hand feeling indecently good. Then I'm stepping in behind her, still fully clothed. My nakedness is absolutely not necessary: the only skin on skin contact I require is my palm against her bare arse cheek.

She's positioned exactly as I asked, bound wrists in front of her, elbows wide like she's doing a plank, head bowed and dark hair falling over pale skin onto the black sheets. Her knees are on the bed, her heels hanging off. I fist my cock and slide it through her flesh, and she pushes back against me in a most gratifying manner.

'Eager little thing, aren't you?' I murmur, and she lets out a laugh-groan of acknowledgement. I cut it off by raising my right hand and bringing it down hard on her arse cheek in a resounding slap, the sound of whose impact rings as roundly, as purely, through the quiet, still air of the room as I hoped.

Her entire body tenses, her skin blooming instantly pink where I slapped her. I give it a little rub and find her clit with the tip of my dick.

The carrot and the stick working in perfect unison.

I do it again on the other cheek, following up with a rub of my hand and a nudge of my dick. This time, she lets out a moan when I strike her. It's low and guttural and hungry, and I find myself answering it with a sharp hiss as I drag my sheathed crown over her silken cunt.

We find our cadence, my slaps and her strangled cries a wonderful harmony of sensation and sound. My dick is throbbing and my head is clearing and my palms are smarting, fizzing headily with the pins and needles that only a good old-fashioned spanking can deliver.

When I can't hold off any longer, when the drag of my flesh against hers is too fucking much and the temptation of her slick, ready cunt *right there* simply too great, I give her one last slap and thrust in. No matter how primed she is, it's tight.

It always is.

I wedge myself halfway in and give her a moment to ready herself for the rest of me as I take in the sight of this pale-skinned, dark-haired woman on the bed for me, arse in the air and bound hands outstretched now, fingers tightly intertwined and knuckles whitening.

Try as I might, I can't help but imagine she's that girl, Natalie. Just for a moment. Just for a fleeting, blessed moment where she doesn't hate me. Or maybe... maybe she *does* hate me, but she wants me more.

Fuck, that fantasy has my cock swelling impossibly, needing to drive forward. Natalie on all fours for me, despising me, despising *herself*, but needing so, so badly for me to fuck all that hatred and resentment and tension out of her that the power of her desire drives away every other emotion. Annihilates every other conflict.

Not that I'd allow her to stay like that for long.

I'd have to flip her over and get her on her back so I could enjoy the sweet look of surrender dawning on her beautiful, contemptuous face as she gave herself over to the inevitable.

'I'm going again,' I huff out. 'You okay?'

'God, yeah,' she pants, giving me my green light.

And go I do. I push into that tight, hot space until I'm fully, gloriously in, and then I begin to move, my drives hard and rough and urgent. The astonishing pleasure of it drives any residual shame and self-loathing from my mind.

'Rose' is a palette cleanser. A fast fuck. A means to an end.

But the means is pretty fucking entertaining.

And the end, when it comes in an unstoppable tsunami of heat as the contractions of her orgasm milk my dick to its own glorious finale, is blessed oblivion.

Just as I intended.

7

NATALIE

S erenity is the rasp of tailor's chalk dragging over wool, the clean, crisp incisions of sharpened scissors slicing through silk as if it's water.

I stand at the edge of the high table in our light-filled attic studio, white-knuckling the edge and watching with a mixture of nerves and gratification as Evan, our pattern cutter, cuts expertly around the engineered panels printed on sumptuous duchesse satin.

The silk mill has done an incredible job with the print. It's so flawless it's as if an artist has taken an actual paint-brush to the fabric, capturing the prettiest daubs of wisteria in all its purple-hued glory, from palest lavender to richest periwinkle.

In actual fact, the flowers were painted digitally and then reworked into shaped panels that exactly fit the pattern of this evening dress, meaning that when the dress is assembled, the wisteria will fall just so, its blooms cascading in the optimum way to complement every pleat. Every dart.

'Nat,' Evan says through gritted teeth, his eyes glued to the fabric.

'Yep.'

'Kindly bugger off. You're creeping me out.'

'No can do. You know this is my therapy.' I gaze at what will be the front panel for the skirt. It's simply sublime. It'll look incredible juxtaposed with the chunky gold hardware that's one of the features of this collection. Incongruous, but incredible.

I run my fingertips reverently over an unprinted section of the fabric. Duchesse satin is one of my absolute favourites to work with, not only because of its lustre, which hits that exact sweet spot between matte and shine, but because of its weight. It drapes like nothing else. I love that we're using it outside of bridal wear. My brand may bear the name *Gossamer*, but I value gravitas in my fabrics just as much, even if the majority of our collection runs towards the diaphanous.

Evan sighs. He's a couple of years older than me, a great, hulking, fair-haired guy who cuts like an angel. The vision for Gossamer may be all mine, but Evan brings it to life. I have a combined business and fashion degree. I draw, and I can sew, but I certainly can't cut at the level the brand requires.

For this particular gown, he draped and draped on the mannequin until we'd got every detail right before making up a toile of it in a cheaper polyester satin that mimicked the weight of the duchesse. Only then did Carrie, our print designer and a digital wizard, transfer the dimensions of Evan's paper patterns into her CAD programme and play with the layout of the print on each pattern piece until her 3D mockup resembled the vision in my head.

No matter how laborious this career, I'll never, ever tire of that astonishing jolt of creative satisfaction that comes from having a dream made real. Of obsessing over the ephemeral perfection of an idea in my head and being fortunate enough to have a team of talented professionals who can draw it from my mind's eye and conjure a flesh-and-blood garment before my eyes, even more beautiful than I could have imagined, as if they're my fairy godmothers.

'You look like shit,' Evan says now. 'You feeling all right?'

'I'm fine.'

I'm far from fine, but I know from experience that his question pertains squarely to my blood glucose, which is stable despite the punishing vinyasa flow I put myself through first thing this morning. My sleep-deprived body complained the whole time, but I didn't entertain its whining. It was worth it. The ritual grounded me, reminded me that I am in control. I get to choose how my day pans out.

Not my body.

And certainly not some dickhead whom karma forgot to call on.

Evan makes a clicking sound with his tongue. 'Want to tell me why you've had a face like a slapped arse all morning?'

'You wouldn't believe me if I did.' He wouldn't, because I still can't believe it. I mean, what are the chances? What are the fucking chances that my past and my present would collide in Alchemy, the one place apart from this studio that I view as a safe space, manifesting in the physical form of an obnoxiously tall, wholly immoral billionaire?

They should be so close to zero that I never need worry about it happening.

Should.

'Try me.' He finishes cutting around the skirt panel and lifts it reverently off the table, laying it over the back of a chair. When he turns back to me, he lifts a quizzical eyebrow. *I'm waiting,* it says.

I cross my arms. Fine. Let's see what Evan thinks. Despite the nausea that rolls through my body every time I think of last night—the shock, the humiliation, the outrage —I'm dying to spill the beans. It's too insane not to talk about. I need to process. Aloud.

'Who's my least favourite person on this planet?' I ask him now.

He narrows his eyes in concentration as his scissors cut down the side of the skirt's back panel. 'Um. That guy who ghosted you last summer? Pencil Dick Darren?'

I laugh despite myself. 'God, no. And we've blocked him out, remember? He doesn't exist.'

'Poor fucker.' He's quiet for a moment, his cutting immaculate, his forehead furrowed, and I know he's processing as he works.

'Omar Vega?'

'Nope. But you're getting a lot warmer.' Omar Vega is an obnoxious but hugely talented Spanish designer operating in a similar part of the market to Gossamer. The differences between us are that the trajectory of his eponymous label has been stratospheric and that he's backed by no other than Adam Wright. Evan and I may or may not take great delight in hate-watching his rising fortunes.

He stops, his head jerking up. 'The bully.'

Evan's never met my brother, but he knows my entire backstory with a level of detail only a friend who's spent every weekday for years with me can.

I nod, and he grimaces. 'What? Did he make the front pages again?'

It wouldn't be the first time I've turned up for work triggered because Adam Wright's smug face was staring at me from the front page of someone's *Financial Times* on my morning commute.

'Way worse.'

His eyes widen. 'Go on...'

I glance around the room. Carrie has her headphones on, and our production manager, Gail, is out at one of our factories doing quality control on the dresses they're currently working on.

'He turned up at Alchemy last night. *With Gen.*'

Evan's usually unflappable, but his face is an absolute picture. 'You are *shitting* me.' He lets the scissors clatter onto the table and straightens up.

'Nope. Turns out he's a friend of Anton's.' That memory drags over me again like nails on a chalkboard, and I shiver.

'Oh, babe.' He stretches out his arms. 'Do you need a hug?'

I shake my head furiously, biting my lip and blinking away the moisture threatening to form in my eyes, because if Evan bestows one of his excellent bear hugs on me, I'll definitely cry.

'Okay.' He lowers his arms. 'Tell me what went down.'

So I tell him about it all. The total horror of seeing Adam. My complete and utter meltdown. Gen being lovely. The curiosity I can't help but have over what went down after Gen went off to have her "little chat" with him.

And, finally, my nerves now, because she sent me a text first thing this morning, asking if I'd come in an hour early this evening to meet with her and Adam so we could discuss "moving forward". Her mention that I'd have to sign an NDA before I spoke to them. And her promise that she'd be with me the whole time. That she wouldn't leave me alone with him.

Fuck fuck fuck.

I wonder if Maddy will be around for a chat later. She's the social media manager at Alchemy and my friend. She's also married to Zach, the club's Finance Director. I've told her about Adam before, and she genuinely will not believe it when I fill her in on the latest.

'Jesus Christ,' Evan says when I'm done recapping. 'I can't believe it. Talk about a bad penny, turning up like that.'

'Right? It seems ridiculously far-fetched, but I suppose these billionaires all hang out together.'

'Yeah.' He scoffs. 'In the Big Dick club. Do you know why Gen wants to talk to you?'

'No clue. Maybe she wants to make him apologise to me for all the devastation he's caused my family? Or maybe he's angling for an Alchemy membership and she won't let him in without getting the go-ahead from me.'

Of all the scenarios spinning around in my head, that seems the most likely. Surely he was there last night to check the place out—as well as its female patrons. Yuck.

'What would you say if that was the case?'

'God, I don't know.' I rub my hand over my forehead. 'It's her club. I'm mortified that I'm causing a fuss. It was so embarrassing last night.'

'You know Gen won't see it that way,' Evan says sagely, making quick work of the rest of the rear skirt panel. 'She'll have been absolutely horrified on your behalf. He gouged your brother's eye out, basically. I have no doubt whose team she's on.'

He's right, of course. Everything about Gen's reaction last night tells me she was heading off to give Mr Wright a giant bollocking after she put me in a prepaid black cab. The cab fare home to Seven Sisters was seventy pounds. *Seventy pounds!* I felt awful about it, but Gen insisted. She really is so lovely.

'Doesn't make me any less terrified for this evening,' I mutter. 'But that's six hours away. I have no intention of spending any more time obsessing over it now.'

I can't. I have fabric orders to put through and a particularly "relaxed" Italian mill to chase up for missing their delivery deadline. I need to price up next season's collection, which is by far my least favourite part of the job and a task I've been putting off and off, and I have a call this afternoon with the woman who does all our social media graphics to discuss the aesthetic for Instagram for the coming weeks.

It's so much. Too much, really. Too many hats. So many balls in the air that if I stop to think about it, the terror hits me like a wall of freezing water.

But, given the epic size of the horrors that await me this evening, right now it feels like a blessing.

8

NATALIE

I was eight when Stephen was attacked. Instead of a full picture, I have blurry snapshots. I'd been at my primary school for almost a year, and I still missed my former prep school. The prep school I had to give up when the successful private wealth firm Dad managed with his oldest friend, Bob, went under, courtesy of a Ponzi scheme good old Bob had concocted.

Bob went to prison, while my parents and lots of their friends lost their life savings. Dad was cleared of any criminal wrongdoing, but the financial regulator found that his lack of awareness and failure to ask questions of his partner amounted to gross negligence and struck him off. He was no longer permitted to work in finance.

Obviously, my full understanding of these details came much later, just as my full understanding of the atrocities Adam Wright inflicted on my brother came much later. I was young, and I was shielded from the worst of both events.

All I knew was that we couldn't pay for private school anymore, so Stephen and I were uprooted from our friends and thrust into the local state schools. We couldn't afford our mortgage anymore, either, so the bank foreclosed on our comfortable, stylish home in a quiet cul-de-sac and we found ourselves in a squalid eight-hundred-square-foot council flat in Croydon. I traded in my beautiful pink bedroom for a tiny box room.

That was the worst part, by far.

I think Mum cried for a solid six months.

That's one of the things I remember most clearly, even before Stephen's attack.

But back to the attack itself. I clearly remember my teacher telling me gently that I was going to the after-school club that day because my mummy couldn't come to pick me up just yet. Auntie Jan came eventually and took me back to her house, where she explained that Stephen was in hospital.

When I was allowed to go visit him, he looked like a mummy, his head and body all bandaged up, with plasters over his nose and just one big black eye peeking out.

I screamed when I saw him. I remember that much.

They couldn't get me me stop.

The man standing before me in Alchemy's airy meeting room is immaculate.

That strikes me as the most unfair part.

He's tall and golden-skinned and wonderfully proportioned, so much so that the designer in me can't help but marvel at how perfectly his frame was built to wear a suit. Rather than look at his face, I focus on his jacket. I swear that's Brioni. It's got to be. Those lapels are definitely hand rolled. Hand stitched. The perfect way it moulds to his body suggests there's a layer of canvas adding structure under that super-fine wool exterior.

Exquisite.

The workmanship, that is.

Guessing the label behind each outfit is a game I play with myself most evenings when I'm welcoming guests at Alchemy. If the people-watching is good here, then the clothes-watching is off the charts. But usually it's a diversion.

Right now, it's a coping mechanism to stop myself from spiralling into all-out panic.

It's my fault for turning up ten minutes late, right on his tail. If I'd been here on time, Gen might have been able to give me a quick low-down on what the fuck is going on. As it is, I only gave the London transport system five minutes' margin for error when calculating my short bus journey from Soho, where our studio is, when I actually needed fifteen. But I was desperate to get that bloody fabric order in before I got changed and made up for this evening's shift.

And now I'm here, and he's here, and he's looking at me, and I'm trying not to look at him, and Gen is standing in a sort of triangle with us, and the awkwardness is off the charts. I'm also conscious that, in my rush and in the face of the severe case of nerves I've had all afternoon, I haven't consumed nearly enough food to match the insulin my pump has dispensed into my bloodstream, a situation I need to rectify and will, indeed, rectify just as soon as I'm done here.

I've got a chicken salad wrap in my bag, barely touched. I tried, but it turned to doughy stodge in my mouth. I'll shove it down as soon as I get a chance, but not in front of him. Not while my stomach is churning with nerves and fear and revulsion, like simply being in the same room as him has me in danger for my life.

'I realise a formal introduction may be unnecessary,' Gen is saying with uncharacteristic stiffness. I don't blame her awkwardness, because honestly, how do you make polite introductions between two people who are linked in the most horrifying way? 'Nevertheless, Nat, this is Adam Wright, and Adam, this is Natalie Bennett, our host here.'

'How do you do?' he asks, and I swear there's a tremor in his voice, but I'm too busy trying not to scoff at his— presumably rhetorical—question to marvel that he may actually be nervous.

Though I'm glad if he is. It would be an offence too far if he was cavalier about this meeting.

I don't grace him with a reply, but I do risk a glance up at his tanned face. At the perfectly trimmed dark beard, the mop of dark curls. At the eyes that you'd expect to be brown but are, in fact, a pale, clear blue. Eyes that a person might find attractive if they didn't know the rottenness of the soul they reflected.

I give him a curt nod. 'Hi.' He's lucky to get that much, frankly. But happily for him, I'm feeling like crap, and I really need to eat, so I'm not going to make this meeting any more difficult than it already is. For any of us.

Gen hands me a clipboard with the NDA on it, which I sign before sitting and tugging the fabric of my dress over my thighs. I'm in my host's uniform, wearing a sleeveless black minidress whose modest crew neck offsets the scan-dalously high hemline. It's definitely not the best dress for sitting on such a low sofa, but I hope it doesn't give Adam, or anyone else, an eyeful of the lace tops of my holdups or the insulin pump stuck to my outer thigh, plainly visible through the fishnets.

My continuous glucose monitor, or CGM, is on the back of my right upper arm this week, covered with one of the cute black patches I've customised for work, embellishing them with the ornate Alchemy *A* picked out in tiny crystals.

Adam unbuttons the single button closed on his lovely jacket, his fingers long and dextrous, their movements easy. He sits, his gaze sliding fleetingly to my thighs before jerking back up to Gen, who's already started speaking.

'I realise this is a difficult situation,' she's saying now, 'and that last night must have been quite a shock for you, Nat, so I appreciate you both coming in today.' She clears her throat. 'And I apologise for having you sign an additional NDA on top of your standard employee one,' she says to me. 'But this one is a little different. You see, Adam is in talks with us currently about buying out Wolff's stake in our joint venture.'

I stare at her in what feels like shock but is floatier, like I can't quite work out what she means, and I suspect my face reflects my confusion pretty well, because she hurries on like she's panicked.

'The talks have been going on for a few weeks, and last night was supposed to be Adam's chance to take a look around the club.' She glances at him. 'He tells me he's still interested in having Wright Holdings acquire it. But, and this is a big *but*, I've been very clear with him that...'

She keeps talking, at least I think she does, but shit. *Shit.* I can't quite work out what she's saying, because I'm getting dizzy, and it feels like my brain is swelling, and my hands are getting weak.

Oh dear God, no.

The pinpricks of sweat over my forehead, down my back, are instant. They're everywhere. I swallow, and I try to clasp my fingers together, but they're all floppy and useless, and now they're starting to shake.

Jesus fucking shit shit *God* no no *no*.

She says my name, and it's all echoey and distant, like she's not sitting next to me on the sofa at all, and then another noise cuts through it.

A shout.

A man's voice, and then a huge, dark shape rising and hurling itself at me. My vision has narrowed to pin-pricks now, and this nausea and general awfulness is rolling over me and over me, but his shout cuts through it all.

'Fuck!'

9

ADAM

She's crashing.

Jesus Christ.

I stand.

'Fuck!' I shout. I take a panicked look down at the huge coffee table between me and Natalie, thinking I'll use it as a launch pad, but it's glass. Better not try putting my weight on it. I sidestep it so I can round the massive three-sided sofa. 'Looks like she's hypo,' I blurt at Gen, whose face drops instantly with realisation and horror.

'Shit,' she says. 'Shit.'

No no no no. This is not happening. *Fuck*. The glassiness in her eyes, the sheen of sweat already forming on her forehead and upper lip, that very particular jerky, floppy flailing that is all too familiar and all too triggering.

I'd know it all a mile off.

'Natalie,' I say more forcefully than I mean to. I get to my knees in front of her and cup her face. It's cold and clammy. 'Natalie, can you hear me? Where's your monitor? Do you have a monitor?' I turn to Gen, who's frozen in shock. 'Does she have a monitor?'

'Yes.' She looks Natalie up and down frantically. 'Oh, it's on her arm.'

I release her face and run my hands up both her arms. Yep. The fabric of the patch hits my fingertips. There it is. It doesn't matter really. I don't need a monitor to tell me she's hypo.

She had a big handbag on her when she walked in. It's by her feet, and it's open. I grab it with one arm and shake it out, emptying its contents all over the sofa next to her. With the other hand, I pin Natalie's shoulder to the sofa. She's flailing more, jerking harder, her hands fluttering ineffectually, trying to slap me away.

'Phone.' I hand it to Gen. 'Try to get into her glucose monitor,' I bark. 'It should be linked.'

She takes it, and I look for long enough to note that she's trying to get Natalie to unlock it with face recognition. 'Natalie,' I say firmly. '*Natalie.* Help Gen to unlock your phone. We need it.'

'I'm in,' Gen says shakily. 'Um, let me see—okay. Freestyle Libre. That sounds like it.'

'Good.' I continue to rummage among the contents of Natalie's bag as I support her. I'm shaking too, my body flooded with adrenaline and dread and God knows what else. There's an opened wrap thingy from Pret, but that won't cut it. Nor will the Snickers bar—there's no way she'll be able to chew it.

'Do you have juice?' I practically shout at Gen. I'm asking too many things of her at once, I know I am. But I need everything now. I need Nat's numbers. I need some form of fast-acting glucose.

'I think so. Hang on.' She stands, her face still on the phone. 'Got it. Is this bad?'

She turns the phone around and shows me the display.

Two-point-two with a downwards arrow showing that her glucose levels are still dropping. *Natalie, you stupid, irresponsible girl.* 'Get me that juice,' I tell Gen shortly, and she runs towards the double doors separating this room from her team's office.

Natalie's getting more agitated. 'Fuck off,' she slurs, the words less clear than her disquiet. 'Fuck you. Devil. Hate you.'

'I know,' I tell her. Even if she didn't loathe me, this kind of hostility, this irritability, is very standard in someone who's hypo. Ellen used to hit me with her tiny fists. 'I know. You hate me, but right now you've got to let me help you. Okay?'

'No,' she whimpers, clawing at my hand on her shoulder, trying ineffectually to swipe it away. She's crying, tears pouring down her face, her mascara a smeary black chaser. I can't bear this. It's fucking splitting me open, seeing her like this. Watching history repeat itself. Where is the fucking juice? I scrabble around her belongings. Surely she's got some sweets, or some gummies or something—

Glycogel.

Bingo.

We never had this for Ellen, but I know what it is. I need to get it into her. If this doesn't work, I'm giving her five minutes before calling nine-nine-nine. She's twisting and turning, and I don't want to make her any more distraught than she already is, but my priority is getting some glucose into her to offset that surplus insulin in her system.

I unscrew the cap and squeeze a large mound onto my shaking finger. 'Natalie, open your mouth for me. I need to give you some gel.'

She arches back, shifting forward on the sofa, the heel of her stiletto grazing my wool-covered thigh as she does. I spy the black lace tops of her fishnet stockings and quickly avert my gaze back to the job at hand, because now is not the time to ogle, and God knows, this beautiful, irresponsible woman is *not* going to get any more ill on my watch.

She's still mumbling, but it's growing less coherent by the second. Her lips are wet with saliva, her cheeks slick with tears and her nose running. My nose is running too. Odd. I sniff hard, gripping her jaw hard with my free hand and sliding my finger in sideways, rubbing the gel over her upper gum as best I can while she thrashes about.

'There you go,' I croon. 'Good girl.' *Please work please work please work.* I've never used this stuff before. I don't know how much is enough, but I'm going to err on the side of caution and give her some more, unless—

Gen appears in the doorway. 'Juice.'

Thank fuck. I release Natalie's jaw. 'Grip her head as firmly as you can,' I order, holding my arm out for the juice. She comes up behind the sofa and cradles Natalie's face in both hands. 'Harder,' I bark. I may even shout it. 'Hold her as still as you can.'

I raise the juice to her mouth and tip the glass to pour a little in. She splutters and spits it right back out, some of it landing on me.

'Fuck's sake, sweetheart,' I groan. 'I need to get this into you, okay? You've got to be brave. I've got you. We've got you. You need to let us help you.'

I try again. Most of it dribbles down her chin, but I get a little in. I swipe the rest off her chin with my hand. This is fucking hopeless—the gel's a better option, clearly.

'Keep hold of her,' I tell Gen and grab the tube again, smearing another line of gel onto my finger. Into her mouth I go, rubbing back and forth as thoroughly as I can in an attempt to get it absorbed. I have no idea how quickly this stuff works.

She's still seizing, but not quite so badly, and as Gen holds her and I rub gel into her gum until I can feel no trace of it, it strikes me that the spasms are lessening.

Oh God is what I think she says, but it's garbled around my finger. I ease it out of her mouth and wipe the back of my hand over the slick of moisture running down my cheek before wrapping my fingers gently around the back of her neck.

'It's okay,' I tell Gen. 'You can let her go now. What's her monitor say?'

She casts around for the phone, which is perched on one of the cushions. 'Three-point-three.'

'Show me.'

She turns it and props it back on the cushion so I can watch the data. The arrow has turned and is bearing upwards. Good. The number is rising more slowly than I'd like, but I can only guess it operates on some sort of delay.

I shift my hands so they're cradling Natalie's face. She's still weeping, but it's less distressed and more piteous now. She's almost childlike like this. I'm well aware that this will be a highly vulnerable position for her to find herself in when she comes around, especially in front of a guy she despises, and I hate it for her.

I hold her for a moment. 'I'll try the juice again,' I say with a hard sniff. 'Natalie? You need more glucose, sweetheart. Okay? Try to take a drink for me. Everything's going to be okay. You're doing great.' I have no way of knowing how much excess insulin is in her system. I suppose all I can do is feed her juice and gel gradually until I see the numbers ticking up to a safe level.

Beats the hell out of pricking her skin to test her blood, that's for sure.

I hold the glass to her lips, dispensing juice with difficulty. It's messy, and a good half of it rolls down her chin with each sip. I notice idly that my hand is shaking, but it's going in. That's the main thing. She's managing to swallow between heaving sobs, and she's attempting to curl a trembling hand around the glass, though I have no intention of letting it go. She's not strong enough yet.

'You're doing so well,' I tell her. Her spasms have lessened now to the point that I don't have to hold her head still anymore, but I keep my hand there for comfort as much as for anything else, letting my fingers smooth down her hair, which has got all mussed up. 'You hear that? You're doing so well.'

I blink away the moisture blurring my vision and glance up at Gen, but she's staring at me with the strangest expression. It looks like concern.

'Are you okay, Adam?'

'I'm fine. Can you get me a towel? Or a whole load of tissues?'

She hesitates, checking me out again. 'Of course,' she says, bustling through the doors. She's back again a moment later with a box of tissues, tugging a few out and handing me a wad.

I get shakily to my feet and take a seat beside Natalie, easing her backwards so her head is supported by the cushions. 'Let's get you cleaned up a little,' I tell her, setting the glass of juice on the coffee table and using the tissues to wipe the tears from under her eyes, the juice from her mouth and chin and neck, and her runny nose.

I ditch the tissues and begin to feed her the juice again. Her head lolls backwards. I know just how exhausted and shitty and intensely vulnerable she'll feel when the worst of this has passed and she's *compos mentis*.

Gen comes around the back of the sofa and takes a seat adjacent to us, watching me. 'This must be very triggering for you.'

'I'm fine.'

'I can't believe I didn't know what to do.'

'Believe me, I'll be having words with Natalie about that,' I say. 'And so should you. It's fucking irresponsible. She should have briefed you all fully.'

Natalie groans and pouts like a child, letting more juice leak out over her full lower lip. I put the glass down and reach for the tissues again.

'But it can wait,' I tell Gen hastily as I mop her chin up. She swipes my hand away, and I grab her wrist gently, holding her hand away from her face. 'Right now, she needs peace and rest, and ideally a full checkup.'

'You're very good with her. I was a mess.'

I have a feeling I'm a mess too, but I shake my head. 'Where does she live?'

'Seven Sisters.'

Fuck that. There's no way she's schlepping all the way back to the arse end of North London, or wherever the fuck it is. 'I want to take her back to mine, get my doctor over. My nutritionist, too. Get her fully checked out and have my chef cook her a square fucking meal.'

'Come on, Adam. You've been great, but there's no way she'll go for that. I can't possibly put her in that position.'

We eye each other over Natalie's head, and it's perfectly clear what she's thinking. Gen's not one to hold back when she disapproves.

'I'm telling you.' My voice is barely above a whisper. 'I swear on my baby sister's eternal memory, I will not harm a hair on her head. You *know* that. And you'd better persuade her of that fact.' I lift the clump of damp, sticky tissues to my face and wipe my cheek.

Her face contorts as if the significance of my oath is too painful for her to handle. 'Fine,' she says finally. 'But only if Nat agrees. I'm not letting you steamroll her, okay?'

10

NATALIE

The Devil himself is sitting right next to me, and he's crying. Actual tears are streaming down his face.

Whatever. I don't have the energy to care. I just feel... ugh. *Horrific.* Sick and shaky and fucking *wiped* like I've just run a marathon, my hands still trembling.

He's holding my hand. Oh my God. I tug it away as hard as I can, and he releases it. It's all sticky. I plonk my elbows on my thighs and bury my face in both my hands, the cloying smell of orange juice hitting me. I just want to curl up into a ball somewhere dark and die. I don't want to be here in this fancy room with Gen and *him* while I'm in this state.

The tears spill over into my hands, and I want to wail at the absolute misery and unfairness of it all. I've had way worse hypo episodes than this, but it's still beyond shitty. I cry harder. Gen's talking, and I think she says my name, but I honestly can't make any sense of it.

Then he speaks. 'Hey. It's okay. You're okay.' I understand that part, and I understand that he's shifting beside me and tipping me forward so he can wrap a strong arm around me and tug me against his hard body.

I should elbow him in the ribs, but I'm too tired. I should be horrified that I've let him get this close, but there's no room in my broken body for that. There's only room for exhaustion, and for the extreme mortification that's creeping over me at the realisation of what's just gone down.

I've just had the most vulnerable experience it's possible for me to have. If I'd got naked and danced on the table it would have been less humiliating. Nothing else can top that.

Besides, his voice is nice and calm and authoritative. Like, if he says it's so, it is. If he says I'm okay, I am. And the arm banded around me feels nice, too. Safe. Strong.

One of the absolute hardest things to accept about type 1 is the extreme vulnerability it forces you to endure, often in very public places, and often in front of total strangers. It's the worst, especially for someone like me, Little Miss Perfect, who always wants to look like she's got her shit together and never wants to impose on anyone.

Believe me, the strangers I've imposed on... the poor, unsuspecting people I've collapsed on and drooled on and flashed my panties at and scared the shit out of.

But nothing beats this. This is the *worst*. An episode in front of *this* guy, when I planned on playing the role of impenetrable ice queen today? It's a fucking joke.

I sob harder. I can't stop. After every hypo, I just want my mum. I want to be babied. It's so bloody miserable.

'Hey,' he says again. 'Natalie.' He holds me more tightly against him. 'It's over. You did great. We just need to get more juice down you, okay? Your glucose is above four now. We're getting there.'

'You're in good hands with Adam,' Gen says, her voice coming closer. 'He knows what he's doing.'

Abdicating responsibility is easy right now. If someone wants to adult for a few minutes, to monitor my levels and feed me juice like I'm three years old, then I'll let them. Gladly. I'm too drained to argue.

I remove my face from my hands. My cheeks are wet, and I can't look at him or Gen quite yet. Instead I look at the coffee table, at the box of tissues and the glass of orange juice, its sides all smeary. To my right, his thighs. *Brioni*, I think. I nod my acquiescence, my head still bowed.

'Good girl,' Adam says. He keeps me in a tight grip while he reaches forward and pulls out several tissues. I raise a hand halfheartedly to take them, but he tuts. 'Let me. Lift your head.'

I do as he says, but I let my eyes drift closed. If I don't have to see it, it's not real, right? He wipes gently over both my cheeks, a little harder under my eyes, and then wipes over my mouth before dumping them and pulling out a fresh tissue, which he holds to my nose.

'Blow.'

Oh, the indignity. I do as he says, and lots of snot comes out. That feels better.

'Excellent,' he says. Now that my nose is clearer, I can smell him. He smells amazing, in a hard-to-define way. Like, if I went into Harrods and made a mix of all their nicest aftershaves. Kind of how their perfume hall smells, but the male version. I'm fucking exhausted. I let my head sag right back till it hits the cushions, though it's not very comfortable with his arm around me.

'Lemme go,' I slur, my bottom lip trembling.

'Nope. Not till you've had more juice. Tell me when you're feeling up to chewing your Snickers.'

'Mmm.' Snickers. God, I know just how well that'll hit the spot—I just need to work up to the effort of actually ingesting it. I open my eyes and stare at the ceiling. The chandelier twinkles prettily at me. It's like something out of a fairytale. A Cinderella chandelier.

'Come on. Juice time,' he says, hoisting me upwards with the arm still banded around me. I want to tell him to fuck off, but I know he's right about the juice.

He brushes my hair off my face before holding the juice glass up to my mouth and letting me drink. I take a big gulp and then another. I haven't looked either of them in the eye yet since that first glance at him. I'm always hyper-vulnerable after an attack, and eye-contact is a step too far. I detest seeing that look of pity and fear in the eyes of someone who's witnessed it; I can't stand knowing the state they've seen me in. That they'll probably never un-see it. That they'll think of it every time they look at me.

'Snickers,' I tell him, pushing the glass away. I can feel my glucose beginning to stabilise, but the hangover isn't going anywhere.

He releases me, thank fuck, though my back feels instantly colder when he removes his arm, and twists, opening the Snickers bar and handing it to me. I accept it wordlessly and take a bite, chomping down on the delicious mix of chocolate and caramel and salty peanuts.

Sooo good.

It gives me the confidence to glance to my left, where Gen sits, her face stricken and her hands clasped on her knees. I can't muster a smile, but I give her a little nod, and she presses her lips together in a gesture of sympathy before asking, 'Are you alright, sweetie?'

'Mmm-hmm.' I nod again and take another mouthful of my bar, focusing on masticating thoroughly so I can absorb its sugar as quickly as possible. I'm well aware she's never seen me like this. I'm always immaculately turned out and immaculately behaved, remembering everyone's name and greeting her members politely. *Professionally*.

She's never seen me crying—last night excepted—and God knows what else: probably fitting and slurring and drooling. Dear God. I have no idea how on earth I'll find the strength to pull myself together for my shift. I'll have to redo my makeup. I must look an absolute state.

On my other side, Adam reaches behind me and rubs my back in circles. I'm stuck in the weirdest place between knowing intellectually that I hate him—*fear* him—and liking the sensation of having a competent adult's hands on me.

It must be primal. Right now, my nervous system knows I'm at far greater risk of being hospitalised with inadequate glucose than I am of having him beat the crap out of me or gouge my eye out in front of Gen.

And, loath as I am to admit it, I understand from my confused memories and from the disgusting mixture of glycogel and orange juice lingering in my mouth that I have him to thank for rescuing me from a worse crash. One where I might have had a full-on seizure or lost consciousness.

How could I be so fucking irresponsible? That's not me. A key subset of my Little Miss Perfect persona is Little Miss Responsible. I blame my nerves over having to sit down with this arsehole.

I risk a glance to my right to see his gaze still trained on my Freestyle Libre app. He may have taken care of *my* tears and eye makeup and snot and drool, but his face is still tear-stained, and those pale blue eyes I was begrudgingly admiring a few minutes ago are reddened.

He looks in far worse shape than Gen. He looks as though I scared the living daylights out of him. I would *not* have pegged Adam Wright, coward and bully and violent thug, for a crier. He looks up, and our eyes meet. His palm is still doing circles of my back, the heat of it warming me through my dress.

'You're getting there,' he says, flashing my phone at me.

'Thank you,' I manage. I'm not sure if it sounds ungracious or simply garbled given my mouthful of chocolate and my compromised motor skills.

'No thanks needed,' he says stiffly. It's too awkward to hold his gaze. My skin should be crawling at this proximity to him, but I feel a different kind of discomfort. Less fear than excrucation at having shared a moment of intense vulnerability with such a monster. My eyes drop instead to his lapel.

'Brioni,' I mumble. Clearly my usual, carefully honed filters have left the building and failed to return.

He gives a low chuckle. 'You've got a good eye. I think she's getting there,' he says to Gen, and I roll my eyes before slumping back against the cushions and letting them drift closed.

'Stay like that, sweetie,' Gen says in a low, gentle voice. 'Just rest. You've been through a lot. When you're ready, Adam would like to take you back to his place so he can get his doctor to look you over.'

No fucking way. Hell would have to freeze over first. I open my eyes and sit bolt upright, but Adam eases me back with a firm hand on my shoulder.

'Lie back and close your eyes,' he says. 'Just *listen*, okay?'

'I'm not going anywhere with you,' I mutter.

'Natalie.' His voice is stern, but it's also low and melodic. I bet he fools all sorts of people with that voice. 'Listen to me. I know you've just had a very rough quarter of an hour, so I'm not trying to give you a hard time here. But the truth is, you had a nasty crash, and you scared the shit out of me and Gen, and I for one won't be able to relax until you've got the all-clear from a doctor, okay?

'Sending you back to Seven Sisters isn't an option. You need to get checked out now, and you need some rest and a balanced dinner. I'm only a couple of miles away.' He pauses. The fact that I'm too exhausted to bite his head off mid-speech is working in his favour.

'I live right behind Kensington Palace,' he continues, 'and I have a car outside right now. Please believe me when I say I'm well aware there's no one you'd rather get in a car with less than me. I know that. But I'm here, and you need to let me help you.'

I roll my head to one side and open my eyes. He's staring down at me with a blistering intensity that makes my face heat.

'I don't need to let you help me,' I whisper, because it's true. I can take the pain of a taxi fare back home, heinous though it'll be. Maybe Gen will let me relax here for another few minutes. Maybe—

'You don't need to, but you should,' Gen says gently. 'I'll vouch for Adam. He's promised me you'll be in safe hands. And there'll be other people around. Right, Adam?'

'Right,' he says hurriedly. 'My butler, at least two maids, my chef, the doctor...' He trails off. 'My PA too, possibly.'

Jesus. Sounds like a circus. Or Downton Abbey.

'My point is,' he says, 'you won't be alone with me at all. You'll be perfectly safe and well cared for. I just want to get you checked over, maybe get some bloods taken.' He pauses again. 'It's really the very least I can do for you.'

I stare at him. It's the most ridiculous, farcical proposal ever, and there is literally no one on the face of the earth who's less welcome and less entitled to see me like this than *him.* I just wish my brain and mouth would hurry up and work together to formulate a coherent argument to that point.

Gen rises and comes to sit right next to me. She takes my hand, and I give Adam some side-eye before I roll my head back around so I can see her, my hand clutching at my Snickers as if it's a life raft.

'Sweetie,' she says in a confiding tone. 'I feel terrible about this. But Anton's away, and this is absolutely not the right place for you to recover, and Adam has these people on speed dial. He'll get a doctor over immediately to his place, and we can all get some peace of mind. I promise you, you're in very good hands. Will you please, please do it for me?'

I close my eyes and gather the flimsiest shreds of resilience from somewhere deep inside my poor, exhausted body.

'Fine.'

11

ADAM

Natalie sits huddled on the other side of my Range Rover, black coat on and arms wrapped tightly around herself as she gazes out the window at Piccadilly crawling past us.

It's pissing it down, which has made the traffic even shittier than normal, but she's safe and warm in here. Still, hostility radiates from her, and I have to give her credit for finding the energy to hate me quite so actively when she must be utterly shattered.

She brushed her hair and cleaned herself up a little in the bathroom with Gen, it would seem, while I waited in Alchemy's lobby and made a hasty, furtive call to Clem, one of my assistants. *Get Dr Dyson to my house immediately. Patient is a type I diabetic. Tell him to bring supplies. And call the personal shoppers at Selfridges and get them to send over a load of stuff asap. I need women's pyjamas, underwear, trainers, lounge wear—all confortable but stylish. And get them to put together a toiletry pack, too.*

I can't imagine how much she'd resent my thinking this, but she's stunningly beautiful.

She was beautiful when she was kissing Gen's arse at the start of our meeting while shooting me what she thought were discreet death stares.

She was beautiful when every bodily fluid her face could produce was streaming and getting all over my hands.

And she's beautiful now, sitting there as streetlights and headlights pan across her delicate features, even if she's clearly drained.

'Can I ask you something?' I venture.

She turns her face, but not her body, wariness in her eyes. I don't blame her. To think this woman and I are connected in the worst way, by the most grotesque thing I've ever done to another human in my life, is as sickening as it is surreal. I'm sure she'd rather be anywhere but here, including on a packed tube back to Seven Sisters.

I push on. 'Have you thought about having alerts set up on your phone for when your glucose drops—I assume they can do that, these days?'

In other words, what the fuck were you playing at? But I can't risk antagonising her any further than my mere existence already does.

'I've got alerts set up.'

I raise my eyebrows, and she rolls her eyes at me.

'I muted them yesterday, okay, because I had a trunk show, and I forgot to unmute them.'

I stay silent, judgement radiating from every pore.

'Look, I'll prove it to you.' She rummages in her enormous bag, which I repacked on the sofa before we left, and pulls out her now-locked phone. A tap on the lock screen shows a series of Freestyle Libre alerts.

'A stunningly effective method for safeguarding your health,' I snap, all efforts at diplomacy forgotten. 'You have to do a better job than that.'

I'm pissed off. I can't help it. I don't begrudge her the continuous glucose monitor or her pump, but God knows, a basic CGM would have saved Ellen's life, had we had them available to us back then.

She gives me a *you can't be serious* look. 'I do a good job, believe me. I'm a highly responsible person, usually.'

'*Usually* won't cut it. You don't get second chances with this shit, Natalie. You can't afford to be this cavalier. All you need is one bad hypo and you're done for.'

Her expression tells me she's taking my advice as inter-ference and not concern. 'You know nothing about me, and you certainly don't have the right to get to know me any better than this.'

'Maybe not, but I bet Gen could have done without having to witness that back there. What the fuck are you thinking, not having briefed your entire team on your condition? Every last one of them should know what symp-toms to look for if you're hypo or hyper, and they should know what to do. You should have a tube of gel in every single fucking desk drawer in Alchemy and wherever else you work. This is basic, basic stuff.'

We glare at each other, and a tiny part of me feels bad for giving her a hard time when she's still recovering, but a far larger part is incandescent with rage and frustration. Gen wasn't the only person who could have done without what was a harrowing trip down memory lane for me.

'You're right, of course,' she says stiffly. 'And my colleagues at my company are all well briefed. I'm usually— I can usually spot them before they get bad, you know? I'm usually in control of it. I don't want the Alchemy guys having to deal with that.'

Despite the shit I'm giving her, I suspect she is usually in control. She seems like someone who prides herself on having it together, who probably despises the lack of control a condition like type 1 gives her. But this illness isn't something to be pushed under the carpet. It's a daily threat, a daily fucking battle. It's running to stand still your entire life, and she'd be far better off if she made peace with that instead of trying to fight it.

'They're good people,' is all I say. 'You can trust them with this. And after today, you can bet Gen will have St John's Ambulance in for a full team debrief. She'll probably have a powerpoint, knowing her.'

She shuts her eyes briefly, as if the thought pains her, but it's true. No fucking way Gen will stand for her and the team not being up to speed on basic hypo management after what went down this evening.

'What makes you such an expert, anyway?' she mutters.

I hesitate, and it's prolonged enough for her to look at me with curiosity.

'A family member had type 1,' I say shortly. 'I'm far too familiar with its dangers, unfortunately.'

That knocks the wind out of her sails. She stares at me, no doubt registering my use of the past tense.

'I'm so sorry,' she says quietly.

'Thank you.' I'm not willing to say more. She's holding me at arm's length, with good reason. Like she said, I have no right to any knowledge of her. But I won't let her have any knowledge of me, either. She thinks she has me sussed, but she's nowhere near accurate, and I won't entrust one iota of Ellen's memory to someone who condemned me long before she laid eyes on me.

I lean my head back and close my eyes, signalling that the conversation is closed.

12

NATALIE

With every minute of this journey, I've grown more on edge. I've allowed this man I loathe to spirit me away and take me to his *home*, for Christ's sake. To his evil, billionaire lair that's probably all stainless steel and cold black marble surfaces in which he can admire his reflection, and punching bags in every room to offer him an outlet so he doesn't beat the shit out of his staff.

He doesn't look like a monster.

He looks like a beautiful, successful, if tired, businessman.

But that tells me nothing. He's probably got some Dorian Gray-type portrait of himself in his attic, only this version gets uglier and more grotesque every time his moral compass slips one rung further.

I can't quite square away everything I know to be true about Adam Wright with the way he looked after me this evening. Despite my ungracious behaviour to him just now, I'm well aware that I'd be surrounded by paramedics if it hadn't been for his quick action back at Alchemy. But that's a puzzle I'm simply too tired to ponder.

We pass Kensington Gardens, though it's too dark to see Kensington Palace, which is set back from the main road. Then we're turning right and stopping in front of a barrier at an actual wooden sentry box.

'Are we going into the palace?' I ask him, craning to see outside.

'No,' he tells me with a small smile. 'That's next door. This is Kensington Palace Gardens—it's a private road.'

There's private, and then there's security guards with assault rifles.

'You must have a lot of enemies.'

He lets out a genuine laugh, and it's startling. Let's just say I avert my gaze from the sight of it pretty quickly. 'They're not for me, believe me. There are a lot of embassies on this road. It's a pretty massive terrorist target.'

'Fantastic,' I mutter as the barrier lifts and the car moves slowly forward.

'If it's any consolation, the Russian Embassy is here, so that's one superpower we don't have to worry about nuking us.'

Better and better. For all its issues, you don't get this shit in Seven Sisters.

After a few hundred feet on what must be one of the widest, quietest roads in London, we turn left and wait as huge wrought-iron gates open automatically. It's too dark to see much, but I spot immaculate box hedges lit by spots along the edge of the gravel.

'Wait there,' Adam says as we pull to a stop. 'Nige will help you.' The driver gets out and comes around to my side, opening the door and helping me down with a kindly hand in mine. It's appreciated, as the car is high, as are my heels, and my dress is short. I'd give anything to be unlocking my front door right now and collapsing face-down onto my own bed.

Still, I thank him politely and walk round the enormous SUV as I gaze ahead of me in astonishment.

This isn't a house. It's a mansion, and it's so breathtakingly, perfectly beautiful that it actually hurts my heart.

Adam Wright lives *here?*

It's official.

There is no justice left in this entire bloody world.

But back to this magnificent, creamy white mansion, its splendour illuminated against the relative dark of its vast gardens. Almost every room downstairs looks to be lit up. On either side of the main entrance, with its shallow flight of steps and grandiose porch, is a huge semi-circular bay window that continues up to the next storey. A glance upwards shows me a further row of picturesque dormer windows punctuating the slate roof.

It's magnificent. Breathtaking. Every creative atom in my body is thrumming at the perfect architecture, the immaculate finish. It probably gets a coat of vanilla ice cream-coloured paint every other week.

The front door swings open, revealing a smartly dressed man who I assume is the butler, and there's a light hand at the small of my back: Adam, ushering me up the shallow sandstone steps flanked with bobbing candles safe in their shiny hurricane lanterns.

'You first,' he says.

'Good evening, madam,' the kindly butler says, and I smile and murmur my greeting.

It's like walking into a hotel. It's *ridiculous*, and there isn't a stainless steel surface in sight.

On the contrary.

A large wooden staircase that's beautifully carved and graciously curved.

A chandelier that makes the one at Alchemy look like it's from Ikea.

A glossy black-and-white chequered marble floor that must need to be buffed every time someone crosses it.

But it's not cold, not at all, because the walls of this huge space are a warm, unexpected buttermilk, and the antique table in the centre is practically collapsing under the weight of its glorious burden of flowers and greenery, and there's a grass-green velvet *chaise longue* that shouldn't work but really does, and there are crazy, oversized paintings jostling for space the whole way up the staircase, and archways over open double doors leading off in all directions and providing all manner of tantalising glimpses into the rooms beyond.

It's quite simply the most beautiful home I've ever, ever been in, and it's nicer than most luxury hotel lobbies I've had the good fortune to sneak a peek at whenever Gen's dragged us out for drinks. It's nicer than Claridges, even. The taste level is off the charts, the art and the flowers and the furnishings exactly, perfectly right, and the smell—that of a florist mixed with expensive candles—nothing short of divine.

'Toby, this is Miss Bennett,' Adam tells the butler as I stand and gape and attempt to pull myself the hell together. 'She'll be my guest for the evening. Has Dyson arrived?'

'Certainly, Mr Wright,' Toby says. 'He's in the drawing room.'

'Good. Send through'—Adam stops and surveys me with narrowed eyes before continuing—'a grazing platter. Nothing too sugary. Plenty of protein. We'll eat properly when Dyson's done his thing.'

We certainly won't, I think, but instead I shoot Toby a smile I hope is grateful and apologetic as I follow Adam, who's already striding off to one of the sets of open double doors.

Oh, sweet Jesus.

The drawing room may just end me. It is *perfection*. It has me at hello with a huge log fire that's crackling merrily in the marble fireplace. I'd give anything to collapse on that nice, thick rug in front of it. Or maybe I should cuff myself to the brass fire surround with its padded leather seat so I never have to leave.

I'd stay forever if it wasn't for the fact that this enchanted palace comes with a royal beast of an owner, unfortunately.

The overall vibe of the room is plush and grand. It's very much a winter room, with its blue-grey walls that look to be covered not in paint, not in paper, but in linen, kind of like an art gallery. And this guy's art budget must rival the GDP of Luxembourg, because there are more spectacular paintings hanging on the linen, each one lit perfectly.

It's the lighting that's the real clincher in here, I realise. Not just the picture lighting, and the dancing glow of the fire, but the dim, low-level lighting courtesy of the numerous silk-covered table lamps dotted around between various clusters of richly-upholstered furniture.

Everything is so damn gorgeous. Everything's been chosen for its decorative value as much as its functional one, and it's all been pulled together so expertly.

Adam Wright sulking into his giant bags of money in a cold, sleek and charmless bachelor pad I can handle. *This* is a far harder pill to swallow.

Alas, my chance at revelling in the sheer pleasure of my surroundings is fleeting indeed, because there's a man rising from one of the armchairs nearest the fire, and Adam is beckoning me over and introducing me and Dr Dyson before hovering expectantly.

'You can leave us to it, Adam,' Dr Dyson says with a jerk of his head towards the door we just entered through. His demeanour is grumpy, but so would I be if I'd been summoned on a house call at seven on a disgustingly wet evening.

Thank God for that. I didn't want to suggest it, but I've had quite enough of him seeing my vulnerabilities for one evening. I can't suffer any more indignities in front of Adam Wright this evening.

Clearly, he's not used to being told *no*. What a shocker. 'I should stay,' he insists. 'I was there for Natalie's hypo, and I'd like to stay and hear what you have to say.'

'Not necessary,' Dr Dyson, who may be my new best friend, says. 'I'll fill you in later where I think it's pertinent. Otherwise, I'd like to offer this young lady a little privacy. After all, it sounds like she's had quite an evening, so far.'

I swallow a smirk as Adam mutters a hostile *fine* and backs away from us.

Thank goodness someone can stand up to him.

13

NATALIE

D r Dyson's examination is as efficient as it is thorough. He persuades me to take off my heels, and I relax into an armchair while he puts me on an IV drip with a cocktail of vitamins and electrolytes that he swears will help me recover my energy. He monitors my glucose levels, takes my blood pressure, my heart rate and my oxygen levels and draws some blood that he says will go straight to an overnight lab for testing.

He also replaces my CGM and examines my pump, just for good measure.

And while we wait for the IV bag to empty, he asks me endless probing questions about my medical history, the last time I had my eyes and kidneys checked, my diet, my day-to-day job and general stress levels, and the events leading up to today's hypo.

'I was really worked up,' I confess. 'I was stressed about the mee—a meeting I was having, and I just couldn't get enough food down me. My stomach was in knots. I thought I'd have time after the meeting to eat my dinner. I miscalculated.'

He frowns. 'There are other ways to compensate if you're going to miss a meal. They're not ideal, but they're better than what happened. Gummies, gels.'

I nod, chastened, because this is basic stuff, and I don't need him to tell me I fucked up. Even if his disapproval is far easier to stomach than Adam's.

When the bag is emptied, and I'm sporting a little round plaster on each arm from the drip and the blood tests, he leaves me to go find Adam. I slump back in the armchair and survey my surroundings. I'm beyond exhausted, and the idea of a long, wet journey home in four-inch heels on tubes and buses is the last thing I feel like, but it'll be good to get home, and it'll feel even better to get out of this dress and these holdups and into my pyjamas.

I just wish I hadn't left my flats tucked under the lectern at Alchemy.

And I wish this armchair wasn't quite so obscenely comfortable, or this fire so warming, or this room so indulgent. I allow myself another cube of ridiculously good herb-infused cheese from the platter the butler, Toby, brought in a few minutes into my checkup.

Dr Dyson returns with Adam a couple of minutes later, both men talking in low voices. As they come around to stand by the fire, I can't help but gape.

Because clearly Adam has used his banishment as an opportunity to shower and change.

Holy shit.

He's in grey jogging bottoms and a form-fitting white t-shirt under an unzipped navy hoodie bearing the Wright Holdings logo on the chest. His hair is damp, his curls raked sleekly off his face and his feet encased in moccasin-style slippers.

He's fully dressed, of course—there's almost no part of

his body left uncovered save for his hands and neck—but it's still... confronting. I'm well aware by now that the man wears the heck out of a custom-made suit, but the sight of casual Adam, dressed so informally in his own home, feels illicit, somehow. Wrong.

I glance down at my legs and hurriedly straighten up in my chair to hide the glimpse of lace I'm flashing. What's appropriate for Alchemy is definitely not appropriate for here.

Before I can say anything, Dr Dyson chimes in smoothly. 'Adam here was suggesting you stay the night, and I have to say I agree. I understand you live somewhere in north London?'

I push myself out of my chair and smooth down my dress. Excellent. He and his doctor are in cahoots to keep me trapped here. 'Yes, but it's fine. Staying here's not an option. I'm going to make a move now. Thank you so much for... everything.'

Flustered, I bend to grab my tote bag, but Adam stops me with a hand on my arm. I jolt away.

'Natalie,' he says in a voice that brooks no argument. 'Listen to me. I'm sure you're anxious to get home, but it's not a good idea. You're very welcome here. I can feed you, and you can get some sleep, and then tomorrow morning I'll get my nutritionist over to run through some ideas, too. I've already texted her.'

Oh, for the love of God. This is bloody ridiculous.

'I have to work tomorrow morning,' I tell him, trying to keep my tone positive. 'And I'm really grateful for everything you've done this evening, honestly I am, but there's no need for any of that. I'll be absolutely fine.'

'I'd feel far happier if you stayed,' Dr Dyson says firmly. 'The last thing you need right now is a long trek across

London. Have some food, go take a long bath in one of Wright's many tubs, get an early night, and his nutritionist can give you some advice in the morning. It sounds like you're out and about a lot with your job. He or she can help you work out a plan for keeping your glucose levels stable when you're on the go.'

I glare at him. This definitely feels like a conspiracy to imprison me here. And his suggestion of a bath—and a sound sleep—almost made me laugh. There's no way I'd ever feel comfortable enough in Adam Wright's house to get naked and bathe, let alone catch a wink of sleep.

I play my trump card. 'I don't have a change of clothes. I don't even have a toothbrush! I can't turn up at work tomorrow looking like this.'

'There's a load of stuff upstairs for you,' Adam says evenly. 'I've had some things biked over from Selfridges. Toiletries, nightwear, some stuff for tomorrow. It's no big deal, but hopefully it'll cover everything you need for one night. I really hope you'll be able to make yourself at home.'

'There, you see?' Dr Dyson looks positively thrilled. 'Now you can have a good night's sleep before you go back to the real world.'

The unpalatable and very inconvenient truth is that I'm still completely wiped. Even after the drip, I feel like Bambi as I stand here. The mere thought of going outside and trying to flag down a cab in this weather feels like a herculean task, dammit. Adam clearly sees the moment I yield, because he smiles at me. It's more of a smirk, and it reeks of victory, and it makes him look even more slappable than usual.

Now I do laugh, because this is ridiculous. Generous, yes, of course. But also more than a little psychotic. Adam

Wright has basically kidnapped me, and the good doctor on his payroll is enabling him.

But Dr Dyson has one thing right.

I do indeed feel like I left the real world behind me when I stepped over this threshold. And not in a good way.

'Pyjamas.' Adam coughs. 'There are robes in the bathroom, but I didn't have any women's nightwear. Obviously.'

He points to the massive yellow Selfridges bag sitting on the huge bed in the centre of this astonishingly chic guest suite. 'There should be underwear in the bag. I haven't touched any of it, of course—my assistant put the order through and one of the maids unpacked. Let me see— leggings, etcetera. I think she got you some athleisure wear, basically. Trainers. The toiletries should all be in the bathroom. Shout if there's anything else you need. Shall we say dinner in half an hour? I've asked the chef to keep it light and simple—we can just eat in the kitchen. I'll get someone to run you a bath once we've eaten.'

Once I've got rid of him and closed the door firmly behind me before checking if it locks—it doesn't—I lean against it and exhale.

This is insane.

Insane.

I'm stuck in the most achingly beautiful, palatial home I've ever seen with the human being who's caused my family no end of pain and destruction. Oh, and with his fleet of staff, of course. And he's bought me half of Selfridges, a gesture I shouldn't accept but probably will, because pyjamas sound really fucking good right now.

Not to mention, this room is utterly perfect. If I'm not

mistaken, the pale green wallpaper adorned with pale pink cherry blossoms is De Gournay, which means that every blossom is hand-painted and that each panel cost a couple of grand. The pink of the roman blinds matches the cherry blossom exactly, and the bed is a huge, white thing of wonder that looks like a marshmallow and probably feels like one.

I may be pissed off as hell to find myself here, with him, but that bed has a siren's call, and it's *loud*.

I push myself off the door and wander over to the pile of clothes resting on it. The tags have been cut off everything— probably his way of ensuring I couldn't insist on any of it being sent back. But those delectable silk satin pyjamas in black and white *toile de Jouy* with black piping are Olivia von Halle pyjamas.

They're five hundred quid *minimum*. I've ogled them through the window of her bijou Chelsea boutique before.

The casual wear is all Varley and Skims. It's gorgeous, obviously.

And it's all my size.

I risk a look in the bag. More Skims. Nude panties and a nude sports bra, both lace-trimmed but tasteful rather than porno.

Fuuuuuuck.

I sigh in defeat as I reach behind my neck for the top of my zip.

14

ADAM

I wonder what she thinks of it. The house, I mean.

I wonder if she likes it.

It's not that I want to *impress* her, exactly. At least, I don't think it is. I'm not the monster she thinks I am. I have no interest in rubbing her nose in how my fortunes have changed, in throwing my wealth in her face when I'm sure she thinks me undeserving.

But I want her to *like* it. It's clear she has excellent taste, and I know, from the dossier I had one of my associates pull up for me today, that she has a stunning—if sub-scale—womenswear label. For whatever reason, I want my tasteful, elegant home to speak to her, to get through to her where I can't. To inveigle its way into that artistic soul of hers.

If I'm honest with myself, I suspect I also want it to work its magic in somehow legitimising me in her eyes. She'll never forgive me, I know that much, but perhaps her opinion of me will grow more nuanced. Perhaps she'll entertain the sentiment that a man who's all monster would never invest in a labour of love to produce something quite so beautiful?

But there's little sign of capitulation in her huge brown eyes when she finds her way to the kitchen. Rather, I detect a wariness, a resentment, that she's found herself forced to accept my help. My hospitality. She's wearing dark grey leggings that mould to her tight little arse and a cropped, blush-coloured sweatshirt. *Thank you, Clem.*

She looks pale and exhausted and perfect.

I wonder if she's ever been spanked by someone who knows what they're doing.

I wonder if she'd ever let herself enjoy it.

She takes in the kitchen, which is my favourite room in the house. It's at its best in summer, when the light streams in from the windows at each end. My architects knocked through a couple of rooms to create this incredible space that runs east-west and is illuminated every morning and evening. The white marble counters lighten it up, but I couldn't resist when my interior designer suggested the pop of colour my duck-egg blue lacquered cabinets bring.

The blue juxtaposed with the rosy gleam of the copper pans hanging overhead brings warmth at this time of year to what could easily be a cavernous space, and the smell is enough to welcome the weariest of guests. Kamyl, my chef, has put together a quick Provençal fish stew at my request. It should be light enough to ensure Natalie gets a good night's sleep, but I've asked him to include plenty of pulses to keep her blood glucose stable.

We sit at the island—it's a little less formal than the dining area—and allow Kamyl to heap steaming stew into our bowls. The saffron gives it a golden hue.

'Thanks, mate,' I tell him, and he gives me a friendly nod of acknowledgment before making himself scarce.

'This looks amazing,' Natalie says faintly, picking up her

fork. I suspect her natural manners are warring with her contempt of me.

'Good,' I say. 'Dig in.'

We eat silently for a couple of minutes. The stew is perfect—warming and fragrant, thanks to all the freshly chopped herbs Kamyl scattered on top. It seems to me Natalie has something on her mind, so I'll give her space and wait for her to spit it out.

Eventually, she does. 'Your home is absolutely beautiful.'

'Thank you.'

'It's not what I was expecting.'

'What did you expect—gold taps?'

'More like chrome and glass everywhere.' She doesn't crack a smile.

'Coming from my background,' I say carefully, 'aesthetics are important to me. And I don't mean appearances —I mean the positive effect beautiful surroundings have on my soul.'

'Yeah.' She slices off a piece of fish with the edge of her fork. 'I get that.'

I know she does, because I've read that dossier. Still, her admission that she is, on some level, able to appreciate and enjoy the delights of my home makes me happy.

Her concession gives me the confidence to ask my next question without too much concern that she'll run for the door.

'So. Do you remember anything Gen said in the meeting?'

'A little.' Her brow furrows. 'Something about you taking a stake in Alchemy?'

'Exactly.' I take a sip of my sparkling water before continuing. 'Now that Wolff Holdings is public, it's coming in for a little investor pressure to divest its share of the

Alchemy JV. The ethical investors—church funds, etcetera —don't like it.'

She rolls her eyes. 'Right. Because what consenting adults do in their own free time is so unethical.'

'My thoughts exactly. But it is what it is. So Anton approached me to see if I'd be interested, and I am. Very.' I pause. 'Do you know anything about my business holdings?'

I swear I can hear the machinations of her internal struggle. I'm sure she doesn't want to admit to knowing a single thing about me.

'You own some luxury brands,' she concedes eventually.

'Exactly. But I've been focusing more recently on service industries at the very high end, hence my interest in Alchemy.'

'Service industry,' she repeats, a droll little smile on her lips. 'I suppose you could call it that.'

I study her. 'You don't approve of it.'

'Of course I approve of it!' she says incredulously. 'I love what they've built. It's fantastic.'

'But you don't partake.'

'That is precisely none of your business, but no. I don't.'

I'd love to ask her why, but I'm not that foolish. I'm also oddly relieved that she doesn't find her way to The Play- room every evening after her shift. After all, she'd have plenty of opportunity to do so. The club doesn't allow guests in after eleven, but it stays open till one. And I can't imagine how many of the patrons who ogle her at the front desk would be delighted to get their grubby mitts on her.

'Anyway,' I say instead, 'your bosses are happy to have me on board, as is the Wolff team, assuming we can agree on a valuation.' I pause. 'But Gen cares about her employees a lot, and she won't go for it unless she's sure you're comfort- able with my being involved.'

'So you want my blessing, is that it?' There's a sharpness in her tone that I should have expected and yet didn't.

'No. Not at all. Well, of course I want it, because I'd like to forge ahead with this deal, but I'm not trying to twist your arm.' I wince internally at my unintentionally violent metaphor. 'I mean, there's no pressure on your part. None at all. But if you want any clarity on my role, or any reassurances, then I'd be happy to give them to you.'

'Will you be my boss?'

I shake my head. 'Absolutely not. I'd have no executive jurisdiction over the London club. Really, I'd be more of a silent partner. Gen and the Wolff team have rolled out a scalable format. New York is opening in a matter of weeks. You won't see any more of me than you do Max Hunter.'

That gets me a tight little smile. 'Believe me, we see a lot of Max in there.'

I grin, amused. 'Seriously? Even though he's ridiculously loved up?'

'The three of them are in there a lot. Darcy still dances there one night a week, but she'll drop it soon.' She appears to rein herself in, realising she's teetering on the edge of an actual, civil conversation.

'Well, I won't be in there more often than any other punter,' I promise. 'So all you'd need to do is endure the occasional sight of me in reception. But again, I understand if that's a bridge too far.'

'I'm not about to derail any of Gen's plans,' she says, rearranging her chickpeas with her fork. She's certainly not shovelling her food down to the extent I'd like to see for her final meal of the day. 'Given I've agreed to spend a night under your roof, I think I can manage checking you in every now and again.'

It might be more often than *every now and again* given

how successful my first visit was, but Natalie probably doesn't wish to know how convenient I found it to have an easy, attractive outlet for my urges last night.

And she *definitely* wouldn't want to know how tickled I am at the prospect of seeing her at the front desk each time I visit.

'Only if you're sure,' I say. 'I'll let you catch up with Gen, and if she feels comfortable moving forward, she can let me know.'

We lapse into silence again, Natalie pushing her food around her plate, me shovelling mine up because it's fucking delicious. My phone lights up with a message from my nutritionist. She's excellent, and I suspect Natalie could benefit from her holistic approach.

'Louise, my nutritionist, will be here by nine tomorrow to see you,' I tell her.

She groans and puts her elbows on the island, resting her face in her hands. 'I have so much to do tomorrow. I really need to get out of here first thing.' She looks genuinely defeated at the mere thought of the workload awaiting her.

I bide my time. 'What is it you do?'

She lifts her face. 'I have a womenswear brand. A small one,' she adds, and I hate that she's felt the need to qualify her achievements in the face of my grotesque success.

'Oh, excellent,' I say. 'So you run that during the day and then work at Alchemy at night?'

'The fashion industry isn't exactly a cash cow unless you have critical mass,' she points out in response to the unanswered part of my question.

'Fair,' I say. 'Still, two jobs and type 1 is a lot to handle.'

Her only response to my unsolicited opinion is a glare. I bet she's a busy little bee. I bet she works that tight little arse off and is responsible to a fault—when she's not fucking up her insulin-to-glucose ratio, that is.

'What part of the market are you in?' I ask.

'Demi-couture.' She spikes a piece of fish and sticks it in her mouth. I wait until she's swallowed.

'And you have a team?'

'Yes.' I suspect the terseness of her one-word answer is a deliberate attempt to shut me down.

'It's an interesting part of the market,' I muse. 'Tough, but every part is tough, to be honest.'

Silence.

'I know you have a lot on your plate, Natalie,' I say, and she jolts like she can't believe I've been indecent enough to use her name. 'But please spare Louise half an hour. She's incredible—she's a very special human. Your body's been through a lot today. Give it this one thing.'

She sighs. *'Fine.'*

'Thank you.'

There's a question on the tip of my tongue. It's so close. I want to ask her how Stephen is. How he *really* is, deep down, aside from the fact that he's apparently thriving in his newish job at Totum, a medical data company founded by one of my great mates, Aidan Duffy.

Aide did me a solid with that one.

But my guess is that if I ask her how her brother is, she'll go fucking nuclear. She'll read all sorts of things into it: that I feel entitled to ask, that I'm digging for information I have no right to, that I'm hinting at my desire for absolution, and none of those is true.

Instead, I say something else I know will piss her off.

'I need you to eat more food. How's your glucose looking?'

She certainly isn't smuggling a phone in those snug yoga

pants, so how she'll answer my question I have no idea. She stares at me like she can't believe what I've just said.

'My glucose is *fine.*'

'And you know this because your phone is right here, where you can hear it if it alerts you?'

'I know it because I feel fine, and because I ate far too much cheese and crackers from that platter in the living room,' she grits out.

'Still, you should eat more. Especially the chickpeas.' I have no way of knowing how much of the snack platter she ate, but believe me, I'm going to check.

She sets down her fork. She has beautiful hands with long, slim fingers. 'Adam. I'm sorry you had to deal with me earlier, but I'm fine. I'm pretty full. And I'll be fine tonight, okay?'

I wonder how many more times I can get her to say *fine.*

'Even so, I'll need you to let me have access to your CGM data tonight.'

If I wasn't so frustrated, I'd laugh at the expression on her face. Sweet little Natalie looks like she wants to rip me a new one.

'You have got to be kidding me.'

'I'm not kidding you. You went full hypo in front of me, you scared the absolute shit out of me and Gen, you're pissing around with your food, and you're my responsibility tonight.' I take a deep breath, willing myself not to get riled. I will do everything in my power to ensure she never spends a second fearing me.

'I need to be able to check that you're stable.' *I won't let another person have a fatal hypo on my watch.* 'We can do this one of three ways. You can give me your phone, which I assume you have no interest in doing, you can add me to the app, which I assume is relatively straightforward to do, *or* we can go old school, and I'll prick your finger every hour, on the hour. Dyson left me some testing kits. What'll it be?'

Our gazes are locked. Her breath is coming quickly. She's doing a far worse job than me of not rising. She pushes her plate away and climbs down from her stool, standing so she's facing me, and only then does she deliver the sucker punch.

'Once a bully, always a bully, I see. I'm going to bed. Thanks for dinner.'

15

NATALIE

I 've bathed in a perfect pink marble bathtub, soaking my body in water that's rich with Epsom salts and Jo Malone bubblebath as I wonder how the fuck I've ended up in this ultimate, if temporary cliché—a gilded cage.

I've indulged in the comfort of a night-time ritual complete with as few of the items from Selfridges beauty department as I could get away with: namely cleanser and moisturiser.

I've brushed my teeth and checked my levels and donned these sumptuously silky pyjamas that slink when I walk across the room.

I've turned off the lights and set my phone on the convenient wireless charger and climbed into a bed so high and soft and warm, thanks to the hot water bottle tucked cosily inside it, that I would happily stay here forever if I wasn't so desperate to put serious mileage between me and the Beast.

It's only now, as I lie on my back in the dark and hug my hot water bottle to my stomach, that I allow myself to face what is really the worst thing about this entire situation.

And that's not my having humiliated myself with a full-on hypo in front of the person I despise most.

It's not being here, having to accept (however reluctantly) the hospitality of a man I hate and having his insane wealth rammed down my throat.

It's not even the niggling, unshakable feeling that in the past few hours, it's he who's behaved immaculately, generously, who's hosted me graciously, and I who've been an ungrateful, churlish little shit. Especially given my parting shot—a shot I can't help but suspect was way below the belt. A shot I regretted as soon as I saw the overt hurt on his face.

It's worse than all that.

It's this secret knowledge whose existence has been corroding my insides for the past few hours now:

If I didn't know who Adam Wright was and what he was capable of in the past, if I hadn't lived twenty years with the scars his despicable crime had left not just on my brother but my entire family, if he was a random, dashing hero whose presence of mind and extreme generosity and stunning home and overall concern for my welfare represented the extent of my knowledge of him, then let me tell you this:

I would be swooning right now.

Swooning.

Hard.

I mean, come on. It would be like I'd fallen into the pages of some excellent *Beauty and the Beast* reimagining, where the beast was Mr Darcy, and he was—some irritating high-handedness aside—utterly, unspeakably perfect.

No transformation necessary.

And I think that awareness makes this entire situation even less tenable than it should be. Being here is a double blow. Not only have I surrendered to the will of a man I know to be capable of horrifying violence, but I've exposed myself to that alluring disguise of his, and boy, is it a good one.

He's so handsome. So commanding. Everything he's done this evening, from reacting to my hypo with actual tears of concern, to the insanely generous Selfridges haul, to Dr Dyson dropping everything, to his insistence that I stay here and rest, feels like a fairytale. Being on the receiving end of that while knowing I can't trust it, I can't enjoy it or lean into it, I can't allow myself to be flattered or hopeful or to flirt gently with my handsome rescuer, hurts my heart a little.

The fantasy is so good, and it's not real, and it's a crying shame.

To milk my *Beauty and the Beast* analogy dry, it's as if he's the anti-Beast. You know, instead of a wonderful man lurking beneath the gruff hostility and the handsome prince hidden under the hideous fur and teeth and claws, it's quite the opposite.

The surface experience is the urbane, good-looking prince in his immaculate castle. At first glance, he's the fairytale.

The animal that lies beneath, and the savagery of which it's capable, is nowhere to be seen.

Unless you know where to look.

When I wake, it's sudden. I lie for a second on my side, my arms still wrapped around the now-tepid hot water bottle, eyes closed and sleep-drugged brain trying to make sense of where I am.

Shit. I'm at Adam's.

And that was a—*snore?*

My eyes fly open. The room is dim, but not dark. My door, which I most definitely shut before I went to bed, is ajar, and soft light from the hallway spills into the room, illuminating what is most definitely Adam on the bed next to me.

What the fuck is he doing here?

My entire body tenses, my fingers gripping the hot water bottle as my brain attempts to process what I see.

He's sitting up against a pile of pillows, legs stretched out, curly head flung back in an uncomfortable-looking position, fast asleep and snoring gently with his fingers intertwined over his stomach. He's lost the hoodie, kept the soft-looking white t-shirt, and gained a tent in his jogging bottoms the size of a bloody wedding marquee.

Oh my God.

Oh my *God.*

I eye it in disbelief. It may be dim in here, but I'd have to be registered legally blind not to be able to make out that thing. It's testing the limits of his jogging bottoms, the jersey stretched taut over his, um, tent pole. It's—*he's*—about two feet away from me.

Close enough that if I pulled my hand out from under the covers and stretched, I could touch it. I could slip my fingers beneath that straining waistband and wrap them around his length.

I could lean over, even, and lick a path through his crown, enjoying the music of his moans as he crossed over into consciousness with my mouth on him.

Now *that* would be a way to wake him up, this delicious, interfering man who just can't help himself. Who's used to getting exactly what he wants, whether he uses his fists or his bank balance to do it.

I may despise him, but I can't deny it's been a while since

I saw any form of dick, let alone one that impressive. And it seems my greedy little vagina doesn't care about his morally corrupt soul or his black heart.

She just cares that there's a beautifully sexy, sleeping man right here with a dick that, from the looks of things, could make every problem in life fade into insignificance.

It doesn't help that, in sleep, he looks like a fallen angel, his dark curls just mussed enough to invite my fingers to rake through them, repose softening his face. He doesn't scare me, I realise. Not when he's like this, looking as innocent as the day he was born. If I'm being completely honest, he hasn't scared me at all since I came around from my hypo to the sight of his tear-stained cheeks.

He's been on my bed for God knows how long—hours, possibly—and he's watched me sleep. I may be mortified by that thought, but I'm not scared by it. I don't feel vulnerable.

Just curious... and aroused.

Very, very aroused.

My nipples are tight little furls. I brush my arm over one of them, and the ache has me biting down on my lip. The silk of my pyjamas feels so sensual against my skin. It's a caress I could do without.

I need to get a fucking grip. And, ideally, more sleep. And I definitely need to get rid of *him*.

I cast my eye over him. If his dick wasn't such a distraction, I'd obsess over the sliver of tanned, lean stomach that's on display courtesy of his t-shirt, which has ridden up. I'd try to read the basic-looking tattoo on his bicep. All I can see is a capital E. I wonder if it's prison ink. It looks like it. I can't square the considerate man lying here amidst his splendour, on *my* bed, with the thug who disfigured my brother and served time.

I also can't square my hatred of him with the pang I feel when I think about him locked up behind bars. Nope. Definitely not going *there*.

My gaze wanders over the fine sight his taut forearm makes and onto the duvet cover. There, lying next to him is a small pile of stuff. What *is* it? I crane my head up gingerly without moving my body.

Oh my God. It's a motherfucking test kit. There are a couple of lancets for pricking my fingers, and I spot a tube of what looks like an unfamiliar brand of glycogel.

It seems our resident heartless thug has been keeping a bedside vigil, primed to test me if he suspects my glucose of plummeting in the night.

It's overbearing, definitely. And unnecessary. And borderline invasive—or outright invasive, even. But it's also comforting to know he had my back, and it's even a little sweet, I suppose.

His fingers have been *inside my mouth* today, and now his dick is pointing north on my bed.

He needs to get out of here before I do something I regret.

Like climb on it.

Or kick him off the bed.

Not sure which.

I do the only thing I can feasibly do, which is to wake him without alerting him to *my* being awake. I roll over heavily, noisily, faking a loud, sleepy sigh and tugging the duvet with me as I go. And then I lie curled up on my side, vagina throbbing and heart hammering and eyes screwed shut, and I wait.

His breathing changes. The bed shifts, and I imagine him sitting up beside me. Realising he's been asleep. There's the faint sound of him gathering up the paraphernalia he brought with him, a quiet curse that makes me press my lips together in amusement while I keep my breathing audibly even. I wonder if that's him registering his boner.

Then he's climbing off the bed.

The door clicks softly shut behind him.

16

NATALIE

It's a testament to the outrageous comfort level of the bed that I found sleep again after Adam and his dick left the premises, but I did. Waking up and getting ready in my room felt almost as if I'd treated myself to a spontaneous overnight stay in a luxury hotel.

I spent way too long letting the shower's epic water pressure pummel me as I washed my hair in a leisurely fashion. While under the spray, I may or may not have allowed myself to speculate idly as to whether that boner of his went down by itself, or whether he had to tend to it in that impatient, commanding way of his. Then I dressed and made good use of the Dyson hair dryer and Air Wrap I found in the bathroom cupboard. Again: fancy hotel.

Of all the life decisions I've made in the past twenty-four hours, putting my makeup bag in my tote bag was one of the best. Sometimes I just leave it at the studio. I turned up here last night looking half dead, and something has me wanting to look far better than that this morning. It's this house, I decide. If I was staying at the Ritz, I wouldn't mooch downstairs looking full emo. I'd make an effort.

God knows, I spend most of my days working hard and unglamorously in a very glamorous industry. I constantly bemoan feeling like I'm some poor little church mouse on the edge of all the fun. This place isn't the Ritz, but it may as well be, and I may as well channel it before I have to leave the bubble and reenter normal life.

The thought is almost enough to take the wind out of my sails. It's dark outside, but I opened my blinds as soon as I woke up. I suspected we weren't overlooked on this vast plot of land. Sure enough, all I could see was the beautiful, barren stillness of Adam's gardens in the moonlight.

How it's possible, in a city of nine million people, to feel so utterly, blissfully, cocooned, I'm not sure. But I'm sure this splendid isolation was worth every penny.

I apply my signature Clean Girl daytime look: primer and a dewy base, only a smattering of powder, lip gloss and peachy cream blush and black mascara, with a shimmery eyeshadow and only the teeniest flick of eyeliner. It works perfectly with the athletic wear Adam gave me. Once my hair is pulled back into a sleek and perky ponytail, I eye my reflection appraisingly in what I fear is the overly flattering light of the bathroom.

My reflection gazes back looking exactly as I planned.

Healthy.

Usually, getting ready in my tiny, damp bathroom is something I grit my teeth and get through. This feels like a huge treat. It's amazing how much of a difference pink marble and heated floors and mirrors can make to a girl.

Around seven-thirty, I drift down the wide, shallow steps of the sculptural staircase and tiptoe into the kitchen. The upstairs hallway is still, a bank of closed doors with no clue as to whether Adam is awake or where his bedroom is, but I sense activity as I enter the kitchen.

Sure enough, the friendly chef from last night, Kamyl, is standing at the island, already prepping a pile of vegetables. Did he go home and come back, or does he live here? There's another member of staff here, too, a South East Asian man dressed like Toby was last night, in a tie and chinos with a sleeveless gilet over his white shirt.

They both turn to smile at me.

'Good morning, Miss Bennett,' the guy who's not Kamyl says. 'I'm Bal. Mr Wright should be down in a few minutes. Can I get you a tea or coffee?'

'Hi Bal. I'd love a tea, please,' I say.

'Of course.' He turns away to grab the kettle.

'Miss Bennett, Mr Wright suggested some Turkish eggs for your breakfast with added black beans,' Kamyl says in his charming French accent. 'May I prepare some for you?'

I resist the urge to sigh and smile at him instead. It's not his fault "Mr Wright" is an overbearing, pulse-obsessed dickhead. 'If it's not too much trouble, that would be lovely. Thanks, Kamyl.'

'It's his favourite,' Kamyl volunteers.

That's kind of sweet, I suppose. I stand for a moment while Bal puts the kettle on, wondering where I should settle myself. But he makes my decision for me.

'May I show you the library? Mr Wright likes to take his morning coffee in there. The fire is on.'

'I'll bring your eggs through when they're done,' Kamyl adds. 'It's warmer in there.'

The kitchen is plenty cosy, thanks to the underfloor heating that seeps through my brand-new socks and makes every step a delight, but I dutifully follow Bal back out into the hallway and through a doorway, and Jeeesus. I want to die of happiness, because this room is extraordinary. Even with nothing more than the light of a grey, dismal dawn outside, it's extraordinary.

It's large and spacious, two of its walls lined floor-to-ceiling with ornate bookshelves painted an eau-de-nil so perfect I instantly want to design an entire collection around it. It has enough minty green to be sweet and enough grey tones not to be cloying. The intricate details of the woodwork are picked out in a dull gold that complements the green perfectly.

The other two walls are papered with a beautiful landscape scene that looks handpainted and is either De Gournay or Zuber—I can't work out which. There's a lovely little fire crackling in the grate and several arrangements of plump armchairs and occasional tables. I'm instantly certain that I could spend days and weeks in this room without coming up for air.

Bal leaves me to it while he makes the tea, and I wander around the room, taking in all the treasures. Some sections of the shelves are filled with beautiful, leather-bound classics, and I have the uncharitable thought that Adam's designer probably bulk-bought these. He's likely never cracked a single one open.

But then the next section is crammed full of business, economics and self-help books that *do* look well-loved, from Tony Robbins to *The Lean Startup*. I spot a few that I've read over the years in my desperate attempts to make this brand of mine viable. And, most enchantingly of all, at the far end of the room, the individual shelves grow larger, with some books facing outwards, like in bookstores.

I've stumbled upon the fashion section.

Oh my God. I thank Bal as he returns with a silver-laden tea tray and a large black wooden box bearing the chic branding of Parisian tea brand Mariage Frères. He's brought me full-on tea porn to choose from, but I barely notice, so taken am I with this even better form of porn: coffee table books.

One of my absolute favourite things to do is to wander around the book department in Harrods, where I can spend hours reverently leafing through the coffee table books on display. They're works of art, and their price reflects it. Some of the books they stock cost a couple of hundred pounds or more and weigh a ton. They're boxed, foiled, embossed, filled with photos of the world's most beautiful women shot by history's most talented photographers and wearing gowns to die for, their likenesses protected by silky sheets of vellum bound into the books.

I run my fingers carefully over a stunning Assouline book on Dior under Raf Simons, its satiny cover a sumptuous riot of black and red. There's a Burberry special edition, its spine showing off the brand's iconic check. Chanel. Vuitton. Saint Laurent.

Forget weeks.

If Bal kept my tea topped up, I could live in here for *months*.

My studio has a few of these books, mostly bought in sales or with birthday money, some of them unearthed by me or Evan in charity shops. I've even managed to get a special edition or two on eBay. But this is another world.

I carefully select a huge, matte-covered Giambattista Valli book and carry it over to the table where Bal has laid out my tea things. After treating myself to a muslin teabag of Imperial Wedding tea and leaving it to steep in the pot of hot water, I sit and crack the book open.

Oh my God. It's so adorable, filled with page after page of the designer's sketches—impossibly pretty frou-frou concoctions worn by the little-bodied, large-headed alien mannequins he's known for.

It's official.

I'm in heaven.

Even if it's the home of the devil.

17

NATALIE

W hen the man himself wanders in with an espresso cup and saucer not five minutes later, it's an unwelcome interruption. At least, it's unwelcome except to my eyeballs, because he looks good enough to grace the pages of any of these coffee table books.

He's in a similar uniform to the ones I've seen him in the past couple of times we've met—black, beautifully cut trousers, white, beautifully cut shirt, open at the neck. But there's something about seeing him here, freshly showered, his dark curls damp and raked off his face, beard immaculate, that motherfucking cologne already wafting over to me, that steals the breath from my lungs.

'Good morning,' he says, and his tone is hesitant, I think. Maybe that's because the last thing I said to him was an insult, or maybe he's remembering that he woke up next to me with a raging boner. Either way, he's on guard, as am I.

'Morning,' I say, closing the book on my lap.

'Don't let me disturb you. I have to head out shortly—a meeting I can't get out of, unfortunately.' His mouth twists like he's pissed off, and I get the distinct impression that he's telling the truth; the early meeting isn't a convenient way to dodge me.

I put the book down on the low table in front of me and stand so I feel more equal with him. 'I'm sorry for what I said last night,' I say, holding his gaze. 'It was really rude, especially after you've been so kind to me.'

He gives a little shake of his head. 'It wasn't anything I didn't deserve ten times over.'

'No.' I press on. 'It wasn't cool at all. And—I regret it.' Last night's parting shot was also the only reference either of us has made to his treatment of Stephen in the twelve or more hours I've been in his home. If someone had told me that I could coexist with Adam for that long without the massive, burning elephant in the room coming up, I'd have scoffed.

This time, I get a nod. 'It's forgotten. I'm sorry if you found me overbearing. I was worried about you, so I tried to take control of the situation. Maybe I pushed it too far.'

I wonder if that apology extends to creeping into my bedroom with lancets and gels and that dick of his and watching me sleep for God knows how long. I'd definitely call that *pushing it too far,* but I suspect he'd die of mortification if I called him out on it. As would I, obviously, so we'll just pretend it didn't happen. He absolutely does not need to know that I woke up when he was there.

When he was hard.

'It's fine,' I say.

His gaze rakes over my body and back to my face. 'Well, you look... much better. You're glowing.'

'Thanks.' I swear I flush. 'I feel much better.'

'Seriously, sit down, please.' He waves his free hand

about. 'Finish your tea. Your breakfast should be here in a couple of minutes, and Louise texted to say she'll try to be here a little earlier, so...'

I stay standing. 'What, no "Turkish eggs with extra black beans" for you today?' I make bunny ears with my fingers when I reel off my not-so-voluntary breakfast order. 'I thought it was your favourite.'

He takes a sip from his espresso. 'It is on Saturdays. I tend to do intermittent fasting during the week.' A pause, then a little smirk creases the corners of his unfairly attractive mouth. 'You know, because I can.'

The jibe takes me a second to absorb, but when it does, my mouth drops open.

'Hang on a sec. Did you just *diabetes* shame me?'

He's still smirking. He looks awfully pleased with himself, and I can't help it. I grin.

'You smug bastard.'

'Yep. But I suspect you already knew that.'

We stand there and smile at each other. It only lasts a moment, but it's long enough to make me flustered. I cast around for a change of subject.

On the table in front of me is a neatly fanned array of today's papers. *The Times* is up top, bearing a front-page photo of the Oscar-winning British actor, Ellery Hart, wearing fucking custom Omar Vega, no less. I point at it. 'Nice work.'

He looks down at it and grins. He really is in a good mood this morning. And no sign of a boner. He definitely jacked off in the shower. The thought of him getting himself off, probably vigorously, probably with those white teeth pressing down on his full lower lip as he reached his climax, makes me feel slightly weak. I should probably sit down.

'That's all Omar,' he says. 'He's such a star-fucker.'

I swallow down another smile, because there's no way I can let Adam Wright have two of them, even if Evan and I hold exactly the same opinion of Vega. 'Harsh but fair.' Clearly, his star-fucking works for him.

Awkwardness descends between us. 'Well,' he says. 'I'll leave you be. Nigel's going to drop me into town, but he'll be back in time to take you to work after you've seen Louise.'

'Oh my God, no. That's really not necessary,' I protest. 'I'll just get the tube.'

'It is. I insist. It's still pissing it down out there. He's under strict instructions to take you wherever you need to go.'

My shoulders sag. I suspect there's no point in arguing with him, or in putting Nigel in a difficult position later if I refuse to let him carry out his orders. I have to admit, a ride in that lovely big Range Rover would be a far nicer way to reacquaint myself with reality than the tube.

'Okay.' I shift from one foot to another. 'That would be great. Thank you so much for looking after me yesterday.'

He hesitates, then comes towards me, holding his espresso cup out of the way, and leans in to give me a double kiss. It's surprising, but also not a big deal at all, because it's more of an air kiss than anything else, his beard lightly brushing my jaw, and it's also how absolutely everyone in the fashion industry greets each other. So it shouldn't feel so... intimate.

He pulls back. 'Thank you for letting me look after you,' he says softly, and then he's gone.

The studio feels particularly drab today, and no wonder. We don't see clients here. Ever. The kind of space I'd want to reflect our brand would cost so many thousands of pounds a month it's not even funny. A shitty, albeit well-lit, attic studio on one of the less cool side streets in Soho is as good as we can get.

Even Soho's taking the piss, if I'm honest. We should be somewhere cheaper, less central. But my Alchemy paycheque subsidises the rent enough to make it barely justifiable. When we see private clients, it's at their homes or in a hotel room or meeting space we book for the occasion. Expensive, but way cheaper than trying to run a client-facing studio.

We take the same approach with trunk shows. It's best, and most fun, when clients host us and their friends at home, just like Gen, God bless her, has offered to do after Christmas.

The studio is passable. Yesterday, it felt fine, but that was before I was treated to De Gournay wall panels and bath-tubs sculpted from slabs of pink marble and florists' worth of bouquets everywhere. It was before I had a chance to remind myself so starkly of what real wealth looks like up close.

It was before I got a reminder of the kind of scale you need to achieve to create value, and generate wealth, in this industry.

It was before I reminded myself that Adam Wright, a guy who's been in prison, for fuck's sake, has achieved success and recognition and the lifestyle to go with it in a way I never, ever will.

Sometimes, when I'm feeling brave enough to be truly honest with myself, I wonder what the hell we're doing here with Gossamer. Creating beauty, sure. Making our clients feel radiant and strong and gorgeous and capable of taking on the world. But with my combined business and fashion degree, I could have taken a dull salaried job that brings home far more and comes with a truck-load less stress.

I've always believed that positivity is a choice. We wake up every morning and we choose to view the world as a good or a bad place. If Einstein said it's the most important decision we can make, he must have been right. I'm the master of reframing. Not *I have to do this*, but *I get to.* I am the absolute queen of faking it till I make it. Taylor Swift has nothing on me.

I work and work and I grind and grind and I smile and smile, and hardly ever do I permit myself the weakness of navel-gazing sufficiently to wonder if I have the energy to keep putting one foot in front of the other on this never-ending treadmill that is running a lovely but sub-scale brand in this gruelling industry.

Today, the single rail of dresses that Gail collected from the factory this week looks paltry. The paint on the walls is more grey than white in this grim November light. My colleagues look tired, and I think for the millionth time that they need a pay rise and then some.

Maybe today is the day where I allow the cracks to show, just a little. After all, it's been a pretty exhausting, ooh, fifteen hours. My illness manifested in its most mortifying form. I was bundled off and pampered by an intimidating, bossy as fuck man who I have excellent reason to despise. He then had the nerve to lavish me with medical experts and disturb my blissful slumber with his sweet little snores and his monstrously big dick.

And then he proceeded to be utterly delightful this morning—by his standards, anyway—and discombobulate me even further.

No wonder I'm feeling flayed open.

'Ooh,' Evan says when I turn up for work, a couple of hours late thanks to the traffic and to an irritatingly invaluable session with Louise, the nutritionist. 'You've never done dress-down Friday before. But your arse looks amazing in those leggings. New threads?'

I dump my tote bag on my desk with a sigh. It's rammed full of my dress and heels from last night, but I left everything at Adam's aside from the outfit I'm wearing. It's not mine to take. And my flat is not somewhere you waltz around in Olivia von Halle pyjamas. I've come away with just the clothes on my body and the best-fitting of the *three* identical pairs of Veja trainers that awaited me in different sizes on the floor of my lovely bedroom.

'You wouldn't believe me if I told you where I got them,' I tell him with a grimace. He's perfectly turned out, as always, in slim-fitting checked trousers that he made himself (obviously) and a black cashmere sweater that's probably Uniqlo but looks a million dollars with the trousers.

'Try me. It can't be a more ridiculous story than the one where you ran into the bully the other day, can it?'

I wince inwardly at the term, the very same one I threw so callously at Adam yesterday and which, high-handedness aside, nothing about his behaviour last night warranted.

'Funny you should say that...' I begin as I make my way over to our crappy kitchenette to put the kettle on.

When I wrap my ridiculous tale up, fifteen minutes later, his face is so totally gobsmacked that I can't resist reaching for my phone and snapping a photo.

He scowls. 'Mean.'

'Stop catching flies, then. Honestly, though, the library

was *epic*. I even saw the full set of those Assouline destination books. You know, the Ibiza one, and Capri...'

'Yeah, yeah.' He stops me with an impatient wave of his hand. 'Tell me about his dick again.'

I groan. 'But I'd much rather talk about the coffee table book porn.'

'Bollocks. Give me the dick porn.'

'It was there. It looked big. It looked hard. It looked like the answer to nuclear warheads and cancer and food inequality and every other problem facing mankind. Okay?'

He chews on the inside of his cheek as if formulating a reply, and I know I won't like whatever he has to say.

'So, in summary, he basically nursed you through your hypo in, like, expert style, he swept you up and took you home, he had half of Selfridges delivered to you, he bought you *Olivia von Halle pyjamas*, he fed you, he crept into your room in the middle of the night to keep a tense vigil through the darkest hours, oh, and he got an epic boner during said vigil...

'What else? Ooh, he owns a palace, he understands the healing power of a beautifully shot coffee table book, and he lavished upon your ungrateful little head medical experts who probably cost hundreds of pounds for a consultation. But you called him a bully. *To his face.* Am I missing anything? And don't roll your eyes at me, missy.'

If I could roll them any harder, my brother wouldn't be the only member of our family in need of a prosthetic eyeball.

Evan pats his hair carefully to ensure it's still perfectly coiffed. 'I'll take that as a no, then.'

'I apologised for the bully comment,' I mutter into my mug. 'And what you're *missing*, dipshit, is that he relieved my brother of an eyeball. Not to mention that his attack sent my dad into an endlessly black guilt spiral over fucking up our lives and our schooling. So forgive me if a few hours of perfectly pitched hospitality and swoony generosity don't quite wipe the slate clean for me.'

He sighs loudly and stretches his arms above his head. 'Mother*fucker.*'

'Quite.'

'Did you talk about your brother at all with him?'

'God, no. That would be a can of worms.'

'Because it'd be too triggering for you, or because you're worried if you let him explain himself, you might hate him a bit less?'

Both. 'The former. There's nothing he can say to justify it. He beat the shit out of a kid half his size. End of story.'

'Jesus Christ,' Evan groans. 'Adam, Adam. Give us something to work with here. Ooh. Maybe he had a lobotomy in prison?'

'That would explain a lot,' I concede.

The giant Selfridges bag turns up at the studio a few hours later, with a sheepishly smiling Nigel attached to it. 'Your stuff, Miss. The boss asked me to bring it over.'

So poor old Nigel has had to come into town twice today on my account. Fuck's sake. I swallow my exasperation and thank him sincerely for his trouble, lugging the bag back upstairs to the studio.

Aside from the pairs of Vejas that didn't fit me, it's all there. The pyjamas, the skincare—the used and unused skincare, the unused underwear, and a couple of spare t-shirts from the original haul, as well as two surprises.

The gorgeous Giambattista Valli coffee table book.

And a little note, handwritten on a stiff white notecard monogrammed with AW.

You forgot your stuff. Thought you might like the book, too. And keep an eye on that glucose :) A.

Dear Lord in heaven, help me to survive this man.

18

NATALIE

If anything has the potential to stoke the fires of guilt that have licked away at me all week, it's dinner with my family. I can't begin to imagine what they'd say if they knew I spent a night quite literally sleeping with the enemy (and his boner).

Which is why they can never know.

Life may have kicked my family in the teeth—and the eye sockets—pretty damn thoroughly a couple of times, but going home isn't the wretched experience it once was. God knows, it took upwards of a decade for us all to find our feet, but we've clawed our way back to a semblance of normality that we can all be proud of.

After five or six years of doing jobs way below his pay grade, Dad was eventually approached by the London School of Economics about a professorship in Financial Systems. The regulator may have banned him from working in the financial sector again, but there was nothing to stop him from teaching that stuff. His tenure's been a massive success, providing a steady income that's allowed him and

Mum to escape the horrors of that council flat and move into a decent semi-detached house in a nicer area.

Most importantly, it's given him back his dignity. His sense of worth.

The biggest change, though, has been in my brother. We call him Winky, which is seriously awful, I know, but always affectionately meant. When he had his accident, one of our aunts bought him a teddy bear with an eye patch. I apparently christened the bear Winky, and somehow the name transferred to my poor brother.

'Hi, Winkster,' I say now, throwing my arms around him. The full-on emo phase that attracted the attention of bullies like Adam Wright is long gone. These days, my brother is a bona fide tech nerd, and he dresses like one. Today he's in a red hoodie bearing the circular logo of Totum, the company he's worked for for the past year or so. I'm fuzzy on what Totum does, exactly, except for a vague understanding that it reconciles patients' medical data between all the trusts in our National Health Service (and their equivalents globally) and massively improves efficiencies of treatment. As a young adult with a horrific eye injury, my brother was under the jurisdiction of about three million eye doctors, so it's no surprise that he's evangelical about technology that improves the flow of information and consistency of care.

Less importantly but more critically, Stephen's ultimate boss, the billionaire Aidan Duffy, is hot as fuck. If he wasn't blissfully married, I'd definitely ask for an introduction— even if my limited experience of hot billionaires is adorned with warning bells and red flags.

'Still drinking the Totum Kool-Aid, I see,' I note aloud, more for the benefit of Anna, his wife. He's my older brother, so mutual piss-ripping is obligatory whenever we see each other.

'He's a total corporate whore,' Anna muses. 'I swear, he has a bigger boner for Aidan Duffy than me.' I grin at her as I release him. I *really* like Anna. She's great fun and unfailingly positive which, given Winky's lifelong potential for anxiety is, I think, a good thing. She is, like my brother, a badass tech engineer—they met at his previous firm, a FinTech startup—but she's far cooler than he'll ever be.

'Never,' I protest. 'You have way better boobs than Duffy.'

'She definitely does,' my brother says, with a lascivious grin at his wife. If they keep this up, my parents will have another grandchild on the way to follow sweet little Chloe, who's asleep upstairs in the full-on nursery Mum insisted on creating in the box room.

~

Mum may not have a French chef, and this kitchen may be poky compared to a certain billionaire's vast space full of blue lacquer and endless marble, but she and Dad have made a life for themselves here, and there's more love around this dining room table than I glimpsed at Adam's palace, that's for sure.

She's made cottage pie, and as I lay my napkin on my lap I'm uncomfortably aware that I'm wearing the sweatshirt and leggings Adam bought for me. When I'm not at either of my jobs, I can't take them off. Aside from the special pieces Evan and I have made for my role at Alchemy, these are the highest quality things I own.

It's been a month since I've been here for dinner, which is not okay. Stephen and Anna are here far more often, but given the amount of time Mum spends looking after Chloe while they work, it's no surprise that their lives are more entwined with those of my parents than mine is. Still, between Gossamer and Alchemy and my hideous commute, I don't exactly do a good job of carving out time for my family.

I'm happy here. I'm comfortable here. I love them all, and they make me happy. Even so, being here reminds me where I've come from. It reminds me of what we all lost, what my parents have, even now, failed to regain in material terms. They've made a decent home for themselves, but it's not what I grew up with, and my brief interlude at Adam's has reminded me all too painfully of just how clawing and nasty and consuming my ambitions are.

If people like him and Omar Vega can make it, then so can I. I know it, and I want it, yet the chasm between the size of my dreams and the harsh reality of Gossamer's lack of scale, lack of progress, gnaws at me every fucking day. My parents are happy now. My brother is happy now. They've made peace with the trajectory of their lives. It's only me who rails against it, who spends her days treading that exhausting, relentless hamster wheel of aspirations that often feel so out of reach as to be a mirage.

Mum breaks my reverie. 'How's your health, honey?' she probes gently. 'All going smoothly?'

'It's all fine, thanks,' I say quickly. I can't tell her I had a crappy hypo this week—it'll make her worry even more than she does. Unlike certain other people I can name, she does her best not to hound me about my blood glucose or breathe down my neck, but I know she stresses about it constantly. It's another burden she's had to bear all these years, and I hate it for her.

I also have zero intention of launching into any story that leads to me disclosing even the slightest interaction with Adam Wright, who's borne the role of fairytale villain for years now where me and my brother are concerned.

No fucking way.

'Actually, I have some health news,' Winky says now, and I beam gratefully at him for taking the spotlight off me. 'I had a pretty intriguing call from my ocularist yesterday.'

Unfortunately, the Bennett family is a collective expert on eye-related medical jargon. Ocularists make and fit prosthetic eyeballs, like the one Winky's had for the best part of twenty years now. It's not awful—the colour of the iris is a perfect match for his brown one—but it's a bit weird, honestly. It kind of stares. He's objectively a good-looking guy, but the prosthesis does him no favours, to say the least.

'Oh yes?' Dad asks, setting down his fork. He and mum exchange one of those glances that hurt my heart—all hopeful and invested.

Winky clears his throat. 'Yeah. He said he's been working with this cutting-edge medical devices company—OcuNova, they're called. They're based out of Cambridge and they have a prosthetic that's meant to be next-level.'

'Next-level, how?' I ask. As I've always understood it, the trauma my brother's eyeball and socket suffered at Adam's hands meant that most of his optic nerves were severed during the removal process. Over the past few years, he's enquired about disruptive technologies, including stem cell treatments. He's always been an early adopter of technology of all kinds and way more open to playing guinea pig for potential solutions than I would be in his place, but he's never proven a good fit for any of the fledgling treatments out there.

I suppose his interest is a function of the industry he works in, as well as the constant handicap with which he lives, but it's been tough to watch him get excited about various options over the years, only to be knocked back over and over.

'Well.' He shifts in his chair and gives us the trademark dorky, adorable grin that used to signal the start of a tirade about Dungeons and Dragons and is now more likely to precede a love letter to Totum. 'It's really cool, actually. Their prosthetics are seriously great-looking. We're talking 3D printed surfaces with irises and even *veins* that would match my real eye. Apparently, their pupils can even change size depending on the light. It's insane.'

I grin at him. That *is* insane. I can't believe shit like this is technically possible. No wonder Winky's geeking out on it.

My dad's shaking his head in amazement. 'That's just incredible. And they think you're a suitable candidate?'

'There's more.' My brother shovels a load of cottage pie into his mouth and we all wait while he chews and swallows, avid for more detail. 'So they're working on lots of AR stuff, too—they have tie-ins with various other tech and biotech firms. Get this: the prosthetic has a camera and an AR system built in, and they're designing various digital overlays.

'Some of them will just enhance what I'm already seeing through my right eye—they'll expand my field of vision, basically, by analysing what the camera sees and marrying it with my actual eyesight—but there's no limit to what else the overlays will be able to provide.'

'Woah,' I say, trying to wrap my head around what he's saying. I'm definitely far less tech fluent than Winky. 'So your eyesight will be half natural, half digital?'

'Pretty much. And it will act like a smart crystalline lens too, so as my range of vision shrinks in my right eye with age, the prosthetic will compensate. So I won't get that annoying thing like you have when you have a TV dinner,

Mum, where you have to keep taking your glasses off to see the screen and then putting them back on to see your food.'

'That's the *worst*,' Mum mutters. 'I gagged on a piece of pork gristle the other night because I was so glued to *Traitors*.'

'Well, there'll be none of that.'

'Do you know what would be amazing?' Dad asks. 'Face recognition that brings up someone's name every time I bump into them at the shops and can't bloody remember their name.'

We all laugh, because Dad's getting worse with names every year.

'That's child's play,' my brother scoffs affectionately. 'This stuff is way beyond that.'

'So they want to work with you?' I prompt, because I'm not sure he's got to the point of his story yet.

'Yep.' He pops the *p* proudly.

Anna leans forward. 'Apparently he's the *perfect* candidate.'

'Of course he is,' Mum says fondly.

'Basically, it's because I'm completely blind in one eye, no optic nerve activity to speak of, but I've got vision in the other so I have a good baseline for comparing the real thing with the digital experience,' he says. 'And Dr Smythe knows I'm an early adopter, so he was pretty sure I'd go for it. I can't believe it. I'm meeting them this week, but I've been poring over their technology all morning and it's bloody incredible. I'm absolutely blown away.'

Anna's gazing at him with so much love and delight, her lips pressed tightly together like she's trying to hold in the emotion.

I know how she feels.

For the past twenty years, my brother's missing eye has been a handicap for him.

Now, it feels as though it could be a superpower.

19

ADAM

I 've stayed away from Alchemy for almost a week, telling myself there's no reason at all for me to go there—even if the team comped me a membership, which is decent of them. I've already looked around the place, sampled the wares, as it were, and set the ball rolling on the transfer of ownership from Wolff to Wright.

No other due diligence is needed. The bankers and lawyers can firm up the details once Wolff's board signs off, which I'm sure they'll do happily. The stake has been a bigger financial PR headache than its tiny presence on Wolff's balance sheet warrants.

The real reason I've stayed away, though, is precisely the same reason I want to show up there so badly.

Natalie Bennett.

God knows, I couldn't find a less suitable person to fixate on. There isn't a woman on the planet who'd find the prospect of the slightest intimacy with me more morally repugnant.

My therapist may insist that I keep women at arm's

length because I still believe, deep down, that I'm unworthy of love. (Rather, he may have insisted once and hurriedly retracted when I threatened to fire him.) Lord knows what he'd say if he thought for a moment I had designs on a woman with whom my chances of making reparations for past unholy crimes are zero.

I know perfectly well what he'd say, in fact. He'd say I'm hoping to win her over because absolution from Stephen Bennett's own sister would be the purest form of absolution I could hope for.

So yes, I steer clear of Alchemy. The irony of my investing in a sex club where I can have any woman I please except for the one I actually want is not lost on me. Seeing Natalie will serve no purpose, ergo reacquainting myself with her enchanting face and perfect body and vicious tongue is pointless.

She endured the hospitality I rammed down her throat with thinly-veiled hostility. She enjoyed my home, sure, but certainly not my company. She may as well have been a fairytale princess trapped in a brute's dungeon for all the graciousness she exhibited. Persephone, even, condemned to Hades' underworld.

Thank heaven she didn't stir while I was stupid enough to fall asleep on her bed. I'm not sure which she would have found creepier—me passed out next to her with a huge boner or me, wakeful and watchful.

It genuinely pissed me off that she wouldn't give me access to her data, that she let her pride and her dislike of me get in the way of having an extra pair of eyes monitoring her while she slept. I haven't had any exposure to type 1 since Ellen died, and I wasn't prepared for how incredibly upsetting it would be to witness Natalie's attack, how power-less I'd feel as I struggled to get her glucose up and, later, as

I lay there next to her with no way of monitoring her short of cracking open a lancet and puncturing the pale skin of the sleeping princess to draw her blood.

That said, the gratification I took from that hour or so of watching her sleep before I succumbed myself had a cause entirely separate from altruism. Not only did she look so peaceful, her beautiful face free from the horrific attack that had contorted it earlier, but all her hostility was gone, too. I was able to gaze down at her for as long as I liked while she slept the tranquil sleep of someone blithely unaware both that their mask had dropped and that their enemy was near.

She makes a fine sight when she's not looking at you as if she'd like to douse you in petrol and throw a lit match at you.

Although, if I'm being honest, she makes a fine sight when she is, too.

I last six days, until Cal, one of the Alchemy founders, proposes drinks at the club, a chance for all of us to informally toast the passing of the baton from Wolff to Wright. Anton will be there, as will Max, Wolff's current CEO, with his boyfriend, Dex, and his girlfriend, Darcy, who happens to be Gen's sister.

This place is incestuous enough to put Ancient Egypt to shame.

I'm also expecting to see Cal's partner, the charming broadcast journalist and documentarian Aida Russell, who's interviewed me a couple of times in the past. It should be a good night. It's the perfect chance to toast the changing of the guard and to catch up with friends, old and new.

It's absolutely not about throwing myself in the path of

any beguiling Alchemy hosts who hate my guts and haunt my dreams. It's a shame the gestures that might make Natalie hate me slightly less—such as my impassioned cold call earlier this week to plead her brother's case to a friend of a friend who founded OcuNova, an impressive ocular prosthetics company—can't ever come to light.

Changing Stephen Bennett's fortunes for the better isn't about improving my reputation. It's about making quiet, necessary reparations when the opportunities arise.

When I enter the lobby and Natalie spots me, it's not outright hostility I detect, but rather wariness. Conflict, even. She's recovered her poise by the time I get to the lectern.

'Hi,' I say softly, taking her in. Her hair is tied back in a long, sleek ponytail. It's a little like the one she sported the other morning, but more glamorous, somehow. Or perhaps it's the heavy eye makeup that provides the glamour. She even has an arc of tiny, immaculately applied crystals above each eyelid. All I know is that she's a vision.

The strapless, boned corset of her top—or dress, I can't tell from here—is crafted from black satin and moulds perfectly to her body, its rhinestone trim sparkling prettily under the chandelier and its cut showcasing the delicate architecture of her collarbones, the toned musculature of her upper arms. The cups are the only parts not done in satin. Rather, they're pleated chiffon, the edges of the fabric frayed, feathering against her skin like the impossibly pretty edge of a parrot tulip.

I'd put money on it being one of her creations. Still, it's skimpy and it's bloody November, after all. The faintest goosebumps are visible on her skin, and I make a mental note to tell Gen to turn the heating up in the lobby.

Far worse, in the split-second that I take her in, my brain

serves up to me the morsel that her nipples are very clearly also feeling the cold.

Not fucking helpful.

I wonder what proportion of the clientele hits on her before they've even made it through to the bar. A decent one, I imagine. The thought irritates me.

'Good evening, Mr Wright,' she says smoothly, and I raise an eyebrow. Mr Wright? Seriously?

'I'd like to think we've graduated to first name terms by now, wouldn't you?'

'Of course. Whatever you prefer.'

She doesn't react. Neither does she say my name. Her impassivity is armour indeed.

'How are you doing?' I ask her. 'It's a general question,' I add hurriedly, in case she takes it as a circuitous enquiry about her glucose levels.

'I'm fine. Thank you for sending the bag over last week. And for the book. You didn't need to do that.'

'It was my pleasure.'

'I'm sure Nigel had better things to do than come back into town on my account.'

'He really didn't.' I lean in confidingly. 'In fact, one of Nige's absolute favourite burger joints is on Brewer Street. So I imagine a lunchtime trip to Soho worked out very well indeed for him.'

That gets me a little smile. 'Well, it was kind, thank you.'

We appraise each other for a minute. She's inscrutable when she's in host mode, and find I don't like it. I'd far rather she was screaming at me, or being exceptionally rude, or giving me side-eye. I don't like that she's behaving as though I'm some random punter who can only expect small talk and barely-interested civilities.

I don't like it at all.

Still, I find myself lingering, hesitant to go on through and bring my brief moment with her to a close.

'Do you know if any of the guys are in there yet? I'm meeting your bosses and a couple of others—Max Hunter and his partners.'

An expression I can't quite read flits over her delicate features—the wispiest of clouds across a clear sky. Disappointment? Disapproval? 'Max just arrived with Dex and Darcy—they've gone on through. And the rest of them are in the bar, too, except for Rafe.'

Rafe already sent his apologies that he wouldn't make it tonight. I know his wife is close to popping.

'Excellent.'

There's a draught of cold air when the doorman lets another member in behind me, but I pause.

She chews her lip, as if she's waiting for me to clear off.

And I bite the bullet. 'Will I—do you ever...' I clear my throat and gesture behind her. 'You know, go next door when your shift is done?'

We stare at each other, and I swear her clear brown eyes widen a little, as though she's caught my unasked questions.

Will I see you in there later?

Do you ever slip through those doors and let any of those hungry, entitled arseholes fuck you?

Would you ever, in some inconceivable parallel universe, let me fuck you? Let me make you feel as good as I know I could, if only you'd let yourself judge me on the man who stands before you today and not the sins I was capable of committing half a lifetime ago?

There's a second where we hold each other's gaze, and I swear our souls speak to each other, before she shuts me down.

'I *never* fraternise.'

Okay, then.

Time to drag myself away and preserve what little is left of my dignity.

20

NATALIE

I t would be truly helpful if someone could please explain the following to me:

Why, up until last week, Adam Wright existed to me solely by name: the thug who ruined my brother's life and the undeserving billionaire who backs some of the biggest jackasses in the fashion and luxury sectors.

And why the hell he is now *everywhere*: saving me from a night in A&E; kidnapping me; dazzling me with his palatial home and thoughtful gifts; creeping into my room while I'm sleeping and putting on a semi-pornographic show for me, and worst of all, *hanging out with my fucking friends?*

Gen knows most of what went down last week—she quizzed me at length when she next saw me to ascertain whether Adam had looked after me well after he swept me away, and it seems my answers reassured her well enough. Still, she made sure to give me a kindly heads-up earlier that he'd be in tonight, but Darcy sure as hell didn't mention anything to me when she rocked up with her gorgeous menfolk half an hour ago.

I don't have to wait long.

It can't be more than fifteen or twenty minutes after Adam goes through to the bar, looking unfairly like a puppy who's just been kicked, that Darcy comes out into the lobby at a sprint. She's in a long, platinum sequinned dress tonight whose deep V plunges almost to her navel, and she looks incredible. No wonder two of the most gorgeous men in London are completely obsessed with her.

Right behind her is Maddy, Zach's wife and another good mate of mine. I love these guys. Maddy's speed is compromised by her five-inch heels. She may be pregnant, but nobody's putting this girl in flats.

'What the fuck?' Maddy begins as Darcy puts her hand up to halt her.

'Okay, tell me I'm crazy, but is Adam Wright, nasty dick-head bully and billionaire you told us about a few weeks ago over drinks the same guy who's sitting next door, charming everyone's pants off? It's the same guy, right?'

The inexplicable rush of resentment at the concept of Adam *charming everyone's pants off* barely has time to land in my reptile brain when Maddy chips in.

'And he's the same guy who's taking over the Alchemy stake?'

'Yeah,' Darcy presses, 'but is he also the same guy who rescued you and, like, kidnapped you last week? My sister just mentioned it in passing to me and I was like, what the fuck are you talking about? But she wouldn't tell me any more.'

She lets her hand fall, defeated, to the lectern and they both stare at me expectantly.

I sigh, because the last thing I need is Darcy or Maddy sniffing around this story and giving Adam's unwelcome prominence in my brain any more oxygen. 'Yes, yes and yes. All the same guy.'

'But, *how?*' Maddy asks, and I laugh, because *my thoughts exactly.*

'Seriously,' I say. 'It's ridiculous.'

Darcy holds up her hand. 'Wait. I'm going to grab a bottle of wine from the office. Give me a sec.'

'But the two-drink rule...' I protest faintly, and she scoffs.

'Oh please. We all know that's to stop drunk dickheads not taking no for an answer and women from getting hammered and then not being able to remember if they gave consent or not. Meanwhile, the only people dicking me down tonight are Max and Dex and they're used to me being tipsy.'

Hard to argue with that.

She returns with a glass of wine filled to the brim.

'Classy,' I observe.

'Says the girl who spent the night with the infamous Adam Wright,' she says airily, and I roll my eyes.

'It wasn't like that at all.'

'Better fill us in, then,' Maddy says.

So I do. I give them bare bones: my hypo here; Adam's presence and his—very unexpected—skill level at reacting to my crisis; his insistence that I go home with him; the feeding and the gifts; the hyper vigilance around my glucose levels; the insane house porn. And as I talk, their eyebrows rise and rise till they're practically in their hairlines.

'So nothing happened?' Maddy asks when I'm done.

I give her my best unimpressed look. 'I had a really bad episode! I wasn't in any fit state to make bad decisions. Besides, I wouldn't touch him with a barge pole.'

'That's not what I asked,' she points out, and I roll my eyes.

'Nothing happened.'

'You didn't see him at all in the night? Because I'm sorry.

I know we hate him. But he's stupidly hot. He's been in there for ten minutes and he's already got women fawning all over him.'

That makes me mad. Madder than I should be. Unless I'm mistaken, he very much propositioned me a few minutes ago, in a spineless, roundabout kind of way.

I bet that guy fucks anything that moves. But the fact that he doesn't have to lift a finger to do so pisses me off.

So I tell them. I tell them about him sneaking into my room at his place with testing kits and a huge erection, and I tell them what he said to me just now. It's childish, and I hate myself for indulging this line of gossip about a guy who I wish would just fuck off and leave me alone, but I know my audience, and I know these two will go feral for it all.

I'm not mistaken.

Their squeals of mirth have one of the doormen opening the heavy front door to make sure no one's being murdered.

'Oh dear God,' I mutter.

Darcy clamps a hand over her mouth. 'I have to say something, and you're going to hate me,' she says through her fingers. 'Two things, actually.'

I take a deep breath. 'Go on.' My tone isn't exactly encouraging.

'One, as Mads said, he's really hot. *Really* hot. I'm sorry, but it's true.'

I give a little nod of my head to suggest I'm not going to fight her too hard on that fact, even if I hate it, because the girl has eyes. No one in their right mind would try to argue that Adam Wright is ugly.

She pulls her hand away, emboldened. 'And... I know what he did to your brother. I mean, I don't know much, obviously, but I know enough. But it's hard to square all that with everything you've just told us. He sounds like he was... *nice?*' She screws up her face apologetically at the last word, and Maddy winces like she can't believe Darcy went there. 'So maybe you guys could find some, I dunno, middle ground?'

'By *middle ground*, she means his dick,' Maddy chimes in helpfully.

I roll my eyes again. 'I figured as much. Look, I know you're trying to help. But I'm not looking for anything from him. I can admit that he may only be ninety-five percent bad, but the stuff he did to my brother—that's a total deal-breaker. Got it? And it's not like he meant what he said to me, anyway. Like you said, he's got women crawling all over him. I'm sure he won't let one rejection keep him down for long.'

I'm sure he's already lining up his next fuck.

I stew for the next ninety minutes.

I don't know what the hell is wrong with me.

I don't know why I have such FOMO, why the idea of Adam partying the night away with Darcy and Maddy and everyone else while I stand out here alone is bothering me so much.

I don't know why the stare of those pale, arresting eyes as he waited for my answer felt grave, a pressure as great as if he were piling rock after rock on my chest.

And I *really* don't know why I feel the need to disqualify said answer, to walk straight in there and prove to him that I am, in fact, capable of fraternising.

On *my* terms.

God knows what he'd do if I turned up and started

hooking up with someone right in front of him. I'd love to see his face. I'd give anything to take him in as his jaw set and his eyes glittered.

I bet Adam Wright doesn't get told *no* very often these days. I have this odd, vague feeling that if I went in there, and he saw me, my very presence would provoke him. To do what, I don't know. I don't allow myself to delve that deeply into the thought.

But the idea is there, like a devil sitting on my shoulder, for the rest of my shift. And it's dangerous enough, enticing enough, that when I finish up at eleven o'clock, I don't change into my flats and grab my coat like I usually do.

Instead, I reapply my lipstick and walk the other way, down the corridor and into the bar area. It's thinned out in here. Not that many people are interested in nursing their two drinks for hours when they could be next door, seeking the kind of pleasure it makes me nervous to imagine.

Adam's not in here, and he certainly hasn't exited the building on my watch, so there's only one explanation.

He's in The Playroom.

In for a penny, in for a pound. I smile at Stan, the burly security guard manning the double doors to the space where all the action happens, and he winks and lets me through. I won't dwell on why it feels like he's cranking open the lid of Pandora's box.

There's thumping trance music and dry ice and dim light and bodies. Lots of bodies. Dancing and grinding and getting naked. I'm not sure what I want to achieve, exactly. I just want a peek. I'll do a circuit of the space and sate that nosy devil, even though Adam's probably in a private room somewhere. He's not going to be just standing around in here.

Suddenly I really, really wish I drank.

There's some kind of performance on the stage. From here, it looks like a pole dancer. I turn away, slinking around the edge of the club. It's so clever, how it's divided into sections with pillars and white, billowy drapes. It gives the illusion of privacy. I'm not sure I thought this through properly, because I told myself I wouldn't look too closely at anyone getting it on, and yet I'll have to if I want to spot Adam. Maybe I'll just look for a head of dark, curly hair atop an unfairly tall, unfairly broad-shouldered body.

It's not until I get to the back part of the space, where the banquette is, that I spot exactly that.

Oh my dear God.

The banquette is really a giant long ottoman, high enough and long enough that several people can be bent over it and laid out and fitted with various hooks and cuffs.

There's only one woman on it right now, and she's completely naked, her pale skin a stark contrast to the black leather.

I draw closer. She has her head turned away from me, so I can't see her face. Her hair is dark. I don't know if she's a member or one of the hosts. Behind her, facing me, is a man who is on his knees, his nose and mouth buried in her pussy so I can only see the top of his head as she wriggles her arse in his face.

But I'm not interested in him, because standing beside them both is Adam. He cuts a tall, commanding figure in the shadows. He's with them, but apart, still fully dressed in his standard white shirt and black trousers.

Exactly what he was wearing the other morning when he bade me goodbye in his library.

He's just standing there. What is he doing—is he *watching*? It certainly looks that way.

Until the other guy raises his head and cranes backwards slightly, and Adam's hand comes down on the woman's backside. *Hard.* She bucks, and I swear I nearly jump out of my skin with the shock. He straightens up, and I'm nowhere near close enough to see his eyes, but I'm close enough to see his face twitch with satisfaction as the other guy gets back in there, licking away, and I'm definitely close enough to see the huge bulge in his trousers.

So he's still a sadistic bastard under all that fine tailoring, under that veneer of wealth and respectability. Uptightness, even. What a shocker.

But that doesn't explain the impression I get that, unlike the violent kid who beat my brother to a pulp, the Adam before me looks to be wholly in control. Turned on, yes. Intense as fuck. But contained. That slap was more of a blow, but it was measured. Choreographed, almost.

He knew exactly what he was doing.

Neither does it explain why arousal soaks my thong in a single warm rush as my pulse finds its home in my clit, tattooing out an urgent staccato.

But none of those things are my biggest problem, because it's at this precise moment that he looks up, and his astonished gaze finds my horrified one.

21

ADAM

F*uck.*
   Natalie stares at me like a rabbit in the headlights before turning on her heel and disappearing
into the crowd.

Not on her fucking life.

I instantly abandon Rose, who approached me at the bar
next door earlier and asked if I'd contribute a few spanks
while some other member went down on her. I was happy
to oblige. It struck me as a practical tradeoff between my
lack of interest in fucking anyone tonight who wasn't the
hostile woman in reception and my decidedly twitchy palm,
a stress response that was as unfortunate as it was
predictable.

But now the dirty little liar who *never fraternises* has
rocked up in the fucking Playroom and has the audacity to
glare at me while I administer a couple of well-timed spanks
as a favour to Rose.

I don't think so.

'Natalie!' I shout ineffectually over the music as I push
through the crowd of bodies. The sheer number of people

in here works against her, as does the length of my legs, and I close the gap before she has a chance to wrench open the door, wrapping my fingers around her upper arm so I can turn her to face me.

Boy, is that a mutinous little face staring up at me. She'd be far safer if she knew how sincerely I enjoy it when women are mutinous. It affords me so much more pleasure when I spank it out of them. Especially when their pupils are as dilated as hers are, and their sweet little tits are heaving like this, and the long, delicate layers of black tulle comprising her dress beg to be tossed airily aside so that the pert little bottom they conceal can be spanked.

'*Wait,*' I order her sternly, and she tries unsuccessfully to tug her arm away.

'Let me go!' she shouts. She's seriously affronted; that much is clear. Also clear is that I have no intention of letting her walk out of here on these terms, so she can go home and seethe with judgement. I put my mouth to her ear.

'Just *wait*. I want to speak to you. Come with me. Just for a minute.'

I take her eye roll as agreement and frogmarch her across the room to the door leading to the private space. One of the hosts, a fair-haired chump in the guys' uniform of tight black t-shirt and black trousers, grins at her, his face positively lighting up as he takes her in.

One of the many fans she has among the staff here, I suspect.

I lean in. 'We need a private room.'

He looks from me to her. That wiped the grin off his face pretty quickly.

'For real?'

'Just to chat,' I lie smoothly. 'Right, Natalie?'

'Are you okay?' he asks her. 'I can get Stan to kick him out.'

I'm about to tell him a stunt like that would be more than his job is worth, when Natalie interjects.

'I'm fine.' Her favourite word.

'Okay then,' he says with a shrug that tells me he's unconvinced at best. 'Room Eight is free.'

I grace him with nothing more than a curt nod as I open the door and lead Natalie down the corridor. We walk in silence towards our allocated room, and I usher her in before slamming the door shut behind us. In an instant, the music dulls to a quiet thud and we're blessedly alone. She backs away a few steps.

I'm determined to have the first word. 'So you decided to fraternise for once, did you? What a coincidence. And let me guess, you didn't like what you saw.'

She crosses her arms over her middle, but it's fucking warm in here and those nipples of hers are still acting like she's skinny dipping in the North Sea. 'You hit women.'

I'd like to think I've been nothing but civil in the face of her relentless hostility for the extent of our interactions, but this takes the cake. 'Oh, for fuck's sake. Don't you dare take what you saw out there and twist that into something disgusting. I would never, ever hit a woman.'

The unspoken hangs heavily between us. *But God knows, I'd hit a man.*

'I was spanking her,' I continue, 'and you damn well know that. And she fucking loved it.'

'How do you know?'

I glare at her in disbelief. 'Because I spanked her last week when I fucked her in here, and she came very, very hard, I'll have you know. And she was on duty again tonight, so when she saw me at the bar she approached me and begged me to use my hands on her again while that guy tongue-fucked her. Consensual enough for you?'

That takes the wind out of her sails. I see the moment she decides to believe me. She swallows, her arms loosening in defeat, fingers swallowed up in the frothy layers of her skirt.

'What are you doing here, Natalie?'

'I don't have to justify myself to you. I work here.'

'So you do. I'm just curious, because I thought you didn't "fraternise". Wasn't that the term you used? Want to know what I think?'

'Not really, but I assume you're going to mansplain it to me anyway.'

I take a step towards her, and she instinctively steps backwards, her back hitting the wall and her head tilting upwards so she can keep her eyes on me as I close the gap. I'm not some dickhead who wilfully misreads women's signals, but it's not contempt I see on her beautiful face as she stares at me, nor is it fear.

Not even close.

I stop a foot or so away from her, planting my hands on the wall and caging her in before I dip my head so I can whisper close to her ear.

'You don't need me to "mansplain" it to you, because your own body is telling you loud and clear. I think you came in to find me, because I think you've been wondering about my question all evening. Wondering what would happen if you did come in.'

'That's ridiculous.' Her voice cracks, and she clears her throat. 'I'm not attracted to violent thugs.'

I dip my head even further so my lips graze her ear, and I swear to God she shivers. 'That's not who I am these days, and I think you know that. I've done a lot of work on myself, and my self-control is positively monastic. So you never, ever need to worry about that.

'In any case, I think you're talking bullshit. But I'll be mature enough to admit it for both of us. I want you so badly I barely know my own name right now, and I would bet a lot of money that if I reached under that little dress and felt your panties, they would be absolutely *soaked*.'

Her breaths are ragged. The perfume emanating from the heat of her skin is subtle enough to suggest she put it on a few hours ago, but it still makes me dizzy.

'I hate you,' she whispers. 'Remember?'

I close my eyes. 'I don't doubt that for a second. But I also don't doubt you want me—maybe even as badly as I want you. And you know I would never, ever hurt you. So why don't you let me make you feel good?' I lower my voice to a barely audible level, so that my words are little more than a caress. 'Because I think you want me to take you to places you rarely let yourself visit, you *sweet* little uptight thing, and the only thing standing in your way of complete and utter transcendence is your own pig-headedness.'

I change tack, straightening up and standing back so I can regard her. Her eyes are huge, beseeching, and her entire posture speaks of defeat, slumped as she is against the wall as though she can barely hold herself up. Her little dress is exquisite: boned satin and glittering accents and the softest, most ethereal skirt—a skirt that would prove no defence against me. It reminds me of her brand.

Gossamer.

It's so perfect for her. Delicate and feminine and ephemeral. She's the dark ballerina in the music box tonight, a beautiful, fragile doll I want to wrench free from her self-imposed captivity and prevail over while I coax unspeakable pleasure from her body.

We stand like this for a moment, my head bowed, my entire body arched towards her, hers open and pliant against the wall. It's as if her body already knows the secrets still evading her head.

She opens her mouth, but the next words out of it take me by surprise.

'I shouldn't want this,' she whispers, almost to herself, as those huge eyes take me in. 'Seriously. Not with you, of all people. What the *fuck* is wrong with me?'

No no no no no. I can't have this. Can't have her beating herself up because I've broken her will. A sudden surge of self-loathing courses through me, as chilling as the flood of relief was warm just now, when she finally acknowledged her internal struggle.

I step forward again and slide my hands under her long earrings and up her neck, finding and cupping her jaw. 'No, sweetheart. Absolutely nothing is wrong with you, you hear me? You are fucking *perfect*.'

She's still staring at me. She looks dazed. Slowly enough to give her space and deliberately enough that she understands I'm in complete control of myself, I bend and press my lips to the side of her neck.

22

ADAM

I linger there a moment. Desire may be an angry scarlet river coursing keenly through my veins, but there's stillness here in this sacred spot. There's peace in the flicker of her pulse, in the elusive ghost of her perfume, in the smooth surface of her skin. She's a shadowy hollow in the woods on a too-warm day; she's a balm for this weary traveller. I part my lips just enough to let the very tip of my tongue slide over her skin with the lightest of tracks.

The sound she makes in her throat is involuntary and shuddery and incredulous, the purest form of surrender. She's acquiesced to me, even if she's not ready to admit it to herself quite yet.

My hands are still braced on either side of her head. Our only points of touch are my lips and tongue against her neck, and the tip of my nose, already dampening as my breath condenses against her skin. I draw one last tiny line with my tongue and reluctantly straighten up to admire the effects of my handiwork.

It's what I wanted to see: her pupils dilating as ink soaks through blotting paper, gaining ground against the deep, clear chocolate of her irises as she trains her eyes squarely on my mouth. Her lips are parted, and I trace the line of her lower lip with my fingertip, just as faintly as my tongue traced the trembling contours of her neck.

I'm waiting for her to come to her senses, to slap my hand away and push off the wall and call time on this thing we're doing, but she doesn't.

I've never touched a woman quite so little and been quite so overcome. This is so much less than when she was crashing. When I forced my fingers inside her mouth and rubbed at her gums and stroked her hair and held her upright. It's so little.

And so much.

I allow myself the merest downward tug of her lip with my fingertip before I withdraw it, watching with something approaching reverence as it springs back into place. I'm so hard I should be thinking only with my dick, yet I've never felt so present. So grounded.

This ballerina corset is a frame showcasing the mastery of her bone structure to perfection. I settle the tip of my index finger in the pale hollow that marks the centre of her clavicle, noting how perfectly it fits, before taking both hands and trailing all my fingers along her clavicle so they form a fan. My skin, still tanned from Miami a few weeks ago, is dark against hers. My fingers look huge. The heels of my hands hover over those pointed little nipples.

I flatten both hands against her skin, slowly, slowly, and I grind their heels over the hard buds. The effect on her is instant. She shuts her eyes, eyelashes fluttering and diamanté arcs glittering on her lids.

'Oh my God,' she whimpers.

'Natalie.'

She opens her eyes. She's teetering on the knife edge of

desire and perceived bad decisions. Not merely bad decisions, but surrender. I'm fairly sure surrender to me would feel to her like the most shameful capitulation to enemy forces—unless I make it worth her while.

'Everything that happens from here is for you,' I tell her, and my dick twitches angrily at this subjugation of its needs. 'Do you understand? All I've wanted to do since I first laid eyes on you is make you feel *extraordinary*.' My voice is so deep it rasps on that final word. 'For God's sake, take this moment for yourself.'

I sweeten my plea with a firm grind of the heels of my hands against nipples so tautly pebbled I swear they could lacerate this chiffon.

Her eyes roll back in her head. 'Okay,' she whispers.

'Okay, what?'

'Don't make me say it. *Please*.'

And suddenly I understand: words that for me would mean consent would for her mean defeat.

'Do you have a safe word?' I say instead, and she looks blank. She's admitted she doesn't come in here—*usually*—so of course she won't have a safe word. 'You can tell me to stop anytime. I promised you I won't lose control. This is all for you.' I pause. 'But I need you to take this top off first and show me these pretty little tits so I can give them the attention they need.'

'I'm not taking my top off for you,' she says as if surprised, and it strikes me that this brain of hers is still lagging far behind her body.

'I think you are.' I keep my gaze on her face as I slide my hands down and roll my fingers over her nipples, pressing them as hard as I can through the fabric.

In my peripheral vision, her hands flutter uselessly at

her sides as her face contorts inches from mine. 'You just want to boss me around. You want to prove a point.'

I don't lessen the pressure of my fingers. 'I promise you, the only points I want to prove are that I'm not the only one in this room with a red-hot attraction and that I can make you feel better than you've ever felt in your life. It would be my privilege to show you what your body is capable of, if you let yourself loosen up enough to allow it.

'And I'd boss you around all day long if I could get away with it, you sweet little thing, but I swear to you, if you let me take charge for the next hour or so you'll be coming so hard around whichever of my body parts you like that you won't give a flying fuck about point-scoring. Now, how does this thing come off?'

23

NATALIE

I ignore his presumptuous question and make one more half-hearted, spat-out attempt to talk myself out of this, as if every moment of deflection will lessen the burden of my inevitable sins.

'You only want me because your ego needs to prove you can conquer any woman you like, especially one who despises you.'

'And you want me because you're far too intelligent to underestimate the mind-melting power of a good hate fuck,' he says evenly, those long, clever fingers rubbing at my nipples through layers of pleated silk chiffon and satin.

God, that's coarse. Even coarser than the way his fingers are abrading my nipples. The mere suggestion of a fuck with him, the pistons of his dick and the cinching of my internal muscles driven not by love but by something far headier, far more base, has those very muscles cramping enough that I shift my hips involuntarily forward into thin air. His hardness isn't touching me, but it's as difficult to ignore as it would be if he was naked.

'Nobody's fucking anyone,' I say in a voice that's despicably breathy.

'If you say so,' he says, still in that mature, tolerant voice that makes me want to slap him, even if the strain visible on his gorgeous face is truly gratifying. 'Anyway, you're wrong. I don't want you because you hate me, Natalie.' He speaks my name like a caress. 'I want you *despite* you hating me. That's a big difference. But I'm not under any illusions here. I'll take any crumb you're willing to throw my way tonight, even if it's the privilege of my tongue in your cunt while you disgorge every obscenity you've been too well-bred to voice before now.'

He has no business being this articulate and filthy and persuasive with such a sizeable proportion of his blood flow having left his brain. But the urgency of his words and the force of his visuals and the supplication in those astonishing eyes are witchcraft.

He's stirring the cauldron, and I'm gazing into its mesmerising depths, as powerless against its allure as a medieval princess is against a fateful pin prick or a poisoned apple. This man's power lies in the very power he's extending to *me,* in the potency so intoxicating it has me stupefied. He's absolving me, preemptively waiving any guilt I should feel at compromising my moral stance so grotesquely and so basely.

It's pointless, because I will, of course, feel guilty to the point of self-loathing afterwards, and it's unnecessary, because I'm already fully aware that I'll let him do whatever he likes to me tonight.

Still, I can't *say* it. I can't stand here and use my words to tell him how badly I want this, how much I need him to put his money where his filthy mouth and striking eyes are and fucking touch me, how swollen, how needy my clit already is at the mere thought of him spreading me out and fucking me with that tongue.

Maybe if I don't admit it aloud, I can tell myself later that I was merely swept along with events. That I didn't stand a chance against Adam Wright's evil sorcery.

Instead, I push myself off the wall and turn sulkily to face it, lifting my hands and bracing against it like Adam did moments ago.

'Ah,' he says, hooking a finger through the bottom of the ribbon tie. 'It's a *proper* corset.' He gets to work, tugging on the bow and loosening the ribbon from the bottom up. I force myself to keep my hands on the wall as he does, because I want every second of this delicious passivity I've gifted to myself to count. 'Who put this on you?' he murmurs.

'Evan,' I say with difficulty, because his movements have the satin lining of the cups rubbing just so over my aching nipples.

'And who's Evan?' He tugs the length of ribbon so swiftly from one of the holes that its rasp is audible.

'My pattern cutter. He made this for me.'

'I bet he fucking did.'

'He's married. To a man.'

I'm not sure why I throw him a bone. It must be the inordinate pleasure of hearing his voice go from measured to roundly pissed off that softens me.

'Glad to hear it.' He pulls out the next section of ribbon somewhat less savagely and keeps working, the corset growing looser around me until it's open and tumbling to the ground and I'm topless, back bared to him and breasts bared to the wall and brain whirring with thoughts: whether he'll kiss me now; how on earth I'll make it seem like I'm not kissing him back with every fibre of my pathetic, traitorous being; how his hands will feel as they map every inch of my skin; why I'm now consumed, lit up, with that filthy thing he wants to do with his tongue.

I don't have to wait long.

'Good God,' he says faintly. There's a featherlight kiss on my shoulder, more of a brush of his lips over my skin than anything else, a trail of his nose, too. Then his hands are on me, warm and large and certain, bracketing my waist, and dragging up my sides, and splaying over my rib-cage— 'you're so *impossibly* tiny'—and finally, finally, reaching my breasts.

'Mmm,' he says wonderingly, 'You feel like satin.' He slides his hands back and forth along their undersides. They're small—far smaller than I'd like and certainly too small to have any overhang—but he's found the ridge, and I shiver. Then he's cupping them, his huge hands covering them entirely, his palms brushing against my nipples and I let out an incoherent curse at the gloriousness of it all.

'Come here.' He keeps his hands on my breasts, tugging me up and against him, the bare skin of my back hitting crisp cotton and firm muscle and the mass of his erection solid against my lower back. From what I can tell, my estimates of his, um, dimensions in bed the other night were pretty accurate.

'God, yes,' he hisses. 'Look at that. Such a pretty little thing. I want to drag you home and play with you for hours.' I moan at that and let my head drop back against his chest, marvelling with what's left of my brain function at how incensed I was to be bundled off to his home last week, when now his threats feel silken. Seductive.

His hands move, fingers toying, pinching, plucking, his neatly clipped beard the softest scratch against my temple, his erection moving against me, although I suspect he's barely conscious of thrusting. I arch my back so I can push my breasts further into his grip, raising one arm to clutch the back of his head. His curls are soft as I thread my fingers through them, and I find I'm able to pull his head closer towards me that way, his warm breath fanning my cheekbone.

I turn my face and let his beard rasp over my skin, my mouth open in a silent invitation.

'Don't worry,' he whispers. 'I'm not going to kiss you.'

'No?' I pant.

'No,' he breaths in my ear. His voice is so low it's almost a growl, and I hear in it every last ounce of the effort it's costing him to hold that self control he promised me. 'I don't make a habit of kissing women who hate me. I'd imagine it's a pretty lonely experience.'

Forlorn, vulnerable Adam is absolutely not an entity I'm equipped for right now. I want him hard and hateful and goading. I want him to show no mercy, take no prisoners.

I reach behind me with my free hand and find his bum, and I dig in as hard as I can with my fingers to all that clenched muscle beneath that lovely wool. Jesus, he's got a fine arse. Not that I didn't notice it the other evening, but it really is spectacular. It feels even better than it looks. I can say precisely the same about his erection, which is now pressed even more snugly into my lower back.

He makes a pleased, surprised noise low in his throat and kneads my breasts harder. 'Look at that,' he groans, and I look down. My skin looks positively milky under his hands. My nipples are the tightest little pink pebbles between his fingers. He's teased them into impossible points, and the ache between my legs is now a relentless, stormy thing, intent on being slaked at any price.

It's a good thing I've already decided to sell my soul tonight.

I stand there and writhe in the fine cage of his body as he strokes and drags those hands of his all over me. And when one hand moves lower, over my navel to the waistband of my skirt, I suck in my stomach to give him as much space as possible.

'More,' I tell him, my head rolling uselessly from side to side, the top of my ponytail digging in to my scalp. 'I need more.'

'I know you do.' His hand slides under the waistband, fingertips grazing the front panel of my plain and not remotely sexy black panties. It keeps moving south until he's cupping me through my panties, his other hand still working my breast, and I swear I could come in ten seconds flat if he just slipped his hand under the fabric and—

'Who do you hate the most right now?' he murmurs in my ear. 'Me, or yourself? Because it feels to me like this greedy little cunt is betraying you pretty badly.'

'Still you,' I lie through gritted teeth, because I despise every inch of my flesh right now while also not giving a flying fuck. I don't care about anything. I don't care if I have to humiliate myself in front of Adam or say whatever he wants me to say or even beg, because I'll beg if I have to. I widen my legs a little, just to make space for that big hand of his, and those long fingers. God knows they'll need it.

He laughs. 'Of course you do.' And then he's pulling his hand out and releasing my breast and gripping my shoulders and spinning me around and guiding me back to the wall.

I look up, bewildered and bereft and thoroughly pissed off.

And he stands there with his crisp shirt and enormous

erection and magical eyes, staring at me, disheveled and aroused and bare-breasted.

He grins like we've been playing chess all this time and this is checkmate.

'If you want me to touch that pretty little cunt of yours, Natalie, then you'll need to show it to me first. I'm not getting you off under your skirt. No fucking way.'

24

ADAM

I t's a beautiful thing to have Natalie Bennett's outraged gaze be the result of denied orgasm and not, for once, the mere fact of your existence.

I'm enjoying this very much.

I eye my handiwork: her perfect little tits flushed from my hands, sweet little nipples hard as marble, princessy ponytail nicely mussed.

It's a truly excellent start.

'I think you want to take it off,' I say cajolingly. 'Your panties, too. I think you want to show me what you've been hiding under all that lovely tulle. I think you want to see for yourself just how *controlled* I can be when you're standing naked and perfect in front of me. And I think you want my mouth on that delicious little clit of yours, too. Imagine how good I can make that ache feel.'

From the way she lets her eyelashes flutter downwards for a moment, I'd say she's imagining, all right.

'Do you spend all your time strong-arming people into doing things they don't want to do?' she asks. 'Because it certainly feels like it.' But she arches her hips off the wall and reaches behind her. God, do I adore this sulky, huffy facade.

But her words have a sting to them, and that sting gives me pause, because she's not wrong. I narrow my eyes, my glib flow of filth halted. 'How the hell else do you think I got myself from a shit-hole prison to where I am today?' I ask her. 'Pretty much the only thing I know how to do is hustle. But if I've misjudged this and you don't want to be here, be my guest.' I jerk my head towards the door.

It feels like a standoff, with her arms frozen behind her and her eyes molten with... what? Rage? Disbelief? I've called her bluff and I've very possibly shot myself in the foot, too, by drawing her attention to the very reason she doesn't want to do this with me, My dick throbs and my heart hammers behind its bars of bone.

Then her arms move behind her, and a zipper rasps.

'I want this,' she says, quietly but clearly, her eyes still fixed on me as she lets her skirt float to the floor in a soft black cloud of tulle.

The little beauty.

'Glad to hear it,' I grit out, taking a step towards her, my eyes going straight to her plain black cotton panties.

'They're not very—attractive,' she says with a self-conscious little laugh that kills me.

I slide my hands over her hips, thumbs brushing the fabric at either side. 'Every single thing about you is attractive,' I tell her, and I sink to my knees in front of her. My mouth lands between her breast bone and her navel, and I kiss the velvety skin there as my hands explore, skimming over her hips and getting a good feel of her spectacular little bottom.

I squeeze it as I dip my head and run my nose over her fabric-covered pelvic bone, and I'm rewarded with a soft sigh from her. She puts her hands on my shoulders and flexes her fingers while I waste no time in inhaling the sweet musk of her arousal. 'Fuck, your cunt smells amazing,' I growl against her, and her moan is music. 'Take them off.'

She releases my shoulders and hooks her thumbs into the fabric. I'm getting far too much pleasure from having it be her, and not me, who reveals this part of her to me, but I'm also in too much of a rush. As soon as she bares her pussy, with its neat triangle of hair, I tug her panties the rest of the way down her gorgeous legs until they're on top of the tulle.

'Jesus Christ.' I glance up for the full effect: Natalie staring down at me, her breath coming more quickly, her face flushed with arousal and anticipation and probably vulnerability and those lovely little tits of hers heaving. This beautiful woman hates me, yet she's permitted me to get her naked, and the enormity of what I've persuaded her to do to hits me afresh.

Do you spend all your time strong-arming people into doing things they don't want to do?

Let's fucking prove to her once and for all that this is what she wants.

'You are breathtaking,' I tell her. 'I knew you would be, but... Hold yourself open for me, sweetheart, and give me your leg. I need a taste.'

'Oh my God,' she says, her voice tremulous. But she's clearly established that being a good, obedient girl for me is her best path to getting what she thinks she wants, which is probably a shameful, cataclysmic orgasm and, presumably, closure.

She's deluded if she thinks she'll get this heat between us out of her system that easily, but I'll play ball. She slings a leg over my shoulder and steadies herself, sliding one hand over my ear and into my hair before reaching down and opening her lips up for me.

It's a sight I'll take to my grave. Her fingers make a *V*, exposing that lovely little pink pearl for me, and it's so swollen and glossy already.

I'm addicted before I even bend my head to taste it.

25

NATALIE

There are entire galaxies in which my having any interaction at all with Adam Wright is a dreadful idea, yet they shrink into some cosmic black hole as he touches his tongue to the millimetres of nerve-riddled flesh that has quickly become my only universe.

It's not just his tongue, though. It's the way his nose presses against my pelvic bone, the slant of his jaw as he tilts his head to bury himself as deep as he can, and the fan of dark eyelashes on his cheeks as he closes his eyes. It's the inhales of my pussy so deep they're practically snorts, and the dig of his fingertips into my arse cheeks, and the abrasion of crisp cotton and hard shoulder muscle against the skin of my thigh.

God knows, the whole effect feels filthy and carnal and heady, so heady I'm in danger of losing my mind and begging this man for everything—for kisses and fucks, for the gift of letting me see him *lose* control. Because he promised me self-control, and he's shaking with the effort of keeping it; I can feel it.

And some strange shift has come about where the idea

of Adam Wright spiralling out of control with *me* feels not even remotely frightening but utterly intoxicating.

The tongue sliding over my clit as his beard brushes my pussy is the singular most perfect thing I've ever felt, so when he makes a hungry sound and pulls his head away so he can glance up at me, I stare down at him, bewildered. What the hell is he doing? He should never, ever stop this. He should do this *forever*.

He stands, and fuck is he tall. And very, very fully clothed.

'I want you on the bed,' he says with difficulty, his hands sliding around my waist and tugging me against him. 'I want to spread you out so I can enjoy you properly.'

His voice is so strained. He's all expensive fabrics and concealed muscles and hard arousal, and I'm soft and naked and pliant in his arms. I like this power imbalance far, far more than I should.

I stare up into his face, at the mouth that's just been on me and the eyes that are taking their fill of me. His words thrill me. They make me feel as if I'm a different type of host, one of the women who work in The Playroom and make their bodies available for the members' every whim.

Like whoever he was spanking just now. He said she was *working* again tonight. He fucked one of the hosts the other night, and he said she loved it, and I'm sure she did. Who wouldn't love being worked over by this man, if they had no prior knowledge of him?

I want him to work me over. I want so much more than his hands flexing on my waist and his tongue dancing on my clit. If he wants to *spread me out and enjoy me*, God knows I won't stop him.

'What are you waiting for?' I ask him now. He smiles like I'm full of surprises and turns us towards the bed.

God, the flash of us in the huge mirror on the opposite wall is really something. Who even are we? I'm tiny and pale and naked, and he's this dark, suited giant intent on devouring me.

And I fucking love it.

I tug my hair out of its ponytail, getting on the bed and edging backwards as elegantly as I can until I'm lying there on my elbows. He's toeing off his loafers immediately and crawling over me as I widen my legs to accommodate him and Jesus Christ is this hot. His proximity. His sheer size as he crouches, *looms,* over me, intensity radiating from him. He's shaking with it as he braces on his hands and surveys me like I'm his property, his little plaything, and I soak it all up. If I was any other woman, he'd be bending to kiss me right now, I'm sure of it. His mouth is *right there*, such a lovely thing, tempting and plump and skilled.

'Your hair is...' he begins. 'It's so beautiful, loose like this. What a delicious little thing you are.' He braces on one hand as he bends to suck my needy nipple and reaches between my legs, finding my entrance and pushing in so hard I gasp. The heat of his finger and the pressure of his mouth are wondrous, and I arch into his touch, finding his hair with my hands, threading my fingers through it.

'Such a shame you hate me,' he muses against my breast. 'I'd love to kiss you. It's interesting, though'—he twists his finger inside me, and oh my dear God—'that you can't keep your legs closed for me, isn't it? And it's positively *fascinating* that you are absolutely soaked.'

That fucker. 'You're such an arrogant dick,' I say, instinctively pushing my legs together, but he chooses that moment to seal his mouth to my nipple and his thumb to my clit and I practically catapult off the bed.

He laughs and looks up. There's a smirk on his face that

I'd really like to slap off. 'That may be, but tell me this doesn't make you want to open your legs wider.' *This* is a measured circle of his thumb pad over my clit, its slickness a testament to my arousal.

'I hate you,' I say, throwing an arm over my face.

'But you love the way I touch you.' He drags his thumb over my clit again and cliffs crumble to clouds of dust. Worlds shatter. 'And I love it, too. If you trusted me more, I'd tie you to this bed, or maybe I'd put these lovely long legs on a spreader bar so I could play with this cunt as much as I wanted.'

I can actually feel myself growing wetter at the thought of Adam dominating me like that, at the thought of submitting to him and his darkness and his kinks, lying there, restrained and only taking what he sees fit to give me.

Him and his body parts being my whole existence.

I groan.

'Imagine it.' He adds another finger inside me, and the burn is real but also... it's heaven. 'Hours of this, hours of teasing and fucking until you've come so many times you don't know your own name and my dick is your favourite thing in the world. Until my mouth has acquainted itself with every single inch of your body.'

'Ugh,' I say. It's the only thing I'm capable of saying, because he slides back down my body, kissing me as he goes, until he can crook those fingers and put his tongue back on me, and *this*, this is all I can bring myself to care about. Not the guilt and the shame of spreading my legs for a man like this, but the unadulterated pleasure coursing through my nerve endings as he fucks me slowly with his fingers and licks me so thoroughly, so lavishly, that I'm incapable of resistance.

'Oh God,' I say as he thrusts and sucks and the molten

heat builds and builds in my core, the pressure and the pleasure consuming me. My abs are cramping, my legs are spread so wide they're shaking, I'm pushing my pussy into his face like the greediest little whore, and, as I go under, there's the strangest feeling of relief that I can let go, that Adam has taken me to a place so pure in this little room that knowing the fullness of my pleasure is all that matters.

'Oh God,' I whimper again, shifting on the sheets, back arching and fingers moving restlessly in his hair and pussy driving into him, 'I can't, oh shit, I'm—'

He drags a hand up my stomach to pinch one nipple *hard* and that, combined with the rough, depraved strokes of his tongue and the pumps of his fingers, has me sailing over the edge like a pebble cast off a cliff. My pleasure is white-hot and pure; it's a rip-tide that sucks every single thing that's not *it* into some kind of vortex. He licks me and licks me and I sob my way through it—I may even scream.

I lie there and let the delirium course over me until it's ebbed gently away and all that remains is the kind of post-orgasmic serenity that's like concussion.

Adam crawls back up my body, planting kisses over my skin as he does, and settles himself heavily between my legs. He's so hard he could probably fuck me through his suit trousers, and so close he'll definitely kiss me. Definitely.

But he doesn't. He hovers above my mouth, his lips glistening with my arousal, and as that serenity morphs into a void, I'm not sure I've ever wanted anything so much as for him to plunder my mouth and fill my pussy.

We stare at each other.

'That was—extraordinary,' he grits out. 'You're dangerous.'

Right back at ya, pal.

'Fuck me,' I propose instead.

He gives a little laugh that contains precisely zero humour and shakes his head, his gaze roaming from my eyes to my mouth and back again before he throws my stupid words from earlier back at me.

'Nobody's fucking anyone, remember? I suspect you'll have a lot of regrets tomorrow—or maybe as soon as you leave this room—and I don't want to add to that list.'

I slide a hand between us and palm that lovely hard dick of his. Christ it's gorgeous, suspended heavily between us, filling his trousers up. 'May as well be hung for a sheep as a lamb.'

He groans. 'I'm serious. I'm trying to be respectful here.'

You'd think I'd *like* a respectful man. You'd think I'd value that quality, especially in someone I'm strongly predisposed to distrust.

Not so much, it turns out.

'Let me make you come, then.'

'Stop it.' He dips his face to my neck, and I'm pretty sure he snorts my hair before pressing a soft kiss to my skin. I wonder if he's aware that he's rolling his hips against my hand.

I thought it was irritating when someone I'm trying to hate acts nobly, but it turns out it's far more irritating when someone I'm trying to hate *and* fuck acts nobly.

'You need to shoot your load. Badly,' I point out. I can't bear that I've got him so wound up that he might actually go back out there and find someone else for his release.

'Don't worry about me,' he mumbles into my hair. 'I'll sort myself out in the bathroom.'

I need him to come. I can't bear the inequality of it. He's seduced me. He's tasted the most intimate part of my body and he's seen me lose control. He'll go home tonight with memories of how my body tremored, how loudly I cried out at his hands. I absolutely have to have the same from him.

He's proven his point.

I want to undo him.

It's only fair.

'Come on me, then.'

26

ADAM

My entire body stiffens, my dick jerking against Natalie's little hand.

I've made peace with the prospect of a quick one banged out in the ensuite here, followed by God knows how many in the privacy of my shower at home, so the vision of ejaculating over her beautiful, naked, *sated* body is the most torturous of mirages.

'You just want to see my dick,' I whisper in her ear, just to piss her off. Oddly, and by unspoken agreement, it seems the more obnoxious I am, the more it increases the heat between us.

'Oh, please. I could have seen your dick the other night if I'd wanted to,' she says, and the surprise of it has me rearing up onto my elbows.

'What do you mean?'

She shoots me a smile I'm sure she intends as smug, but in truth the sight of her lying under me, flushed and as relaxed as I've ever seen her in my company, has me enraptured.

'I know you came into my room the other night. I woke

up and you were fast asleep, snoring with all these lancets beside you and the fucking Empire State Building in your pants.'

Shit. I had no idea. It's on the tip of my tongue to apologise for what I know is a move that will have royally pissed her off, but I stop myself. She's here, isn't she?

'And what did you think?' I ask instead, pushing up onto my knees between her still-spread legs and putting my hand to my belt buckle. My poor cock is an aching, miserable bar, and her eyes are glued to it.

'Beyond the fact that you were a crazy psycho with no boundaries who was far too obsessed with my glucose levels?' she asks. It looks as though she's talking to my dick and not to me.

'Beyond the fact that I was concerned for your safety after you hypoed all over me, yes.'

I unbuckle my belt and undo my hook and eye and unzip my flies and palm my cock through my boxer briefs. Her greedy little stare doesn't waver. Fuck, that feels amazing.

'I didn't know whether to ride it or push you off the bed,' she says, crossing her hands behind her head. This sight of her beneath me is fucking spectacular, but her response has me barking out a surprised laugh.

So she was interested, on a physical level at least, even then. Jesus, that must have pissed her off. I'm astonished she didn't act on her impulse to shove me to the floor.

I tug my shirt tails up, pushing down the waistband of my boxer briefs and extracting my sensitive cock as gingerly as if it was an unexploded grenade which, honestly, is not a bad analogy for how it feels right now.

'So you didn't take a look? You didn't fancy a little peek?'

It appears she's far too busy fixating on the sight of my

hand moving slowly up and down my rigid length to have heard me. Her mouth drops open, which is unhelpful, because it makes me want to lean forward and ram the whole thing down her throat, if I'm honest.

'You could have.' I employ all my abs to help me lean to the left and pump some of the lube that's on the bedside table. As I settle back in place, I close my eyes briefly at the sensory delight that is the cold gel on my hot, hard dick. It's nowhere near as fine a home as Natalie's cunt. Or ass. Or mouth. But having her greedy, horny little eyes on me is almost as good.

Almost.

'You could have slipped one of those little hands in and had a feel,' I continue, 'or pulled my dick out. I would have loved waking up to that.'

'Sounds like a pretty compelling reason *not* to have done it,' she retorts, but I don't miss the tilt of her hips in front of me. She wants me as badly as I want her.

I ignore her. 'I wonder if you could even close your hands around it,' I muse aloud, my own hand working harder. Precum is now weeping from my slit, and it seems I'm not the only one who notices, because when I glance up at her, she's licking her lips.

'Nobody likes a gloater, Adam,' she manages, but it's breathy. I bet she's kicking herself.

I grin and lean forward, bracing on one arm so I can really let my dick have it while I hover over her. Alas, my performance will be less protracted than I'd like for optics. 'It's less awful if it's true. Where can I come?'

She swallows. 'My boobs. My stomach. *Not* my face— you haven't earned it. And if you get it in my hair I'll kill you.'

God, I love it when she's like this. I had the impression

from Gen when I spoke to her that Natalie was meek, if anything, but she's not like that with me. Not at all. If I'm the only person she shows this side of herself to then I'm a lucky man.

Her excellent banter notwithstanding, the sight of her alone is enough to have my orgasm hurtling through me, fevered and urgent. She said I can come on her tits, and they're so small, so perfect, almost flat in this position, her delicate nipples still furled and taut.

It's an invitation like no other.

As I cross the finish line, that control I've been lauding snaps, and I let her have with my words what I can't with my body.

'Jesus fucking Christ, you are *beautiful*. Going to come all over these gorgeous little tits, but you bet I wish it was your cunt I was fucking. It was so tight, even with my fingers. Imagine how tight it would feel if I fucked you. Have you thought about it? Huh? Have you fantasised about how it would feel to take this cock? How full you'd feel?'

If her body is a vision, then her face is a picture, eyes wide and lips parted. She's breathing almost as heavily as me as she takes in the sight of me looming over her and the filth of my words. God knows how beautiful she'd look trussed up and restrained for me.

Earning that level of trust from her is a privilege I can't conceive of, so I focus instead on her eyes, her mouth, her tits, the soft, supple skin of her stomach, and the need in me makes my body shake and my scalp prick with sweat and my abs spasm, and veins are surely popping in my neck and forearms as I jack the everliving fuck out of myself, fucking my hand as violently as I can, panting like I'm running a bloody marathon as my body prepares to deliver the most staggering orgasm.

The heat that floods me as it does is like molten treacle coursing through my balls, my veins. I jerk and jerk and come, shooting rope after thick white rope over her hips and stomach and tits, painting her with the creamy evidence of my astonishing desire for her. Her gasps ring in my ears alongside the wet smacks as I brand her, and it's beautiful.

I thrust and thrust into my hand until I'm spent and I've adorned Natalie with all my arousal. 'God,' I say, looking down at my creation. *'Fuck.'*

She watches in what appears to be stunned, breathless silence as I release my dick and use my fingertip to trace shapes on her skin with my cum. I swirl it in. I rub it over one dusky nipple and then the other, which has her moaning softly. I wish I could lower myself on top of her and kiss the breath out of her lungs while my seed lies sticky between us. I wish I could drag her into what I know to be an excellent shower next door.

But I know, even through my post orgasmic haze, that I'm on borrowed time here.

I've been on borrowed time all night. This has been a stolen moment, a fleeting portal to another kind of existence with Natalie.

My eyes flicker to hers, and I see peace in them. Satisfaction. She's not embarrassed—yet. She hasn't come to her senses—yet.

And I'd rather get her sorted out and into a cab before I see that hatred return to her eyes again.

'Let's get you cleaned up,' I say, running cum-slicked fingertips down from her breastbone to her navel. 'And I'm going to need a serious running commentary on how to get you back into that corset.'

Her little laugh tells me she appreciates my attempt at levity, however lame my joke might be.

But as I reluctantly extricate myself from between her legs and climb off the bed in search of a washcloth, I can't help one last glance at her laid out like this on the sheets, covered in *me.*

I can't help but commit it to memory.

27

NATALIE

When anxiety strikes, keep busy. That's my MO, anyway. If my anxiety is a maelstrom inside me this morning then I'm a whirling dervish, whizzing around the studio like a cartoon character inside one of those tiny cyclones that keeps them spinning. Keeps them productive.

My ridiculous orgasm should have helped. God knows, the concussion-slash-bliss lasted as Adam cleaned me up and put me in a fluffy robe so I'd be covered up while I wove all that ribbon back into my corset, loosely enough that I could step into it.

It endured as he escorted me outside and bundled me into a black cab which he insisted on paying for up front as he instructed the cabbie to take me all the way home.

It endured as he leaned into the cab almost shyly before pressing a kiss to my cheek.

And it even endured through the shower I took when I got home—a brief one, because my tiny, grotty bathroom in my tiny, grotty flat is fucking freezing.

But this morning, I'm in the weirdest mood. It doesn't

help that all my worries from yesterday have come rushing back in, more taunting and insidious than ever. It's as if that hour in that room with Adam was a stopper that plugged the dam momentarily, and once that stopper was removed, the deluge was waiting to do its worst.

It also doesn't help that I feel really odd about what happened last night. It's part shame—the kind of guilty, *how the fuck could I have done that* shame my girlfriends have complained about countless times after drunken one-night-stands, the kind my forced sobriety has mostly protected me from. I have no idea what I was thinking, what possessed me to go along with it, what gave me the courage to say the stuff I said.

I told him to come on my boobs, for God's sake!

It's part vulnerability, too. I feel fragile and exposed and a bit shaky. It seems Adam Wright is getting all my most vulnerable moments, the sexy and the not so sexy.

But I'm self-aware enough to know what it isn't: regret. Because every time I allow myself to think about what went down in that room, I get this delicious, fluttery clenching low in my stomach. It was so ridiculously hot I could never, ever regret it.

It's possible the memory of Adam looking at me with hooded, hungry eyes from between my legs is branded on my brain forever. And the visual of him jerking himself off more aggressively than seemed possible *or* advisable while looking positively feral will live rent-free in my head for the rest of my days. Dear God, it was so damn big, that thing. So *angry*.

I made him lose his self-control, and he was a beast, and it was bloody fabulous. All of which makes it pretty difficult to regret.

'So we now know the Loch Ness Monster is an actual thing,' Evan muses. He's been obsessing over the final version of a paper pattern for a bias-cut evening dress all morning. Once he's happy with it, Carrie will digitise it and send it to the grading agency to be reproduced across the spectrum of women's sizes. Actual Haute Couture brands tend to make each pattern from scratch, but as a demi-couture, we re-use our most iconic patterns and definitely the "blocks" off which they're based.

He's also been obsessing over Adam's penis all morning, which is as irritating as it is unhelpful... and as unsurprising. He was intrigued by the nighttime boner situation, so it stands to reason that Adam having unleashed the full force of it on me last night has made him unbearable.

'Mmm-hmm,' I say absently, my eyes glued to the browser window showing our bank balance. It's horrifying. Beyond horrifying. I need to pay one of our French mills tomorrow before they'll release the three hundred metres of excruciatingly expensive custom jacquard we ordered, but paying it will mean there aren't enough funds for payroll next week unless we have a bonanza weekend on our website, which I doubt.

Sales have been *slow*. It's that horrific time of year where an unseasonably mild October meant no one was buying new season collections that month, and November is always a write-off because everyone waits for Black Friday to buy anything at all. The world and his wife will discount then, and we won't, both because mid-season discounting doesn't reflect well on our brand and because it trains customers not to shop at full price. Inevitably, though, that means we'll see none of the wallet share from the biggest shopping weekend of the year.

So here we are, with my entire life savings sitting in unsold inventory, and a hideous cash flow model that always, always works against us, and insufficient funds to pay my amazing, hardworking team, and it's all enough to make the anxiety that's been coursing through me all of yesterday (well, *most* of yesterday) and this morning turn to fully fledged panic, a panic that twists my stomach like two hands might wring out a wet dishcloth.

'I don't get why you're being so blasé,' Evan says now, and and I press my lips together before answering, because what I want to shout at him isn't appropriate or cool. He may be one of my best friends, but he's also my employee. I'm the business owner, and our finances are my problem, no one else's. Neither Evan nor Carrie nor anyone else can ever know how close they come to not being paid every single month.

They can never know how fortuitous it is for them—and for me—that my Alchemy pay cheque hits my personal account the day before Gossamer's pay day is due each month. And they can *definitely* never know how often I have to top up Gossamer's bank account with my own Alchemy salary. Or that Alchemy is pretty much paying my bills on its own, because my original plan to pay myself a small salary from the business is categorically not an option right now.

It will be, at some point, but there are always so many bills to pay, so many parties clamouring for their funds—mills and factories and the landlord for this studio, obviously. It's a never-ending tunnel of keeping the panic to a manageable level while I spin plates and run to stand still and try very, very hard to keep the following from myself and from everyone else: that this dream of running a beautiful fashion brand has become more of a nightmare, and that *I can't see the dimmest, tiniest speck of light at the end of that tunnel.* Not any more.

But I won't say any of that to my lovely Evan, who works so fucking hard and is so fucking loyal to me, despite the fact that he could easily get snapped up by a bigger brand. He claims he's here for the autonomy a small brand gives him, but I know better.

Nor will I say any of it to myself. I may have no idea what lies ahead for us, but spiralling over that fact prevents me from doing what I need to do: keep my head down and focus every day on living to fight another day. Another week. To make another payroll.

So I plaster on a smile for my dear friend and I tear my eyes from the horrible sight on my screen. 'Definitely not blasé,' I manage. 'Not with my track record. Just trying to get through the to-do list.'

I force myself to banter with him for a few more minutes, because God knows he doesn't deserve to have a miserable cow for a boss. But when the doorbell rings downstairs and he ambles off to answer it, I let my eyes drift closed. The tears are there. They're so close that my lash line is damp. My entire face aches from holding it in. There's a well of pressure building behind my face, and it's all I can do not to let it release.

I try taking slow, even breaths in and out. Maybe I can trick my body into regulating itself. Maybe I can breathe away that bank balance. That invoice from the mill that's blinking at me on my screen. They're waiting for me to send them a payment confirmation before they'll release the fabric, and I really need DHL to pick it up by tomorrow. If they don't, we'll lose our slot at the factory.

But I'm so fucking exhausted, and I know my antics last

night—delicious though they were—didn't help. It's hard enough holding down a late-night job when I'm a morning person, but it's far harder when I'm getting naked in my place of work afterwards and crawling into bed at one in the morning. Even without ill-advised sexy times, I'm burning the candle at both ends, and the candle is feeling pretty useless. Exhaustion is making me less resilient when I need every ounce of resilience I can muster in this business.

A tear rolls out of my tear duct and down the side of my nose, and I dab it carefully with a tissue so as not to mess up my perfect makeup. Maybe I'll go treat myself to a fancy coffee that I can't afford. The caffeine hit will be worth the investment. Sure, it'll make me even more jittery, but I'll also be more productive, and that can't be a bad thing. If only I could find the energy to get up from my chair.

It turns out I don't need energy to get up. I simply require a big fat shock. Because when I jerk my head up at the two sets of heavy footsteps clomping up the narrow staircase that leads to the front door and see Adam Wright standing in my studio, I'm out of that chair like a rocket.

28

ADAM

S he's not okay. It's obvious as soon as I look at her.
Fuck.
I shouldn't have pushed her like that last night.
Shouldn't have been so bloody selfish as to bundle her into
a room with me and sweet-talk her into something she's
clearly regretting. But even as I mentally berate myself, I'm
grateful that I listened to my gut and followed up with her
today. Because the red-eyed woman who's shot to her feet at
the sight of me is not the same post-orgasmic one I tucked
into a cab last night.

This Evan guy who answered the door to me and is, I
now know, an exquisite cutter, looks from me to her as
though he's even less certain that letting me up here was the
right thing to do. I ignore his hovering and stride towards
Natalie, extending one of the two lattes I just picked up at an
artisanal place on the corner. It was a typically pretentious
Soho coffeehouse but it smelt like heaven. I have no idea
what she drinks, but this seemed like a safe bet.

She looks from the cup to me as she accepts it, and our
fingers brush.

'It's a latte,' I say. 'I hope that's okay.'

'It's perfect. And this is my favourite coffee shop. Thank you.'

'Excellent.' We stare at each other for a moment. She definitely looks teary, which I absolutely can't have, but she's polished perfection in skinny jeans and a black, slim-fitting sweater with little pearls in her ears, her glossy hair pulled back. So elegant, so stunning, as always. There isn't a hair out of place, and I can tell her makeup has been immaculately applied, but beneath it she looks fucking exhausted.

'Can I talk to you?' I blurt out, wedging my free hand into my coat pocket and breaking our gaze to glance around the space. It's a decent size but by no means huge, and rails on wheels cover most of what space there is. On the rails hang dress after dress, each in its own clear plastic garment bag, and behind them I see picking boxes containing folded garments.

It seems the left-hand side of the room is used for pattern-cutting, sewing and designing while the right-hand side is a makeshift warehouse. I guess they do their own fulfilment direct from here, which is laborious and possibly not the best use of prime Soho real estate when that side of things could be outsourced to a third party fulfilment centre in a location where square footage is far cheaper. They'd be better off refurbishing this entire place and using the extra space as a showroom for clients.

Natalie looks around, too, no doubt taking in the fact that we have company and that her colleagues appear *very* interested in my having turned up out of the blue. 'Um, yeah. Sure. Why don't we...' She trails off.

Behind me, Evan claps his hands. 'Gail, Carrie, how about we take an early lunch? We'll give you an hour, sweetie,' he adds to Natalie.

'Have a seat,' she says, sinking back down into hers with weary resignation. I do as she suggests and wheel over a swivel chair from the table nearby so it's facing her. Once I've set down my coffee and shrugged off my coat—a move that has her eyeing my body with what looks like memory in her eyes—I take a seat opposite her. She really does look pale.

'Do you need to grab some lunch?' I ask once the others have cleared off. It seems to me the most diplomatic way to ask her if she's keeping on top of her blood glucose levels, but it gets me a tired eye roll.

'I think my favourite thing about last night was that you didn't once ask to see my CGM.'

Ouch. But also—interesting that she's gone straight there. I wasn't sure if she'd opt to ignore our scorching hookup.

'My bad.' I pick up my coffee cup. 'Seems I had other things on my mind. And, from the excellent memories I have, I wouldn't have guessed that was your *favourite* thing about last night.'

'Maybe you should stop trying to guess what I'm thinking then,' she retorts with a flush.

'I can't imagine you'll welcome more interference, in that case, but you looked a little upset when I walked in. I stopped by because I wanted to check you were okay with what had gone down'—unfortunate choice of words, but I forge gamely ahead—'and you weren't regretting it *too* much.'

Jesus, that sounds like a plea for her to admit the exact opposite. I'm not sure what I'm expecting—probably an outright denial that she's upset or a vehement protestation that she hasn't given her orgasming all over my tongue a second thought.

As usual, she surprises me.

'It has nothing at all to do with last night. You just caught me at a bad time.' She looks down at her coffee cup and carefully peels the lid off it. I survey her.

'Work stuff?' I guess.

She shrugs without looking at me. 'And then some.'

I'm treading carefully here. 'So you're okay about last night? You don't have any more regrets than I'd expect?'

She sighs. 'Not everything is about you, Adam, shocking though that may be. But I have far bigger things to worry about right now than how much I should slut shame myself, so honestly, you should just leave me to it.'

'You know,' I begin slowly, 'I don't know the ins and outs of running a luxury brand like you do, but I do know how fucking brutal things can be in this industry, so if you want to talk it through with someone who has some grasp of the lay of the land then I'm happy to listen.'

That gets me a mirthless little laugh. 'Yeah, right. I'm sure things are brutal over at Omar Vega's.'

Gaining her trust and, perhaps, the opportunity to help her, is more important than discretion right now.

'They're difficult. Omar has to be kept on a tight rein, creatively and financially. He's very much Creative Director only. His decisions on what to produce and how much he can spend doing it are driven by the Finance Director and the merchandising teams. He's told how many dresses to design versus trousers and jackets each season. He's told what colours will be most commercial.

'What I'm trying to say is that he's operating within far tighter parameters than you are and he only has to wear one hat. You have to wear all of them. You're CEO and FD as well as creating. It's tough. So please know how genuine I am when I say I'm impressed and I'm sympathetic.'

What I *don't* explicitly say is that Vega is an unhinged coke head who's a fucking liability, and that Natalie has more professionalism—not to mention discipline—than a guy like him could ever hope for. Right now he's playing ball, but Vega's perception of his disposability is vastly different from mine and that of his management team.

I also don't say that my ability to provide level-headed advice right now is being seriously tested by the sight of Natalie's neck, slim and pale and showcased to perfection by her low, sleek bun. That I had my nose and mouth buried in that neck last night, let alone in more sacred, delicious places, seems miraculous to me.

'Well, thank you for saying that.' She sounds not prickly, exactly, but brusque. Still, it's not a total brush-off.

'Cash flow problems?' I hazard.

She stiffens, wrapping her delicate hands around her coffee cup. 'Understatement.'

'Can I ask how bad it is?'

There's a pause where she's clearly evaluating my entitlement to any of her confidences. Then she sighs, yielding. 'There's a supplier I need to pay tomorrow. It's a hefty invoice, and it leaves payroll next week looking... difficult.'

I grimace. 'Okay. Will they give you credit?'

'They don't do terms,' she says quickly. 'They've made that clear before. They have a strict policy of not releasing the fabric unless they've got their payment, or at least proof that it's been sent.'

'Have you pushed them recently to see if they can change that?'

'No. There's no point.' Her shoulders are rounded like they're bearing the weight of the world, and it kills me. I need to tread carefully here. She must feel so alone in this, yet I'm not someone whose help or pity she wants. I'm sure this invoice is looming large in her head, but I bet it's no more than ten grand. Obviously, that's still a sizeable chunk for a company of Gossamer's size, but it's also something I could write a cheque for right now and not bat an eyelash.

Not that that would ever be an option in this reality we have. So I'll give her the next best things: advice and perspective.

'Look.' I lean forward and rest my elbows on my thighs, steepling my fingers and enjoying far too much the way her gaze brushes over my hands and back to my face. 'You'd be amazed at what they may be willing to do if you just put your cards on the table and ask. If you're not already aware, then you need to be very clear that you're not the only person in this industry who can't pay their bills.

'I mean, the entire fucking fashion sector is built on sketchy shit and everybody constantly cajoling and begging and going quiet when bills are due. It's a bloody nightmare. The cash flow model is heinous, and you guys, as a small outfit with no economies of scale and no critical mass are always going to get squeezed at both ends.'

'Why did you get into it, then?' she asks.

'Same reason you did, I assume. I enjoy beautiful things. It's been my gift to myself after years and years of grafting in tech. Now I get to help talented visionaries like you bring those visions to life. But I'm not a charity. The sector's inefficient, and I like efficiencies. Vega and the other brands I own all share the same central functions—book keeping, HR, that kind of thing. That's a massive swing factor in improving their operational efficiencies. It also gives us more clout when purchasing—we can demand better terms from suppliers.

'And I'm playing a long game. These core businesses are never going to make great margins, but I'm interested in the product extensions, licensing agreements, all the things that can build a lifestyle brand. Omar Vega doing a collaboration with Pottery Barn or Ruggable? *That's* what gets me excited.'

She smiles a little, and I hope I've reminded her that she's not alone in this. That the rest of the industry is on its knees with her. Not that that makes her imminent cash flow squeeze go away.

'It gets me excited too,' she admits. 'Our print designer is so talented. I'd love to see her prints on home furnishings down the line. But that's not going to happen if I can't pay this bill.'

Time for the ultimate push. She's made it clear in the recent past how much she detests it when I interfere. She may not like me, but I know from last night that she trusts me on some level, and she's also not stupid. I'm a successful guy with a portfolio of relatively high-performing brands in her sector. She'd be crazy not to pick my brains or use my expertise to help herself out of this crunch.

'If you're open to showing me your numbers,' I tell her, 'then we can go through them together and make a plan.'

I just need to text my assistant and get her to cancel my next couple of hours.

29

NATALIE

The thought of having a man as successful, as competent, as Adam look through the car crash that is my numbers makes me feel sick. My P&L is a source of great shame to me—a constant, conditionally formatted prompt for me to judge myself on what I've failed to achieve in the four years I've run Gossamer. The horror of its sea of red washes over me afresh every time I dare to pull it up. Even opening it makes me feel sick.

I do, of course, because denial on that scale is spectacularly unprofessional. Still, confronting the rows and columns that tally my achievements is the least palatable part of my job.

My fingers hover over my laptop keyboard as I stare at him. It doesn't help that he's so fine. So handsome. I could have swaddled myself in his beautiful black wool coat when I saw him standing in the doorframe. I know, without even touching it, that it's double-faced cashmere.

He's in a variation of his usual uniform today—steel grey trousers, a crisp white shirt, open at the neck, and a pale grey merino V-neck sweater. His beard is immaculate, he looks as though he's had twelve hours sleep, and his wavy hair is raked back with just the right amount of product.

Don't get me started on his light eyes and full mouth and huge hands, because they're perfect.

And they were on me last night.

All of them.

There's a push-pull with Adam. It's all driven internally, of course, but the conflict I feel between wanting to hate him and wanting to impress him is exhausting. It strikes me that there'd be nothing worse than having his pity. It would kill me, I know it would.

'They're not pretty,' I tell him now. My numbers, that is.

'Spoiler alert,' he says quietly. 'Nothing bad will happen if you show me your numbers. I won't laugh. I won't judge you. But I *may* be able to help you a little. Whatever's stopping you, don't let it. There's nothing on the other side of that fear, I promise. Absolutely bugger all.'

So Adam Wright is a hot male version of Oprah with British swear words. Excellent.

'Okay,' I say with a sigh, and I open up the cash P&L we run and slide my laptop across the desk so he can see it, too. He scoots his chair closer until he's right next to me and peers in, long fingers flexing on his coffee cup.

'How often is this updated?'

'Weekly by my book keeper. She's freelance.'

He nods. 'Do you have a pen and a piece of paper?'

'Sure.' I open up my large notebook to a blank page and hand it and a biro to him. He draws rough slashed lines along and down it and gets to work, scribbling years along the top and key metrics down the side: revenue, gross margin, operating margin, net margin, before populating it.

I watch in something approaching awe. I'm far more qualitative than I am quantitative. I think in ideas, not numbers, and, while I've worked hard to build a strong grasp of the metrics pertaining to my business, it doesn't come naturally. Clearly it does for Mr Maths Machine next to me, however.

He rips out the page and starts a new one, firing questions at me in a way that's focused rather than abrupt but still makes my brain panic at being put on the spot. What's the average production cost for each collection? How many collections do we do a year? How many drops in each collection? Average spend per photo shoot? What are my main marketing and advertising platforms? How much of each season sells through at full price? How heavily do we discount?

And so it continues for a good half an hour, during which my colleagues stay thankfully out at lunch. Adam also maps out a cash flow timeline for a typical production schedule, from the outlays we have to make up front right through to when we can expect our first sales.

Finally, he throws down the pen and sits back in his seat. I stare at him like a patient waiting for her doctor to tell her if it's terminal.

'Well? How bad is it?'

He blows out a long breath before answering. 'You've got to tighten this up.' He draws a big circle around the production schedule. 'You're getting shafted by your suppliers *and* your stockists. It's not cool. I can help you with that, if you'd like.'

'Yeah,' I admit. 'It's been even worse since we started stocking a few of the big retailers. Their terms are brutal.'

'They really are. But everyone in this chain is benefiting except you. You'll have more sway with your suppliers. You need to push them to accommodate you better. Call every single one of them and talk up a big game about how well everything is going, how you're getting picked up by the big retailers but that changes your working capital requirements and you're looking for suppliers who can partner with you on this exciting transition.'

My face must show my scepticism, my distaste. I know he's right, but I can't help it. Unless the other party is Adam Wright, confrontation is my biggest horror. I'm awful at uncomfortable conversations and I'm equally useless at both hustling and haggling. I can't negotiate for shit, and I've always taken pride in appearing to be a counterparty for all my suppliers and stockists that's reliable and professional, who's got everything under control.

But while going cap in hand to these partners might terrify me, I also know he's right. Without the credit lines and deep pockets its larger competitors have, Gossamer simply can't survive this cash flow model in which we're bogged down. It's financial quicksand.

'I don't know,' I say lamely, despising myself for my lack of backbone.

He takes out his phone. 'Pull up the invoice.'

'What are you doing?' I demand.

'Renegotiating your terms. Let's start with these guys who are breathing down your neck.'

I make a face I hope communicates my lack of comfort and pull the invoice up on my screen. It's for just under nine grand which, in my world, is an enormous chunk of cash.

'Okay,' he says. 'Who's your contact there?'

'Gui Mercier.'

'Is he in Accounts?'

'No, he's my sales rep there.'

'Let's call Gui then.' He pauses. 'How long have you been buying from them?'

I consider. 'Three years at least.'

'Ever been late with a payment—ever had the goods sitting on their warehouse floor because you can't afford to take delivery?'

'Never.' I shake my head.

'Excellent. Watch this.'

30

NATALIE

He crosses one ankle over its opposite knee and sits back in his chair, grinning at me like he'll enjoy this. I watch him with a mix of interest and preemptive second-hand embarrassment, because I'm already dreading what he's going to say and already turned on by him metaphorically getting his dick out.

The spiel starts as soon as he's connected with Gui.

'*Bonjour*, Gui. This is Adam calling from Gossamer in London—I'm Natalie's new Finance Director. How's the weather in Lyon today?'

I raise my eyebrows at that gigantic detour from the truth, but he presses on.

'Yeah, pretty miserable here, too. And thank you— I'm excited.'

A pause, during which he presses his mouth into a grim line.

'She's wonderful, I agree. So talented. And it's a fantastic brand. Lots to get my teeth into. I'm calling around our most valued suppliers to introduce myself, but also to share an update from our end. Do you have five minutes?'

There's a brief silence before he nods and continues.

'So I don't know if you're aware, but we've had some big wins on the wholesale front recently—Net à Porter's picked us up which we're thrilled about.'

I frown. I certainly didn't tell him that, which means he's been checking us out.

'Yeah, it's a big win, and they're very committed to building out Gossamer's offering. We may even be doing some exclusive stuff for them.'

This guy is a major, major bullshitter.

'But obviously,' he continues, shifting in his chair, 'it means we have to completely reevaluate our entire supply model as well as our cash flow. I understand from Natalie that we're still operating under the same terms with you guys that we put in place when we started, but we'd like to think our relationship with Tissus de Pascal has really solidified since then.

'We're very committed to moving forward with you as a trusted partner, but as our model evolves, we're looking for partners who can evolve with us.' A pause. 'Thank you for saying that—it means a lot. Anyway, we're looking for terms more akin to net ninety, going forward. That should give us the leeway we need to accommodate our wholesale clients at the other end.'

My jaw drops as Adam waits, his tense expression at odds with the jovial tone he's adopted for the call. I can hear Gui's voice faintly, but I can't make out what he's saying. There's no way on earth Tissus de Pascal will grant us ninety days' credit. Absolutely zero.

He holds eye contact with me and licks his lips as Gui speaks. Then his entire face breaks into a smile, and it's a beautiful moment. I gape like a groupie.

'I understand. No, completely. That makes total sense.

I'll have to check with Natalie, but I'm confident we can make net sixty work.'

He's bought us *two months* of credit with them? Holy crap! That's beyond incredible. I beam at him, and he holds his finger up.

'Thanks, mate,' he continues. 'I appreciate your support —it feels good to be on the same page. I'm assuming we can put that in motion for the shipment I understand is forth-coming this week, yes?'

I hold my breath until he nods, his grin not wavering. 'Okay, great. So if you can send Natalie an amended invoice that'll be great, and we'll get the courier booked in once you've confirmed the shipment weight. Yep. So happy to have connected with you, Gui. You have a great day. Thanks —*au revoir.*'

'Oh my God,' I say in a rush as soon as he's ended the call and thrown his phone onto my desk. 'Thank you, thank you. Sixty days?! That's insane!'

My brain is racing. The big fat axe that's been hanging over me all week hasn't gone, but it's sure as hell lifted from the back of my neck.

'Now you need to do that with every single supplier,' he says, waggling a finger at me.

'I will,' I tell him. 'I can't believe they rolled over so easily.'

'I had the distinct impression he's a fan of yours,' he says sternly. 'But it's also a function of you and how you've carried your relationship up until now. He can't see your P&L. He's judging you on what he knows, and you've never given him reason to doubt you before, so why would he start now? The important thing will be coming good with the money when the credit period is up.'

'I will,' I say again. 'I didn't even know there was wiggle room with these guys.'

'Everyone in this industry will take what they can get, but they're often decent people, too. And there's never any harm in asking. There's only upside.' He hesitates and pulls himself up to standing, reluctantly, it seems. 'If you want to have a chat about longer term stuff and how to optimise your model for scaling, I'd be happy to.'

I stand too, and then we're facing each other, my face tilted up to his.

'You've done enough. This is way below your pay grade.'

'Bollocks,' he says. 'I like it. I find it interesting, and I've looked closely enough at your brand to know it's worth it. Always remember that the potential of your brand and its financial health are very different. Don't judge the former on the latter.'

I nod, feeling oddly emotional. He's been so kind. With a single phone call, he's alleviated the pressure I've felt and given me breathing space that I'm determined not to waste.

'I won't.'

He pockets his phone and puts his hands on my shoulders, letting them slide down my upper arms. Once again, this beautiful man I'm not supposed to like has made me feel seen and cared for and valued. I stare up at his face. I can't know the truth and not tell him.

'I don't hate you, you know. Not really.'

It's little more than a whisper, but his fingers flex on my arms before he slides one hand around the back of my neck, caressing it so lightly it sends a flurry of goosebumps over my skin.

'I'm very glad to hear that,' he says gruffly. We stand and gaze at each other as he strokes my neck, and I have the impression that he's searching for an answer in my face. He must find it, because he dips his face, his perfect mouth closing over mine.

His kiss is soft and hard all at once. It asks and it tells; it begs and it plunders, and all of it, his lips and tongue and breath and teeth and fingers, weaving magic and spinning my body and my soul until I'm a whirlwind of sensation and emotion and I don't know which way is up.

I know his arms are full of me, though, and his kiss is *intentional*, and I know it would be a crying shame if I didn't overdose on him while I have this random window in my dingy studio in the middle of the day.

So I do.

I drag my hands up his merino-clad arms and over his broad shoulders, and I entangle my fingers in his hair, and I slide my lips, my tongue, against his as I marvel at feeling him harden against my stomach in real time. I saw a lot more last night, of course, had a front-row seat to how angry, how hungry that monster dick could be, but this is different, somehow.

If last night felt like a battle where each of us wielded our need to undo the other like a weapon, then this is the most heated sort of truce, our dancing tongues the white flags, our roaming fingers the olive branches, our mutual surrender more evident with every ragged breath.

How long the kiss lasts I can't say. It's eternal and all too brief, the moment where Adam pulls carefully away from my mouth and settles his lips instead into my hair the most crushing dissolution. I collapse my face against his shirt, his sweater, my breath coming hard, my hands tracing the splendid planes of his back.

There are a thousand things I could say, thoughts I could voice, and they all seem as redundant as each other in the face of *that*.

'Are you working this evening?' he murmurs into my hair, his arms more a cocoon than a cage around me.

I mumble my assent.

'If I swing by when you're done,' he asks haltingly, 'would you come home with me tonight?' He releases me and takes a step back so he can pin me with that clear, pale blue gaze. 'I can't—I want to move forward with you, but I'm conscious that there's a lot to say first. There are some things I'd like to show you.'

31

ADAM

There are times for brushing things under the carpet, for locking the monsters in the closet and hoping they'll stay there. And there are times when the only way forward is through, when the most fearsome confrontations can yield the greatest blessings.

I'd like to think I proved that to Natalie today on some small scale with that phone call. I demonstrated that nothing lies on the other side of fear except the possibility of reward.

And it's time I took my own advice, because I'm conscious that these moments with her have been gifts. Glimpses into an astounding chemistry that could, I'm hopeful, be more, but not as we stand currently. I'm frankly blown away by the things she's let me do to her so far, but if I want to get any further with her, I need to take that hand I've held close to my chest and lay every last card on the table.

If I'm to have even the briefest future with her, then I need to shine the brightest, most unflinching of lights on my past. My only comfort is that she can't possibly think any worse of me than she already does.

When I turn up at Alchemy, ten minutes before the end of her shift, it's immediately obvious that two guys are chatting her up. They're typical finance bros and, although her smile is polite and professional, it looks to these hopeful eyes like it's strained. When she spots me, her face lights up to an extent that's beyond gratifying, giving me the confidence to do what I do next.

And that's to stride down the hallway, past the two guys, lean over the lectern and kiss her full on the mouth, my hand wrapping around her neck in a signal I hope reads *MINE - BACK OFF.*

'Hi,' I murmur when I release her.

'Hi,' she returns dazedly. She puts her fingertips to her mouth, but she can't hide her smile as Douche One and Douche Two clatter off down the corridor in search of a more available conquest.

I've asked Bal to put our food in the library. I had the impression Natalie enjoyed this room last time she was here, and her happy sigh when she pads in on stockinged feet confirms that. The night is cold, but in here it's wonderfully cosy, thanks to the drawn curtains and the fire that casts golden shadows over the bookshelves. I spend most of my time at home in my bedroom or study, but this is my favourite room in the house.

'Let me guess,' she says. She glances at the tray of food on the coffee table, but there's none of the irritation she exhibited last time. 'High protein and slow-release carbs?'

'You've got it.' I slide my hands around her waist and tug

her against me. 'There might be some cardio later, if I play my cards right,' I murmur against her ear. 'Best to refuel while you have the chance.'

Her laugh is music. 'Is that right?'

My fingers flex on the small of her back. I'm growing addicted to this spot. 'That, or you'll be running for the hills. Either way, you'll need your energy.'

She draws back, suddenly serious. We both know this conversation has to happen. I can't expect her to take any more leaps of faith than she already has without knowing the full picture, and I'm well aware I need this for myself. If we're to have anything more than a few libido-fuelled hookups, then I need her to know the real me, for better or for worse.

My attack on Stephen has been the elephant in the room since she first laid eyes on me at Alchemy, and, while I'd like to think some of my actions have allowed her to view me as the man I am today, I can't gloss over the episode that has defined my entire life's journey—as well as Natalie's perception of me until now.

I wait until I've tucked her up on the sofa under a soft throw and she's happily spooning the contents of a chia seed pudding bowl into her mouth before I extract the large leather-bound box from a cupboard under my business books. She eyes it, her eyebrows raised in question.

'This all feels very serious.'

'It is serious.' I sit down next to her and put the box on the coffee table. 'What I did to your brother is the worst thing I've ever done, no question, and I don't ever expect you or your family to forgive me. But I'd like to give you a little more context, if you're prepared to listen.'

'Why?' She doesn't say outright that nothing can ever

justify my actions, which I appreciate. Her face is curious, but I don't see judgement there.

'Partly for selfish reasons. Maybe it's *mainly* for selfish reasons. I told you I'd like to move forward, but I can't ever expect you to agree to that unless I'm an open book. But also —I'd like you to have all the facts before you make a decision.'

'Okay,' she whispers, spoon suspended above her pudding.

'You look pale. Keep eating.'

She rolls her eyes, but I suspect she's picking her battles, because she takes another spoonful of chia seeds. I twist my body so I'm facing her as much as possible on the sofa.

'I picked on your brother at school, I won't deny that. I picked on lots of kids.'

She flinches almost imperceptibly, and it takes all the discipline I've honed in the past two decades to give her the space she deserves to process and judge rather than reaching out to her.

I plough on. 'I was a total dick at school. I was… unhappy and bored, and most of the teachers had written me off, and things at home were… really rough.' I lay my hand on the lid of the box. 'But if it's okay, I'd like to show you what my mental state was at that time. If I'm completely honest, I barely remember the attack itself. What you need to know is that *this* happened five days before I beat your brother up.'

Here goes.

My mouth is dry as I lift the lid off what is essentially a shrine to a soul far too young, far too pure, to have been so short for this world. She used to cry on me and laugh with me. She used to hug me so tightly and smile so brightly, and while her memory is dazzling, her body is dust. Even after two decades, I will never, ever fail to feel that fact as the most searing pain, as a void so cavernous it astonishes me.

It's an effort to hold myself together when I'm brave enough to open this box, and I despise that the innocence of Ellen's memory is so inextricably linked to an event so horrific, so shameful. I tarnished it that day, and I allowed my demons to set in motion atrocities that impacted lives far beyond our own family's, and I'm so fucking ashamed I'll never live it down.

On top of the pile of keepsakes and photo albums is, as always, the order of service from Ellen's funeral. It's a low-quality black-and-white photocopy, printed on shitty paper and folded in half to make a booklet. But the photo on the front, a school photo, is one of my favourites. Mum had been sober enough to do her hair that day, and she was so pretty with her French plaits. They even had little bows on the end. You can't see it in the printout, but they were red, to match her sweatshirt.

But it's her smile that gets me. So bright. So trusting. You can see the trust radiating off the page. She always had faith that her big brother would be there for her, to look out for her and to monitor her levels and see her through when she was so little, so vulnerable.

And I fucking failed her.

32

NATALIE

I put down my pudding so I can take the thin piece of folded paper Adam hands me. As I glance over the front of it, it's as if my brain is wading through treacle, so slow am I to piece it together.

Order of Service.

In memory of Ellen Grace Wright, aged 10, who is now with the angels.

On the front, there's a grainy black-and-white formal school photo of a beautiful little girl with immaculate, fair-haired plaits, a huge smile, and what I swear is my old school uniform.

I look at the date.

Oh my God.

Oh my fucking Christ.

No no no no no.

I jerk my head up. Adam's looking at the paper, his face contorted with grief and disbelief and God knows what else.

'No.' I say, my tone pleading. This can't be true—please Lord, no. This is too much, too horrific.

'My little sister'—he clears his throat, devastation

evident in his voice—'died in her sleep five days before I lost my shit.' He pauses. 'She had a bad hypo, and she went into a coma, and...'

Oh my God. Oh my God. I clamp a hand over my mouth, because I can't bear it. My brain is a tornado of thoughts. Every time he's tried to feed me, tried to check my levels, I've been a total bitch. I thought he was an overbearing pain in the arse. I hypoed in front of him, for Pete's sake! Even through the haze of the aftermath, I recognised how upset he was when I came around.

He lost his little sister.

And when he attacked my brother, it was five days later.

I tug the blanket off and crawl over so I can straddle him, burying my head in his neck and wrapping my arms around him as tightly as I can, as if I can squeeze all that grief and horror and regret away. The tears come instantly.

'I'm so sorry,' I say against his skin. 'I'm so *fucking* sorry.' I'm apologising as much for my irresponsible blood glucose management and ingratitude as I am for the unthinkable loss he's endured.

'Thank you,' he whispers, putting his arms around me. We stay like that for a few moments, me weeping quietly against him, until I pull up and sit back on his thighs.

'Do you want to tell me what happened?'

He gives a little nod, almost as if he's telling himself he can do this. 'My, uh, mum was an alcoholic. Still is, probably. We're not in touch. My dad worked his arse off, usually on night shifts. Ellen developed type 1 when she was six or seven. She was eight years younger than me, and I was the oldest—I've got another sister, Quinn. But I took on the role of caretaker, because Mum wasn't capable. I went along to the doctors appointments with her and Mum, I spoke to her teachers about it, and when she wasn't at school, I looked after her most of the time. I set an alarm for two every morning so I could do a pinprick test on her. This was before CGMs and integrated pumps and all that stuff, obviously.'

'Jesus,' I mutter. I remember those days well. The difference was, I had two parents who treated my diabetes as their utmost priority and cared for me with endless love and indefatigable commitment.

Little Ellen Wright didn't have an adult capable of providing that for her, only a loving brother who was still a kid himself.

'Yeah, well, we had our ups and downs, but we got through it. But'—he closes his eyes for a moment—'I had a new girlfriend, and her parents were away one night so we made a plan that I'd go stay at hers. I remember I was so worried about leaving Ellen, but Mum had been dry all week and she swore she'd be fine. I fed Ellen and tested her before I went over to my girlfriend's.

'Mum was fine when I left. I'd set the alarm by her bedside table so she could do a middle of the night check, but she drank two bottles of wine and passed out and, I dunno. She swears the alarm didn't go off, but I'm ninety-nine percent certain she turned it off in her sleep.'

I stare at him in horror.

'And my sister never woke up,' he concludes with a kind of quiet finality that chills me to the bone, as if I was still expecting, somehow, that his story would take a happy turn.

I close my eyes at the horror of it. I don't want to know who found her, how Adam took this blow. There must be so much pain inside him—I have no idea how he lives with it. How he goes about his life with the ball and chain of such a loss weighing him down.

But he does, and he has, and the last thing he needs is

me flaking out because even the thought of what he's been through is too much to handle. So I open my eyes and I force myself to glance down at Ellen's happy little face again.

It's an emotional tsunami to absorb, but it strikes me that the guilt must be the worst part for Adam. The regret. The what-ifs. And the anger at his fucking mother, who couldn't be trusted to keep her daughter alive for a single night while her son blew off some steam, explored a new relationship.

It makes me sick to my stomach, all of it.

'I can't bear it,' I tell him now, cupping his face in my hands. 'It's horrific. The poor little thing. And poor you. None of it was your fault.'

'It was, though. I should never have gone to stay at Lisa's. I was the only person Ellen could rely on, and I wasn't there, and I just...' He trails off. 'One fucking decision, and she died because I wanted to get my dick wet.'

'You can't think of it like that,' I plead. 'I sincerely hope I'm not the first person to tell you that this is categorically not your fault.'

He shrugs. His face is stricken. In the short time I've known him, I've never seen him so defeated. 'It doesn't matter whose fault it is, because she died as a direct result of my not being there. So you can cut it any which way, but I wasn't there, and she died. Anyway, it gets worse.'

I steel myself for more horror, and he pushes on. 'Not worse than Ellen dying, obviously. Nothing could top that. But Dad found her when he got home from work. Mum was still unconscious. We'd agreed that I'd go straight to school from Lisa's and Dad would get Ellen ready for school.

'So he called nine-nine-nine, obviously, and the cops turned up with the ambulance. Apparently it was clear Mum was in a bad state so they breathalysed her, and after

Ellen was declared dead they arrested Mum for negligence and involuntary manslaughter.'

'Good,' I mutter through clenched teeth.

'You say that, but she was in holding and missed the funeral. They had social services crawling all over us—I was eighteen, so I was all right, but they were talking about taking Quinn into foster care. Dad was fucking destroyed—he blamed himself, too. But honestly, I was Quinn's best chance of a remotely normal childhood, until...'

He stops and tugs his lower lip between his teeth.

'Until you got yourself arrested,' I finish with a mirthless laugh of disbelief, because holy fuck. You can't make this shit up.

33

NATALIE

He lifts me gently off him, settling me next to him. I curl into the warm bracket of his arm as he rifles through the box with his free hand. If I'd been asked a fortnight ago, I would have said Adam Wright was one of the most diabolical, immoral men I could think of.

Now I'm growing dangerously suspicious that he's one of the most upstanding, loyal, dependable, despite how he treated my brother.

'I think I said it earlier, but it was all a bit of a blur,' he says, pulling out the original colour photo of Ellen and handing it to me. It's one of those typical professional school photos, complete with brown and gold cardboard frame. She was a skinny little thing, but otherwise healthy looking, with dark blonde plaits and a gorgeous grin. Her front teeth still look too big for her face, and her incisors are missing.

'She was such a beautiful little girl,' I murmur. 'What year was she in, when she...'

'Year Five,' he answers absently.

'I was in Year Three when you—when Stephen was

injured. So she must have been a couple of years ahead of me at St Benedict's. Anyway, sorry. You were saying?'

'Yeah.' He sighs heavily, shifting next to me, his arm still clamped around me. 'About your brother.'

It's the oddest thing. Suddenly, the horrific damage he inflicted on Stephen feels like the least relevant part of this story, which is ridiculous. But the tragedy surrounding the events that autumn feels far more enormous, far harder to stomach, than the injuries Stephen endured.

I put a hand on his thigh and keep it there, a quiet sign, I hope, that I'm here to understand but not to judge.

'It was a few days after the funeral,' he says. 'Mum was in prison. Dad was on compassionate leave from work, thank fuck, but he was a mess. Quinn was refusing to go to school, but I went straight back in. There was no way I could hang around that fucking house. I was ignoring Lisa, I was furious with everyone who'd failed Ellen—Mum, for being so fucking weak and the system, for not realising Ellen was in danger, and mainly myself.

'Your brother pissed me off, I'm not going to lie. He was a whiny little shit, always moping about and looking down on the rest of us, and he just—he rubbed me up the wrong way. I was so fucked up, and people like him made me see red. I mean, what the fuck did he have to complain about?'

Not much, apparently. Stephen and I had had our own issues over the year leading up to that attack. Our instant, unwelcome transition to relative poverty was, until then, the defining moment in our lives. I know now how unhappy, as an intense, introverted kid, he was at his new school, even before Adam beat the shit out of him.

Even so, Adam's right. Stephen had little to complain about compared to him.

'One day I saw your mum dropping him off at the gates,'

he says, his voice strained. 'Fuck, this is hard. I wasn't doing well. Dad was barely functioning, I was looking after Quinn, everything was up in the air and Mum was still on remand.'

Adam doesn't sound like a man who's made billions and proven himself the world over.

He sounds like a scared, angry, messed up little boy.

He picks up my bowl and spoons up some chia seed pudding with a shaky hand, twisting so he can hold it up to my mouth. 'Seriously, you need to get more food down you.'

I obey silently, sucking it off the spoon while I wait for him to continue. I can't imagine how hard it is for him to relive this at all, let alone with a member of Stephen's family.

'I remember—um—she gave him this big hug and handed him his lunchbox, and I was like, for *fuck's* sake. He's *eighteen*, and he's a weird, miserable fucker, and his mum is coddling him like he's a fucking five-year-old and Ellen had no one who could even keep her *alive*.'

He makes a strangled sound. I sit there, my hand on his thigh, my body frozen less with horror than with pity so great it feels as though my heart is bleeding. Almost like all those reported sightings by saints of the Virgin Mary with her bleeding heart seeping through her clothes. My heart may as well be beating, bleeding, outside my body for all the clawing, wretched pain pulsing through it.

Of course, Adam's missing a tonne of context. Mum was in pieces after Dad's firm went down. She was used to being a stay-at-home mother in a lovely house in a nice neighbourhood, and she was probably completely unmoored in those days when Adam observed her with Stephen. I was too young to remember it properly, but her clucking around us was most likely an attempt to do anything within her power to provide us with stability and herself with meaning in a world that was no longer recognisable to her.

Not that it matters. Whatever the reality, Adam saw the narrative he chose to see, which was a vignette of family life so far removed from his own lived experience that it must have felt unbearable.

'It's okay,' I say. And I mean it. He's okay in this timespace continuum where he's put these horrors behind him to achieve unimaginable success, and I'm okay with hearing his honesty. I can handle it. He can share his truth. He can recall his version of those bloody events.

I'll take it all.

'It's no excuse, though,' he grits out.

'I'm not here for excuses,' I say softly, rubbing his thigh. 'I'm here to get to know you, remember?' I nudge him with my shoulder. 'Because I think you're someone worth getting to know.'

He reaches across and covers the hand on his thigh with his own. 'If you want to go home after this, I'll understand. I'll get Nige to take you.'

'Adam, I've spent two decades hating your guts and rueing the day you were born. I thought you were a total fucking psychopath who didn't deserve a second chance, let alone the success you've had. The only way is up, my friend. Believe me.'

That gets me a little chuckle and a kiss to the top of my head, both of which I'll take.

'Thank you,' he whispers. 'Right. So... I saw them, and I basically saw red. I was with some of my then-mates, who were just hangers-on, really. Typical sheep. Anyway, we followed your brother across the playground and I just let rip while they held him down.

'I went absolutely. Fucking. Mental. It was like I was in

some kind of frenzy. I wanted to punch his face in until I shut him the fuck up—I don't know. I can't really remember. I just wanted everything to go away, all this rage and—helplessness, and he was the outlet.' He shrugs. 'Simple as that. Wrong place, wrong time. And I don't remember going for his eye, I genuinely don't. The only thing that stuck with me afterwards was that his lunchbox fell and it split open on the ground and two tangerines rolled out. I remember them rolling across the astroturf and thinking *good*.

'I've thought about those tangerines so many times. How lovingly your mum made that packed lunch for your brother, and how it all went to waste.'

The man who beat my brother to a pulp is sitting beside me, describing his actions in sickening detail, and I should be feeling many things right now. I am feeling many things, obviously, but I'm not sure my emotions are the exact ones they should be.

The tangerines, though. There's something about the thought of them that makes my bleeding heart haemorrhage harder. It bleeds for Mum's heartbreak, for Stephen's pain and loss, for Dad's guilt that his business failure had put Stephen in harm's way. It bleeds for the young, horrified girl who screamed at the sight of that mummified boy in the hospital bed.

And it bleeds for little Ellen Wright and her terrified sister, her devastated father, and her poor, broken brother. The brother who I take in my arms now.

'I'm so sorry,' he says, over and over, his voice cracked with emotion. 'I'm so *fucking sorry*.'

I hold him tighter. 'I know you are. I know.'

And I do.

34

ADAM

S he's not leaving.

Reliving this particular chain of events from twenty years ago is always draining, whether it's with my therapist, a journalist, or a group of men in one of the many rehabilitation sessions I do with current and former inmates.

But none of them are quite as draining as treading that exhausting path, pushing through the chokehold of weeds such as waste and grief and deep, deep regret, in front of my victim's sister, a woman I'm increasingly mesmerised by and, as luck would have it, a woman who suffers from exactly the same condition as Ellen.

I have to believe the universe is giving me another chance, a chance to care for someone consistently enough that they thrive. I have to believe history isn't so cruel as to repeat itself.

Natalie isn't Ellen.

'Here's the thing, though,' I begin haltingly. 'I'll never forgive myself for going to Lisa's that night, but I've done enough work on myself to know that's the most thankless kind of *what if.* What I did to your brother, though... That was all me.

'You can rail and rail against circumstance and luck and accidents of birth and shitty parents. But at some point, you have to take responsibility. It was my fists that did all that damage, and I had to deal with the most epic fucking shit-show because of it.'

The awful truth is that I didn't fully comprehend the graveness of my crimes against Stephen Bennett until I began pre-trial prep with my feisty state-appointed lawyer, because I was far more consumed by the enormous act of self-sabotage I'd committed. That I'd robbed Quinn and Dad of my support, my presence, in the most spectacular fashion and at a time when my family had never needed me more consumed every fucking hour I spent incarcerated.

'You mean your sister?' Natalie asks now.

'Yeah.'

'Did your dad get to keep her?' she asks in a voice so soft it's like she's terrified of what my answer will be.

'Yeah. By the skin of his teeth. But it wasn't pretty. Imagine—me, mum and Ellen all gone. Just like that. The poor girl had a shocker, totally fucked up her GCSEs.'

She winces. 'Oh God. It's all so awful. Is she—is she okay now?'

'She's doing pretty well. She's a sculptor—she's really talented.'

I put Quinn's life on hold when I went to Lisa's that night, and I really stomped all over any chance of normality for her when I beat the shit out of Natalie's brother. That year I was in prison she spent in survival mode, and I've spent the past twenty years making amends.

Nat's silent for a second, leaning into me, her hand on

my thigh, her touch showing me that, incredibly, she's here for me.

'And what about you?' she asks.

I frown. 'What about me?'

'Well, how did you cope in prison?' She hesitates. 'Did you fall apart? Because God knows, it would have been the obvious thing to do. You were grieving and in massive shock.'

I consider the question. I can see why that would be her assumption, but the reality was pretty different.

'In the beginning, maybe. But I'd already fallen apart, to be honest. I'd say putting your brother in hospital was my lowest low. I was still so fucking angry when they arrested me, but I was probably still in shock, too.'

She bites her lower lip and nods.

I clear my throat. 'I had this lawyer, Anne. She was probably only forty, but she felt ancient, and she was fucking terrifying. Told me our only hope was to make the judge sympathetic to our case, given the circumstances.'

'Surely they were black and white? You'd just suffered a horrific loss, *and* you were basically Quinn's best option as a guardian. Shouldn't they have taken that all into account?'

I smile at the moral outrage on her beautiful face and slide my hand around her neck. 'Hey. You're not supposed to be on my side, remember?'

She purses her lips disapprovingly but doesn't argue.

'I think that worked both ways. The judge didn't see me as fit to care for her, given the stunt I pulled. He ordered that I get some therapy in prison, but that was about it.'

'Was it juvie?'

'Nope. I was eighteen, so I got the full works.'

'Shit,' she says faintly. 'Was it... horrific?'

It was horrific and relentless and inhuman and devastating, but I was so broken by that point, so wracked with guilt, that I barely cared.

'It wasn't fun,' is all I say. It was my cross to bear, and I ruined Natalie's family as well as my own, so I have no intention whatsoever of allowing her to feel any more sympathy than necessary.

'So how did you get from'—she waves the hand on my thigh around—'there to here? I mean, who the hell pulls that off outside of a rags-to-riches novel?'

That makes me laugh, because a journalist once used that very analogy in an article about my so-called meteoric rise.

'Anne, my scary-as-fuck lawyer, gave me a real talking-to when I got sent down.' She was utterly furious, and I know she was furious on my behalf, rather than *with* me, but she sure as hell channelled that fury into a hell of a bollocking.

'She told me that I'd already proven to myself and everyone else how royally I could fuck up an already terrible situation with my actions, so I'd better make sure every action from now counted.'

I remember she said I could choose to be a victim or I could choose to be proactive. She told me my sentence could be a spectacular waste of a year of my life or a period of readjustment. Reprioritisation. A time I could use to lay the foundations for not only the kind of life I wanted for myself, but the kind of man I wanted to be.

The kind of man I wanted to be.

Her anger, her vehemence, was probably the biggest compliment I'd received at that point in my life. Her insistence that I counted, that my future and my potential counted, was the seedling I needed—tiny, but with potential buried somewhere deep inside its DNA.

In the same way that a humble acorn carries within

itself a universe of promise, the ghosts of future metre-wide trunks and scalloped leaves, of shelter and abundance equally, so did this exhausted, terrified, angry kid carry in himself that kernel.

Anne, God bless her, was the first person to plant that seedling, to suggest that betting on myself was the smart thing to do.

She was also the first person to thrust a metaphorical mirror in front of me and demand that I acknowledge my own agency. My actions had consequences—I'd proven that beyond a shadow of a doubt—and if I wanted to change those consequences, it was down to me to act accordingly.

Less philosophically, but more urgently, I knew the day I got out was the day I'd start making it up to Quinn and Dad. And I didn't want to waste a minute.

'Well, you clearly made your actions count,' Natalie says now. 'And it's all very well to have people say these things to you, or even to believe them, but you made things happen. That's a big deal.'

I shrug at that, because there were people who found me, who helped me, who dragged me out of that pit of despair, even people who should have walked away.

'You know I met Anton when I was in prison,' I say, stopping to laugh at her horrified expression. '*He* wasn't in prison—I was. At the time, he ran this kind of entrepreneurship programme at the place I was in and at a women's one. I signed up because I was bored out of my brain and I'd already wrecked my chances of sitting my A Levels.' I shrug. 'It was something to do, and I fucking loved it.'

Understatement. That programme put a fire in my belly like nothing else had, even before I'd got myself banged up.

'You're kidding me! You've known him all this time? My God, he must be so proud of how far you've come.'

'He was until his wife got mad that her husband's protegé had beaten up your brother,' I tell her with a smile, and she grimaces.

'Yeah. I can't imagine incurring Gen's wrath is fun for anyone, even the mighty Anton Wolff.'

I shudder as I think of how pissed off she was that evening, how utterly outraged on Natalie's behalf. 'Tell me about it. You've got a badass woman in your corner there.'

'She won't believe it when I tell her I spent another night at yours—willingly, this time. But go on, tell me about this programme.'

I grin at the memory. 'It was a theoretical case study about this failing packaged consumer goods company—it was a Harvard Business School one, if you can believe it. I think that was probably part of his plan: giving us an HBS case study was his way of saying he believed in us.

'Anyway, I was the youngest person there, and definitely the keenest. I got some flack about it from the others. But I was fucking obsessed. He gave us each a folder and it had all sorts—P&Ls, balance sheets, qualitative stuff, sector themes, everything.

'We had to come up with a plan for their board to vote on. Their financials were really shaky. Everything was on the table—raising equity, taking on more debt, divestments... whatever we thought would stem the outflows. He came back once a month, and I had more questions every time he showed up.

'I spent hours and hours analysing the financial statements, trying to work out what the fuck all the acronyms meant, trying to understand how they flowed, reverse-engineering them. In the end, he brought me more accounting textbooks, and I spent an embarrassing amount of time with them, too.' I glance up and halt at the expression on her face. She's staring at me with so much emotion, and, from where I'm sitting, none of it looks like hatred. 'What?'

'I'm imagining eighteen-year-old Adam in a prison cell with just a pile of textbooks for company, and I'm trying really hard not to lose it,' she whispers, her hand sliding up my neck so she can scratch at my beard with her fingernails.

'Hey.' I lean my forehead to hers. 'I deserved everything I got. Your brother lost an eye because of me, remember? And besides, it was the best thing they could have done for me. I came out of that place with a handful of people who believed in me and a sound understanding of the basics of business and finance. If I'd stayed at school, there's no way I would have pulled it together enough to get my A Levels, and God knows what I would have done.'

She's still scratching softly at my beard, and it feels so good. 'How did you get a job, if you didn't have any A Levels?'

I smile against her mouth. 'Anton took a chance on me,' I say, and then I kiss her.

There's a time for talking.

There's so much more to say.

But it can all wait.

35

NATALIE

A dam's mouth is firm against mine. It's the second time he's kissed me properly, his little charade of possession at Alchemy aside, and it's as intentional as that one in my office was earlier. No other man has ever kissed me like he means it quite so much. He twists his body towards me and slides his hands up my neck and cups my jaw and angles my face, as if the details matter. As if he wants the fundamentals of this kiss to be flawless.

If this is how he kisses, with hungry slides of his lips against mine and desperate drives of his tongue, his fingers clawing feverishly at me, then I can't imagine how intense it will be to have him moving over me, pinning me down against his bed.

He was right last night—of course I loved the push-pull of what he deemed hate-sex (or hate-oral, at least). It was hot beyond belief, and every smug smirk and self-confident jibe from him had me spiralling higher. But this is arousing in a completely different way. It's raw and honest. We've stripped ourselves bare tonight, and when he takes me off to that bed of his I'll go willingly.

More than willingly.

Somehow, I suspect that will be more consuming for both of us than my endless denials and barbs last night.

It's so much, like this. He overwhelms me with his size and his strength and the heat of his desire, his hands now roaming over me, one cupping a shoulder bared in this asymmetrical dress I'm wearing as the other tugs at my hair. He smells delicious, and the noises he's making at the back of his throat are so low and *male*, and oh my God.

Maybe it's a good thing he didn't kiss me last night, when I was still telling myself I hated him. I couldn't have withstood this onslaught—I wouldn't have survived it.

My heart is invested now, too, after listening to the horror of his story. It's still beating, bleeding, outside my body for this beautiful man who has so many reasons to think me a hostile audience and still chose to trust me enough to share the most harrowing details with me. I kiss him harder, as if hoping that the intensity of my need for him can act as some kind of eraser for the memories that still haunt him, some kind of harbinger of oblivion.

He *felt* dangerous when I saw him only as a thug, a blunt instrument shrouded in Italian wool and hand-rolled lapels, his presence in this beautiful house as incongruous, as undeserving, as a beast seeking refuge inside a Fabergé egg.

But now that he's lifted the mask and shown me his true self, now that he's wearing his wounds and welts as openly as if his skin was coloured with them, he *is* dangerous.

Because I'd like to think that no matter what I let him do to me last night—*asked* him to do to me, in that dim little room where he peeled me like a piece of fruit—I would have held firm inside while my body prostituted itself and betrayed twenty years of firmly held hatred in favour of his delicious mouth and capable fingers, in favour of the carnal pleasure of having the white ropes of his arousal paint me like I was his whore.

Tonight, when he peels me open in the astonishing, heartbreaking light of his revelations, he'll find this particular piece of fruit ripe for the picking, a sweet, unctuous mess for him.

I want his pain. I want his bruises. I want to wear his heartbreak like a brand; I want to exsanguinate that bleeding heart of his and take it all in some sick, grandiose transfusion of his anguish to me.

He slides a hand over my breast and palms me hard, his life line and heart line dragging over the tightly furled bud of my nipple through the fabric of my dress, my bra.

'Have you had enough to eat?' he whispers hoarsely against my lips.

I'm a goose in a *foie gras* factory right now, but I don't say that, because the poignancy of Adam having spoon-fed me as he recounted, relived, his little sister's death is not lost on me.

'I'm good,' I tell him, my fingers working in his thick curls. 'I want you to fuck me.' It feels so good not to hold back, not to try to shield myself with the semblance of dislike or the pretence of indifference. It feels so right to rub my face against his beard as I kiss him, the memory of its abrasion of my pussy a real, vital thing between us, to inhale him so hard it's like I'm snorting, to lean into him, to take and take.

If this is how I am with his kisses, there's no doubt he'll have me begging once I'm in his bed.

'You sure?' he asks, the check-in sounding so reluctant I almost laugh. It's reassuring to know he's as opposed to applying the brakes as I am.

'God, yes.'

Arousal has my skin sensitised, a heavy need blooming low in my belly at the thought of Adam consuming me.

Obliterating me.

36

ADAM

There's a war being waged under my skin as I kiss her. My memories are always there, but I can usually keep them on a low simmer. Tonight, my conversation with Natalie has my emotions threatening to boil over, the thin lid of my sanity clattering from the force of the convection currents raging below.

So much conflict.

So much need.

I suspect this woman can slake it all... *if* she allows me to dominate her in the exacting, perfect way I require right now.

Whether she climbs over me to straddle my hips or I drag her here, I'm unclear. But her thighs are clamped down around mine, her stretchy black dress riding up enough that its slit reveals the lace trim of her stocking to my greedy fingers as my hand roams up her leg and around to grab her arse.

My other hand is in her glossy hair, clawing at great big fistfuls of it as I hold her head in place. The heady floral notes of her scent bewitch me, the breathy little moans deep in her throat the most entrancing encouragement to sustain the deep, probing strokes of my tongue inside her mouth.

I use the hand on her arse to tug her closer to where my dick is threatening to punch through my trousers, and she obeys like the little beauty she is, grinding down on me, rubbing that warm little pussy against my impossibly angry hardness, and all the while kissing me back, her lips, her tongue, just as demanding as mine.

Her hands are shaking with need, and they're everywhere: in my hair, on my face, scratching at my beard and pulling at my curls and fumbling with the buttons on my shirt. I adore this openly greedy side of her, but the chances of us getting all our clothes off before I'm inside her are nil.

The clothes can wait.

I can't and, from the looks of things, neither can she.

I cup her breast hard with one hand while attempting with the other to ruck up the long, stretchy skirt of her dress so it's around her waist. There are still too many layers of fabric between us, but I'm getting there. Once it's out of the way, I allow myself a moment to enjoy the smooth perfection of her bare arse cheek, the velvet softness of that expanse of skin between the top of her stocking and her thong.

'Rub yourself against me,' I order her through our kisses. 'Mmm. Tell me how it feels.'

She grinds down harder against me, and I thrust up to meet her. 'It's not enough,' she says, the pout clear in her voice.

'No. It's not. You want my dick, don't you?' I hiss the words through my teeth as I slide my hand over her thigh to the useless, soaking scrap of fabric covering her cunt and rub my fingers against it. I'm not sure what feels better: the wet heat of her on my fingertips or the extra friction my hand is giving my poor cock.

She rolls her forehead against mine and pants out her reply. 'Yes, so badly. I need it.'

'Such a sweet little thing.' I tug down my zip in brusque, excruciating increments. 'And such a glutton for my cock. Exactly the way I want you.'

I thought I'd feel victorious at having her writhing and grinding and rubbing that sweet little pussy against me, at having her so desperate for my dick, but, given what's transpired between us this evening, I don't. If anything, I feel... grateful. Humbled. She's letting me in, figuratively and, it seems, literally. If anything, it's less a coup and more a miracle.

She too wedges a hand between us, slipping it inside my open flies and palming me through the jersey of my boxer briefs. I groan into her mouth before pulling back slightly.

'Imagine how tight it'll feel inside you,' I tell her, pulling back enough to admire the glazed prettiness of her eyes.

'I haven't been able to think about much else today,' she whispers, and I reward her honesty with a hard kiss.

'That's my good girl. Why don't you put this on me so I can fill you up just as much as you need.' With difficulty, I lean to one side so I can extricate my wallet from my trouser pocket and pull out a condom. My plan is twofold—let her sink down right here, impaling herself on me at her own pace so she can adjust to my size. Then I'll stand us up and fuck her against one of those bookshelves, because Lord knows, I'll have little leverage in this position.

She shuffles backwards sufficiently to release my cock from the waistband of my boxer briefs. I don't miss the sensual way her teeth sink down into that delectable bottom lip as she takes my bare, achingly hard shaft in her hand with something approaching reverence.

'Oh God,' she murmurs, letting her eyes flutter closed for a moment. 'You're so perfect, Adam.'

Our eyes meet. Hold. 'So are you. Wrap me up, sweetheart.'

She glances behind her at the closed door.

'No one's coming in. I promise you.'

I'll take her to bed shortly, but I need to take her here, first, in this room she's entranced with, where we've shared such searingly raw confidences. I'll fuck her hard against the books she adores and ruin her, just like she's ruining me.

We're both still as she tears the condom wrapper, pinching the tip of the latex and positioning it on my crown before rolling it down me. She's slower and less deft than I would be, and I marvel at the focus on her beautiful face as she performs her ritual, rendering something that's usually perfunctory anticipatory and delicious. But as soon as it's on, I'm tugging her back towards me so she's forced to widen her knees.

'Come on, sweetheart,' I urge her. 'It's time to feel me.' I slide my fingers between us and hook the flimsy thong out of the way, allowing myself a moment to appreciate how impossibly silken and wet and welcoming she feels for me. My dick is so engorged it may snap off if it can't sink inside her body right away.

She whimpers as I circle her clit. She's every bit as swollen as I am. I replace my fingers with my dick, dragging its sheathed tip through her wetness before notching it at the place right at the centre of her, the place whose tight heat will, I know, suck me in, choke me, wring everything from me.

I won't be the one 'taking' her, I realise now. Not in the

slightest. She'll take me, and she'll milk me dry as surely as a vengeful goddess might demand that a sacrificial lamb be bled out for her, and this sinner—this willing, willing victim —will welcome every blessed moment of it.

37

NATALIE

He has my thong pushed aside and the impossibly wide, blunt head of his dick wedged against my entrance and an anguished expression on his beautiful face that tells me he might actually die if I don't sink down onto him and grant us both what we so badly need.

The room is quiet, the only sounds the reassuring crackle of the fire in its grate behind me, the rasp of breaths already laboured with anticipation, and the wet noises of my body preparing to take Adam in. This is no sex club. This is raw and intimate—a mirror shone on every denial, every insult, I've hurled at him, the light of honesty it's reflecting so blinding I can't escape it.

There's nowhere to hide.

I wouldn't want to, anyway.

My body is humming. Alive. My blood is warm treacle in my veins. I wrap my fingers around his hand and start to lower myself down. God, it's like nothing else: the shockingly thick head of him, that low sound of approval, the way he glances up at me through his long, dark eyelashes like he, too, can't believe this is actually happening.

If I let myself get intimidated by the size of this thing, I'll clam up. There's fear at the edges, but mostly I just feel a blind, raging need to fill myself with him, so I keep moving, my free hand bearing down on his shoulder for balance and leverage and probably reassurance as I bear down.

He fills me, inch by glorious inch. We're both shaking.

'Nearly there, little one,' he croons through gritted teeth. 'It's taking every ounce of effort I have not to thrust up into you.'

'I want that,' I tell him, and he gives me a pained chuckle.

'You have about thirty seconds to get used to it before I take over.'

I shimmy further down with a sharp inhale. I'm wet, but he's fucking enormous. Still, the burn has nothing on the pure, carnal pleasure that's flooding my lower half at the stretch of him. At the intensity of it all. My body continues to take, and take, and I roll my hips, and he's there, touching a part of me that's *so* deep inside. The feeling is like no other.

We stare at each other in wonder. Adam slides a hand under my hair and around my neck, tugging my mouth to his.

'Feel how fucking good that is?' he murmurs.

I smile against his lips. 'Mmm-hmm.' And, as he kisses me with rough, hungry strokes of his tongue, I drag myself up the length of his dick before pushing back down. It's such a tight fit that my skin pricks with sweat.

'Mmm. Do that again. Let me see you ride me.'

I lean back slightly in his lap. Next thing I know, he's tugging my dress up from my hips, up, up, until it's at my shoulders. I raise my arms and let him pull it off completely and throw it on the floor.

Oh my God.

When I glance down, past the black strapless bra and my bare stomach, the sight where our bodies meet is obscene: my black thong yanked aside and his huge dick disappearing inside me. My mouth makes an O, because it's so indecent like this—and so, so hot.

He's staring, too. 'Fucking look at that. *Jesus.*'

I drop my forehead to his, clamping both hands to his shoulders and starting to move again, far more slowly than we both need, but the sight of his length disappearing and reappearing has us both transfixed. He lets me do it a couple more times before he's wrapping a vice-like arm around my back and edging forward on the sofa.

'Hold on tight,' he grits out. I koala myself around him as he stands, his arms around me and his dick still inside me. God, his leg muscles must be made of steel.

As soon as we're upright, the dynamic changes. He's been humouring me, letting me play with my new favourite toy. He's let me take my time, and shimmy prettily up and down it, and get to know it a little, but when I look up at him, at his pupils swallowing up those rings of pale blue and the almost unhinged desire etched on his face, it tells me the tables are about to turn.

He walks me backwards until my back hits a bookshelf and then, holding me tightly with one arm, reaches behind me and unsnaps my bra. There are no straps to untangle, so it comes off with a single snap and I'm practically naked in his arms.

'Better,' he grunts. He's breathing heavily, looking between us at where my now-bare breasts are smushed against the crisply starched cotton of his shirt, my nipples sharp, needy little points that chafe deliciously against the fabric. They're not the only needy things—his dick is still pulsing inside me, ready to show me what it's capable of now he has me where he wants me.

As he wrestles his eyes away from my boobs and up to my face with a slow, seductive smile, it occurs to me that being naked in Adam's arms and shoved up against one of his beautiful bookshelves may be what perfect happiness feels like.

Or it would if the ache deep inside, where that blunt crown presses so promisingly at the most intimate core of me, wasn't quite so insistent.

'Give me this,' he says gruffly, his soft beard abrading my chin as he bends to capture my mouth, 'and I'll take you upstairs and worship you for the rest of the night.'

'Please,' I beg, because I want all of it. I want hours and decadent hours of Adam spreading me out on his bed and feasting on me, just as I want the carnal kick of him taking me hard and fast up against his beloved books.

I want every single treat this man sees fit to bestow upon me.

'Mmm. That's my girl.' That hoarse, throaty *mmm* may be the best sound I've ever heard. 'Hold on.'

I wrap my legs and arms more tightly around him, fingernails clawing at his shirt. 'I need you naked,' I say sulkily. 'It's not fair.'

He grins, and it's positively wolfish. 'Life's not fair, little one. All in good time.'

'Is it because you have a hairy back? Don't be embarrassed. I'm willing to overlook—*ohmyohmygod.*'

He pulls out of me and thrusts up, hard, stealing the air from my lungs.

'That's one way to shut you up,' he says, his voice ragged, and then he moves again.

Oh fuck, this is so much better than my dainty little moves on his cock. He's using it on me like a weapon, size and strength combining into mighty shunts that create a halo of sensation reverberating out from where he's hitting me.

'Again.'

'That I can do.' He captures my mouth in a kiss as he drags that dick of his out and jams it back inside me, even harder than before. I keep him in a headlock with one arm so I can claw at his hair and tug his face as close to mine as humanly possible. I want nothing to exist but him and his mouth and his dick and these shoulders. I'm falling down an Adam-shaped rabbit hole and I never, ever want to come up for air.

'Need this hard and fast,' he grunts against my mouth. 'Okay?'

'Okay. Do it hard.'

'Can you come like this?'

'I'm seconds away,' I manage.

His response to my confession is a strangled groan and a renewed assault on my pussy the like of which I've never known. This is Adam, unleashed and animalistic, fucking me like he's been born to do this and nothing else.

I've wondered about this. I've thought about it endlessly today. I know he was holding back last night, and I know why. I bet he didn't hold back with that woman he fucked and spanked the other night.

This is how he likes it.

This is what he needs.

And it's *me* who's giving it to him.

Somehow, everything I feared about him, everything I

despised, has morphed, shifted, until it's unrecognisable. The strength, the intensity, that primitive side he hides so well these days under those expensive disguises—it's all here, at the fore, and to be the object of it all is as wondrous, as heady, as being in the eye of a beautiful storm destined to wreak havoc wherever it strikes.

It's this knowledge, as much as the fast rolls of his hips and the relentless drives of his dick and the stunning fury of his kisses, that has my body growing molten around him, that has the flesh of my inner walls swelling and sparking with sensation. I cling to the now-damp cotton across his shoulders. My moans turn to whimpers as I bury my head in his neck and suck on the skin there.

It's so much. I'm only human. It's impossible to withstand this onslaught—unthinkable, even. My clit is rubbing against the fabric of his flies, adding an unnecessary but incredible layer of stimulus. And I'm spiralling, falling and soaring, so hard, so fast, like a junkie spinning into euphoria without the slightest care for how she'll survive it.

'Jesus, I can feel you getting close,' Adam grits out against my ear. 'So *fucking* good. You're such—a—tight—little—thing.'

He fucks me as he forces out the words, and the thought of being his tight little thing has any remaining defences crumbling as my body surrenders to his offensive in spectacular, cataclysmic style.

38

NATALIE

His room looks like a hotel room, right down to the fancy turn-down service it's received. I gaze at it dreamily from where I'm draped across his arms like some swooning heroine from yesteryear—which is not unlike how I feel. He may have put his dick away for the time being, but given I'm naked aside from my holdups and a worse-for-wear thong, I'm glad we didn't encounter any members of his household staff during our dramatic journey upstairs.

My first impression of the room, perceived through my post-orgasmic haze, is less of the details and more of an overall impression that lighting, textures, and deep, moody colours have been expertly woven to balance sensuality with serenity.

In more basic terms, it's the perfect space for Adam to fuck me into that very soft-looking mattress and then for me to recover in his arms.

He lays me on the bed. The sconces bracketing the fireplace are on, and the bedside lamps cast a rosy glow through their delicate pleated silk crinolines. The only other lighting comes from the picture lights illuminating several striking paintings that I bet cost a fortune.

But he's looking down at me as though I'm by far the most priceless thing in this room. Under the heat of his gaze, I stretch like a cat.

He leans forward, planting his hands on the bed and looking me over. 'Time to lose the thong.'

I scoff. I don't think so. 'Get those clothes off, mister, and then we'll talk. Unless you really do have a hairy ba—*eeek!*' My words turn to a squeal as he makes a grab for my ankles and tugs me down the bed, towards him.

'You'd better help me, then,' he says, and I scramble to my knees at a speed that makes him chuckle. But I don't care, because I'm finally, *finally* getting to unwrap my delicious present, and I couldn't give a shit if his back was an actual pelt. (Well, maybe I would. But I'm pretty sure it's not.)

He licks his lips and brushes his palms oh-so lightly down my upper arms as I undo his buttons. His shirt is so perfectly tailored to his body that I have a fair idea of what awaits, but I can't wait to get my greedy little eyeballs and lips and hands on all that skin and hair and muscle.

Dear Lord. The sight of dark hairs appearing as I get his shirt open has my mouth watering. I tug his shirt tails impatiently out of his waistband and finish the job before reaching up. My palms go to his chest, to that warm skin and soft hair and hammering heart of his before I smooth the shirt off his shoulders with nothing short of reverence.

'You're so beautiful,' I whisper, because he really is. His beauty is astonishing. Outrageous. That light tan, and those rounded shoulder caps, and the perfect dusting of dark hair that fans outwards from his breast bone to his nipples and then tapers south, cutting the most alluring line of symmetry between the defined slabs of his abdomen.

What hits me hardest, though, is the tattoo on his bicep. That rough, jagged *E* I spied when I found him asleep on my bed what feels like a million years ago spells *ELLEN*, and the sight of it makes me want to weep. I run my fingertips over it. Our eyes meet, and I hope mine tell him just how desperately sorry I am for his pain.

His shirt is still hanging from his wrists, and he holds his arms behind his back as he attempts to disentangle himself, Houdini-like, from his sumptuous cotton shackles, because his liberator is helplessly, hopelessly distracted.

A glance upwards reveals an expression on his gorgeous face that's anguish and desire and disbelief all in one. I run my hands over his pecs, gliding them down his stomach, my fingertip tracing the darker hollow of his navel. I want to use this man's torso as a pillow—a firm, hairy and decidedly soft-skinned pillow.

I follow my fingertip with a kiss to his navel. Mmm. So soft. But I'm going in. My hands halt on his belt buckle. I've already put a condom on him, and I've just had him inside me, for crying out loud, so it's ridiculous, but I'm a little apprehensive. This time, I get to see it up close.

It's hard again, which shouldn't be a surprise. I'm sure Mr Adam Wright doesn't indulge biological trifles such as refractory periods. I yank his belt buckle open and unhook the closure on the top of his trousers before lowering his zip and pushing them down. He's freed his hands from his shirt, and he slides them both around my neck now, cradling my head as I run predatory palms over the fantastic bulk protruding from his black boxer briefs.

'Not sure I've ever seen you so focused,' he quips, but his voice is shaky.

I glance up at him. 'You should show me your dick more often, then.' A tug on his waistband has his beautiful cock springing free, *right* in front of my face, and oh sweet baby Jesus, it's so bloody gorgeous as to be ridiculous.

'I got it out just as soon as I was confident you wouldn't take a bite out of it,' he quips. 'Though even last night, I couldn't be one hundred percent sure.'

I grin up at him as I wrap my hand around it. 'I'm way too self-serving to injure this thing. It's my new favourite dildo.' It's a joke. I've never used a dildo. But I'm not telling him that.

'Jesus,' he groans. 'When you say things like that, I—and fuck me, you really can barely get those little fingers around it.'

We both look down at where I'm holding him. I flex my fingers around his girth. I love this dynamic as much as he does: his size and mine. The fact that physically he over-powers me. It makes succumbing to him so much sweeter. I want him to cover my naked body with his and nail me to this bed with his dick.

'Luckily, I have a mouth, too,' I tell him, and I stoop so I can taste him.

I take that huge, smooth crown between my lips and slide my tongue along his slit, spreading the bead of precum that's already appeared. This first touch has him groaning and sliding his hands through my hair again.

'Your mouth feels so good on my dick,' he hisses.

Good. I shift on my knees, crouching further so I can explore his underside. Cup the soft sac of his balls. Trace a line with my tongue up the big vein that runs along his length and then take all of that big, blunt head into my mouth. I suck decadently, loving the male taste of him, loving the feel of his velvety crown against my flickering tongue.

'Good God, woman,' he grits out. 'Too fucking good.' And then he's pulling out of me and pushing down my thong with hooked thumbs and flipping me onto my back and crawling over me, kicking his trousers inelegantly off as he goes and reaching back to tug off his socks.

We're here.

We made it.

I'm flat on my back on his enormous white bed, naked aside from my hold-ups, a gloriously, perfectly naked Adam ranging over me on hands and knees, his body huge and golden, the expression on his face almost worshipful as he gazes down at me, and that dick of his pointing straight at me like a loaded gun.

I can't help it. I break out into a grin. 'Come here.'

He smiles back at me as he lowers himself down on top of me, and God, the weight of him, and the sheer size of him, and the softness of his skin against mine—it's all exquisite.

'Am I too heavy?' he murmurs, pushing up onto one elbow so he can brush some hair off my face.

'No.' I hook my fingers around his neck and tug him down. 'I want all of you.' *I've wanted it like this for longer than I care to admit.*

'Okay then. Tell me if I'm crushing you.'

'There are worse ways to die,' I mumble as he flattens himself over me and presses his face into the crook of my neck, inhaling deeply into my hair. I raise my knees and wrap one leg around him as best I can, exploring the gorgeously bunched muscles of his arse with the sole of my foot. I want so much of this man. I want to get to know every single inch of him with my hands and lips and tongue—I may even indulge in a nibble here and there.

We lie there for a moment. My breaths are shallow—my lungs are far too squished under this enormous pile of man for proper inhales—but I may just be perfectly happy. Adam's dick is pulsing, trapped between our stomachs.

He reaches one hand down to the leg I have propped up and gently traces the outline of my insulin pump, secured beneath my hold-up, with his fingertip. He may be obsessed with my blood glucose levels, for reasons I now understand far too clearly, but he gets my illness. There's no awkwardness, no need for me to apologise for or explain away the funny little contraptions stuck to various sites on my body. As long as he's confident I can withstand whatever delicious form of cardio he throws at me, he'll embrace this aspect of me without question.

He raises himself back up onto his forearms and I gaze up at him, dizzy with desire and knocked sideways at the emotion this intimacy with him is prompting.

'You tired?'

'Nope. Absolutely not. Not even a little.'

'Okay, then.' He laughs and shifts his weight off me, and I pout.

'I just want to see you better,' he says, running his knuckles up over my pelvic bone and stomach to between my breasts with a touch so light it makes me shiver.

'Ogle away. Believe me, I'm doing the same.'

He hesitates. 'Will you let me tie you up? Just your hands —above your head. I want to do a lot of very bad things to you, and it'll make it even more enjoyable for both of us if I have you restrained.' He pauses, uncertainty written on his face. 'Only if you trust me, that is.'

39

NATALIE

L ast night, I distrusted him and resisted him and despised myself.

Tonight, I trust him.

Such a huge shift in such a ridiculously short time, but I can't help it. The man crouching over me on his bed with ardent eyes is not the man I thought I had a fully formed view of. He hasn't changed at all, but my opinion of him has done a one-eighty at whiplash-inducing speed.

He let me in. He let me see him, and by showing me himself he's obliterated my fear so fully it's as if it never existed.

Adam gave me a gift tonight. He revisited the most unconscionable horrors, recounting them to a woman he had every right to believe would throw his part in them back in his face. And it seems no hardship at all to reward that faith in me with the greatest gift I can give him in this moment.

I reach up and trace a path across the place where the clean line of his beard meets his cheek. 'I trust you,' I whisper. 'You can do whatever you like to me.'

Somehow, I know he won't push my boundaries tonight. While my head is a quagmire of confusing, unfamiliar thoughts about relentless palms and pink, stinging flesh, I know he'll play it safe. I suspect he wouldn't spank me tonight even if I begged him to.

There's a flash of emotion across his face, as unmistakable as it is fleeting. 'That's my girl,' he says hoarsely, pulling the silicon-lined top of my sheer black hold-up away from my right thigh and manoeuvring it with infinite care over the site of my insulin pump before sliding it down and off my leg. The other follows more easily. It's not until he gathers them, flexing them between his hands with what looks like malicious glee, that I understand his game plan.

He's going to tie me up with my own stockings. Tame by his standards, I'm sure, but more exciting for a girl who's never experienced even the most basic form of bondage. My four other sexual partners were all vanilla as fuck compared to this guy.

It's not just the stockings that have my heart rate ratcheting up. It's all of it—the forcible way he nudges my legs further apart so he can kneel between them; the sheer size of him looming over me; that hard, dark jut of his erection right above my stomach; the way his abs and shoulder muscles contract as he holds himself upright even as he orders me to bring my hands up so he can bind them together.

It's quite a sight. I already feel hopelessly, wonderfully overpowered. Apparently, my face says as much, because he glances down and laughs.

'*Look at that smirk*. Could it be that my innocent little Natalie's worked up already?'

'Maybe. I hope the main event doesn't disappoint,' I bluster from my position of clear physical disadvantage.

He shoots me a malevolent smile that is way sexier than it should be. 'That kind of backchat won't earn you any favours. We're doing this my way. You just focus on keeping those little hands above your head and enjoying the ride. Understand?'

The look between us would ignite if there were flammable liquids present. Is there anything hotter than this moment, where you sign your soul away for the promise of delicious, dirty orgasms and you're poised on that precipice of desire and anticipation?

If there is, I haven't found it. And I certainly haven't experienced anticipation this intense with any of my exes.

I meant what I told Adam.

I trust him.

But he's just enough of an unknown entity that the promise of what he's capable of sends a thrill through me. He fucked that woman, and spanked her, and she loved it enough that she begged him to do it again—the spanking part, anyway. Maybe all that should put me off, but it doesn't.

It makes me want to be the one he unleashes himself on.

'I understand,' I say, sealing our filthy covenant.

'You're so heavenly when you're being obedient,' he croons as he crawls back down my body. 'Don't ruin it by trying to run this show. Let me show you just how incredible it can feel to yield to me.' He punctuates this with the lightest brush of his lips across the area south of my navel, just above my bikini line.

'Okay,' I say with a shiver.

'Mmm. So soft,' he murmurs, dropping a line of kisses along the same spot. It's heaven, but his mouth is about three inches higher than where I need it. My orgasm downstairs may as well never have happened, given the greedy, urgent way my body is primed for his mouth. His dick. Whatever he'll give me.

He moves closer to where I need him. 'I haven't stopped thinking about this sweet little cunt of yours since last night. Do you know I got myself off again in the shower when I got home, just thinking about how you tasted? Thinking about how pretty those little pink nipples looked covered in my cum?'

I moan in response to that, because his words, and the way he's saying them, are so damn sexy. If Adam Wright masturbating in the shower to memories of my body was anywhere near as vigorous, as violent, as the way he got himself off at Alchemy, then it's a travesty I missed it.

'Show me later,' I whine, tilting my pelvis in a way I hope puts my pussy closer to his delicious mouth.

He chuckles. 'Maybe another time. I'll be far too busy shooting my load inside you tonight.'

With that, he pushes my legs even further apart with two large palms and bends to lick my centre. Dear God, the sensation of being spread out for him while he licks the most intimate part of me is beyond words. His licks are hard. Rough. There's no warming me up for the onslaught—and it is an onslaught.

'Keep your legs open nice and wide for me like a good girl,' he instructs, before moving one hand to splay over my stomach, pinning me to the bed as he finds my entrance with the other hand and pushes two fingers in, hard. I rut into his tongue and his fingers, my entire consciousness shrinking to the sight of Adam's dark, curly hair between my legs and the terrible, wonderful sensation of him finger-fucking me as he laves my clit.

I wish I could move my arms.

I wish I could reach down and claw at his hair with my

fingers and push his face even further against me so he can barely breathe.

But I can't, and the forced helplessness stokes the flames of my arousal.

'Please, harder,' I beg, and he groans against my flesh.

'Jesus Christ, I am so fucking hard.' His breath is warm against my clit. 'Fuck knows, it was hot when I knew you were fighting it last night, sweetheart, but knowing you want it now is a million times hotter.'

I can actually see that toned arse of his rutting in the air as he thrusts uselessly. I vow to milk his dick harder and better than any vaginal muscles have ever, ever milked him.

'I'm so close,' I gasp. 'Make me come, and you can be inside me in about ten seconds.' He gives a pained laugh.

'God, I love that. I love how much you need me. I can do it in five.'

It might be an arrogant promise, but it's an accurate one, because I'm *right there*. With that, he adds a third finger and twists while pushing down on my stomach and making his tongue even more taut, and all the gorgeous, shameless, insane heat washing over me crests, and I'm molten lava as I fall apart around him.

He licks me through my climax, holding me in place as I writhe and thrash and cry out, and then he's pulling his fingers out and scrambling to his knees as he braces over me to tug desperately at the drawer of his bedside table and pull out a condom. As he rolls it on, I lie there and admire the view: Adam looming over me on his knees, huge and tanned and hairy, that dick pointing straight at me as he sheaths it.

Last night, he unleashed it all over me.

Tonight, he'll unleash it inside me, where it belongs.

40

NATALIE

As he lowers himself down on top of me, I groan with the sheer pleasure of his weight, his skin. He reaches up and brushes some stray hairs off my face, his fingers lingering on my jaw, eyes flickering over my face like he can't quite trust what he sees.

'Think you can come again?' he murmurs, and I laugh.

'Highly unlikely. I've never even come twice in one night until now. A hat trick feels excessive.'

He grins. 'Seriously? That's shit for you, but I love it for me.'

'I told you last night. Nobody likes a gloater.'

'I'll gloat even more when I've given you a third,' he says, lowering his mouth to mine, and I close my eyes and allow the indulgence of it all to wash over me: his mouth, his heaviness, that body, and the promise of his thick crown nudging at my entrance.

Our frantic fuck up against the bookshelves in his library where we scratched the most urgent of itches was beyond hot, but this is... incredible. *Terrifying*. I draw my knees up and stretch my arms out lazily above my head as he pushes inside me, wide and hungry and insistent. It's so intense like this, being tied up for him. Surrounded by him. Consumed by him. The way his tongue entangles with mine. Those delicious sounds he makes low in his throat, like I'm driving him to a place of wildness. Savagery. And, *God*, the feel of him working his way inside my body, dragging against my needy nerve endings.

When he bottoms out, we both groan at the pleasure of it.

'Jesus, I'm in,' he says through gritted teeth. 'You're the tightest, sweetest, loveliest thing I've ever felt, sweetheart.'

This feels sacred. Awe-inspiring. He moves, his mouth not leaving mine, his arms caging me in in a way that makes me feel cocooned. There's a tsunami of emotion working its way up from my stomach to my throat. I can barely think straight amid this maelstrom of sensation. I wasn't lying—I probably can't come again—but this goes way beyond orgasms. Having him on top of me, inside me, feels elemental, as if the place where our bodies are joined is some kind of super circuit, a switch throwing what I believe and who I am into sharp relief.

I'm making noises, I realise, little whines that are delighted and pleading in equal measure. I hope he can hold on, because I never, ever want him to stop. There must be a God, because those long, powerful pumps of his stay rhythmical as he fucks me.

'Dear God,' he grits out, releasing my lips so he can bury his face in the crook of my neck, 'I could die a happy man right now.'

'Please don't die. I'm not finished with you yet.' I wish I could raise my arms and loop them over that glorious, tousled head of his. I wish I could touch every inch of his body. But he asked me for this, and it seemed like he wanted it very badly, and right now I'll do anything within my power to make this beautiful, kind, damaged man as happy as possible.

'I'll try to hang in there.' He raises himself back up. Before I quite know what's happening, he's sliding out of me and flipping me over before tugging me up onto my knees with a firm arm banded around my stomach. I squeal, but as he plunges into me from behind, the squeal turns to an embarrassingly guttural moan, because *hoooooly fuck*, that's deep, and it's so, so good. I don't even attempt to get up onto my elbows, instead letting my cheek press into the smooth cotton of the duvet and my arms stay outstretched.

Adam digs the fingers of one hand into my hip, holding me in place while he fucks me. This new position has unleashed something in him. He's pounding into me harder, faster, than before. His other hand trails up my spine before he reaches around to squeeze my breast.

'When I say,' he says in a hoarse voice, 'that this is pretty much *all* I've thought about doing to you since the moment I laid eyes on that hostile little face of yours... *fuuuuck*.' He punctuates that expletive with a particularly savage thrust that has me grunting like a farm animal and shunting up the bed a little while my inner walls celebrate, because Christ Almighty, if this guy isn't in very real danger of giving me a third orgasm.

'Really?' I manage, deciding I'll attribute the breathiness in my voice to the fact that his dick has pumped all the air out of my lungs. I'm not sure if it's demeaning or hot that he's wanted to bend me over and fuck me senseless this whole time.

Definitely hot.

And probably a little demeaning, but who gives a flying fuck?

Not me.

'Really. Oh God, this is... you look so fucking beautiful, bent over for me. You should see how glorious your tight little cunt looks, taking me in, over and over.'

I have never been spoken to like this. *Never.* I think all my most recent ex was capable of was the occasional *yes, baby* or *take it.* Adam's filthy words have desire roiling in my stomach and suffusing the entire area about which he's waxing so poetically with a glowing, sparking heat.

He likes me bent over for him. Oh God—I wonder if this is how he fucked *her* when he spanked her. It must have been, surely? It would be the obvious position. Something darker spikes inside me, something envious and adversarial. God knows, I'm a total newbie at this stuff, but I want to be the woman who turns him on more than anyone else. I don't want him holding himself back, treating me with kid gloves and then fantasising about—or worse, *going to*—other women for the stuff that gives him his real kicks.

All of which gives me the courage to ask, albeit in a small voice, 'Have you thought about spanking me, too?'

He groans and shunts deep inside me. 'Jesus Christ, sweetheart. Warn a guy.'

'Is that a yes?' My voice sounds weird, given one ear and cheek are plastered to his bed. I wish I could see him.

'It doesn't matter. This is—this is way more than enough, believe me.'

'Will you spank me?'

'*No.*' He sounds angry as he pulls almost all the way out and drives back in. 'I don't want you worrying about that stuff, okay?'

'I think I want you to.' I let that bombshell lie there. For a moment all I can hear is our ragged breathing and the sounds of flesh slapping against flesh.

'If you think so, then we can discuss it another time, when I've got my shit together.' *Thrust.* 'Because I'm so close to blowing, sweetheart, and the idea of pinking up this little arse of yours isn't helping.'

He pauses for a second and does something with his hips that has his dick kind of gyrating inside me, and it feels so sublime that I forgo my retort in favour of a moan.

'That's my girl,' he says. 'You like that, hmm? You like having my dick buried this deep inside you?'

'Uh-huh.' *Jesus, yes.*

'God, I'm loving how much you want my cock,' he croons. He's stroking both my arse cheeks now, and I know I'm not the only one imagining him spanking me. 'Who knew a sweet little thing like you would have such a greedy cunt?'

Fuck, fuck, fuck. It's all too much—it's too dirty, both what he's saying, and being bent over like this with my bum in the air. The heat is building. My entire lower half is glowing. I feel radioactive—I could light up the national grid with the energy I'm producing. The heat is achy and insistent and wonderful, and I'm fluid and helpless in the face of Adam's verbal and, um, penile, barrage.

'I'm going to—' I stutter before I burst like a balloon, impossible, ludicrous pleasure coursing over me in wave after wave as he fucks me through it.

'Oh Jesus fuck, thank fuck,' he mutters. He gives me another couple of strokes before going impossibly rigid and jerking out his own release deep, deep inside my body.

41

ADAM

N atalie saunters back from the bathroom, naked and still sleepy and impossibly beautiful. She also looks far too mischievous as she climbs up onto the bed and crawls towards me.

'Get over here.' I hook an arm around her and tug her close against my body before pulling my heavyweight duvet over us.

'You know what would be awful?' she muses. 'If your staff forgot to fold the end of your loo roll into that little triangle one day. Can you imagine if you had to hunt for the end of the paper all by yourself? God knows what those lost two or three seconds of your time would cost the British economy.'

I stifle a chuckle. She wants a spanking? She's coming dangerously close to having her wish granted. 'Three orgasms last night and you're still giving me a hard time? I was sure I'd fucked the back chat out of you.'

'Nope.' She nestles against me, tucking her head under my chin. 'And don't change the subject. Please tell me you don't actually make your staff do that.'

'Of course I do. Discipline is in the details. If I let them slack on the small things, it'll be a downward spiral.'

She pulls away, outraged, and spots the grin on my face.

'You're a dick.'

'I've never claimed to be anything else.'

She raises her eyebrows, and I sigh.

'Of course I don't tell them to make stupid fucking pointy bits. They just do it—all of them. I have no idea why.'

'Glad to hear it.'

'Look, I've been in prison, for fuck's sake. I wasn't above resorting to wiping my arse with torn-up squares of the *Mirror* when I'd run out in my cell and the screws wouldn't replace it. Do you honestly think I'd insist on pointed ends for my bog roll?'

She sucks in an audible breath, her face anguished. 'Oh my God. I hate that for you.'

'Hey.' I trail my fingers down the delicate structure of her spine. 'We've talked about this. I deserved it, remember? And I've faced a lot worse than newspaper chafing. It's all good.'

'I know, but—it's just so grim. I can't bear knowing that you went through all that.'

We gaze at each other for a moment, our faces inches apart on my pillow, before I speak.

'I want you to know, in case I haven't made it clear enough already, just how sorry I am for what I did to your brother and what I put your family through. I'll never, ever stop regretting it. I'm unspeakably ashamed of what I did. After leaving Ellen that night, it's the biggest regret of my life.'

'I know,' she whispers. I can see from the soft, open expression on her beautiful face that it's the truth. She puts a small hand over my poor, wounded heart, and I let my eyes drift briefly closed at the simple pleasure of her touch.

I hesitate. 'Can I ask how he is?'

'Sure.' We lie, limbs entangled, as she tells me about his job, about which I know broad brushstrokes, and his potential prosthetic. While I'm aware, of course, of his candidacy, I'm genuinely delighted to hear how thrilled he is, how fascinated by the technological opportunities it presents for him, how excited he is about the potential quality of life improvements it offers. I'm even happier to hear of the love he has for his wife, Anna, and their baby girl, Chloe.

While I can never, ever take back the horrific injuries I inflicted on him, I can rejoice in the rush of ease that comes from knowing he didn't let them define him. He has a full and happy life, no thanks to me.

All I can do is continue to surrender all of that pain and guilt, to atone for my past sins, and to make reparations to the Bennett family wherever possible. This beautiful, compassionate, forgiving woman next to me has no idea of the extent of those reparations, and I hope she never will.

But since that tenure I eased the way for her father to procure at the London School of Economics over a decade ago now, the ability to in some small way play fairy godfather to the Bennett family has allowed me to live with myself just that little bit more easily. It's selfish, in a way.

'It sounds like he's a trooper,' I tell her now, covering the hand on my heart with my own.

'He is.' She smiles fondly. 'He's the best.'

'Still an emo D&D weirdo?'

'I cannot *believe* you went there. No, he's not, thank you. He's a total tech nerd.'

'Glad to hear it.'

She pushes me so I roll over onto my back and hoists

herself up onto one elbow. I look up at her. That usually-perfect hair is messier now. It looks like she's had a damn fine fucking, actually. Her lips are still a little swollen. She is a sight for sore fucking eyes.

'Anyway. Talking about my brother feels like a spectacular waste of time right now.' She looks down as her fingers brush against the hair on my chest and sucks in a breath. 'I hate to inflate your ego further, but you really are revoltingly gorgeous.'

I smirk. 'Revoltingly, hmm?'

'Yep.' She pushes the covers down so my entire torso is exposed and traces a line between my pecs, over my navel, and down my happy trail. 'God, you're just... this is...'

Finally, she's lost for words. My dick, which is already semi-hard, stirs. 'I wouldn't go any further unless you intend to finish what you started.'

Our eyes meet. Hers are alight with mischief. 'Is that a threat or a promise?'

'Definitely a threat.' I hold her gaze as her mouth curves into a smile.

'Sounds like a good way to start our morning. What do you usually do with your Saturdays, Mr Wright.'

'I work. And you, Miss Bennett?'

'I work.' She grins, but I frown. I opt to spend my weekends working because I love it and because I don't particularly love socialising—or relaxing. I suspect Natalie does it because she has to, because between trying to keep her company afloat and putting in the hours at Alchemy, she's always at a time disadvantage.

I let it slide. I don't want to make her feel self-conscious, nor do I want those work-related worries that had her in tears yesterday to stage a reappearance. I'm confident that the blissed-out, orgasm-drunk woman who fell asleep in my arms last night was entertaining precisely zero thoughts of cash flow or overdue invoices, and I'd very much like it to stay that way.

'I should clarify,' I say, 'I never begin my weekends with a beautiful, naked woman in my bed, so this is uncharted territory for me. I could definitely be led astray today, if you're game.'

She laughs. 'Oh, come on. Adam Wright, billionaire playboy extraordinaire, sleeps alone? Yeah, right.'

With one move I have her flat on her back and my body pressing down on hers, my now fully hard dick twitching between us.

'I'm serious. I don't spend the night with women. I never, ever invite them back here, and I always leave theirs the same night.'

She stills beneath me. 'If you tell me you let me stay so you could keep an eye on my blood glucose levels, I'll strangle you with my bare hands.' There's determination on her little, heart-shaped face, but vulnerability, too, and my heart constricts.

'That's quite a violent streak you've got there, sweetheart,' I say lightly. 'And if you think I *let* you stay, you're delusional. There was no way on earth you were getting out of here last night. I wasn't letting you out of my sight.'

She doesn't reply, but her expression softens. 'Is that a fact?'

'Yeah. In case you haven't noticed, I've spent the last couple of weeks pursuing you. Wooing you at the club with my dastardly oral skills and at your office with my world-class negotiation prowess... If you think last night was a one-time thing, you are sorely mistaken.'

She swallows. 'Okay. Um. So, then, we should probably lead each other astray. What do you suggest?'

I grin. I do have one idea. Any other woman would scoff, but I have a feeling Natalie will bite my hand off. 'I do actually need to go into the office for an hour or so. But I wondered if you'd like to come with me and check out Omar Vega's studio?'

If I wasn't lying on top of her, I think she'd sit bolt upright. 'Ohmygod. Are you serious? I would kill, like literally *kill*, to have a snoop around.'

I smirk at the strength of her reaction. 'I thought so, you devious little angel.'

'Wouldn't it be a bit immoral, though?'

'I don't see why not. It's not like I'm showing you his confidential information. It's good for you to see how a larger brand lays out its workspace—it'll give you something to visualise. Aim for.'

'I'd love to. I'd love it so much. When can we go?'

I laugh and move over her so my dick leaves no room for misjudging its intentions. 'Not so fast, my little corporate spy. First, you're going to show me your levels. And then, if you don't need feeding right this second, I have some plans for you.'

42

ADAM

ost London-based fashion brands have their studios in East London, near to where the majority of the factories are located. There are outliers, of course, most notably Victoria Beckham, who chose an enormous Georgian mansion in Hammersmith to house both her offices and studio space.

Omar Vega is another outlier. As Nige drives us over to Victoria, I explain to Nat that when I started up my own tech company, OfficeScape, after leaving Wolff, I based it in Victoria. Since my shift towards investing in luxury, I've kept my entire stable of brands under one roof. Hence, Vega and his team hang out in the same building as a variety of my other businesses.

'What does OfficeScape actually do?' she asks me, adding hurriedly, 'explain it like I'm five.'

I laugh. 'It fits out and furnishes massive office spaces using AI. Say you're a tech firm and you're expanding to a new twenty-floor office in Hong Kong. OS will take the floor plans and input best working practices in terms of productivity and wellbeing, and then it will spit out proposals for how to lay out various divisions and workers within those divisions. It'll also come up with interior design schemes, furnishing suppliers, budgets and sustainability metrics. Oh, and it can drive the entire ordering process for fitting the buildings out, too.'

She raises her eyebrows. 'Holy crap. That's amazing. I didn't even know that was a thing.'

I stroke her thigh. 'More and more. Traditionally, all those roles have been carried out by different people— different firms, even. But for rapidly expanding companies, it's a godsend. And obviously the technology has come a long way, too. The programming infrastructure I built it on fifteen years ago is nothing like what exists today.'

'How did you even come up with the idea?' she asks, looking genuinely fascinated.

'I think I mentioned that Anton took a chance on me— he gave me a job straight out of prison, didn't make me go through any of the usual channels. God knows, my CV wouldn't have got me through the front door.

'Basically, he brought me in as a very junior member of the Corporate Centre, which is the part that oversees the entire enterprise.' I blow out a breath. The magnitude of his trust in me, of what he did for me, still affects me today. It's no understatement to say he took a chance on a fucked-up kid and made the world my oyster.

He made me do my Business Studies A Level, which I completed in a year thanks to all the material I'd poured over endlessly while I served my sentence. A part-time MBA followed, funded by a Wolff Holdings bursary and essentially credentialising me for the business world.

'I got involved in so many different projects, I can't even tell you,' I continue. But one of the biggest was helping with the expansion of their Madrid office, which was a new

Southern European headquarters for them. I did a tonne of the budgeting and cost analysis around it, and it gave me a pretty good idea of the overall process—it was a logistical nightmare of epic proportions. But it gave me the idea that surely things could be streamlined, and it kind of went from there.

I shrug. 'I knew technology had to lie at the heart of it. I did some homework and pitched it to Anton. He loved it. Told me to go for it. He let me use company resources to test out some of the technology. In the end he invested—he seeded the entire thing.'

I'm silent for a moment. I didn't just benefit from Anton's extraordinary generosity, nor his unshakable belief in me or my ideas. I undoubtedly profited from being at the centre of a company that, while massive, was still at its heart so entrepreneurial. Having access to Wolff's hive mind, tapping into it, was akin to my fledgling company being nurtured by one of Silicon Valley's finest incubators.

'Sounds like investing was a smart move on his part,' Natalie muses, and I grin, because making my mentor even richer after everything he did for me has been one of my greatest privileges.

'Yeah. Thankfully, it all worked out and he made a pretty hefty return.'

'Of course he did. And then you pivoted, basically, into luxury goods?'

'Can you tell I have a soft spot for them?' I ask in return, and she grins, pawing at my sweater again. Not that she's stopped since I put it on earlier. I don't tend to opt for overt designer logos, preferring quiet luxury, so I'm fond of this understated Brunello Cucinelli sweater. It's cream cashmere, form-fitting, with camel intarsia bands across each bicep. Simple, but beautifully knitted from the finest cashmere in the world.

Not only could my little fashionista name the brand on sight, but she looked a little shell-shocked when I put it on. She muttered something about how good it looked with my skin tone and then stroked my chest while mumbling about defined pecs.

I think she approves.

Nat—I'm guessing I'm allowed to call her Nat now that she's allowed me inside her body three times—looks every inch the stunning fashion entrepreneur in the understated outfit I had Clem send over from Selfridges yesterday after securing Nat's promise that she'd stay the night. She's in a black cashmere polo-neck, tight jeans and Golden Goose trainers, but her hair is pulled back in its trademark sleek ponytail and her makeup is glowy and perfect.

She doesn't look like a woman whose insatiable new lover kept her up half the night because he couldn't keep his hands off her—though it seems from the way she's stroking my bicep through my sweater that I'm not the only one suffering from that problem.

'Luxury goods are the ultimate indulgence for me,' I confess now. 'The OfficeScape stuff is great—I get off on all that problem-solving and streamlining. I like smooth processes. Which is odd, because there's nothing that gives me more pleasure than the total opposite—like knowing how much care and attention has gone into crafting the world's most desirable goods.

'And I'm not talking about huge logos, obviously. I'm talking about the labour of love that is hand-combing the most cherished cashmere goats on the planet and artisanal practices that are passed down from generation to generation and which require years of apprenticeship to master. *That's* what floats my boat.'

'Exactly!' Her brown eyes are shining with fervour. 'That's what I love most, too—that's why I chose the higher end of the market.' She pauses and returns her hand to my thigh. 'Do you think some of that fixation comes from having done time? I mean, if you were using newspaper as loo roll at one point, then maybe being able to enjoy possessions purely for their beauty is something you've aspired to? It's the ultimate sign that you've moved on.'

It's something I've not only pondered at length over the years but discussed ad nauseam with my therapist. 'There's definitely an element of that,' I admit. 'My therapist thinks it's a combination of rewarding myself for having turned things around and establishing safety cues. And it goes way beyond prison. If I grew up mired in uncertainty and deprivation, it stands to reason I'd try to surround myself with enough of a material buffer to mimic stability—or something like that, anyway.'

'That makes sense,' she murmurs.

'I think'—this part is harder to admit, especially to Nat —'there's a redemption angle, too. I get to invest in and enjoy the best life has to offer. I've got the money, after all. I charter yachts and commission art because I can.

'And I know that sounds flippant—I mean it as the opposite, really. I never take a single instance for granted. I marvel at my good fortune every fucking day. But it's something I've cultivated very, very intentionally, this ability to surround myself with beauty and ease and to be able to sit with that without guilt or shame or self-recrimination. Does that make sense?

'At the end of the day, luxury makes me happy, pure and

simple, and I'm finally at peace with being happy, I suppose.'

'That's as valid a reason as any, and it's probably how lots of people feel. I'd guess the market is split between those who buy high-end because of the status it implies or the need they have for validation and those for whom beautiful objects and experiences crafted with care bring them a deep, intrinsic happiness.'

'Especially at a time when fast fashion is threatening to overrun our planet,' I agree.

'*Especially* now. And, honestly, I have very similar feelings to you about the whole issue. My dad's investment company went bust when I was seven, and he wasn't allowed to run money anymore. That's why my brother and I ended up at St Benedict's. We lost our lovely house—we had to live in a council flat for years and it was *grim.*'

'I'm so incredibly sorry to hear that,' I murmur. I know far more about Nat's childhood than I intend to let on, so vague sympathy seems the best policy for now.

'Thanks. I had nothing like the kind of trauma you and your family lived through, obviously, but it was still pretty shitty for a long time. My mum was depressed, and then...'

She trails off.

And then you beat the shit out of Stephen and put him in hospital, minus one working eye.

She doesn't need to say it.

I dig my teeth into my lower lip.

'Anyway,' she continues, flustered, 'it wasn't like we were mega-rich before, but we were comfortable, you know? And I had this bedroom that was all pink and white with a gauzy white canopy over my bed. I loved that room so much. The entire bed was so covered in soft toys I could barely fit in it.'

I smile, but my heart is breaking for her. No, she didn't

lose a sister or have a waste-of-space mother, but I'll warrant she lost a huge piece of what made her feel like herself when Noel Bennett's crooked business partner brought them down.

She's such a lovely person. She tries so fucking hard, all the time. I've only known her a couple of weeks, but it's evident in everything she says and does. That she felt so helpless, so bereft, makes me fucking furious.

'It all went,' she says with a little shrug. 'The flat they moved us to was tiny. I got the box room, and I could only bring a few toys with me. It was such a little shit hole. Anyway, my point is that yeah, running a fashion brand is far harder work than I could ever, ever have imagined, but I'm so happy that I spend my days helping to create beautiful things that make people happy.

'We're not saving lives, but there's something so indulgent about it all, you know? Being surrounded by creative talent and gorgeous fabrics fills my soul—that's the crux of it.'

She has a beautiful soul, and after everything she's been through I'm so fucking relieved she's finding a way to feed it —even if that way is far more rife than I'd like with stress and financial woes.

I'd love to take away all her headaches and allow her to focus only on the work that makes that soul of hers sing.

As I unfasten her seatbelt and pull her into my lap, I vow this to myself:

If it's in my power to do it, I will.

43

NATALIE

I'm not prepared for the sheer scale of the huge glass building that looms over us as we thank Nigel for the lift and step from the car.

I glance up at Adam. 'This isn't all yours, is it?'

He laughs at the awe on my face. 'Welcome to Wright Holdings' European headquarters.'

It makes sense, I suppose. I know he's worth billions. There have to be some seriously large businesses supporting that valuation. But still—holy crap.

'Nice,' I mutter, and he laughs again, taking my hand. 'Come on.'

A huge man waves us through the revolving doors at the front of the building with a grin. Once inside, Adam shakes his hand and greets him by name, asking after his family. The lobby we find ourselves in is enormous—all glass walls and gleaming white floors and low white sofas.

The air is thick with the smell of the oversized floral displays that punctuate the huge space, and I spot perfectly fanned piles of glossy magazines on the coffee table as I walk past, featuring everything from Architectural Digest to the current French Vogue. The coffee table itself is at odds with the perfect whiteness of everything else. It's hewn from a lustrous, irregular-shaped piece of wood—olive or euca-lyptus, maybe—that adds warmth and character to the otherwise intimidating space.

If the rent on my tiny Soho studio cripples me each month, then I can't compute the cost of this vast lobby that just exists without any real function beyond setting the tone for visitors to or associates of Adam's businesses.

We pass an immense white marble reception desk with waterfall ends that probably houses a row of immaculate blond receptionists during the working week but is now empty save for another security guard. When we reach the bank of lifts, I cast my eye up the companies listed for each floor.

'Are all your companies based here?' I ask him.

'Depends. Everything I've founded or want to keep a close eye on—our friend Vega most definitely included—is here.' I giggle at that. 'But if I buy companies as a going concern, then I tend to leave them where they are unless they're in dire need of restructuring.

'We've acquired a handful of luxury office furniture brands in Milan and Amsterdam. OfficeScape was throwing so much business their way that it made sense to bring them in house and improve their cost efficiencies, but it also made sense to leave their manufacturing bases where they were.'

'What else do you own?' Omar Vega I know about, obvi-ously. I'm also familiar with Elysian, a beautiful high-end yoga brand focused on technical fabrics in statement prints.

'Soft luxury, mainly. We own Whitechapel Leathers, though their production is all in the East End, and Obsid-ian, which does luxury leather tech accessories. When we bring them all under the same roof'—he holds an ID card to the scanner and presses the button for the lift—'we can make vast improvements. Obsidian and Whitechapel now share the same suppliers, and all our companies use the same centralised HR and accountancy functions. Little things like that can slash a tonne of cost.'

He may think of them as *little things*, but they're not. They're huge efficiencies. Not only is Gossamer's cost of goods sky high, but we have lots of fixed costs, like our book keeper and audit firm, that are far bulkier line items on our P&L than our top line warrants.

It sounds like a dream.

'Do you want to go straight to Vega?' he asks as we enter the lift.

'Sure. But I want to see your office later, too.' Now that we're here, I'm getting greedy. I want to sniff into every corner of Adam's empire; I want to breathe in the air of success that he and his thousands of employees do; I want to spend a couple of hours feeling steeped in the abundance mindset that is so infectious in places like this.

And I want, on a less professional note, to see where my super hot new fuck buddy sits and runs that empire. Because if I find Adam attractive right now, in his jeans and gorgeous cream sweater, I might just die if I get a glimpse of him in CEO mode.

'Sure thing,' he says easily, pressing the button for the tenth and final floor. When we step out of the lift, I'm positively dazzled with the natural light that's pouring in. Victoria isn't an area overrun with high-rises, so at this height, Vega's studio is bathed in uninterrupted winter sunlight.

The smug, high-maintenance twat even has first dibs on our limited supply of sunshine, for fuck's sake.

Once my eyes adjust, what strikes me most about this

space is that, unlike our poky studio, this vast floor in this fancy building is designed as much with beauty in mind as much as function. I'm certain, given Adam's background, that every inch has been designed to be productive and commercial and ergonomic and all the rest.

But, categorically *unlike* Gossamer's shabby home, there's nothing utilitarian about this space. Every detail has been carefully plotted to provide inspiration and wellbeing to the fortunate people who spend their days here.

The floor is white and gleaming, as are the tops of every desk and cutting table I can see. The only items on display are items that are *supposed* to be on display: the sleek iMacs, the perfect tiles of framed campaign shots on the walls, and the draping mannequins.

Oh dear lord, the mannequins.

I drift forward without quite realising it, drawn to a linen-covered one wearing a half-finished sheath dress. The entire thing is crafted from ultra-fine horizontal strips of scarlet satin, their perfectly frayed edges softening what could be a severe silhouette. It's breathtaking in the flawlessness of its execution. I run a reverent hand over the hundreds of thin bands, appreciating how the satin flutters under my touch.

'Like it?' Adam says from behind me.

I turn to see that it's me he's appraising, hands in his pockets, and not the craftsmanship in front of us.

'It's perfect,' I tell him.

'Go on.' He jerks his head in the direction of the vast space to our right. 'Have a snoop. I won't tell.'

I take him at his word, heading past the banks of desks, which probably belong to the production, design and merchandising functions, towards the huge cutting tables. Evan would lose his life. Each table must be twelve feet long at least, affording space to cut even the most audacious, extravagant patterns from the fabric.

Best of all, Vega's fabric collection lies under each table. I assume the bulk of the current season's fabric is at the factories, but every fashion brand accumulates excess fabric, which is often used when sampling future collections. On the shelves under the table at which I'm standing lie roll after roll of tweed. I recognise the fabulous, metallic-heavy signatures of two of the top mills, Mahlia Kent and Linton, both of whom are beloved by brands such as Chanel and Balmain. The rolls are organised by colour: from duck-egg blue to azure at one end while pink shades ranging from salmon to magenta lie at the other.

Willy Wonka's chocolate factory has nothing on this. It's dazzling, the sheer scale of Vega's resources. The fun I could have playing with these fabrics.

The magic I could weave.

What really hits me hard, though, is when we get to the far end of the room, only to find that it's actually an L-shape. Around the bend is a sumptuous area that is clearly where Vega sees his most important clients. The flooring here is walnut, the walls a pale pink silk that also covers the changing area, and the fixtures rose gold. It's feminine and indulgent and stunning.

And hanging on that silk? Photo after photo mounted on perspex, showing the great and good of the entertainment industry wearing Omar Vega's admittedly gorgeous creations.

Margot Robbie in aqua-coloured ruffles on the red carpet at Cannes.

Emma Watson at some premiere.

Queen Rania of Jordan in a frothy emerald green tea-dress.

A sketch of a silver sequinned dress commissioned by Taylor Swift, signed with Vega's trademark flashy scrawl.

Images that credentialise the man who dressed these women as the real deal.

And just like that, the childlike excitement I felt at being let loose in this inner sanctum dissipates, leaving only a crashing, sickening sense of imposter syndrome.

'It's so beautiful,' I tell Adam, giving him a smile I hope reflects none of this. Clearly, I'm a worse actor than I give myself credit for, because he takes my hand and pulls me down to sit next to him on a plum-coloured velvet sofa that's supported God knows how many famous bottoms.

'Remember what I told you,' he murmurs into my hair as he wraps an arm around me and pulls me to him, 'raw talent and commercial potential and financial strength aren't the same things—well, neither is a business's size. This isn't all *him*. Sure, it's built around him, but we have three hundred people working for this brand, and that's not including any of the centralised functions I mentioned, nor the PR agencies we pay an arm and a leg to every month.

'This is a machine, and it's a fucking cash-hungry machine at that. All this gloss is the result of massive investment and hundreds of people who are very, very good at what they do. It takes an astounding amount of time and money and hard work to translate one person's vision into *this*.'

I nod a little too vigorously. 'I know,' I say, my throat so tight it aches.

'That wisteria dress I saw on your mannequin yesterday,' he continues. 'You know more about this stuff than me—a lot more—but I swear to God, you put that up on the rail over there and get some celebrity in and she'll bite your hand off to get her mitts on it. It was spectacular. Exquisite.

That hardware you had going on on the shoulders? Just beautiful. Honestly, sweetheart, I'm not exaggerating. From what little I've seen, your creative talent is just as good as his. Better, possibly.'

I start to roll my eyes at what is an absurd proclamation from a businessman who's astute enough to know better and most likely still sex-drunk, but he reaches up with his free hand and grabs my chin gently.

'Listen to me. The only thing separating you from Omar Vega is circumstance. *The only thing.* And if you'd like to chat at any point about taking steps to change the circumstances of your brand, then I promise you I will do anything in my power to support you through the process.'

44

ADAM

She doesn't seem to believe me, and it pisses me off.

'It's so easy to feel intimidated by all this,' I continue, waving my hand around the space. 'But it's just a snapshot of where a business stands at a certain point in time. Your journey may not be on the same timeline as his, but that doesn't mean you won't get there.'

'Sometimes I think I'm delusional,' she admits. 'Like, what the hell am I even doing? It feels as though I'm just trying to stay afloat every day. What's the point? The company's maxed out its credit cards. It feels like such an effort to keep it going, and I'm so focused on survival that there's no oxygen for growth.'

I release her face and take her hand. 'That is very, very standard for a business of your size. There's this toxic rhetoric out there that things should be easy, or that a company's viability rests on how quickly it can grow, but that's bullshit. I meant what I said about circumstances. Vega has a lot of advantages that you don't.

'But I hear what you say about feeling deluded, too. If a business is a dead horse, I firmly believe you should walk away.' I pause, squeezing her hand. 'Forget the bills and the struggles for a moment. What's your vision for the brand? Why did you start it, and do you still stand by that vision?'

She sighs. 'I felt that there was a place for a beautiful British brand that has craftsmanship and sustainability at its core. I don't want to have to cut corners or compromise on the craft *or* the ethics—that's why I positioned it in a less price-sensitive part of the market.'

I nod. 'Smart.'

'And I know there are better designers than me out there. I know there are people who are more commercial, who have more celebrity relationships and are just better at hustling... But I truly believe in my bones that our aesthetic has a place in the market. And I really, really believe in our prints. I think they have so much potential beyond clothing.'

'Like what?' I ask, my interest piqued. 'Pull up your Instagram, will you?'

She rummages around in that enormous, grotty handbag and extracts her phone, pulling up Gossamer's Instagram account before handing the phone to me. I scroll through the feed. It's nowhere near as curated as Vega's or most of our brands' feeds—clearly, she doesn't obsess endlessly over the grid layout like Vega's team does—but it's stunning, an endless palate of pastels, and delicate florals, and exquisite detailing. If I was a woman, I'd fall into a drooling, swooning heap over this stuff.

'So that's the wisteria you said you spotted,' she says, pointing, 'and we have a peony print this season, too.'

The feed shows me what my glimpse of that dress in her studio didn't: the up-close detail of the prints. They're hand-painted and dreamy, with daubes of watercolour so well printed that they feel like original canvases.

'They're stunning,' I say.

'I love them. And I really think they'd do so well for other lines, too, especially home furnishings. Curtains, wallpaper, tablecloths—even place mats. They could also be amazing as yoga gear.'

'I agree.' They're British and romantic and feminine and highly commercial. 'Have you ever approached anyone? Athleisure brands? The big home furnishing guys like Osborne and Little? Licencing the prints could be a great form of passive income for you.'

She shrugs. 'Not yet. I can't imagine anyone would be interested—we don't have the clout to collaborate with a big brand.'

'You don't need clout when you have aspirational prints like these. I can put it to Elysian if you like?' Our yoga brand is still smaller than I'd like, far smaller than the giants like Alo and Sweaty Betty, but we're pumping serious money into it, and it's gaining a reputation for being the brand of choice among the most discerning yogis, to the point that we're looking at opening a Santa Monica popup next spring. Collaborating with a truly British womenswear brand could be a nice hook to test out stateside.'

She gasps, then stops herself. 'No way. I don't want favours just because we're sleeping together.'

I laugh. 'If you think I'd let my dick get in the way of my business brain, you're sorely mistaken. I'm a commercial animal.' I lean in. 'This is what I'm talking about when I mention circumstances. Vega has tonnes of unfair advantages. I'm giving you one—an in with a brand that could be a wonderful partner for you. It's just an intro. No skin off my nose. It'll be up to you and your fabrics to seal the deal, not me.

'When these kinds of doors crack open, you elbow your way the fuck through them, got it? *That's* the difference between you and brands like Vega. They've been given opportunities. You haven't, necessarily. That changes now.'

She's still looking uncertain, and it makes me want to kiss her and shake her. 'Don't be too British about this,' I warn her. 'You've got to hustle.'

She nods. 'I know you're right. Okay, if you're sure, then thank you. I'd love an intro.'

'Good. I'll set up a coffee with Claudette, the founder. She'll like you, and I think you'll like her. And speaking of hustle, how many of your suppliers have you managed to renegotiate with so far?'

She squirms. 'Two or three.'

'Keep trying. There are no silver bullets, okay? This industry is fucking brutal. Anyone who thinks it's fun or glamorous is deluded. You take the breaks when you get them: introductions, cash flow reprieves... That's how you buy yourself enough time to make an impact.'

She nods again, more decisively this time. 'I know you're right. I keep wondering if I'm missing something.'

'I'll take a more detailed look at your numbers, if you like,' I offer. This is the side of incubating start-ups that I love. While I adore luxury products, it's the numbers, the growth prospects, the trouble-shooting, that get my neurons firing. It all feels like one giant puzzle. And now that my business interests are so broad and my perspective birds-eye at best, I love getting myself stuck into the weeds of small businesses.

Her eyes are wide. 'Really? That would be great, but you've done so much already. I don't want to take up any more of your time.'

Jesus Christ. I pull her up onto my lap, sighing heavily into her glossy, lavender-scented hair. 'Sweetheart. If you consumed every single minute of my day, I'd be a happy man. This is your baby—how can I not be interested in it? You've built a beautiful brand. Let's at least see if we can find it some oxygen.'

I don't mention my ulterior motive. I'd like to see if her business is viable from an investment perspective. I may not be able to hope for a romantic future with Nat—her family would never, ever stand for that—but perhaps we could have a business relationship. I shove aside the thought that it's a terrible idea to even consider investing in the business of a woman I'm fucking, because I'm not interested in those kinds of thoughts right now.

If I'm right, Gossamer has real potential. I suspect the debts she's so worried about would be pretty small for us to swallow, and she wouldn't need a tonne of capital up-front —mid-six figures, maybe, to fund an increase in production and get some new projects off the ground.

As for Natalie herself, I'd back her every day of the week. Not only is she the perfect representative for her classy, feminine brand, but she's articulate and smart and creative and focused and relentlessly disciplined. While the latter makes me worry for her wellbeing, she's every inch the kind of founder I love to back.

The more I think about it, the more my gut tells me she could do great things with this brand with the right kind of financial help, personnel support, and mentoring.

I have another test up my sleeve, and this is a fun one.

'If it makes you feel better, you can help me in return,' I murmur into her hair.

She turns and grins at me. 'Is *help* code for *blow job*?'

'Not in this instance, though I'm not above accepting sexual bribes. But while we're here, tell me what you think of Vega.'

Her eyebrows wing up. 'The man or the brand?'

'Both, though I'm more interested in the latter.'

She slides off my lap and turns in a circle, gazing at what she sees. 'Well, you know the brand a lot better than me.'

'Just like you know Gossamer better than I do. But an outside perspective brings its own value. *And* you've already admitted to stalking the brand, so I suspect you have many, many thoughts. I don't want nice, polite Natalie. I want scathing Natalie. Like how you were with me when we first met.'

That gets a laugh. 'Fine. So you want feedback other than that he seems to be a complete twat?'

'That's a given,' I deadpan.

'Okay, then. Well, for a high-end label, your total lack of sustainability strategy—or messaging—is a disgrace.'

I cross my arms. 'Go on.'

'There are many people who can't afford to vote with their wallets when it comes to the sustainability of their clothes or their food or anything else. But your clients can.'

'I agree.'

She sets off across the room, and I follow her, amused by her vehemence and interested to see where this leads. She stops at one of the cutting tables and points underneath. 'I mean, stone-washed denim? Really?'

'It was for an Eighties collection, I think,' I protest weakly.

'Yes it was. Last season. And there was no suggestion at all on your socials that the denim came from overstock. Have you any idea how much water this would have used?'

I have some idea. Too much. And she's completely right.

'What would you do if you were his CEO?' I ask her.

She leans against the cutting table. 'Give him iron-clad boundaries to work with. He wants to use stone-washed denim, he gets his team to source excess rolls from somewhere. Don't tell me you guys lack the manpower.'

'We do, but it's harder at his scale,' I argue. 'We need to be able to ensure consistency of supply.'

'I get that, but frankly it's a lazy argument.' She scratches at her forehead. 'There's this quote I read once that still haunts me. *The last thing the planet needs is yet another sustainable fashion brand.* I lost sleep over that one. But I do my best. That's one of the reasons we've grown more slowly —we spent a lot of time focusing on becoming a B-Corp.'

I frown. 'That's a big undertaking for a company of your size.' I'm not entirely sure it would have been the best use of her time or energy.

'Yes, but we wanted to get the right learnings and processes in place *before* we scaled. Now that stuff is second nature. But you have a hell of a lot more infrastructure to help you work around those constraints, so the question is, why haven't you?'

She's glaring at me, and I fucking love it. *This* is the Natalie who first transfixed me, and the world doesn't see enough of her.

'The past few quarters since we acquired Vega have been about improving profitability,' I admit. 'I told you we've put some very strict parameters in place around what he can and can't design, and what he can spend.'

'Well, that's lovely for your wallet, but all that tells me is that you have the perfect structure to implement even more controls,' she argues. 'He needs to be kept accountable. Look at that sequinned dress. I bet those are plastic sequins.'

'Probably.' I cringe inwardly, because I have no clue at all and I know she's right—about the sequins and the rest of it.

She narrows her eyes at me. 'It's not okay, Adam. This is a big brand, and it's only getting bigger. Make it part of his design framework, and your workflow, and your bloody marketing efforts, for God's sake. Talk about it! But only when you've done the work to get the basics right. The days are gone where designers can design whatever the fuck they want with no regard for the true cost of their products.'

I grin broadly at her. 'What else? Tell me.'

45

NATALIE

I have to talk to my brother. This... thing with Adam is consuming me so rapidly, so ardently, that I'm going up in flames. I don't stand a chance at withstanding his onslaught.

If it was purely physical, I could walk away. (I couldn't, actually, but I'd like to think I had more of a chance of withstanding him that way.) But it's not.

It's everything.

Every moment, every gesture.

It's the way he comes to fetch me after every single Alchemy shift, even though his chef Kamyl let slip the other day that he's usually early to bed and early to rise.

It's the quiet times when I'm draped over him in his beautiful library and we're both reading.

It's his obsession with getting Kamyl to concoct the most delicious high-protein meals and snacks for me with slow-release carbs aplenty.

It's the hours and hours he's spent pouring over Gossamer's numbers over the past fortnight, grilling me on the most random points and making suggestions that are utterly brilliant and incredibly helpful.

Last night, he spent the entire car journey home from Alchemy quizzing me on the price of printing on silk habotai for various meterages, and he introduced me to Claudette from Elysian via email the day we visited his offices. I met up with her earlier this week, and we hit it off right from the start. She loved the mockups Carrie did of our prints on her signature yoga pants and crop tops, and I think this could turn into an actual collaboration. It's a dream come true.

He's a dream come true.

The thing I can't square in my mind is the reality of this kind, brilliant man I'm falling so hard for with the outdated but entirely justified view my family has of the monster who put Stephen in hospital and derailed his life. I've come around because I gave him a chance, took the time to get to know him. But how can I possibly ask them to do the same?

Before I speak to my brother, I'll sound out my mum, I decide. She's the calmest, the softest, of all of us. She tends to look for and find the best in people. Maybe she can advise me.

Maybe I can get her to fill Stephen in on the fact that I'm falling for the man he hates while I quietly escape to the other side of the world.

But before I speak to Mum, I'll chat to the girls. I owe them an update, especially my lovely boss, and they tend to be cool and non-judgemental in a way other people in my life are not.

They also may be more impartial than Evan, whose giant boner for Adam has him shipping us so hard I swear I might find myself at the top of the aisle.

We meet up at an ancient but fantastic pizzeria in

Mayfair before Alchemy opens, and it's no understatement to say I've been looking forward to this *all day*. While I'm endlessly grateful to Adam and Kamyl for respectively obsessing over my needs and creating the most delicious meals for me, sometimes a girl just needs a fucking pizza. So when Dr Wright isn't around, I go big.

Even if managing the blood glucose requirements for metabolising pizza is a gigantic pain in the arse. I've increased my basal dose of insulin today—that's the low, longer-lasting stream that works away in the background, processing glucose when I'm not actually eating. I'll increase my bolus dose too, right before I eat.

What can I say? It'll be worth it. Every bite will be sublime. Pizza may not be the ultimate health food, but God knows, it's good for the soul.

After a hearty toast to the absent Belle, who's due to pop any day now, our evening begins with a discussion of the opening party for Alchemy's swanky New York outpost in a couple of weeks. Maddy's not going. She claims to want to stick around for Belle, but I suspect she's staying for the baby cuddles. It'll be good practice for her, I suppose. At six months pregnant, she's glowing and gorgeous.

Gen and Anton will be flying in, and she says Cal and Aida will, too. It makes sense—not only is Cal Alchemy's events manager, but he's not one to miss a party. Darcy, Max and Dex are also going.

'Max has booked a suite at the Aman,' Darcy says with glee. 'We're going to make a few days of it and combine it with some Christmas shopping. Oh my God, I'm so excited! I can't wait! I've never been to New York—can you believe it?'

'Me neither,' I say. 'You're going to have the best time!' I'm genuinely thrilled for her, but I can't help but feel a shameful pang of envy at the thought of Darcy strolling down Fifth Avenue with an adoring man on each arm. Adam's been consistently incredible, but he's made no mention of New York at all.

Surely he's planning on going? He is the brand new part-owner of Alchemy's overseas operations, after all, and the opening of the New York flagship is a biggie.

Maybe he'll go without me?

The thought of it makes me feel physically sick: Adam in some glamorous Manhattan sex club, all tall and gorgeous and commanding, the glossy women of New York fawning over his model-grade looks and British accent, begging him to exercise that twitchy palm that he won't unleash on me.

Ugh ugh ugh.

'You all right, babes?' Maddy says. 'You're white as a sheet.'

'I'm fine,' I say hastily. 'Just hungry.'

I don't miss the panicked look the others share. Ever since my hypo at work, they've treated me like an unex-ploded bomb.

'Let's order, then,' Gen says, waving a waiter over.

We order and request some bread and olive oil while we wait. When a basket of focaccia squares swimming in oil arrives, I mentally calculate the additional insulin I'll need. This stuff looks delicious.

After stuffing a couple of wedges of focaccia soaked in the most delicious, peppery olive oil in my mouth, I begin to relax. Gen talks about the silver flapper gown she's picking up from Alexander McQueen next week for the speakeasy-themed opening party. It sounds dreamy. McQueen is one of her go-to brands—she adores all the hidden corsetry it offers, not that she needs it. Her curves are spectacular. I'd kill for boobs and hips like hers.

Adam loves your small boobs, a little voice reminds me. *He adores how delicate you are. He tells you all the time.*

It's true. He's not one to hold back on the compliments. I may not be anywhere near as voluptuous or goddess-like as Gen, but I have never, ever felt so desired as when Adam Wright's skilful hands and worshipful gaze are on my body. I sip my lemon-flavoured San Pellegrino and watch with amusement as Gen and Darcy knock back their first glasses of Tuscan red. They must be thirsty.

It reminds me that Adam has never drunk in front of me. I know he drinks—he has a well-stocked, glass-fronted wine alcove-thingy in the kitchen, and he's tasted of whisky or wine a couple of times when he's gone out for work dinners before picking me up from Alchemy, but he's never so much as cracked open a beer in my presence.

He must refrain because he knows I steer clear of alcohol.

The thought of it is a rush of warmth to my heart, and it emboldens me. New York isn't important. It's the countless small but thoughtful gestures that he makes every single day that are important.

'Actually, I have some news,' I confess once our pizzas have been served. My *quattro formaggi* is steaming in front of me, and I can't resist picking up a slice and taking the most enormous bite before I resume. Jesus Christ, that mouthful of carbs and cheese is *the* best taste in the world. Maybe I should just pump myself full of insulin and subsist on pizza all day, every day. Adam can shove his black beans up his arse.

The others exchange a look that's knowing and not a little smug.

'What?' I demand.

'If you're planning on coming clean about Adam Wright,

it's not exactly news,' Maddy says. 'Just saying. Fuck, this baby is a whore for simple carbs.' With that, she shovels a good half of her slice of pizza into her mouth and groans theatrically.

I can relate, and I'm not even eating for two.

'Really?' I ask now, my gaze darting between them. 'How come?'

'You've been terribly quiet on the whole front since you last updated me,' Gen says gently, 'and given how vocal you are about him when you dislike him, I wondered if the quietness spoke volumes. Besides, Ben came clean to me a couple of weeks ago that Adam asked him for a private room for the two of you.'

I gasp. 'Oh my God, that's so mortifying.'

'What?!' Maddy squeals. 'I can't believe you didn't tell me!'

She aims that at Gen, who fixes her with the iciest of glares. 'It's called client discretion. Nat and Adam are entitled to their privacy at Alchemy just as much as anyone else.' She turns back to me. 'I would have checked in with you, but you've seemed very happy this past couple of weeks, so I let it slide.'

I shut my eyes in mortification, but they fly open when Darcy hits me on the arm.

'Oh my God. Did you have *all* the hate sex? We told you you should, didn't we?'

I groan and screw up my face. 'Um... kind of?'

Maddy pushes her enormous pizza plate away so she can put her elbows on the table and glare at me.

'Spill it, Bennett. All of it. *Now.*'

46

NATALIE

I groan. Where to start?

'Just so we're clear,' Darcy says, shaking her gorgeous auburn hair off her face. 'You hate him, but you're fucking. Right?' She's definitely overdressed for a pizzeria in a low-cut black dress that has her amazing boobs on display, but who cares?

'Not really,' I say.

'Ugh! Enough vagueness!' Maddy shouts. 'I'm a horny pregnant person! I need all the salacious details!'

'Keep your voice down,' I grit out as Gen rolls her eyes at Maddy. 'Okay, fine. Obviously I had my weird little sleepover at his place where he actually looked after me amazingly and I was an ungrateful bitch.'

'And he got a boner in your bed,' Darcy reminds me helpfully.

'And he got a boner in my bed. Um—that night that Ben mentioned, Adam had asked me if I ever came through to the club. I said no, remember? I saw you guys that evening. But I couldn't resist going in for a little peek after my shift.'

Maddy squeals and clenches her fists, and I glare at her.

'Sorry,' she says, looking chastised. 'Please proceed with your delicious tale.'

'Well, I went through to The Playroom, and there he was, spanking one of the hosts on the Banquette while someone else went down on her.'

'I fucking *knew* he'd be into that,' Darcy says, slapping the table. 'You can tell just by looking at him, can't you? He looks so stern.'

'*Anyway,*' I say pointedly, 'he saw me flouncing off and he came and grabbed me and dragged me off into a private room. He told me the woman he was spanking was someone he'd fucked previously, and that she'd asked him to do it.'

'It was Rose,' Gen says, wrinkling her nose like she's not sure if this is information I want to hear. She's holding her pizza slice more elegantly than I would have thought possible.

'Oh.' My stomach does a flip. 'She's really sexy.' God, he fucked Rose. And spanked her. And she loved it. Maybe that's why he hasn't spanked me yet—maybe he likes doing it to little sex kittens who know what they want rather than uptight women who may well run a mile.

'Don't overthink it,' Gen orders in her firmest voice. 'Keep going.'

'Well, we had a very, um, *hot* time in the room.' I don't know why I'm shy about this. These three have got up to all sorts of mischief I couldn't dream of. 'He kind of seduced me, and he was so smug and insufferable and I was more turned on than I've ever been in my life.' Their rapt faces make me smile. 'We didn't have sex—he undressed me and went down on me and then he straddled me and came all over my chest.'

Gen grins in a *that's my girl* kind of way and gives me a

very small and discreet hand clap while Maddy and Darcy look like they might expire.

'Why didn't he fuck you?' Darcy wants to know.

'I may have... begged him to, in the moment, but he refused. Said he didn't want me having any more regrets than I already would. He wouldn't kiss me, either. He said it would be too lonely kissing a woman who hated him.'

Maddy clasps her hands over her chest. 'Be still my heart!'

'Let's remember Adam isn't exactly blameless here,' Gen says. 'He's put Nat's family through hell.'

'Amen to that,' Darcy says.

'But I gather things have developed from there?' Gen asks.

I swallow the mouthful of pizza I've snuck in. 'You could say that. He came to my office the next day to check if I was okay and he found me upset about some work stuff. Money's been a bit tight, and I had a massive invoice that was due for payment before the mill would release the fabric.

'Anyway, he was amazing. He sat me down and made me tell him the problem, and then he got on the phone with the mill in France and renegotiated our terms then and there. He bought me sixty days' credit, and he told me to go away and do the same with all our other suppliers.'

'Well, that's impressive,' Gen says. 'What a thoroughly decent thing to do. I'm so glad he could help you.'

'Me too.' I shrug. 'It made me realise that, whatever shit's gone down in the past, maybe the man he is today isn't all bad. I kissed him after that, and it's escalated since then. I've spent pretty much every night at his place, and he's helped me so much with work stuff. He's the kindest man I've ever met.'

This declaration is met with stunned silence.

'Honestly, it's true. He looks after me so well. He has his chef cook me amazing meals that won't spike my blood sugar. And he comes and gets me every night after my shift. He doesn't even send his driver, and I know it's making him tired, but he shows up every time.'

Gen smiles, and I can see in her smile how thrilled she is for me. 'The doormen may have mentioned that to me, too,' she says with a wink. I should have known I couldn't pull the wool over Gen's eyes.

'So... you're dating?' Maddy presses. 'It's serious?'

I sigh. 'I don't know. It seems to be serious, but we haven't discussed the future at all. The elephant in the room is that I don't see how we can go public to my family, like, ever. I need to talk to my mum about it.'

'How have you come to terms with what he did to your brother?' Darcy asks. 'Have you just decided to forgive him and let bygones be bygones?'

I hesitate. I don't want to betray Adam's confidence, but I don't think the headlines of his story are a secret. 'He's told me a lot about what happened then. It's beyond horrific. Let's just say he was a victim, too. He had an alcoholic mother, and his little sister had just died. He beat my brother up five days after the funeral. She had type 1 diabetes.'

Darcy and Maddy gasp. Gen merely presses her lips together sympathetically.

'You knew?' I asked her.

'I made Anton tell me the full story,' she admits. 'I was so angry after that first time you recognised him. But I figured it was Adam's story to share with you.'

I nod. 'Like I said, he was a victim just as much as my brother. He was in a seriously bad place. That judge really did a number on him. But I'm not sure whether I can ever persuade Stephen to give him a chance.'

We're all silent for a minute. Maddy sighs and picks up her pizza slice. 'Well, that's depressing. Poor guy.'

'Tell me about it.'

'But he seems like a keeper,' Darcy insists. 'It sounds like he's doing everything right.'

I nod. 'He really, really is.'

'How's the sex?' Maddy asks with a grin.

I laugh. 'Um, yeah. It's amazing.'

'Spanky spanky?'

'Not so much.' I hesitate. Maybe these women can give me some advice. 'I know he's really into it, but he won't lay a finger on me.'

'That makes total sense to me,' Gen muses, tucking a lock of immaculate platinum hair behind her ear. 'For years and years, he's been the bully who landed your brother in hospital. I'm sure he's on his very best behaviour with you.'

'I know you're right.' I sigh. 'But I trust him implicitly. I've told him that, over and over.'

'Have you been spanked by anyone before?' she asks.

'No.'

'So you can see why it would be high risk for him. He has no idea if you can handle it. Do you like the idea of it?' Her voice is gentle but probing.

'Yes? I don't know why. I'd never thought about it before, but I really like the idea of Adam doing it. But I don't know if it's because I really want it or because I know he loves it and I want to be able to give him that. I don't want random women like Rose sharing that with him and not me. Does that make sense?'

'It does, but you have to do it for yourself, babes,' Maddy tells me. Her voice is so kind.

'I know you're right. I don't love pain—I don't want him to hurt me. But I love the idea of him... disciplining me, I suppose?'

They all grin in tandem.

'Amen to that,' Darcy drawls, saluting me with her wine-glass. 'Pretty much the first thing Max ever did when we met in Cannes was threaten to put me over his knee. It was so fucking hot.'

'Do they spank you?' I ask her tentatively.

'Max, yes, a lot. Dex sometimes, when Max tells him to. And I don't like pain either. You should see me getting waxed. I'm pathetic. But being put over Max's knee like a naughty girl has me practically coming there and then—I fucking love it. I can't get enough of it.'

'Me neither,' Maddy offers. 'Spreadsheet spanked me that first time he fucked me, at Slave Night, and he practically had to peel me off the ceiling. I fucking *loved* it.' She turns to me. 'Think about it. I bet Adam would be so good at it. Doesn't it turn you on, imagining him putting you over his knee or getting you on all fours, and then peeling down your panties and spanking you while he finger fucks you? Imagine how serious he'd look. I'd put money on him being a natural disciplinarian.'

Oh my sweet baby Jesus. I squirm in my seat as Gen lets out an amused snort. How is it that Maddy's characteristically crude words have just painted such a scorching hot image?

She's totally nailed it.

Adam Wright, disciplinarian.

I can feel his hands on me, stinging me, while those long fingers pushed inside me.

I need this from him.

47

ADAM

'Please,' Nat slurs from her position on my pillow. She's drunk with either exhaustion or desire—I'm not sure which. I press my lips together to swallow a smile, because she's something else when she's like this— lying in my bed, dark hair fanned across my pillows and those eyes huge and beseeching. Even in her silk pyjamas, she's impossible to resist.

'No,' I tell her far more decisively than I feel. 'You're shattered.'

'I'm not, honestly.'

'You were dead on your feet when I picked you up. You were actually swaying.'

I swear, something has to give here. I've picked Nat up from Alchemy three nights this week. On the evenings that she hasn't been working, we've met up in town and travelled back to mine together. She's burning the candle enough as it is without adding sex marathons into the mix, but I assuage my guilt over being one more demand on her time with the knowledge that the comfortable drive to my place is far shorter—and less exhausting—than her lengthy tube commute back and forth to Seven Sisters would be.

That's a circuitous way of admitting that she's spent every night this week here with me.

I'm worried about her. Even without the burden of a chronic illness to manage, she has too much on her plate. I get that she values being a part of Alchemy. That she adores Gen and the rest of the team. I get that it pays the bills. But if she's really serious about building Gossamer, then we need to find a way for her to focus her time and energy there and not on what is merely a short-term financial crutch.

That she's nightly fodder for whatever over-sexed, overly entitled dickheads frequent Alchemy is beside the point.

'I hear orgasms are good for quality of sleep,' she says now, her voice soft and seductive, and I roll my eyes, because if I think I stand a chance against this assault on my heart and my cock, then I'm sorely mistaken.

'Is that so.' I fondle the top button of her pyjamas and gaze down at her from my position perched on my elbow. 'That rationale only applies when people actually get some sleep, Miss Bennett.'

She smiles, cat-like, and reaches up, sliding her hand around the back of my neck. 'Okay, I admit, I'm tired. But I've been standing in that lobby all evening, fantasising about you. I told the girls about you tonight, and I just want you inside me. Is that so terrible?'

I bat away the glow of pleasure that she's told her friends about us and make one last-ditch attempt to protect her from herself, because she needs to fucking sleep.

'Maybe I should tuck you in in the spare room,' I say sternly.

'That's never stopped you and your monster hard-on from seeking me out before.'

I burst out laughing. 'Touché, sweetheart. Touché.'

A moment later, I'm sucking in a sharp breath through my teeth as I get the final button undone and let her pyjama top drop open. She's the most exquisite creature I've ever laid eyes on. Her skin is pale and creamy, her stomach flat above the elasticated waistband of her pyjama bottoms. Her little pink nipples are already hard and begging to be pinched. Rolled. Tormented. She has a small, perfect freckle on the underside of one breast, and I trace it with my fingertip. She shivers.

If things were different between us, I'd be flipping her over before she could react and letting her feel the force of my palm.

What am I saying?

If things were different between us, I'd be making plans for us to spend Christmas together. Possibly booking a trip to the Caribbean for New Year's, if I could be sure she'd manage the jet lag. Jet lag is brutal if you have type 1.

I spend every day devising ways to coax her back here for the night, and she comes, willingly. I'm drawing her in— we're drawing *each other* in, becoming hopelessly besotted and helplessly entangled. If I ever thought it was hot when Nat fought her attraction to me, her utter submission to whatever this is is something else entirely.

Forget the trappings of wealth and respectability I've accumulated. Forget the validation, the plaudits I've earned from the business world. The pure-hearted willingness Nat shows to be with me in every way she can is the most humbling gift I've ever, ever received.

Which makes my certain knowledge that we have an expiry date even more cruel. Because we're still hiding in the shadows. I'm under no illusion that I doomed this perfect relationship to failure the day I took my fist to Stephen Bennett's eye.

A stronger man would walk away, would never have started anything in the first place. He would have left Nat alone. He wouldn't have sunk to seducing her, to gaining her trust.

But I did.

And I'm not strong enough to walk away.

Not yet, anyway.

I shake the cold, clawing sense of doom off. No point in fixating on that when I'm about to enjoy my new favourite activity. Making Natalie Bennett come undone.

'So'—I push myself up so I can straddle her—'you've been fantasising about me all evening at work, have you? What did I do to you in these torrid and most unprofessional fantasies?'

She hesitates, eyelashes fluttering as I let my palms slide over the silken skin of her stomach.

'You spanked me.'

Jesus Christ. *This woman.* She seriously has no sense of self-preservation. Now it's my turn to shiver, even as her words have me thrusting forwards so my flannel-clad cock nudges against her pelvic bone. As it does, I slide a couple of fingers under her waistband and stroke the skin there.

'Jesus fuck,' I mutter. I rear up onto my knees so I can slip these silky pyjama bottoms right off her. The sight of her neat little triangle of dark hair almost fells me. *She's letting me undress her. See her naked. Touch her. Do what I want with her. She's fantasising about my spanking her, for God's sake.* There's something so innately vulnerable about the sight of her naked body beneath me that has my heart twisting in my chest.

I tug down my own pyjamas while I'm at it and settle

back top of her for story time. She widens her legs, raising her knees so I can lie flat against her. We're both naked now, and the relief I feel is extraordinary. This is as it should be. Against my better judgement, I ask, 'What did I do, exactly?'

She smiles up at me. There's a hint of self-consciousness on her face, but it's warring with desire. Trust. 'You showed up at the club and dragged me off to one of the rooms.' She takes a deep breath.

'You can tell me,' I urge her. 'I mean, you're making it very fucking hard for me to behave here, but if you're shamelessly exploiting me in your fantasies, I deserve to know about it, right?'

She runs a hand up my bicep. 'You definitely weren't the one being shamelessly exploited. So you got me in this room, and you told me I'd been a bad, bad girl, and then you put me over your knee and pushed up my dress, and you spanked me over my panties.'

Fuuuuuuuuck. 'Were they white?' I breathe.

'Absolutely. White cotton. And then you slid them down, very slowly, and you started fingering me as you kept on spanking me. I came so hard.'

I stare at her. As far as spanking fantasies go, it should be pretty basic stuff.

But it's not.

Because it's *Nat's* little white panties and *Nat's* pretty little bottom I'm spanking and *Nat's* pussy coming all over my fingers, and she's right, she's so fucking right. We shouldn't do anything else but that.

I move against her, my cock seeking her core, and she opens wider for me.

'Sweetheart,' I groan against her pink mouth, 'we've talked about this.'

'No we haven't,' she insists. 'Not enough. You always tell

me you don't want to do it because you don't trust yourself. Well, guess what? I trust you enough for both of us. I know you're not a violent thug. Your secret's out. You're a really, really good guy. And if we both want this, then why the hell shouldn't we try it?'

'You don't know if you'll like it,' I argue. Christ, I need to bury myself so deep inside her that she'll never be the same again.

'No, but I know that if I really hate it, then you'll stop. Right?'

'Of course.' I stroke her hair.

'So give me one little spank. Pretty please?'

I reach down and press my palm to her bottom so I can squeeze. 'First you're begging me for an orgasm, now you're moving the goalposts. You're not playing fair.'

'Funny. I thought you'd love it when women beg.'

'I love it when *you* beg,' I say through gritted teeth. I release her arse and wrap my arm around her so I can flip us over. She lands on top of me, gazing down at me, her face already flushed, and God knows I will give this woman every last thing she desires, in bed and out of it.

'Ride my cock,' I tell her, and I draw my hand back so I can administer a stinging slap to her arse. Her look of shock and her surprised yelp are fucking wonderful. Her jaw drops.

'Did you like that?'

'It stung, but God, yeah.' She pushes herself upright, planting her palms on my pecs.

'Good. That's all you're getting for now. If you want me to spank you properly, then I will, but let's do it at the club. I'd rather take it out of the bedroom in case you don't enjoy it.'

Her brown eyes dance with delight. 'Seriously?'

I laugh at her reaction. 'Yes, my beautiful, dirty little minx. Now open the drawer.'

She beams at me and reaches over to open the drawer of my bedside table, frowning when she finds that it's empty of condoms. I removed them earlier when I replaced them with the printout from my latest sexual health checkup. They're in the bottom drawer now.

'Where are they?' she asks. 'We didn't use them all up, did we?'

I laugh. 'Not quite. But take a look at the paper. I'm clean. I'm not planning on going anywhere near another woman, sweetheart.' I pause, stroking my hands up the slim thighs straddling me. 'I don't know if you're on the pill or not. I'd never want to make any assumptions. But if you want to go bare, I'm game. If not, no worries. The condoms are in the bottom drawer.'

There's a beautiful smile spreading over her face. 'I have a coil in, and I hadn't slept with anyone for over a year when I met you. I had a test when we broke up, so I should be good to go.'

Taking a woman's word for it when she says she's on contraception is the ultimate rookie error when you have my financial status. That's the theory, anyway. But this is Nat, and in our dynamic, all the trust runs one way. She's taken an enormous leap of faith to trust me after everything I've put her family through, and there isn't an atom in my body that doesn't have the utmost faith in her.

'I haven't been bare with a woman for years and years,' I tell her now, my cock twitching at the way she licks her lips.

'Good,' she says as she rears up, wrapping her slim fingers around my erection, which is so desperate for release that I could erupt right this second.

The sensation of pushing into the tight channel of her body, into that slick heat, of having my flesh drag against hers with nothing between us, is so intensely pleasurable that I may black out. It's not just the sensation, though. It's the sight of her above me, her pale skin and taut pink nipples, the sight of my dick disappearing inside her beautiful body inch by inch. It has me feeling all kinds of emotions that lie heavily on my chest, pressing down just as much as she's doing with her hand as she feeds me in.

There are so many things I could say. Things I won't say, shouldn't say, shouldn't *feel*.

'You are so beautiful,' I say lamely instead, fingers flexing on her hips. 'You're the most beautiful woman I've ever seen.'

Forget the sights I just described—the disbelieving, bashful smile that spreads over her face at my words is the best of them all. I rear up, propping myself on one hand so I can cup her face and kiss her.

'Really?' she murmurs against my lips.

'Really,' I tell her. In response, she sinks down, rolling her hips to accommodate me somewhere gloriously deep inside her body as I bottom out. I groan into her mouth, my tongue coaxing hers, because she was absolutely fucking right, as always.

This is far better than sleep.

'Well, you're the most beautiful man I've ever seen,' she says a little shyly. 'Every part of you is so perfect.' She shifts, wrapping her arms tightly around me as she buries her face in my neck. 'I—I don't know how to handle it, really.'

In a minute, I'll lie back down so I can thrust inside her properly as she rides me. I'll give her that friction she craves so badly.

But for now, just for a moment, I band my arm around her, and I sit with this.

This sensation.

This emotion.

This staggering, terrifying, awe-inspiring intimacy we're sharing.

48

ADAM

I've just caught my new girlfriend staring at my old mate for the third time since I introduced them twenty minutes ago in the bar at Alchemy. It's her night off, and this evening is supposed to be about my carrying her off to a room and spanking that pretty little arse until it's perfectly pink and she's begging me to fuck her.

It's *not* supposed to be about watching her make eyes at Gabriel fucking Sullivan.

I lean in, putting my mouth to her ear. 'Should I be jealous?'

She starts and giggles. 'No, not at all. It's just—'

'Just what?'

'Don't you think he looks like the devil? Like, if the devil was in human form, *that's* what he'd look like.'

I can't help it. I guffaw so forcefully I send champagne splashing over the rim of my flute and onto my trousers. Bugger.

'I'm serious.' She brushes ineffectually at my thigh. 'He looks... satanic.'

I laugh again. 'Do you know what his former profession was, until he succumbed to the dark side a few months ago?' I whisper in her ear, enjoying that delicate floral scent on her skin, the way she shivers at the proximity of my mouth. I cover the palm on my thigh with mine and intertwine our fingers.

'What?' She turns to face me.

I say the words against her lips. 'A *priest.*'

She throws her head back and laughs, and I sit there grinning at the beautiful sight of my girlfriend when she's tickled pink. 'You're pulling my leg.'

'Nope. He was a man of the cloth. And leaving the priesthood was a source of great distress to him, so when callous little wenches compare him to Satan it's pretty fucking rude.'

She's still laughing when she returns her lips to mine. 'Don't tell him, then. God, he must have had a very female-heavy congregation.'

I shake my head at her. 'Got a thing for priests, do you?'

'Hot ones, yeah. Me and every other woman out there. I blame *Fleabag.* Do you know there's a full-on confessional in one of the rooms downstairs? Rafe had it installed.'

I laugh. 'Did he, now? Kinky bastard. There won't be any of that happening once his wife pops.'

Her perfect little tongue peeks out and licks a line along my lower lip. 'I bet you'd look hot in a dog collar. We should try it sometime.'

I thread my fingers lazily through her glossy mane of hair. She looks glorious tonight in a short, sexy red dress. I know for a fact that, just as we've agreed, she's wearing pristine white panties underneath it.

Perfect for being spanked.

'Just say when, you dirty little sinner, and I'll be there.

God knows, you'll carry out your penance on your knees for me.'

It's not until a little later, when Darcy's turned up with Max and their other partner Dex and Nat's scooted away from me to chat happily with Gen and Darcy that we guys have a chance to catch up more closely.

'You look shattered, mate,' I observe to Gabe. I suspect Nat's take is correct—he definitely has a look of the diabolical about him, and that tortured demon thing he's got going on is certainly a hit with the women, even if the shadows under his dark eyes are more black than purple.

'Burning the candle,' he admits with a sheepish swipe of his hand across his forehead.

'Oh yeah?'

The Sullivan family office is a behemoth. Gabe's grandfather emigrated from Ireland, he and his sons—Gabe's father included—amassing enormous fortunes by winning contracts to rebuild huge swathes of the east London docklands. Gabe ostensibly left the priesthood to take over the management of the family wealth when his old man retired. It's a full-on family office: they have several billion pounds of assets under management. I've always had the impression there's more to the story than that, but he holds his cards close to his chest. Contrary to any perception his looks may encourage, he's a thoroughly decent guy, even if he's intense as fuck.

'I'm pretty stressed at the moment. And when I'm stressed, I need to let off steam. You know what I mean,' he adds with a meaningful jerk of his head towards The Playroom.

'Fuck knows how you lasted as a priest.'

That gets a tired laugh. 'Nothing about being a priest was stressful—except the celibacy part, obviously.'

'Is Alchemy your only outlet, then?' I ask, amused, because I'm sure he doesn't find it hard to get dates.

'It's the most time-efficient and least emotionally painful outlet,' he admits, and I chuckle. 'I don't have time for dating or remembering to call women. That's a full-time job in its own right.'

'Alchemy definitely knows its target customer,' I muse. I'm pretty sure mega-successful, time-poor guys like Gabe, who would otherwise be fending off gold-diggers left, right and centre, are precisely the reason the club is thriving as much as it is.

All of which bodes very well indeed for my new stake in its overseas JVs.

'Yeah. It's fucking impossible to stay away from. Hence I'm here at ten o'clock at night, champing at the bit to get my dick wet next door when I should be at home, out cold on the sofa with a pile of reports on my lap.'

I'm tempted to keep taking the piss out of him for being a horny former priest, but an idea hits me before I get the chance. 'You know,' I say slowly, 'Anton may have an even more time-efficient solution for you.' I lean over Gabe to tear my mentor's attention away from Max, his successor and closest friend.

'What's that dodgy agency you pretend very hard not to own? Celestial or something.'

'Seraph,' he and Max chorus. Max's entire face brightens with a dirty grin at the thought of it.

I nudge Gabe. 'Think I might have found Seraph their next punter.'

Gabe's frowning. 'I'm not familiar. What kind of agency?'

Max and Anton exchange a conspiratorial glance.

'Executive assistants,' Anton says. 'The best in the world. They all have MBAs from the top schools.'

'*Full service* executive assistants,' Max interjects. 'These women will meet every need you didn't know you had during office hours. I swear to God, you'll never need to go looking for sex again.'

I laugh, because it's all dodgy as fuck and also absolute genius, if you think about it. Anton founded Seraph during one of his marriages, as far as I remember, but he definitely made use of it before he met Gen.

'What was the name of that EA you had?' I ask, screwing up my face with the effort of recalling her name.

'Athena,' he says quietly with a glance over at Gen, who's in full swing and oblivious to the turn our chat has taken.

'Jesus fucking Christ, Athena,' Max groans, letting his head collapse in his hands. 'She was so fucking sexy. And so *obliging*. Good God.'

'What was the score with her?' Dex asks, looking as bewildered as Gabe is. Max raises his head and leans over to him, whispering in his ear as he threads his fingers through Dex's. I watch in amusement as Dex's eyes widen. 'Oh, wow.'

'Wow is right,' Anton says.

Gabe's gaze is flitting from him to Max. 'How does it work, exactly?' I'd put money on that casual tone of his being studied.

Anton shrugs. 'Pretty straightforward. We launched it precisely for men like you, my friend. Cash rich, time poor, too stressed, and can't be fucked with the high-maintenance women you most likely attract. The EAs Seraph offers are ridiculously smart, completely overqualified, and absolutely stunning. And they'll remove every single stress from your working day like you wouldn't believe.'

'They'll run your diary and ride your cock,' Max offers cheerfully, and I snigger.

Anton shoots him a withering look. 'Oh, to have had your marketing expertise when we launched it.'

'Anyway,' Max continues blithely, 'Athena was Anton's EA. Lovely girl, and sometimes Anton shared her with me like the good mate he is. She's a spectacular fuck.'

'I took the best they had to offer for myself,' Anton says, smug bastard. 'Obviously. And she was worth every penny.' He gives his friend a sly sideways look. 'That's why, when you take bonuses into account, I paid her more than I ever paid Max.'

Gabe, Dex and I fall about laughing at the look of utter disgust on Max's face, but he recovers well.

'God knows what kind of bonuses you gave her, but she can keep them. She was young enough to be your daughter, you revolting old lech.'

Anton grins widely. 'She loved it. So did I. But'—he slaps Max hard on the thigh—'I have zero regrets about parting ways with her. I think you and I can both safely say we lucked out with the beautiful Carew sisters. And with you, too, Dex, of course,' he adds hurriedly.

Dex coughs. 'Touching, thanks Anton.'

But I don't miss the softness on his face as he and Max eye-fuck each other. Trust Max Hunter to find epic, ever-lasting love with a seemingly wonderful man *and* a stun-ningly beautiful woman.

When Gabe recovers from his laughing fit, he looks trou-bled. 'I don't know. Paying for it seems... excessive. I mean, is it even legal?'

'We manage the paperwork so it's all above board,' Anton says smoothly. 'So don't worry about that. Just think of it as a turnkey solution, if you like. One incredible woman meeting all your needs before you even know you have them. She'll have everything running smoothly. Honestly, an executive assistant from Seraph will just make all the pain points go away, on all fronts. You'll never look back. It's astounding, really.'

Gabe swirls his ice cubes around in his now-empty tumbler, not meeting Anton's eye. 'And you say this Athena is the best.'

'Everyone on their books is great. But Athena's a very special person—incredibly adept on all fronts, if you catch my drift. You really would be in very capable hands with her. I have no idea if she's working at the moment, but just say the word and I'll make some calls.'

'Thanks.' Gabe sets down his tumbler and stands, tiredly, it seems. 'I appreciate it. It's a lot to think about, though. I'll let you know, if that's okay? I'd better head next door and get myself sorted out. Good seeing you all.'

'Try not to fall asleep on the job,' I call after him.

Poor, exhausted fucker.

I glance over at Nat. She's laughing at something Darcy's saying, head thrown back, white throat on display. Her long legs are crossed elegantly, the short, flirty hem of her scarlet dress showcasing toned thighs.

Yep.

It's definitely time to take my girl next door and intro-duce her to the mind-blowing transformation a firm hand can have on her sexual experiences.

49

ADAM

The sex Nat and I have in my bed is terrific: hot, intimate, intense.

But we've come here tonight for a specific reason—to push her boundaries and take the insane chemistry between us to the next level.

She's already given me the greatest, most precious gift: her total trust. Now it's my turn to give *her* a gift. Tonight, I intend to show her just how sweet complete trust and total submission can feel for her.

Tonight, I intend to show her another side of myself. A darker, more shadowy side, as well concealed as it is integral to the man I am, the needs I have.

There's no doubt I'm falling hard for Nat. I'm unspeakably grateful for every part of our fledgling relationship. I want her on her terms, and I'll do everything in my power to ensure she feels safe, cared for, when she's with me.

But if she enjoys what I have in store for her tonight, if it unleashes some part of her that's remained hidden even from herself until now, then God help my heart, because the sky is the limit for what she and I can share together.

We've prepped for this. Discussed my plans, her limits. She has a shiny new safe word, *organza*, that's as feminine and delicate as my girlfriend. But when I close the door of the private room behind me with a soft thud, there's no denying the intoxicating mix of apprehension and anticipation on her face.

'Come here, beautiful,' I say. My tone is a caress, but the command in my words is unmistakable.

She does as I ask, and I watch her like a tiger eyeing up its supper. She's immaculate tonight. I know she felt self-conscious about joining us for drinks as my girlfriend, so I suspect it was a—wholly unnecessary—desire to make a good impression that had her pulling out all the stops, but God knows there's another benefit to the way she looks, and that is that every single perfect detail makes me want to undo her all the more.

Her lips are scarlet, just like her dress. She must have touched up her lipstick when she went to the loo just now. Her hair is in a sleek ponytail, a segment of hair cleverly concealing the hair tie. She's in sheer stockings and a pair of black patent Louboutin pumps that I insisted were more of a gift for me than for her when I bought them last weekend.

The dress itself is apparently one of her samples, and it's fucking magnificent: a classy little fit-and-flare number with a round neck, capped sleeves, a nipped-in waist, and a short, flirty skirt that'll flip up so fucking nicely when I have her on my knee.

Before I show her what we're both capable of, I have another job for her. One that will remind her who's boss tonight.

When she stops in front of me, I wind her ponytail around my hand and tilt her head so she's looking up at me.

There's a small smile playing on her red lips. The way they curve has me licking mine in anticipation.

'First things first.' My voice is low. Even. I'm in control here without raising it a decibel. 'Get on your knees and take my cock out. I want to see that pretty lipstick make an even prettier ring around it.'

I wait. Her eyes widen slightly, and I imagine it's a departure for her, having me speak to her like this. I haven't been this dispassionate since that first night in this same room, when I had the time of my life coaxing her into betraying every last one of her principles for the prize of my mouth on her cunt.

'Of course, sir,' she says, just as evenly, and I press my lips together to prevent a smile.

My perfect little Nat. God forbid I should forget what a worthy adversary she is when she's riled.

Every single time.

She sinks to her knees gracefully, her palm brushing down the front of my shirt as she does. As she unzips my flies, she glances up. The sight of her upturned face, her huge doe eyes, her crimson lips, is so perfectly pleasing that I allow myself to strum her lower lip gently with my thumb. It's so soft. So pillowy.

When she opens for me and slides those lips up the length of my fully hard cock, I practically pass out. Her mouth is fantastically, wickedly, wet. She drags it back down my length, her little tongue moving over my throbbing crown with the most decadent licks and a ring of scarlet branding my cock with her mark.

Quite right.

I close my hands over her ears and work her head up and down. I won't be able to withstand the devilish skill of her mouth for long, but I can't bring myself to pull away just yet. Instead, I stand, paralysed by desire, as I fuck her face. Her hands claw at my thighs, and the little noises she's making at the back of her throat are winding me even higher.

Fuck it. I'll make her get me off like this. It'll take the edge off, allow me to prolong her pleasure before I'm sinking into her like a man crazed.

'Hmm, make me come, sweetheart,' I grit out, my fingers flexing on the sides of her head. 'Show me what this sinful little mouth can do before you earn my hand on your arse and my fingers inside your pussy.'

The sound she makes around my cock is strangled and hungry, and fucking hell. She's so damn good at this. She has a hand wrapped around my base as she laps at me, her saliva smoothing the fine, fine drags of her mouth up and down as she takes me in, over and over, like *such* a good girl.

'You're so good,' I hiss. 'So obedient. I'm going to fuck you so hard after I've spanked you. Just wait and see. You won't be able to sit down for a week.'

My words have her moaning more loudly and working me harder, and I marvel at the miracle of having this exquisite woman on her knees for me as my arousal spirals around me. I'm at the centre of the most perfect storm, helpless against its force as it whips me into a state of utter frenzy. The heat shooting up my spine, searing my balls and cock as the latter hardens impossibly and I shudder my orgasm into Natalie's warm, willing mouth.

I can barely stand. This is a full-body onslaught. It's been building since I sat down with her and our friends next door, all too aware of those little white panties under that stunning scarlet dress. Of the silken skin of her arse waiting for my hands to mark it.

And now it's her turn.

50

NATALIE

Adam helps me off my knees. They're stiff from the floor, and my legs are shaking from the intensity of what just went down. He tilts my face up to him and gently uses the pad of his thumb to wipe away the tears I shed during his face-fucking, sucking his thumb into his mouth.

That was pretty brutal, and I fucking loved it. I loved how he used me, how commanding he was, how insanely hard his dick was when I sucked it. I *adore* having that effect on him. He's breathing hard, his pupils still blown out, his irises thin rings of pale blue, gaze darting over my face as though he can't believe I'm real.

He pulls his thumb from his mouth. He has the most perfect mouth I've ever seen. The most perfect *face* I've ever seen. I hook my hand around his neck and tug him down for a kiss. I'm so turned on, so desperate for more of him. His mouth is soft, but his kiss is hard, and I lean into it. I'll take whatever I can get, though God knows, I'll need far more than this to relieve the ache between my legs.

'You are extraordinary,' he whispers against my lips when he breaks the kiss. 'Are you wet for me?'

'So wet,' I manage, my eyes locked on his.

'Do you need to come?'

'So badly.'

'Do you need a good spanking first?'

Jesus Christ, what is it about those words? Why, at the mere thought of Adam putting me over his knee and letting rip on my bare bottom, am I a puddle of lust on the floor?

'God, yes, please.'

'Such a good girl,' he murmurs, releasing me and strolling over to the bed, tucking himself back in as he does so. He sits on the end, as far back as he can get, so the end of the bed hits the backs of his knees.

Then he pats his lap. 'Come here. On your stomach.'

Oh my God. I'm not sure how to do this elegantly. I climb onto the bed and lower myself down so I'm draped sideways across his lap, along the end of the bed, my pelvic bone pressed against him and my elbows propped on the black satin sheets.

I've been so intimate with Adam these past few weeks, in so many ways, but everything feels different tonight. The air is thick with the tension of what he's about to do to me. What I want him to do to me.

Nerves are sparking in my stomach as he puts one hand between my shoulder blades to indicate that I should flop my shoulders downwards and lie prone as his other one brushes upwards between my legs, burrowing under my dress until it finds the top of one of my stockings.

One by one, he rolls the nylon down my legs and tugs them off before flipping the skirt of my dress up and over so my bum, in its virginal white panties, is on display for him. Despite the warmth of the room, the air feels cooler on my exposed skin, and I shiver as he caresses me through the fabric, his deft hands roaming over white cotton and pressing between my cheeks. I can't see his face, and those lost social cues make the anticipation even more delicious as I await my fate.

'Mmm,' he murmurs, rubbing my bum, grabbing at the flesh before stroking down my thighs and circling back. 'I've wanted to do this since pretty much the first time I laid eyes on you.'

'Really?' I croak.

'Mmm-hmm. And *definitely* since you stayed that first night and were such an ungrateful little brat.'

I laugh, despite myself. 'I was provoked. And you were seriously thinking of spanking me then?'

'Yeah.' He runs a single fingertip under the rear elastic of my panties, and I suck in a breath and widen my legs slightly, because I need him to touch me. I need him to stop teasing me, winding me higher with his words and his fingers, and just get to it.

'You were in those leggings that Clem got for you,' he continues, 'and your arse looked so fucking peachy, and you were so bloody hostile, and I knew if I bent you over the kitchen island I could shut you up very effectively. Unfortunately for you, I've finally got my chance.'

He punctuates this ominous statement by running his finger down, down, under the elastic of my panties, until he hits my pussy, and swiping through it languorously. I practically shoot off the bed.

'Oh my God,' I moan.

'Wet, aren't you?' he croons. 'Think how good it's going to be after I've spanked you a few times. Fuck, these panties are sexy. I need you to count for me, sweetheart. If you can last till ten, I promise I'll reward you.'

I've barely had time to react when he pulls his finger away and his hand comes down hard on my right cheek. The sting and the sound are equally shocking, and I let out a little cry before he smooths his hand soothingly over my smarting skin.

'One,' he prompts when I don't say anything.

'One.' My voice is shaky.

'Good girl.' He slaps the other cheek. Oh Jesus.

'Two.' I scrabble at the sheets. It's not like it's particular painful. I think it's more the shock, and the lack of control, that's bothersome.

When he's spanked me five times, he rewards me by pulling my panties right down and exposing my bottom, rubbing one hand over my bare skin as he reaches between my legs with the other and pushes a couple of fingers roughly inside me. I'm so sensitive there, and holy fucking Christ, it feels so good. I moan loudly and wriggle.

'Stay still,' he orders, massaging my bum as he finger fucks me slowly. I groan, because staying still is almost as difficult as staying quiet.

'Jesus,' he rasps. 'You're wetter than I've ever felt you, sweetheart. A couple of spanks and my filthy girl is practically spurting all over my fingers.' He drives them in again. He's not lying. The sound of my greedy body sucking him in is *loud.*

'Fuck,' he says, sounding anguished. 'On second thoughts, get up on your knees. I want this greedy little cunt in the air for me.'

God, yes. I want that. I want to be even more exposed to his magic hands. He removes his fingers, and I pull myself up so my bum is in the air and my chest is pressed to the bed, as if I'm attempting some kind of cobra pose.

'Ready?' he asks before using his left hand to press my

shoulders down and administering spank number six. This time, he doesn't attempt to soothe my skin but instead immediately jams his fingers back inside me, and the jolt of stimulation is so gloriously intense that I gasp as I push against them.

'I really think you're enjoying this,' he muses in a voice of quiet satisfaction.

'I am,' I plead.

He pulls out his fingers and strikes me, harder this time. Back in they thrust as I count aloud, twisting inside me in a way that's borderline brutal and so fucking good I might actually die.

By the time we reach nine, I'm so aroused I can barely count. I may still be flinching at each spank, but Adam's diabolical spin on Pavlov has my insatiable pussy overriding the pain in favour of the reward it expects each time.

'Ten!' I scream in victory and anticipation.

'Good God,' Adam groans. 'Such a good fucking girl, letting me spank you like that. You did so well. Feel this, sweetheart.'

This is those magical fingers again, but it feels like three this time, because the burn is real. He keeps his other arm banded around my shoulders as he works my pussy with deep, deliberate strokes. And when his thumb finds my poor, swollen clit, I press the side of my face deeper into the mattress and my pussy into his hand.

I don't know if it's the spanking-related endorphins (with which some googling has acquainted me), or the relief of not only surviving but adoring Adam's "punishment", or the simple pleasure of a gorgeous, stern man putting me over his knee and then finger-fucking me into oblivion as I writhe upside down on his lap, but I'm on the brink.

He pauses. 'Say *please, sir, make me come.*'

'Please, sir, make me come,' I gabble. I'll do anything, say anything, to get my mitts on this promised orgasm.

'That's my very good girl. *Now* you can move that gorgeous little arse,' he tells me, and I do. I drink in every bit of sensation I possibly can. His movements are rough, his fingers invasive, probing and rubbing me as hard as they can. It's too intense, too glorious, this relentless assault on my most aroused parts, and when the searing heat grows too much. I'm flooded, engulfed, with the molten lava of my orgasm as it takes me under.

51

ADAM

There's no going back from this dynamic.

Nat, so prettily on her knees for me, sucking my cock so well.

Nat, pliant and shuddering and greedy on my lap as I spanked her arse and finger fucked her little pink cunt.

And now, Nat, a post-orgasmic heap of long, pale limbs and crumpled red silk, lying face-down on the bed as I grow impossibly harder beneath her.

'Roll over, sweetheart,' I say gently to her after removing my fingers, and she does so with what feels like the effort required by a body leaden with pleasure. I gaze down at her flushed face, her smudged mascara, glassy eyes.

She'll do very nicely indeed.

Nope, there's definitely no going back from here.

'Clean up the mess you made on my fingers like a good girl,' I say, sliding them into her mouth. Her eyes widen, but she sucks obediently until I remove them.

'How do you feel?' Her dress is twisted, its skirt still bundled up around her waist, panties down around her knees. I smooth a hand up her thighs and over the neat strip of dark hair on her pubic bone, and she shivers.

'Like I want you to put me over your knee every single hour of every day from now on,' she slurs, and I laugh. I'm a missionary of the Church of Corporal Punishment, my beautiful, sensual girlfriend my newest and loveliest recruit.

I'm desperate to push inside her while she's like this—swollen and sated and glowing. I wrap an arm around her shoulders and another under her knees and manage to get us both to standing.

'Turn around, sweetheart,' I tell her, unzipping her dress at the back as soon as she does and letting it slide down her body and to the ground. Her bra follows, and I get down on one knee to tug her panties the rest of the way down until she's naked. I pause for a moment on bended knee, trans-fixed by the sight of her before me, by this perfect bottom, its cheeks still pleasingly flushed from my ministrations.

With a hand lightly on each of her hips, I lean forward and kiss each pinked-up cheek in turn. As I rise, I trace the delicate bumps of her spinal column with my lips until I'm standing behind her and burying my face in her neck as my dick flexes against her lower back.

Ravenous as I am to be inside her body, I'm loath to sully a moment that her trust in me has distilled to an essence of such perfect purity. I slide my arms around her waist, and she crosses her own, pressing her palms to my forearms.

'You are the most exquisite woman I have ever met,' I confess into the silken sanctuary of her neck. 'The most exquisite, and the most extraordinary.' She says nothing, but turns in my arms, her mouth finding mine as though she needs my kiss to set a seal of truth on my words.

I know how she feels. Nothing about the way we are, the path we've forged, feels believable.

As our kiss amps up from exploratory to desperate, this glut of unfamiliar emotions, as enthralling as they are unsettling, morphs into blinding physical need.

'I need you on your hands and knees,' I say hoarsely against her mouth, my hands doing laps of her back and arse. 'Face the headboard.'

She smiles. With the way my dick is painting her skin with precum, she can't be surprised I need this outlet.

'Of course, sir,' she says, turning away from me, and it strikes me that what I'm about to do to her will mirror that first night in here with that other woman—Rose, wasn't it?

I almost laugh at how discomfited I felt when I realised I was fantasising about Nat when I fucked her. She seemed a lovely woman, but God knows, the pleasure of watching my naked girlfriend crawl up that bed is akin to one's first view of a real Monet after knowing only poor counterfeits.

This is what I want. Who I want. Her pale skin and now-messy dark ponytail, the curve of her spine and the narrowness of her waist and the vulnerability with which she exposes all her most sacred holes to me in this position is a veritable gift. She's a madonna, and I intend to show her just how she should be worshipped.

I shed every last item of clothing with impressive speed and climb onto the bed, nudging her legs apart with my knee and closing the space between us, smoothing one hand over her hip and arse as I wrap the other around my cock and swipe it experimentally through her still-slick pussy. Nope. No need for lube here.

'Nat, Nat, Nat,' I murmur. 'What a very soaked girl you are.'

She groans. 'Hurry up, for god's sake.'

'Whatever you say, princess.' My tone may be amused, but I'm deadly serious. Whatever this beautiful woman wants, she gets. *Especially* if it's my dick buried deep inside her body.

My fingers flex on her hip as I push in. It's awe-inspiring, every single time we do this. But to be sinking into her when she's just let me spank her, when the clean smacks of my hand have echoed through the air and she's come all over my fingers, is another privilege entirely. I push my way in, grunting and sweating, revelling in the luxurious way her plush inner walls blanket my length, welcoming it even as she shifts to accommodate me.

I'm in, and here's that quiet moment of stillness and awe again before I move, as we marvel at how perfectly we fit. How right and good and elemental it feels in a way I'm not sure anything has before.

'You ready, sweetheart?' I ask in a voice more cracked with emotion than I intended, and I'm rewarded with the turn of her head and the swish of her ponytail and the astonishing radiance of her smile as she takes in the sight of me, reared up proudly behind her, primed to take her.

'More than ready.'

I roll my hips and grin at the breathy sound she makes. This is the best fucking game in the world.

'Tell me how it feels.'

'So full.' She drops her head back down, her shoulders flexing as I drag my length slowly, slowly out. 'And so—*God*, so intense.' A pause. 'Emotionally, I mean. It's a lot.'

Yes. Yes it is.

'I know.' I smooth a hand down her back. 'I feel it too, my sweet, sweet girl. Let me show you.'

I slam back into her and lose myself in staggering pleasure: the tease of my flesh dragging against hers; the sight of my hard, angry dick disappearing inside her over and over;

the impossibly delicate architecture of her beautiful little body.

The climax to which she brought me with her perfect lips around me just minutes ago is forgotten, a ghost of pleasure past, the promise of the delight to come the only thing upon which my hungry body and my soaring soul can fixate.

As I fuck this beautiful woman harder and harder, her own thrusts and whimpers and pleas a constant feed of oxygen to the fire burning inside me, the intensity of it consumes me. I don't stand a chance as she pushes back against me, more and more greedily each time, as she begs me in a voice rendered hoarse by her own need to fuck her harder.

She crests, crying out and taking it all so beautifully as her internal muscles clamp around me. But it's my name on her lips that finishes me off.

'Sweetheart, I—' I begin. 'Dear God, you're so beautiful. Feel what you do to me. Can you feel it?'

I mean, of course, the impossible hardness of my cock as it swells. As I hold still against her and spill and spill and spill.

But as I collapse over her, wrapping my arms around her stomach and shoulders before hauling her up against me, it strikes me that she can't possibly comprehend the enormity of what she does to me.

52

ADAM

I have a perfect winter's Sunday planned for me and Nat today: a walk in Windsor Great Park followed by lunch at a fantastic pub just outside the palace gates. The pub may be ancient—and tiny—but those in the know come far and wide for its roast sirloin.

All of which makes it extremely exasperating that I've woken up feeling bloody awful and realising that the mere thought of roast beef makes me want to hurl.

I don't get sick these days. It's a point of pride for me to maintain my immune system in ship-shape condition. I follow an anti-inflammatory diet, for the most part, designed by my nutritionist, Louise, and executed by Kamyl. I take enough supplements each day to make me rattle. I don't drink much—especially since meeting Nat. I make regular use of both the ice bath and infrared sauna in my basement. I meditate and adhere to a workout regime that balances the obligatory weights and cardio with more somatic movement to maintain my mind-body connection.

That is to say, someone who manages their wellbeing

and immune system in the tightly controlled way that I do has no business feeling this bloody horrific.

I lie there for a while, careful not to wake Nat, who's slumbering peacefully next to me, as I edge the covers off me. It's still dark outside. I'm boiling hot and my head feels like a power drill has taken up residence inside it. The pain is so bad I can barely move. I try to turn my head towards Nat, but a flash of agony sears my skull.

Fuck.

I'm unsure how long I spend in this tortuous state, but at some point, a dim grey light bleeds into the edges of my blinds and Nat rolls towards me, tucking her lithe, naked body against mine. It's a move I'd usually treasure, but I'm too fucking hot to endure any further human heat.

Thankfully, she rolls right away as though I've scorched her.

'Woah. You're like a furnace.'

I groan my agreement, and she puts a hand to my forehead.

'Jesus, honey, you're burning up.' She scoots onto her knees and gazes down at me, her lovely face tight with concern. 'How do you feel? You definitely have a fever.'

'Don't feel my best,' I croak, because I'm not one to whine. There's precisely nothing to be gained from self pity. I learnt that lesson a long time ago. 'I'll just...'

I'll just grab some meds is what I'm thinking as I attempt to swing my legs over the edge of the bed, but I find I have neither the energy nor the mental capacity to construct the end of the sentence. Nor, it seems, do I have the energy to get out of bed.

'No!' Nat shouts. 'What are you doing?! Don't move. Stay there.'

She leaps out of my bed and pads over to my bathroom,

where I hear her rummaging around in the medicine cabinet under the huge vanity. She emerges and comes around to sit on my side of the bed.

'Let's get you dosed up, and then I can call Dyson?' Her voice is hesitant, and I nod. The retainer I pay him is certainly hefty enough to warrant disturbing him first thing on a Sunday morning. This feels like a textbook flu, so there's not a huge amount he can do. But at the very least, he can administer an IV or two and help me feel slightly more human.

Nat busies herself with popping capsules from the Nurofen and Lemsip packets. She lays them on my bedside table and grabs one of the extra pillows from the floor before slowly, carefully, putting her arm around my neck. Even with her help supporting my weight, the effort of raising my head enough to insert the extra pillow behind it is agony. I suck in an involuntary breath through my teeth.

'Poor baby,' she says, bending to kiss my forehead. She stuffs the pillow behind me and I lean back against it gratefully. The shock waves of pain recede as I still, and this elevated position feels better for the pressure inside my head, full stop.

She feeds me two of the capsules before picking up the glass of water I took to bed and holding it to my lips. I swallow, and then swallow the next two capsules. I'm not the biggest fan of pharmaceuticals, but fuck knows I'll do anything to relieve this pain in my head and the terrible cramping in every muscle in my body. I feel a hundred years old.

'Thanks,' I murmur, letting my eyes drift closed. 'Just give me an hour and then we can get going.'

I hear a little laugh. She brushes my hair off my face before placing a damp washcloth over my forehead—she must have grabbed it from the bathroom. It feels wonderfully cool, and I hum my appreciation.

'You're not going anywhere, mister,' she whispers. 'Your only job today is to rest and get better. Okay?'

I frown, and the washcloth shifts. 'But what about...'

'Nothing.' She readjusts the washcloth and gently presses down on it with her hand. 'Today we're chilling. I'll cancel the pub.'

For fuck's sake. I had very specific plans for today, and they involved showing Nat what my Aston Martin is capable of before strolling around Windsor with her like a lovesick puppy and feeding her forkfuls of Yorkshire pudding. Sundays are precious when you work as hard as she does. I wanted to make today count. At least once Dyson gets here, she can escape and salvage her day. See her family, maybe. Catch up with some friends.

But I don't have the energy to say any of that.

The next hour is a blur. Dyson shows up with a nurse who sticks a needle in my arm, telling me this IV should sort me out.

'Trish will stay with you,' he tells me. 'Nasty fever you've got, though plenty of rest and fluids should do the trick. Looks like a standard flu to me.'

While I'm pretty sure I pay him far too much for that kind of vague diagnosis, I'm also aware that there's not much doctors can do to treat the flu except manage the symptoms and provide relief.

Trish is far too chirpy for my liking. She can't be far off retirement age, and while she seems capable, she's already exhausting.

'Don't worry, my dear, I'll stay right here,' she trills in a soft Edinburgh accent. Oh dear God.

'Just stay downstairs, thanks,' I tell her hurriedly. 'I'll call if I need you.'

'Right you are, dearie,' she says with a beam and thankfully takes her leave with Dyson.

I squeeze Natalie's hand. She's been sitting beside me on the bed this whole time. 'You can head off, too,' I tell her. 'Trish will keep an eye on me.'

'Are you kidding me?' she asks. 'Of course I'm not leaving you! I'm staying right here. Just let me grab some breakfast and I'll be right back, okay?'

Of course she needs to eat. I hate that I didn't think of that. I hate that she's here, fussing over me, when I should be the one caring for her, making sure she has everything she needs to stabilise her glucose levels.

'Go,' I growl, feeling frustrated and shitty and guilty in equal measure. 'Go and feed yourself. I'll be fine.'

She hesitates before bending to drop a kiss on my cheek. 'I'll see you shortly.'

I'm alone in my cell. My dickhead of a cellmate, Ronan, is in the infirmary—lucky twat—but they don't have room for me. A brutal flu has swept through the prison, felling an alarming number of inmates and staff. That's what I hear, anyway. They've locked us down, but I'm far too ill to leave my cell even if I wanted to.

Jesus, I'm burning up. I soaked through my sheets last night and they fucking stink, so I pulled them off and threw them on the floor. Now I lie on my bare, rubber-covered mattress, slick and revolting with sweat, in a world of pain.

I swear I can feel my pulse pounding in my skull, so badly does my head throb. Every muscle in my body is atrophying. I'm as weak as a kitten. With the staff decimated by illness, the only care we're getting in our cells is a couple of capsules of paracetamol with our meals three times a day and the recommendation to drink as much of the metallic-tasting water from our in-cell washbasins as we can to keep our fluids up.

I open my eyes with the intention of rolling off my bunk and crawling over to the basin. I'm on the bottom bunk, but even that seems an impossible mission right now. My vision is pin-pricks—probably dehydration. I remember collapsing en route to the bathroom when I was younger and suffering from chickenpox. This feels like that: a helpless, hopeless chaos of delirium and misery.

Even Mum was a better caretaker than the screws are.

I've been in here for four months. I thought spending Christmas Day behind bars with only my relentless grief and guilt was a low point, but this is the fucking pits.

I close my eyes again.

I hear a voice. 'Addy. It's okay, Addy.' A plastic stethoscope is pressed to my chest. A tiny hand soothes my sweaty brow. 'Nurse Ellen is here.'

I've told her so many times that Addy's a girl's name. It used to make her laugh so much, the little monkey. Still, I fucking loved it.

'Addy's sick.'

I know she can't really be here. But it seems so real, and this hallucination is a blessed silver lining—a message from my baby sister that I'm not entirely alone in this godforsaken hell-hole. I'm not prepared to open my eyes and face reality just yet.

The puddle of sweat on my mattress has cooled, and

now I'm shivering uncontrollably. Jesus fucking *Christ*. From somewhere in my broken, dehydrated body, the tears appear, and I begin to weep.

'Adam.' *She's saying it correctly now. What happened to* Addy? 'Adam, honey. It's me. You're okay.'

'Ellen,' I whisper. Fuck, my mouth is dry and my lips feel like they might crack open.

I'm pretty sure she sobs. 'No, honey. It's Nat. You're okay. I'm here.'

Nat? At her name, at the jolt of recognition that rocks me as I traverse that trippy chasm from delirium to lucidity, I open my eyes. Ellen's gone, drifting backwards through some celestial portal, no doubt, but I swear I can feel her presence. My first rational thought, though, is relief. Yeah, I'm still shivering, but I'm in my bed. In my *home*. Not in that cell that will haunt me for the rest of my days. And my beautiful Nat is here.

I'm safe.

'It's okay,' she croons, taking the now-cold compress off my forehead. I look up at her, startled and unsure, my heart pounding. My face is wet with tears, but her beautiful brown eyes are tear-filled, too. Why is she crying?

'Jesus, you're shivering,' she says, sniffing and blinking briskly, like she's trying to pull herself together. She grabs a tissue from the bedside table and wipes the tears from under my eyes. 'Let me grab Trish and we'll change your sheets. They're soaked through.'

'No.' With what feels like herculean effort, I reach up and snag her wrist. 'Stay with me for a sec.'

'Okay,' she says softly. 'Of course.' She extricates her

wrist and rounds the bed so she can climb on and snuggle up next to me. 'You were asking for Ellen.' Her voice is so quiet and hesitant. 'I didn't know what—are you all right?'

God, I feel so stupid. She must think I'm a nutter. My voice sounds thick, sluggish, as I hasten to reassure her. It hasn't caught up to my inner panic. My confusion.

'I was having a nightmare, I think. I'm not sure. I dreamt I was in prison—or remembered.' It must have been a flash-back of some description. It was precisely the same as that horrific bout of flu I had my first winter there—minus the saintly apparition of my late baby sister.

None of the unpleasant physical symptoms of being ill or having a fever come close to the horror of that terrifying hinterland in which I just found myself. It has me deter-mined to stay awake. I can't bear to be sucked down into that dystopian twilight again.

'It's over now,' she says, stroking my hair off my head. 'I'm here. You're safe.'

53

ADAM

My continuing physical misery aside, I feel pretty damn contented to be sitting in the library with Nat. Yesterday was a blur of pain and sweating and even fucking hallucinations. This morning, I'm nowhere near ready to head back in the office, but I'm feeling strong enough to allow her to tuck me up lengthways on the sofa, pillows stuffed behind me and a cashmere throw over my lower half.

She's sitting at the other end of the sofa, by my feet, her laptop on her knees. To my immense frustration, she refused point-blank to go into work today, just like she refused point-blank to leave my side yesterday after she found me weeping like a baby for my dead sister.

Fuck that was horrible.

And mortifying as hell.

When I continued to drone on about how embarrassed I was, she remarked that it was far less embarrassing than when she drooled all over me during her hypo. I won't admit it, but I suppose I take her point. At least my little display of vulnerability wasn't in front of someone I actively despised, like hers was. I don't like appearing vulnerable to Nat, though. It's really important to me that I'm someone she can depend on to be there for her when she needs me. Involuntary downtime doesn't factor into that dynamic.

Nat looks pretty engrossed in her work. She swore blind that she'd get more done from here than in her studio with her team to distract her. She also promised that working out of my library, with its crackling fire and stash of Hermès throws, was preferable to freezing her tits off (her words) at work.

I take advantage of her apparent focus to slowly extract my phone from where I've hidden it between the sofa cushions.

'Put that down,' she says without looking up.

'I'm just checking the weather,' I lie. 'Anyway, I'm fine.'

'Spoiler: it's going to be cold and rainy all day. And you need to rest. *Put it away.*'

The strength of my sigh makes her laugh. 'Isn't it annoying when you feel fine but a certain person keeps fussing over you like you're on death's door?' she asks me with a perky smile.

Checkmate to her. 'Yeah. It certainly is,' I grit out.

'Will you be okay for two minutes if I pop into the kitchen? I want to talk to Kamyl about the broth I've asked him to make for you.'

'Honestly, tell him not to bother. I'll just have some toast or something.'

'Hmm.' She pretends to ponder. 'It's so frustrating when a meddling busybody overrules what you want to eat, isn't it?' she asks now. 'Like, for example, when you'd love some pancakes and someone keeps asking Kamyl to serve you up legumes.'

I poke her in the side of her thigh with my big toe. 'Isn't

it just.'

We smirk at each other.

'I think you'll live,' she pronounces, setting her laptop on the floor. 'I'll be right back. I want to make sure he's putting ginger and lemongrass in it.' She pauses at the door and beams at me. 'I'll be back in a second to breathe down your neck once more. Enjoy your reprieve.'

I roll my eyes at her departing back. How the tables have turned. She's definitely milking this situation to her full advantage.

'What do you normally do when you get sick?' she asks me as I carefully sip my steaming hot and truly excellent bone broth. The lemongrass and ginger and fresh herbs are wonderfully fragrant, and it's light enough not to turn my stomach. The bowl is on a tray which is balanced on my knees, and I'm leaning forward as I take spoonfuls in order to minimise the chances of boiling hot liquid hitting me in the gut—or the nuts.

'I don't get sick. I haven't had a bug like this in years.'

'But if you did,' she insists.

'I dunno. I'd do what most adults do. Dose up. Suck it up. Deal with it. And I've got Dyson on speed dial as well as a fleet of staff to tend to me, which makes me luckier than most.'

'So you wouldn't have anyone who—' She stops herself.

'Who what?'

'Who cared for you, to look after you.' She presses her lips together like she's worried she's said the wrong thing.

'I'm a big boy, sweetheart. And I've never had anyone to look after me. Not really. Not until I could afford Kamyl and

Bal and the rest of them.' She looks like she's going to cry, so I press on. 'Look. I didn't know my childhood was fucked up for a long time. Kids tend to embrace their own lived experience as 'normal'. I've never been able to decide if that's a blessing or a total travesty.

'But as it turns out, I was essentially neglected for a long time—we all were. So this is how I deal with it—by making sure I'm well looked after by people who I can rely on to show up for me, and by making sure that I in turn look after them well. It's a wonderful covenant. It works for me, anyway.'

I wholeheartedly believe this. You can't choose the caregivers who bring you into this world. You can't control their all-consuming demons any more than you can control the relentless work responsibilities they face. My mother and father were both absent for entirely different reasons. I've made my peace with that; I understand that none of it was my fault. So when you can cherry-pick the most wonderful employees and lay out to the word exactly what you require of them?

It's bloody miraculous.

But Nat's not staring at me as though it's miraculous.

Carefully, she gets to her feet again and picks up a light mahogany chair from its place in front of the antique roll-top desk. She proceeds to set it next to me and sit on it, placing my tray on her lap.

I blink at her. 'What are you doing? I'm ill, not totally incompetent.'

'You need to learn,' she says softly, 'that there are people in this world who will take care of you because they can think of nothing more they'd rather do. Open.'

I'm pretty sure the word *open* should be preserved for me, for my most commanding Bedroom Voice, and that it should refer to her long, slim legs and not my mouth. Way to make me feel like a ninety-year-old invalid.

Nevertheless, I open my mouth and allow her to spoon some clear, fragrant broth in, mainly because her face is so pretty and her expression so earnest that I'd rather die than reject her sweet gesture and risk hurting her feelings. She's in leggings and a dusky pink sweater that's seen better days, her hair pulled back and her face makeup free.

She looks like an angel sent to have mercy on the undeserving.

'If you're going to do the nurse thing,' I quip, 'we should at least get you a proper costume.'

She shakes her head at me and refills the spoon. 'Very funny. Here.'

'I'm deadly serious.'

'There will be no boners today, thank you. You're recuperating.'

I suspect my poor, flu-ravaged body wouldn't be capable of an erection even if she did rock up in full *naughty nurse* mode, but I have no intention of admitting that.

'What a wasted opportunity,' I mutter before closing my lips around the warm metal of the spoon.

She studies me. 'I don't think so.'

'What do you mean?'

She hesitates and puts the spoon down on the tray. 'I've been getting the distinct impression that you're uncomfortable having me look after you.'

'I'm not uncomfortable,' I hasten to reassure her. 'I just feel guilty. It's shitty for you. We've only been together for a few weeks—you didn't sign up for this. *And* you're missing work. I look like shit, and I'm all sweaty and snotty and revolting. You should beat a hasty retreat and come back when I'm my usual, sexy self again.' I wink at her, but she doesn't rise.

'You really don't get it,' she says, picking up the linen napkin from the tray and twisting it in her hands. 'Do you?'

'Get what?' I ask.

'I don't *want* to be anywhere else.' She clears her throat self-consciously. 'I just want to be here with you, in any capacity.' Her beautiful, expressive eyes keep flitting from my face to the napkin she's wrecking. 'I'd rather be here than at work, missing you. And I'd *definitely* rather be here if you're ill with only paid employees to look after you.'

My heart contracts painfully at her words, but she keeps speaking.

'Listen to me. I care about you, you idiot. I'll take you any way I can get you, and there's no way on earth I'd leave you when you were ill. I hate that you're feeling crap, and I'm going to do everything I can to make it all the slightest bit less grim for you. Do you understand what I'm saying?'

I nod, not trusting myself to speak. *She cares about me.* I hoped it was true—I suspected it was—but I couldn't be certain that she felt anything beyond a physical attraction and a connection borne out of our common career experiences.

She sets the tray on the coffee table and comes to sit on the edge of the sofa. I shuffle my bum to make room for her. She has her hands on my face when she says, 'Adam. This is really important. I know you didn't have anyone to look out for you when you were younger, and it makes me so fucking furious that that's your frame of reference. But this is what people do when they care about each other. They look after each other *because they want to*. I promise you, there's nowhere else I'd rather be today than right here with you. Oh, and you may be sweaty and snotty, but you still have my absolute favourite face. So stop trying to get rid of me, okay? Because I'm not going anywhere.'

Her lips are so soft when she brushes them lightly against mine. She holds my face, and I slide a hand around her neck as we stay like this for a moment.

'I love having you here,' I whisper, because it's true. I may still be feeling like death warmed up, but the contentedness in my heart is real, and it's complete. 'Thank you for being you,' I add, because that's the crux of it. Somehow, against every single odd the universe has attempted to throw at us, I've met a woman who sees me. Who cares for the man I am today and forgives the man I used to be.

If we can be this good, this happy, when I'm ill and we're tucked up together in my library, how incredible a force can we be out in the world?

I have no idea if Nat can ever bring her brother around to accepting me, and even less idea of what she would do if she were forced to choose between us, though God knows, I'd never let that happen. I'd prostrate myself at Stephen Bennett's feet and beg his forgiveness for the rest of my life if it meant preserving his relationship with his sister.

Still, Nat's admission has made me greedy. I want everything for us; I want to give this relationship oxygen. I want to walk down Regent Street with my girlfriend for all the world to see. Both of us have had our fair share of shit, of constraints to deal with, in our lives.

That ends now.

I have infinite means these days, and the world is our playground. I want to woo the hell out of this extraordinary woman and lavish upon her every pleasure her heart could desire.

I wind her ponytail slowly around my fist and tilt her head so I can whisper in her ear.

'How do you fancy a trip to New York?'

54

NATALIE

When I suggest to my mum that we meet up for lunch, I'm careful not to give her the slightest inkling of the bombshell to come. I don't for a second pretend that I have an agenda beyond an overdue girlie catch up, mainly because I haven't quite decided how I'll confess that the man who maimed her son so violently is whisking me off to New York for Christmas shopping and kinky sex.

Fuck fuck fuck.

The collapse of Dad's firm may have hit Mum the hardest initially, but it was also she who rallied the hardest in the wake of Stephen's attack. I don't know if it was her inner caregiver being stoked into resilience and action by such a horrifying challenge to her maternal instincts, or whether the attack simply put into perspective everything we'd been through so far.

Either way, she was a fucking trooper.

I know Mum felt lost when we lost our home and our savings. I know she had to grapple with an entirely new identity along the way. And I'm hyper-conscious that it was she who held us all together in the aftermath of what Adam did to Stephen.

But somewhere along the way, she learnt a word that altered the course of her life.

Surrender.

You can't change the shit that happens to you, so all you can do—the only way you can reclaim any power—is to choose how you react to that shit.

It's worked brilliantly for Mum. I can't say she's managed to transform its power to me, though. I'm far more of a pusher. When things get hard, my MO is to push harder and attempt to control everything around me.

It's worked really well for me so far. *Cough.*

Mum opts to come into town and meet me at the studio before we slip out for a coffee and a sandwich. She's always been my biggest cheerleader. She kept all the endless drawings I did of beautiful dresses when I was a little girl, and it was she who gave me the confidence to apply to fashion school when my teachers were pushing me towards more traditional Arts degrees.

She looks as elegant as ever. Her penchant for investment pieces stood her in good stead over the "lean years" (that's definitely a euphemism). She wore her beautiful clothes to death—she was definitely the only mum on the St Benedict's school run in a Burberry trench.

These days, the designer clothes from nice boutiques are long gone. Mum's wardrobe comes squarely from the high street, with the exception of a few silk scarves—and one gorgeous shirt-waister dress—that Evan's made for her (he's such a sweetie). Still, she's a beautiful woman who knows how to dress for her boyish body shape and has an eye for putting an outfit together, and it shows.

Today, she's in a nice camel-coloured crew neck and

similar coloured slacks, with chocolate brown loafers and a burgundy-and-white scarf made from last winter's leftover silk twill. Her light-brown hair is in a neat bob, and she has her wedding pearls in her ears. The sight of her always makes me feel a bit weepy, but these days it's a good kind of weepy.

She even has some money of her own now. While I'd love to be earning enough to treat her to the occasional weekend away, at least Stephen and Anna are paying her. They insisted that they'd rather have Mum mind Chloe than any nanny, and that they should pay for that privilege. She won't take anything near market rate, but I know it's helped boost both her coffers and her confidence.

'You're glowing,' I tell her when I've released her from our hug.

'Thanks, sweetie.' She pats her bob. 'I've been following Verity's anti-inflammatory diet, and I swear I look less bloated.'

Mum is an *enormous* fan of Vitality with Verity, a wellness platform for women of a certain age. I'm not sure whether Maddy or I were more excited when I discovered that Verity is none other than Maddy's mother.

'Ooh, that reminds me. Maddy got her new book signed for you.' I dig around in my tote bag. This thing is revolting. Adam teases me about it, but my entire life is in here, and if I don't want him buying me underwear from Selfridges every time I sleep at his, then the tote bag stays.

'Oh my goodness!' Mum actually claps her hands together in glee. 'That is so exciting! I think I'd die if I met her in person.'

'Well, that's unfortunate, because you definitely will. Maddy says you're invited to her baby shower when she has one, and she'll introduce the two of you then.' I extricate the book from a tangle of stockings and hand it over triumphantly. It's called *Find Your Zen,* its cover featuring a stunningly beautiful brunette who looks exactly like a Charlie's Angel and also exactly how I imagine Maddy will look in twenty-five years.

Lucky Future Zach.

Maddy tells me that Verity's next book will be called *Find Your Drive* and is all about reigniting menopausal and post-menopausal women's libidos. She said her mum has not only been asking her the most horrifying questions about how she and Zach keep things interesting but has been angling for an invitation to Alchemy. While the idea of Maddy explaining St Andrew's crosses and spanking to her mum is beyond hysterical, I've already decided that's one book my mum will *not* be getting a signed copy of.

She and Dad can work that stuff out for themselves, thank you very much.

After Mum's finished squealing over the book and the prospect of toasting Maddy's unborn child over mimosas with Verity herself, I lead her over to the racks of samples to show her the wisteria collection we're producing for spring.

'This is just stunning, darling,' she says, holding up the dress with the gold hardware and engineered panels that Adam was so complimentary about when we were in Omar Vega's studio. 'What an absolute showstopper. Where are you shooting it?'

'We're just doing a studio shoot for spring,' I say brightly. 'But we've got a guy making us a backdrop of silk wisteria. It should be lovely.'

That's what I tell myself, anyway. The truth is that a studio shoot is far more cost-effective than a location shoot. Not only is the hire fee way cheaper, but we can get far more shots under our belt in a day in front of a single backdrop than we can if our photographer needs to set up for each shot in a different location.

With cash being this tight, dropping an additional ten grand or more on a location shoot is simply not an option, so we need to get creative. While I'd love to sell the dream properly, I'd settle for just selling clothes. I try not to think about Omar Vega's latest shoot: zany, futuristic-style dresses shot on location at Kensington Palace. Obsessing over his probable shoot budget is plain unhelpful (though I bet Adam would spill the numbers if I asked).

I suspect Mum can read right between the lines of my phony perkiness, but she just smiles and says, 'I'm sure that will look lovely, darling. And isn't this print *wonderful?*'

'I can definitely find a spare metre to knock you up a little *carré*, Adelaide,' Evan tells Mum, referring to the French word for *square* and the term Hermès uses for its scarves. I roll my eyes. He's a pretentious arse-licker, and I adore every bone in his body.

'Really?' Mum breathes, fingering the dress reverently. 'Oh God, I'd love that. But isn't it a bit thick for a scarf?'

'We're printing it in twill, too,' he says with a wink at her. 'For these shirts, see? Ooh—I'll get that. You ladies carry on.'

That is the doorbell.

'Thanks, hon,' I tell him, pulling the wisteria shirt out so Mum can admire the hidden buttonholes. I'm hoping to steal this sample for myself once we've shot it. It's to die for.

It's not until I hear the jumble of male voices and the clatter of footsteps that I belatedly understand what's happening on the stairs. And it's already far too late when I spin around to find the very fine and most unwelcome figure of Mr Adam Wright standing in my studio.

55

ADAM

U p until I register the two women in front of me, my brain has been preoccupied with whether I can persuade Nat to believe I was just passing by. I'm holding in my gloved hand a takeaway box from an organic cafe down the road that's stuffed to the gills with harissa chicken, grains, and some kind of miso-roasted aubergine thing that looks delicious.

It's not that I believe my girlfriend willingly skirts danger with her eating habits, but I know how fully immersed she can get in her job. We're both workaholics, but only one of us has a body that attacks its own insulin supply, so here we are.

Now, though, I register the panic on Nat's face at the same time as I spot the slow recognition on Adelaide's face. After all, I've changed a lot more than she has. I'm no longer a shaven headed, angry kid.

'Sorry, Nat,' Evan says breathlessly from behind me.

'Mum, I—' Nat begins, her beautiful face stricken.

'Hi, Adelaide,' I say warmly.

'*Adam?*' Adelaide asks incredulously.

Nat's head whips from me to her mother. '*What?*'

Since meeting Nat, I've assumed she isn't aware of the steps her mum took to build a relationship with her son's attacker all those years ago. She's certainly never mentioned it. And, given Adelaide's insistence at the time that her visits weren't something she was disclosing to her family, I've never had any reason to think she'd make her daughter aware of them.

Therefore, I've never so much as hinted at the extent to which Adelaide has helped me. There was a moment the other night, when Nat was fretting about how to sit her brother down and come clean about our relationship. She mentioned that she might sound her mum out first, and I made some vague comment to the effect that her mum might be more amenable than Stephen. Nothing more than that.

So when Nat sees me grinning at her mother and Adelaide positively beaming at me, I get the feeling that this will be a bombshell of epic proportions for her.

Adelaide, it seems, is handling my appearance far better than her daughter. 'Oh my God!' she cries, coming towards me, her arms already outstretched. 'How on earth are you here? Do you two *know* each other?'

'Hi, Adelaide,' I say, opting for full-wattage charm as a master stroke of deflection. 'You look fantastic.' I allow her to envelop me in a hug whose genuine warmth has my throat constricting with emotion. While I've never forgotten her kindness, it's only now hitting me how much of her compassion and empathy she's passed onto her daughter. (The origin of Nat's impressive feistiness I'm still unclear on.)

'Oh, stop it,' she trills, hitting me playfully on the arm and drawing back so she can look at me. 'Look at *you!* So handsome! And looking so well! Goodness, it's wonderful to see you thriving.'

We beam at each other for a moment while Nat stalks over to us. 'Uh—do *we* know each other? How about how *you two* know each other?'

She crosses her arms and glares at us, and I hastily release her mother. A quick glance around tells me Evan and the rest of the team are staring at us with indecent interest and that a speedy migration of our little soap opera moment would be wise.

'I'll explain,' I tell her, hastily swallowing the *sweetheart* I was about to tack onto the end. It seems both these women have a bombshell incoming, and I'd like to retain control of this rapidly unravelling situation to whatever extent is possible. 'How about I take you both around the corner for some lunch?'

'Mum and I were supposed to be going for lunch,' Nat says, still glaring at me.

I'm wavering between apologising for messing up their lunch plans and pointing out to her that urgent disclosure by all parties is now more pressing when Adelaide speaks.

'Let's do as Adam suggests. I want to know how you two know each other.'

'*Ditto,*' Nat growls with a death stare as she grabs her coat borderline violently off a nearby hanger.

The most expedient option available to us is Soho House on adjacent Greek Street. I usher the three of us into the club and request their most discreet table. Thankfully, the host has a small private room tucked away on the second floor. There's a cosy fire crackling in the small grate, but the energy emanating from my beautiful girlfriend is positively arctic.

'Talk,' she says, shimmying out of her coat and throwing it on the sofa on one side of the room.

Adelaide and I exchange a glance, and I realise that, as the only party privy to both of these clandestine relationships, I should probably clarify with the broadest brushstrokes what the hell is actually going on here.

'Adelaide, Nat and I are dating. We've been seeing each other for a few weeks and I know she's been wanting to talk to you about it.' I turn to Nat and take her hand. 'Sweetheart, I haven't seen your mum for years, I swear, but she was very, very kind to me after I was sentenced.'

Both mother and daughter react in different ways, albeit with equal levels of emotion. Adelaide's little laugh is one of utter delight and wonder, whereas Nat's huge brown eyes fill instantly with tears.

'Did you visit him?' she asks her mum in a whisper. I'm vastly encouraged by the fact that she hasn't tried to pull her hand away from mine.

Adelaide opens her mouth, and I sense she's going to offer some justification or apology, but she doesn't. She glances at our joined hands and gives a simple nod. 'Yes, I did.'

I wait. I want to give Nat space to process. To ask her own questions. Her view of what happened two decades ago, of the man I am, is vastly different from what it was a few weeks ago, so I hope she can find it within herself to retrospectively forgive her mother for taking an action that might, until last month, have felt like a betrayal of their family.

'More than once?' she asks.

I remain silent and defer to Adelaide.

'Yes,' she says, looking at me now. 'I visited Adam monthly, I think, for as long as he was in prison. Is that right?'

I nod. 'Yeah. And then we kept in touch by email after I was released. She knew about the job with Anton,' I tell Nat. 'We had coffee years later, too—maybe five or six years later?'

A glance at Adelaide is all I need to know that she remembers. She needs no reminder of how the tables had turned by the time that overdue coffee rolled around, how much I was thriving under Anton's tutelage, working my arse off for Wolff while I built OfficeScape.

She needs no reminder of her own intense concerns back then over Noel's lack of meaningful work. Of how, days after our coffee, I emailed her to let her know that Anton and I had had an excellent lunch with one of the deans at the London School of Economics and extolled the virtues of Noel Bennett's expertise in the very Financial Systems professorship he was looking to recruit for.

It was an inadequate gesture of thanks towards a woman who had shown me such forgiveness and compassion in the face of the most inhuman act of my life—towards her own son, no less.

'It was just a quick catch up,' I say lamely. 'We haven't really chatted much since then.'

'Wow,' Nat says, shaking her head.

'Are you okay darling?' Adelaide asks, leaning forward with concern.

'Yeah.' Nat's voice is so low, so shaky, that her words are barely audible. 'God, I had no idea. But I'm so, so glad he had you.' Her bottom lip trembles on the *you*, and she presses her hand to her mouth. 'Jesus, he had no one else. Thank God he had you.'

'Oh, my darling,' Adelaide says, her voice tremoring. 'Don't worry. He had me. He had his fabulous lawyer. And that lovely man, Anton. We looked out for him.'

'But how?' Nat says. 'I mean, how come you ended up visiting him?'

'Your mum is a very generous, compassionate person,' I tell her. 'And somehow she found it in herself to see beyond my incredibly fucked-up persona and reach out.'

'It wasn't like that,' Adelaide protests, shaking her head disapprovingly. 'The entire trial was ridiculous. Obviously, Noel and I had no idea, until we sat through it, quite what Adam had been through. It was awful. Just awful. And somehow, that judge failed to show any regard whatsoever for the future of a young man who'd been dealt such a deeply, deeply tragic hand. So I sought out Anne, his lawyer, after he'd been sentenced, and I got her to persuade Adam to agree to a visitation.'

She leans over and pats my hand. 'I wanted to look him in the eye and tell him that I knew that crime didn't define him. I wanted him to know that someone on the outside saw him, and cared, and was sorry that he'd been let down so very badly.'

Nat is crying now, big tears rolling down her cheeks. She nods. 'Good. That's good. And did Dad and Winky know you were visiting him?'

Adelaide draws back. 'God, no. Your father was so distraught—he blamed himself for putting your brother in harm's way, as you know. Still does. And you were still so little, and Winky was healing. I didn't want him to think for a moment that I wasn't firmly in his corner.'

She pauses and takes a sip of her water, considering. 'I

regret that, actually. I was trying to protect him, but really, I only perpetuated a silly myth that I should have tried to debunk. A myth that someone who commits a crime like that must be all evil. When everyone at this table knows that is categorically not true.'

Jesus fuck, my eyes are misting. I give us about three minutes before we're all holding hands around the table and openly weeping.

'Amen to that,' Nat says with almost comedic emphasis. I release her hand and wipe the dampness from her nearest cheek.

Adelaide catches the gesture and smiles at us fondly. 'And would you like to expand upon how you've come to join the Adam Wright fan club? Though, god knows, he's an easy man to be a fan of. He's such a good boy.'

I laugh, because it's been a very long time since anyone has described me as a good boy.

Nat grimaces. I suspect she's more worried about confessing her hypo attack than any other part of our story. Maybe I can help her downplay it.

'It's definitely an interesting story,' I tell Adelaide, picking up my menu. 'But how about we order before we get stuck into it? I'd feel a lot better if we got your daughter some lunch.'

56

NATALIE

For some reason, the relief I feel isn't due to knowing that Mum is already a fan of Adam, that she's one less family member to get on board.

Not even close.

Instead, it's thanks to this incredible revelation that somehow, amid all the pain and panic and worry of Stephen's horrific maiming, she found it within herself to recognise his attacker as a lost, terrified, betrayed boy and to do something about it.

Every time I imagine her visiting him in prison, the tears well up again. My brain is reframing what I know of Adam's sentence, piece by piece. Yeah, it was horrific for him. It was a travesty, really. But he had my mother in his corner: one of the warmest, strongest, most compassionate people I know.

I hope that, over the years, the knowledge that one member of the Bennett family saw him and forgave him and was actively *rooting* for him gave him that extra reassurance that his future was worth fighting for. That *he* was worth fighting for.

What an extraordinary gift to have given him. What incredible generosity, humanity, to have shown him.

'Oh, sweetheart,' Adam says as I lose it again. He reaches into the middle of the table, where napkins and cutlery stand in shiny silver julep cups, and shakes out a linen napkin before pressing it gently to my face. 'It's okay,' he says. 'We're all good. Everyone's great. There's nothing to be sad about, honestly.'

'I know.' I nod my head like a child. 'I just can't believe it. For some reason, the thought of you being there for him in that place makes me so emotional,' I say to Mum.

She purses her lips sympathetically. 'I take it you know the whole story, then?'

I nod again. 'Yeah. And it makes me so angry.'

'I'm glad,' she says. 'I'm glad you know what a good boy he is.'

That makes me giggle. '*Such* a good boy,' I say, wiggling my eyebrows at Adam, who's looking very much as though he wants to put me over his knee here and now.

Fine with me.

'But I'm still waiting for *your* story,' Mum prompts gently. 'Can I assume you met through Anton Wolff?'

My mouth falls open.

'I always wondered if your paths would cross,' she continues. 'When you told me about that lovely lady, Gen, marrying him, it seemed such a coincidence to me that your boss was marrying Adam's old boss, but I just put it down to one of life's fun little morsels of happenstance.'

I give Adam a slow smile before answering her. 'We met through Anton,' I confirm. 'Adam came in one night with him and Gen, and I recognised him instantly. I kind of had a meltdown when I saw him. Gen had to bundle me up in a cab and send me home.' I grimace at the memory, and

Adam takes my hand under the table, squeezing it reassuringly.

'I'm not surprised,' Mum says. 'It's not like you had any sense of who he really was as a person.'

'Exactly. Anyway, it turned out he was in talks with Gen to buy Wolff's stake in Alchemy off him, so Gen called me in for a meeting with Adam to see if we could work things out.' I hesitate and hold up my hand in warning. 'Please don't freak out, okay? But I was so stressed about the sit-down that I didn't eat enough, and I ended up having a hypo in the middle of the meeting.'

Mum's horrified gasp has me pausing, but I push on. 'I know, I'm not proud of it. But Adam was amazing. He totally nursed me through it, even if I wasn't at my *most* gracious.'

Adam laughs. 'She was an ungrateful little horror, more accurately. Not that I can blame her.'

'I can only imagine,' Mum murmurs. 'But Adam, that must have been horrifically upsetting for you.'

He attempts to deny it, but I butt in. 'It was, and I was awful. Just awful. Obviously, I didn't know anything about Ellen at the time, and I just thought he was this overbearing pain in the arse. Anyway, he basically kidnapped me and took me back to his place and forced all sorts of doctors and chickpeas and nutritionists down me, and he even made me stay the night.'

I glance over at him, and the softness on his face, in those pale blue eyes, as he listens to me recount the story almost fells me.

How far we've come since then.

How profoundly wrong I was about him.

I let my eyes drift closed for a moment as I brush my thumb over the back of his hand under the table.

'It's kind of gone from there,' I conclude lamely. 'He

looks after me so well, and he's a major, major feeder. Oh, and he's been incredible with Gossamer, too.'

Mum's been watching us as closely as she's been listening, it seems. She cocks her head and regards us thoughtfully.

'Thank you, Adam, from the bottom of my heart, for looking after my little girl. Even if she is an ungrateful little horror, as you say.'

'She's improving,' he teases. 'Slowly.'

I pout like the brat I am.

'And it's serious?' Mum presses. 'It certainly seems that way.'

'It's still early days,' I hedge, right as Adam says firmly, 'It's serious.'

I swear my heart does a full somersault.

It's not until our soups and salads have arrived that I broach the topic of Stephen. The conversation has flowed non-stop, actually. Mum wanted to hear every detail about our relationship, although clearly the version we've given her is highly sanitised.

'I was actually going to tell you about Adam today, Mum,' I confess between spoonfuls of my deliciously velvety butternut squash soup. 'That's why I suggested lunch. I was hoping you wouldn't totally freak out and that you'd be able to give me some advice about how to tell Winky.'

Adam sniggers. 'I still think it's seriously fucked up that you call him Winky.'

'He can take it,' I say airily. I turn back to Mum. 'But obviously I'm worried that he'll be a lot less amenable to getting to know Adam properly than you've been.'

Mum frowns. 'Oh dear. Yes, I can see that he might go off the deep end. But at the end of the day, you're an adult and you're entitled to be in a relationship with whomever you choose, as long as they make you happy, which I can see Adam does.' She shoots him a smile. 'I imagine your best bet is to try to persuade him that Adam isn't the man Stephen thinks he is, or ever was, really. I can talk to him, too.'

'No,' I say quickly. 'It needs to come from me.'

'I agree, darling, but if your news doesn't land well, I can talk to him afterwards.' She turns to Adam. 'I'll come clean about my visits to you in prison. That man has no idea what you've done for him. I assume you were behind the Totum job?'

'What?' I demand through the roaring in my ears.

Adam groans, shooting me a panicked look. 'Jesus, Adelaide.'

'What? I follow you on Instagram. You're always hanging out with Aidan Duffy. It didn't take a genius to make the connection.'

'You got Stephen his job?' I ask, my mind racing. Fuck, I can't believe this. Neither can I believe I didn't work it out for myself. 'Does he know?' I ask Mum.

'I didn't get him anything,' Adam says firmly. 'I simply asked Aide to take a look at his LinkedIn profile. Your brother earned that job on his own merit—Aide says he's a very fine programmer.'

'He definitely doesn't know,' Mum says to me now.

'And it's going to stay that way, got it?' Adam says, glaring at me. 'It was an intro. Nothing more. Let's not make a big deal of it.'

'What about this new prosthetic thing he's so excited about?' Mum asks him. 'That seemed to come out of the blue. Know anything about it?'

The panicked looks Adam's shooting me just keep on coming. I'm torn between amusement that Mum is blithely laying bare his apparent secret side hustle of fairy godfather to my brother and a rush of emotion so *strong* it's threatening to overwhelm me.

Adam is such a good man. Such a kind man. And clearly, a man who seems to believe he still has to make reparations to Stephen, all these years later.

'Good God, Adelaide,' he grumbles to Mum. 'You need to work on your discretion.'

Mum sits back and crosses her arms with a satisfied smile. 'I knew it.'

'It was a single phone call,' Adam insists. 'A mutual friend hooked me up with the CEO. But again, Stephen will get that eye on his own merits. He may be a good candidate, he may not. There's absolutely nothing I can do about that.' He turns to me. 'And for the love of God, I won't let you ever use this stuff as leverage when you're pitching my good name to your brother. Never. Understand?

'He accepts me, or he doesn't. Either way, we'll deal with it. You're not getting rid of me that easily. But I don't ever want him feeling beholden to me, because the truth is that I ruined his life, and if I call in a million favours on his behalf, none of them will change that fact.'

'Yeah,' I say quietly. 'I understand.'

Mum opens her mouth to speak, then pauses. When she finally speaks, her words are measured. 'I truly believe, Adam, that you didn't ruin his life. You altered the trajectory of it, yes. He suffered a lot of trauma and a great loss, but he's fine. We're all fine.

'Of all of us, you're the one who's suffered the most unimaginable losses, and look at you. I don't need to tell you that a good life can be forged from the ashes of tragedy. You don't need to worry about Stephen anymore. It's not your job, you hear me?' She winks at him, and it's filled with affection. 'Just focus on my daughter for now.'

57

NATALIE

I should speak to Stephen alone, I really should.

But maybe if I spill the beans to him when Anna's around, he won't bite my head off.

That's not fair. He deserves to hear this from me, one on one. That's all there is to it.

Although... Anna's his wife. She deserves to hear it just as much as he does.

If I meet up with him alone, then he'll just end up storming off home and giving her some massively skewed version of the truth, and then she'll go all mama bear and call me, and I'll tell her *my* version of events, and she'll be horrified on my and Adam's account and she'll hang up and bollock Winky, and it'll all be a giant mess.

Yep.

I'm definitely bringing Anna along for the ride.

Maybe I can use her as a human shield if the shit really hits the fan?

I purposely leave my chat with Stephen until the day before Adam and I are due to fly to New York. I'm intent on getting my secret relationship off my chest so I can enjoy what I know will be the most exciting trip I've ever been on, and there's some comfort in knowing I'll be putting an ocean between us if my brother really loses his rag.

The memory of our impromptu and ridiculously emotional (not to mention eye-opening) lunch with Mum is as much of a balm to my conscience as it is a warm blanket around my heart. That my mother knows and adores Adam is crazy and wonderful and miraculous.

When he disappeared off to pay the bill at his insistence, she hugged me so tightly and told me how absolutely thrilled she was for us both and how certain she was that he would make me happy. I won't allow myself to have her level of faith over our future—it's been less than a month since we started fooling around, after all—but her insistence that we're good together is a definite comfort. She seems equally excited for both of us. Not only is Adam a "good boy" and therefore a worthy suitor, but she also seems relieved that he has me in his corner.

If only she knew how fully and irrevocably I am in that man's corner.

As I walk the short distance from Clapham Common tube station to Stephen and Anna's lovely Victorian house, I remind myself that I have nothing to be ashamed of here. Yes, my relationship status will be a blow to my brother, but I know that the man I'm dating is the very best kind of man there is. I'd stake every last pound I have on the strength of Adam's character.

I just have to find a way to persuade my brother, the victim of Adam's ugliest, most depraved moment of existence, that one hate crime does not a man define.

Gen's allowing me to start late tonight so I can have this chat, and she's very sweetly told me not to turn up for work if I'm too upset afterwards. Adam has been texting me all evening with little messages of support, and belief in me, and gratitude that I'm taking this stand for him. I know how guilty he feels about every single part of this, and I hate it for him.

My stomach is in knots, but I've been careful to supplement the light dinner I managed to get down with a load of gummies. The last thing I need is a badly-timed hypo.

When I arrive, I find to my delight that Baby Chloe is still awake. My God, she's divine. She's had her bath and smells like baby shampoo and talc and heaven. She's in the softest pale pink onesie, and she blows bubbles and clutches at my hair as I bounce her on my lap. Not only am I delighted to get my fix of snuggles, but I'm selfishly hopeful that her presence will make this conversation less intense than it might otherwise be.

Only one way to find out.

I feel sick as I clear my throat. Winky and Anna know I have something specific I want to talk to them about. God knows what they're imagining, but it sure as hell isn't the truth. I remind myself that there's no way around this. Not only do I owe this conversation to my brother, but I owe it to Adam, and it's that that spurs me on.

He's fucking wonderful. He floors me with his kindness and steadfastness. Absolutely floors me. There is no way on God's green earth that I'll let him feel for a second that I'm ashamed of his past, that I'll keep our relationship in the shadows.

Even as I prepare to tell my brother something that might devastate him, and even as I brace myself for the worst, this new and wonderful and magnetic North Star shines brightly in my soul, reminding me of my purpose and giving me the kind of courage I never, ever have in any confronting situation. God knows, I can't even renegotiate terms with my fabric suppliers without baulking, and this is the most horrifying conversation I've ever had to have.

But it doesn't matter, because my North Star is as follows:

My relationship with Adam, and his importance to me, deserves to be legitimised in every single way.

'So, the reason I wanted to chat,' I say, craning my head to keep my hoop earring away from Chloe's grabby little paw, 'is that I've met a guy, and it's still new, but it's getting serious really quickly.'

There's a split second where Winky and Anna both look shocked, but then they grin at me.

'But that's amazing, sis,' Winky says. 'We thought it was going to be something bad. You had us worried there.'

I grimace. 'It's a bit more complicated than that.'

'Is he treating you well?' He asks quickly.

'Yeah. He's treating me like an absolute queen. Honestly, he's amazing, and...' I trail off with a little shrug. 'He's just amazing,' I say lamely, making a mental note to pull myself together and ramp up my rhetorical skills.

'Okay...' Anna says, frowning like she's trying to read between the lines. 'That's fantastic, right?'

My inhale is shuddery. Jesus, this is hard. It's hard for me and for Winky and for Adam, and ugh. Just *ugh*. 'He had a tricky time when he was younger,' I said. 'He's the best man I've ever, ever met, but he had a really rough upbringing, and it made him do some terrible things.' I sniff. *Seriously, Natalie. Get it together.* I glance up at them and see only sympathy on their faces.

'He, um'—I stroke Chloe's cheek, taking comfort in the

velvety softness of her skin—'he did, like, a *really* bad thing, and he—oh my God, Winky, I'm so sorry.'

Anna's still trying hard to figure out what the hell is going on, but I see the second it lands with my brother. His face hardens instantly.

'You've got to be kidding me.'

'What?' Anna asks him.

I shake my head. 'I know how awful it—' I begin, but he's on his feet and looming over me. He starts shouting.

'You're seeing Adam *Wright?* You cannot be serious right now!'

'Steve!' Anna cries as I shrink back against the sofa, cuddling Chloe to me and pressing her little, soft head between my breast and my hand in the hope that she won't hear her father screaming at her auntie. Winky's the least aggressive guy on the planet, but historically there's been no speedier way to wind him up than by mentioning Adam's name, and I've never, ever seen him this furious.

He turns to his wife, gesturing at his prosthetic. 'She's fucking the guy who did *this* to me. Have you no self respect at all? Jesus fucking Christ.' That last bit is to me.

'Listen to me,' I plead, but it's eminently clear that my brother is *not* in listening mode. He's spiralled so deep into his sympathetic nervous system that the blinkers—and the ear plugs—are well and truly on. It seems I've massively underestimated how triggering this revelation would be for him.

'No.' He points his finger at me. 'You listen to me. What the bloody hell are you thinking? Meet him at your fancy sex club, did you? I cannot fucking believe that you'd spread your legs for the guy who put your own brother in hospital just because he's bagged himself a few billion.'

'Holy shit, babes,' Anna says, getting off the sofa with a

massive sigh. 'Not in front of Chloe. And calm down, for God's sake. You can't talk to your sister like that.'

Clearly Anna has not received the memo that being told to calm down has never, ever resulted in anyone actually calming down. Not in the entire history of humankind.

I get his reaction, though. In my brother's eyes, Adam Wright has been a two-dimensional, piece of shit bully for the past two decades. Just as he's been in my eyes until very recently.

Anna walks over and takes Chloe gently out of my arms, and I let her. She presses her lips together sympathetically and gives me an encouraging little nod. I appreciate it. I suspect she doesn't want to get too stuck into the discussion without a full set of facts, unlike my brother, who has no clue quite what an incomplete picture of Adam he's working with here. The question is whether Winky will ever be willing to entertain some new perspectives.

'I get it,' I tell him softly. 'But you couldn't be more wrong about him. When he did what he did to you, which was awful—completely horrific—he was so messed up. His little sister had just died, like *days* before he attacked you, his mum had been arrested for causing her death... He was barely functioning, and he was in so much pain he didn't know which way was up.'

Winky rolls his eyes. (I'll never be the one to tell him it's less effective when one of them is glass.) But there's something there—a flash of surprise, maybe? I'd swear some of what I've just told him is new information for him.

'Spare me the sob story,' he says now. 'I can't believe you'd sell out on your family like this. It's so fucking disloyal, it makes me sick to my stomach.'

I told myself before I came here that this was about Stephen, not me, and that I'd suck it up if he wanted to hurl insults, then I'd take them if it helped him to process. But I can't deny it's devastating to stand here and have him accuse me of selling out on our family, after every fucking thing we've been through together.

Jesus, there's so much I want to say to him.

Mum adores him.

She visited him.

He saved my life.

He got you your job.

He got you your shot at a new eye, for Pete's sake!

But I don't. I won't go there. And while I want Winky's absolution with an intensity that's terrifying, I don't technically need it. This evening is about my doing the right thing and providing my brother with information he's entitled to have.

It's not about earning his blessing to date Adam.

I'm not sure what to do, really. This has landed badly, really badly, and I don't want to turn and flounce out of the house, but I also don't want to stay here and be a punching bag while Winky works through his anger. I have the upper hand here. I came here knowing the facts, and he's been blindsided, therefore it's right that I should hold space for him and not resort to insult-slinging.

'Listen,' I say, standing up and hauling my bag over my shoulder. 'I know you're angry. If you have questions for me, I'll stay and answer them. But I get that you're going to need some time with this, and I'd rather not stand here while you basically accuse me of being a gold-digging whore. You know where I am if you want to chat.'

I sling my coat over my shoulder, plant a soft kiss on Chloe's silken cheek, and get the hell out of there.

58

ADAM

One of the many fucked-up ironies of my life is that I've seen fit to surround myself with items of great beauty, to identify aesthetics as one of the profound, constant pleasures of this human experience, all the while having robbed another man of half his eyesight.

If anything haunts me, it's that. Stephen Bennett isn't blind, but he's halfway there. If anything happened to his other eye, he'd be blind because of me. And yet I have the gall to continue blithely surrounding myself with beautiful things.

Another fucked-up irony?

His sister is the most beautiful being I've ever had the pleasure of feasting my eyes on.

I used to tear myself to pieces with guilt. *I took away his fucking eye.* For years and years, I had an eyepatch that I kept hidden at the bottom of one of my bedroom drawers like an addict might hide his stash. In particularly dark moments, I'd put it on, covering my left eye for hours or days on end.

This is how Stephen Bennett feels every single day, you

callous thug. The discomfort, the inconvenience, the blurred black-grey where half of any view I looked at should be. When I started making serious money, when Anton would drag me on business trips to visit his offices in Hong Kong and New York and San Francisco, I'd squirrel the eye patch away in my luggage and put it on when I had the chance.

This is how half of Victoria Harbour looks, dickhead, I'd taunt myself from my balcony in The Four Seasons Hong Kong. *This is how half of Central Park looks. A bit shitty, isn't it?*

The day I stepped foot back in the very same prison where I was once incarcerated, as part of my plan to deliver the same business course through which Anton had once saved my life, was the day I threw that fucking eye patch away. The habit of surreptitiously closing my left eye when I'm overwhelmed still lingers, though.

I do exactly this as I regard my girlfriend in profile. She's bathed in the dazzling sunlight you only get at thirty-seven thousand feet, and her expression is far more pensive than I'd like to see on a woman who's being whisked off for what she claims to already know will be the best weekend of her life.

Unfortunately for my masochistic tendencies, we're close enough that even a one-eyed view of her is perfection.

She's worried about her brother, and I'm worried about her. I based myself at Alchemy the other night so I could be around her all evening. She insisted on working her full shift despite Gen's offer to bail, so I planted my arse on the big sofa where Nat scared me shitless with her hypo and caught up on some work. And while she's given me a detailed run-down of how their conversation went (in a word, disastrous), I know she's trapped inside her own head.

I fucking hate it.

I lean forward and plant a kiss on her temple, and she

gives me a little smile, leaning in towards me. While I'd love us to be travelling alone on my jet, Dr Dyson is sitting down at the other end of the aircraft. Changing time zones is complicated for diabetics, and jet lag is fucking brutal. I'm taking no chances with either the administration of Nat's insulin as her body clock adjusts to Eastern Standard Time, nor will I tolerate jet lag robbing her of her joy on this trip.

We've both already done an IV bag of electrolytes and vitamins to preempt dehydration on the flight, and we'll do more when we get to our hotel.

'Brie?' I enquire. We've been grazing on a delicious platter of smoked salmon and all the usual accoutrements, various cheeses, and gluten-free charcoal crackers.

She shakes her head at me. 'No thanks. I'm stuffed.'

Hmm. I'm not sure the amount she's eaten would 'stuff' anyone.

'Is your stomach still in knots?' I ask her, leaning my forehead against hers and sliding a hand around the back of her neck.

'A bit, yeah. Is it weird that I wish I could be a fly on the wall during dinner tonight and that I'm also really glad I'm putting thousands of miles between us?'

'No,' I tell her. 'It's not weird in the slightest.'

Stephen and his wife, Anna, have been essentially summoned for an early supper tonight when they pick Chloe up from his parents' place, and Adelaide appears intent on letting rip a few truth bombs—though none surrounding any meddling I've done in Stephen's life in recent years, thankfully.

I've been clear since my earliest days in therapy—in prison, actually—that Stephen Bennett's forgiveness is not only a gift I can never hope or deserve to ask for, but a vali-dation I shouldn't need. The only way to move from hating to liking yourself is to accept yourself. So there is no part of me at all that craves anything from him.

This is about Nat, and her relationship with her brother, and the injustice that she should feel judged or even resented by him because of me.

'The good thing is we'll be five hours behind,' I tell her now, tipping my face up so I can brush my lips over her forehead. 'I'm sure your mum will update you when they've gone.' I really hope for her sake that's true. I'd love to see her enjoying everything I have planned for tomorrow and beyond with the weight of all this gone from her shoulders.

'Mmm-hmm,' she says. 'I'm sure you're right.'

'New York should be very Christmassy,' I say, hoping for a subject change. 'Hopefully it should get you in the mood.'

I pull away enough to see a genuine smile flash across her beautiful face. 'Oh my God, I'm going to die from excitement.'

'What do you usually do for Christmas?'

She shrugs. 'I just spend it with my folks. Stephen and Anna tend to alternate between seeing our family and hers, but her parents are going on a cruise this year, which is great for us—it's Chloe's first Christmas.'

I grin. 'Sweet. Christmas is always a lot more fun with kids around.'

'Yeah.' She snuggles against me on the spacious cream leather sofa. 'I can't wait. I have a feeling Mum'll go crazy on the present front.'

I laugh. Adelaide definitely will.

'What do you do?' she asks. There's a quiet, tentative tone to her voice as if she's treading carefully.

'I usually have Dad and Quinn over for dinner, and then they stay the night. I cook, and it's usually pretty quiet.'

Quiet is a euphemism for sombre. There are far too

many ghosts at our Christmas dinner table. Ellen loved Christmas so much. One Christmas Eve, she got herself so overexcited that she threw up.

'Do you ever hear from your mum at Christmas?'

'No. She knows that's not an option.'

She snakes an arm over my stomach and around my waist. Considering how light and delicate it is, it feels wonderfully anchoring. 'Do you know where she is?'

'No.' I hesitate. 'She's in Scotland, I think. I was so worried she'd come looking for Quinn when she got out of prison, but she didn't. Thirteen or fourteen years ago, when I had enough money, I hired an investigator to track her down and keep an eye on her. She was in Aberdeen when he found her, working odd jobs. She'd been fired from a job in a hotel bar, shock horror.

'Anyway, he's on an annual retainer. He knows where she is, and he knows not to tell me unless he sees her making a move anywhere near London—then he'll call me straight away. I never want to see her again, and I know Dad and Quinn don't, either.' I stroke the arm on my stomach over her cashmere sleeve. 'It's best this way.'

'I'm so sorry,' she murmurs. 'It's so shitty, but I get it.'

I hesitate. 'You know, if you wanted to come by over Christmas, then I'd love you to meet them. I don't want to drag you away from your family, but maybe when you come back to London—Boxing Day? No pressure,' I add hastily. We usually trek down to Croydon to visit Ellen's grave on Boxing Day, but maybe we can move things around this year. Try to make some new memories, and even, if Nat's up for it, bring her along on our little pilgrimage.

I'd like *both* my sisters to meet the woman I'm falling hard for.

She straightens up and I instantly drown in her big brown eyes. 'Really?'

'Of course. They'd love you.'

'Do they know about me?'

'Quinn does,' I tell her. 'Dad doesn't... yet. I didn't want to tempt fate.'

Her mouth turns down at the corners, like she's in pain on my behalf, and she leans in to press a soft kiss to my lips. 'I'm not going anywhere. And I'd love to meet your family.'

'Good,' I murmur against her mouth.

'I do have an important question, though,' she says, pulling back and brightening.

'And what's that?'

'Do you decorate your house for Christmas? I can't imagine how beautiful it must look.' She gives me a grin so hopeful that I feel like I'm kicking a puppy when I answer.

'Not really. I get someone in to put up a tree in the hallway, but that's about it.'

Her face falls. 'Seriously? No garlands? Adam, that's awful! You could go so crazy on that staircase with tons of fresh greenery.'

I shrug. 'It's only me there most of the time. And the staff, obviously. I can't be bothered.'

She raises her eyebrows, unimpressed, and I laugh and straighten up in my seat.

'Miss Bennett. I happen to have the enquiry form from the guys who do the tree sitting in my inbox. Would you be at all interested in running with this special, festive project? I think we could find a way to expand the remit if you think you're capable of assuming more responsibility?'

She sits bolt upright. 'Seriously? You'll let me kit your entire house out?'

'I'll let you brief a team of professionals on how to kit my entire house out, yes,' I clarify, sliding my iPad towards her and wondering exactly what I'm letting myself in for. Nat's a very classy woman with excellent taste. I'm assuming she'll do an incredible job.

Far more importantly, *this* is the kind of smile I've been trying to put on her face for the past two days.

59

NATALIE

Max may have swept Darcy and Dex off to the Aman, which I'm sure is all modern gorgeousness and understated luxury and neutral palates, but my boyfriend knows me well, it seems. I suspect he's not surprised by my reaction to The Pierre, where he's booked us a suite.

Whenever I've dreamed of New York in the past, *this* is what I've imagined. The Pierre feels old world and old money and decadent, with its frescoed rotunda and well-heeled patrons and huge bowls of pink and white flowers everywhere.

Oooh—I wonder if we'll see Tory Burch? She's a major idol of mine, and I'm pretty sure she lives here.

But none of this has anything on our suite, which is incredible and absolutely massive. It features platinum-coloured silk on the panelled walls and low grey sofas and even a mahogany dining table. Our bedroom is almost as palatial as Adam's is back home, but my absolute favourite part is the terrace that lies beyond the smart French doors.

Not only is it chic as hell with its wrought-iron furniture, but it has a gobsmacking view straight onto Central Park. Granted, late November is not the best time to hang out on a high Manhattan terrace, but I'm determined to cosy up under some blankets later and enjoy the view.

Adam takes me out for a late lunch and a wander around the neighbourhood. I fall fast and hard for the Upper East Side. It's every bit as iconic as I've dreamed of, with its chic boutiques and art galleries. I particularly love the leafy side streets off Madison, their brownstones to die for.

It's on one of these streets in the seventies that we sit for a late lunch of *moules marinières* and obscenely good fries at a charming little bistro with starched white tablecloths and rickety wooden chairs. I'm in heaven. I thought I'd be feeling worse, but the magical concoction Dr Dyson gave us and the plane nap Adam insisted on in an actual double bed have me fighting fit and raring to go.

It feels good to be here, to put some physical distance between me and not only my brother but my unpaid invoices and long hours. I've only seen a tiny part of Manhattan, but so far it's delivering precisely the shot of inspiration and wellbeing that I've always suspected it would.

It's not until my phone lights up with a voice note from my brother towards the end of lunch that I allow myself to consider the real world. Why would I? I'm in a dreamy bubble with the kindest, most handsome, most attentive man I've ever, ever met, and I'm not sure I'm ready to reenter the real world. I eye my phone suspiciously. I'm afraid that if I listen, and he goes off on some slut-shaming, disappointed rant again, my precious little bubble will burst.

I put my phone in my bag. Once we're in Central Park, and Adam's fetching us hot chocolates from a kiosk with stern instructions to me to adjust my insulin first, I put in an ear bud and settle back on a cold bench and press *play*.

Hey. My brother's awkward greeting fills my ear. There's a pause, and then he starts talking. *Jesus. Look, I know you're in New York—with him—so I didn't want to call and disturb you. I wanted to say... I had a long, long chat with Mum and Dad, and my brain's a bit all over the place, to be honest, but what's very clear is that I owe you an apology. You definitely caught me off guard the other night, but I was a total shithead, and I'm sorry.*

There's a huge sigh. *You have more integrity in your little finger than anyone I know, so I should never have said those things to you, and I'm so sorry, Natster. Obviously, I don't think you're a slut—that was a horrific thing to say to my little sister. I was just so fucking shocked.*

I shift on the bench. The cold is seeping through the thick wool of my coat and chilling my bum, but the sky is clear and blue, and the park ridiculously picture-perfect, flanked as it is by elegant uptown skyscrapers. I cross my arms tightly over my chest to keep my boobs warm and sigh as I keep listening, my breath a cotton-wool cloud in the crisp air. In the distance, a busker is singing Coldplay very well indeed.

But look, my brother continues. *It seems there's a lot of shit that I wasn't aware of and have never wanted to be made aware of. I don't know if you remember this, but I didn't even go to the trial, except to give evidence. Mum and Dad thought I was too fragile. So I honestly didn't know anything about Adam's circumstances, and frankly, I was horrified. I mean, Jesus Christ, what that family went through was beyond horrific.*

He gives a little laugh. *It's funny how black and white things seem when you're young, isn't it? We're so incapable of accommodating shades of grey. Obviously, there couldn't have been more than one victim. Obviously, I was the* only *victim. But Mum was pretty bloody adamant tonight. Not sure I've seen her so militant before. She's very, very clear that he was a victim of circumstances as much as I was, and that he's a seriously good guy these days.*

I mean—he exhales heavily through his nostrils—*I'm not sure I'm ready to buddy up to him, you know? I've lived with this narrative, I suppose, for want of a better word, for a long, long time. But I'd like to think I'm evolved enough to make an effort to see the good in someone if people whose judgement I trust, like you and Mum, really believe it's there.*

I let out a little sob, because God knows I needed to hear this. I needed to know that my brother might, eventually, come around to accepting the idea of his sister being with the man he's always hated.

The same man who's walking towards me now in the golden New York winter sunlight in his beautiful black cashmere coat, his face tight with concern for me.

The man whose face is my absolute favourite face in the world.

Look, my brother says as Adam sits down next to me, taking the lid off my hot chocolate to let it cool down, *the only thing I care about is whether he's good for you. At the end of the day, all that matters is that he's not a violent man these days and he'll look after you the way you deserve. And Mum seems ready to join the Church of Adam Wright, so that gives me some comfort, I suppose. So have a good trip, yeah? I'm sorry again. And maybe we can—I dunno—all meet up and have a beer or something over Christmas. Love you.*

'Are you okay?' Adam asks me, putting his free arm carefully around me as he hands me my hot chocolate.

I remove my ear bud as I look up at him and smile.

'Yeah.' I nod, drinking in his face, his eyes. His everything. 'It sounds like he's coming around to the idea.'

'Really?' he asks. His voice is strained, like he can't quite believe it.

'Really,' I tell him. 'My mother can be very persuasive when she wants to be.'

'Don't I know it.'

I lay my head on his shoulder, the strains of *Yellow* and the scent of roasting chestnuts floating around us.

60

NATALIE

The theme for tonight's opening party may be *Speakeasy*, but this is ridiculous.

I regard my reflection in one of the several full-length mirrors in our suite. I packed the outfit Adam so enjoyed taking off me that very first time—my crystal-studded corset and tulle skirt—but he kiboshed that plan with a trip to Chanel down on Wooster. The result is that his net worth is at least five grand less than it was this morning and I look as close to a supermodel as I'll ever get.

Like I said, ridiculous.

The dress is short and gold, with a square neckline, thick shoulder straps, and fluttering cascades of sequins on tulle that hide my insulin pump. It features a gold sequinned camellia on the chest and is basically the most beautiful dress I've ever, ever worn. I feel like Taylor Swift.

Adam had the hotel concierge sort out hair and makeup for me at a nearby salon, and my hair is a glossy curtain that's been pinned up in a sleek ponytail. My makeup nods to the Twenties while still being sleek and modern, just the way I like it.

I can show up to Alchemy like this. I can be on the arm of one of the most eligible men on either side of the pond and feel worthy of him. I twist in front of the mirror, admiring my adorable black patent Mary Janes (also Chanel) and bending one leg, flapper girl style.

Adam comes up behind me, and I take great pleasure in eye fucking his reflection. He's wearing a black tux that's so beautifully cut I could weep—clearly Brioni has angels on its payroll—with a white tie. He slides his hands over my hips in a way that feels proprietary, and I shiver. I'm so worked up I could bend over for him here and now. Forget Alchemy. All I need is a bed—or a nice soft rug.

Fuck the rug. I'd ride this man on the parquet.

We haven't had sex since yesterday morning, a fact my vagina is all too aware of. Last night, I was so jet-lagged, and so tired from touring the Frick and the Met that I passed out before he was even finished in the bathroom, and he's refused to lay a finger on me today. Not even when we had our jet lag-busting siesta.

He says it's more fun to 'keep our powder dry' for tonight.

I wholeheartedly disagree, and I remind him of our difference of opinion by grinding my arse against him.

'You little minx.' He grabs my ponytail and tilts my head so he can slide his lips down from just below my ear to the strap of my dress. 'You know the more you tease me, the more intense it'll be for you tonight, don't you?'

'Mmm-hmm.' My voice is breathy, and I keep grinding. Sequins be damned. Adam has alluded more than once to having orchestrated a 'surprise' for me this evening, and I'm pretty sure he doesn't mean his dick. I have no idea what he has planned, but I bet it's kinky as hell.

Rather, I *hope* it's kinky as hell.

Alchemy's new Manhattan home isn't in a fancy brownstone, as I would have imagined, but in a huge former warehouse in the Meatpacking District. According to Adam, the team (especially Gen) had their hearts set on a brownstone, but getting permission for a sex club in any exclusive Upper East Side neighbourhood was a non-starter.

This is more discreet, too. Adam points out that guests who wish to come and go anonymously can use the underground parking garage to avoid the paps. Makes sense, I suppose.

There's no discretion tonight. For those souls brave enough to flagrantly enter a sex club in front of a sea of cameras—of which my boyfriend is apparently one—there's a full-on red carpet out the front. Adam gets out of his side of the town car (look at my American lingo) that brought us here and comes around to open my door. When I step out and get to my feet as elegantly as I can, my hand in his, the cameras flash, and I belatedly congratulate myself on the timing of coming clean to Stephen.

Having him see this shot in the *Daily Mail* would have warranted a fun conversation.

The ground floor is gorgeous. It's a totally different vibe to the London club—more industrial—but it's still incredible, with its high ceilings and polished concrete floor and sheer *size*. It looks like there are several bars, their facades paying homage to the London venue's backlit pink onyx one and their jewel-coloured bottles shining under the hanging copper lamps.

A glance around tells me a lot of the guests are here for a good party. The champagne is flowing, and hot shirtless guys wearing only black trousers and bow-ties are doing the rounds with trays of drinks, but they're also discreetly stamping the guests' hands each time someone takes one. No one's getting upstairs with more than two stamps on their hand, but I suspect it won't matter for a lot of tonight's partygoers, who are here to look beautiful and get papped and have a great time.

You can have a lot more fun with scale here than you can in a London townhouse—or a New York brownstone, for that matter. The stage is enormous, its red curtains hanging at its sides. Two beautiful women are spinning in golden hoops suspended from the ceiling, their crystal-dusted body stockings leaving almost nothing to the imagination.

Uh oh. I hope Max and Dex are willing to restrain Darcy tonight. One drink and she'll be climbing up there to show off her talents. I've never seen her in action in the The Playroom, but I've heard her dancing is world class—and seriously sexy.

The people here really are beautiful, especially the women: toned and glossy and expensive. They must have invited so many models along tonight. I smile to myself. Cal did well—this is an incredible party. I recognise a few of the patrons from London, the guys in particular. What a shocker that they've shown up here. I bet they bit Cal's hand off when he invited them. I get a lot of greetings and smiles and compliments, even a couple of kisses on my cheeks before my glowering, gorgeous boyfriend scares them off.

'They'd better not think for a single second that you're fair game tonight, just because you're not on the front desk,' he growls in my ear, his fingers flexing on my waist.

I pat his arm. 'I'm pretty sure nothing about the way you've got me in a death grip says I'm fair game.'

'Sorry.' He has the grace to look embarrassed, but he doesn't loosen his hold on me. 'I just know what dodgy fuckers these guys are. Give them an inch, and they'll take a fucking mile.'

'Nobody's taking anything except you,' I tell him, tilting my mouth up for a kiss.

The music tonight is fabulous: a speakeasy vibe but with a modern, sexy pulse. As people drink up and warm up, the dancing gets going. The lights strobe, and I enjoy the sight of beautiful bodies in expensive threads giving it their all. I finish my mocktail—a delicious cinnamon and vanilla concoction—and drag Adam to the dance floor where the other Alchemy London representatives are letting rip.

'We've never danced,' I tell him, shimmying in front of him.

'Not vertically, anyway,' he drawls, hooking me at the waist and drawing me closer. I slide my thigh between his legs and start to move, throwing my arms around his neck. He gazes down at me appreciatively. I never, ever go out dancing, but God, I love it, and this slinky, sparkly dress was definitely made for dancing in.

'Excellent point, Mr Wright,' I purr. Fuck, he's hot with that dark, dangerous look in his eyes. I reach up and tug at one end of his perfectly tied white tie so the ends fall flat against his dress shirt. It's a good one—it even has those little screw-in black and silver buttons. He watches me in amusement.

'May I remind you that the downstairs area has a strict clothes-on policy?'

'Tell that to Cal.'

He laughs. Cal's gone full gangster tonight in natty black and white spats, a white shirt, and red braces—suspenders, I suppose the New Yorkers call them. But his tie is long gone, and that shirt is now almost fully unbuttoned. I don't think Aida, who looks sensational in a short black dress with chevrons of jet beading, has played any part in undressing him. I think this is all Cal's handiwork.

From the way he's dirty dancing with her, I give them twenty minutes before they disappear off upstairs. I've already seen Gen, looking resplendent in custom McQueen, leading Anton up the huge, shallow metal staircase in the centre of the vast room. Clearly she has higher priorities than networking this evening.

I allow myself to soak it all up: the jaw-dropping surroundings, the sexy music, the glamorous women in their designer attire. This kind of sensory input is like crack for me. It's pulsing through my veins, morphing into pure creative inspiration in my head.

Tomorrow morning, I'll lie in bed and sketch some of the ideas that are coming to me even now, because a speakeasy theme for Gossamer's next Autumn/Winter collection would be divine. Gold and black. Short and flirty. Sequins for days. It would make for perfect Christmas party wear.

As the ideas whip around inside me, another more primitive part of my brain is aware that my boyfriend is hardening against me. He's not the only one getting worked up. Dancing with him, in this glorious, decadent place, has me on fire on all fronts. Thanks to the caffeine-laced IV Dr Dyson administered before we headed out for the evening, I feel on top of the world. I'm energised and excited and yes, aroused.

'I can dance until you fall asleep in my arms,' Adam whispers in my ear. 'But anytime you want to go upstairs and see your surprise, just say the word.' His voice deepens seductively as his hand tightens on my bottom. 'Just remember, once we get up there, you hand everything over to me. Your power and your pleasure. Got it?'

Oh *God.* My pussy clenches at the thought of it, and I remember that the dancing part of the evening, fun and sexy though it is, is just a warmup.

The main event—my surprise, whatever it is—awaits us upstairs.

'Let's go,' I say quickly, and he laughs and kisses me on the cheek.

'Christ, I love how predictable you are.'

61

ADAM

Following Nat up the broad industrial staircase in the centre of the room is the best kind of foreplay, especially given how conscious I am that she's not wearing panties tonight. We bypass The Playroom and head straight for the next floor. The highly specific surprise I've booked for her is in one of the private rooms.

'Room twenty-four, please,' I say to the young woman standing at the entrance to the long corridor that stretches ahead.

'Name please, sir?' she asks with an appreciative glance at Nat.

'Wright.'

'Certainly Mr Wright. Enjoy your evening.' She hands me a heavy, old-school iron key that feels pleasantly cool and appropriately weighty as I close my fingers around it.

'I'm sure we will,' I say, curling my arm around Nat's sequin-covered waist as I draw her down the corridor.

Space is certainly at a premium here. The doors are far more spaced out than in London. But the key difference, and the one Nat clocks immediately with an amusingly audible gasp, is that every single one has a large viewing window.

Some showcase dim, empty rooms, quietly waiting for a spectacle to unfold within.

Some have their scarlet curtains drawn, the bleed of golden light at their edges the only sign that the room is occupied.

And some are gloriously, seductively open, beckoning passersby and voyeurs alike to stop and sample the delights of the tableaux they showcase.

It seems there are already voyeurs aplenty. One window has drawn a small crowd, and we stop, Nat still pulled tightly against me. My gaze lands on a couple watching. Her back is to his front. She has crimson-coloured hair in a vintage-looking updo and is wearing a cropped black corset and black leather leggings. His hand is down the front of said leggings as they watch, and, judging by the way she's grinding against his dick, I'd say he's hitting the spot.

I smile to myself. I wonder if I could ever get my beautiful little minx to capitulate so fully that she'd allow me to touch her like that in public. My instincts say no, but God knows she's surprised me so far.

A glance through the window shows two fucking huge Black men spit-roasting a voluptuous red-haired women. All three are naked, writhing, the sheen of sweat on their skin suggesting they've been at it for some time. A shot of desire spears through me, causing me to harden further.

I notice belatedly that there are a couple of old-school telephone receivers hooked just below the window. I pick one up to see if my hunch is correct, grin when I hear that it absolutely is, and put the receiver to Nat's ear.

She gasps again and turns scarlet. 'Oh my God.'

Yep. I suspect she just had a sample of what the guy fucking the woman is saying to her.

'You've got to be Alchemy's most shockable employee by a country mile,' I tell her as I lead us away from the window, and she swats me.

'Shut up.'

'It's true. And I think it's adorable.'

'Does our room...' she begins. 'Does it have a window?'

'It does. And a curtain. And a mute button for the microphones. I'll allow you to decide how brave you're feeling.'

She mutters something under her breath that I don't quite catch, but it sounds amusing, in any case.

We reach room twenty-four, and I guide her through with a hand on the small of her back, immediately locking the door and pulling the velvet curtains closed over the viewing window, which is actually a two way mirror. I want to give her privacy while she ponders what she wants. The microphone under the window defaults to off, so we're safe on that front.

I tug her against my front as we take in the room. It's far bigger than the ones in London, but the look and feel are similar: sculptural wall sconces and midnight-blue walls and ornate lacquered cabinets housing all manner of toys. There's a massive bed—it must be eight feet across—kitted out with metal hoops, just like in London. On the far wall, brackets support a selection of spreader bars, and I'm reminded of my extreme interest in rigging Nat up on one of those sooner rather than later.

But none of these delights are what's holding her attention right now, because, planted in the middle of the empty space in front of the bed and in prime position for the viewing window is a wonderful example of an antique spanking bench. It looks to be made from oak with burgundy leather padding. From the lower branches for the recipient's—or *victim's*—arms and legs, leather cuffs hang open.

'Is this the surprise?' she asks, turning to look up at me. All sorts of thoughts and emotions are travelling over her face, and I'd give a lot to be privy to them right about now.

'Yes.' I trace the outline of her lower lip softly with my thumb pad. 'Do you know what it is?'

'I have some idea,' she mutters. 'But you'd better enlighten me.'

'It's a spanking bench,' I say in a quiet voice, watching her face for a reaction. 'All it does is put you in the perfect position for me to spank you and do whatever else I like to you. The restraints mean you'll be secured, but it also puts you more at my mercy, which I think and hope will give us both great pleasure. What do you think?'

I keep my face neutral—no mean feat, given the mere thought of having Nat naked and cuffed to that thing is wreaking havoc with my dick. I've fantasised about this ever since Cal sent me the floor plan for this place and asked me which room I'd like dibs on, but seeing Nat standing right next to it is another story.

'I'd like to try it,' she says, wriggling.

'Are you imagining it right now—is that why you're squirming?' I ask.

'Yeah,' she confesses, looking up at me through her eyelashes. 'I dunno—it just feels... exciting, knowing I won't be able to move.'

I nod encouragingly. 'It's supposed to. I figured you'd be ready for this. You've let me tie you up before, and you've let me spank you. This is more of the same, just with the intensity ramped up. You should know that once I've got you up on this thing, you're my little fuck toy, to do what I like with. Do you understand?'

She swallows as she nods, and I swear her eyes are growing glassier by the second. I fucking love that we both get off on this dynamic equally.

'Tell me your safe word.'

'Organza.'

'Good. Curtains open or closed?'

Her eyes dart to the window. 'Closed.' She pauses. 'For now.'

'That's my good girl. I'm going to blindfold you. It'll help you submit to me and add to your sensory pleasure. Okay?'

'Okay.' She licks her lips, and the corners of my mouth curve up into a smile. I love all the facets of my girlfriend: her feistiness (with me, at least), her courage, her ambition, her extraordinary compassion, her softness when she chooses it. I'd never, ever want her to be a pushover. That would be boring as hell.

But when she opts to put herself in my hands, to shed her inhibitions and transform into a delectable, pliant kitten, it takes my breath away.

I slide a finger over her delicate collar bone. 'Now, stand very still so I can admire my beautiful little toy while I take off your dress.'

62

NATALIE

A dam moves around me, and I shiver as his fingers brush the nape of my neck. He unzips my dress slowly. It falls to the floor, heavy with sequins, and I step carefully out of it.

'Turn around.'

He may be the one calling the shots here, but I've never felt so potent as I do in this quiet room with every last ounce of this powerful man's attention trained on me, every bit of desire *for me*.

I stand before him in a black lace bra, matching suspender belt and fine fishnet stockings, all courtesy of a productive trip to La Perla yesterday with Adam. I'm still in my Chanel heels, but even so he towers above me.

I want to ask, *like what you see?* But the stark hunger on his face makes the question redundant.

'Just perfect,' he murmurs, and reaching around, he unhooks my bra. I shiver again as he slides the straps down my arms and the lace cups snag on my taut nipples. His white tie lies flat against his shirt, just the way I left it, and a dark curl has escaped his Twenties-style slicked-back hairdo. He is a sight for sore eyes, and he's going to unleash himself on me at any moment.

He moves to stand next to the bench. 'Now, sweetheart. This bench has been designed specifically for naughty girls just like you, who need to be punished and need to be fucked. I want you to watch me cuff you, and then I'll put your blindfold on.' He bends and slaps the main, upper padded part hard, and I jump. 'Up you get.'

I approach the contraption with caution. He's right—it's not a huge departure from what we've already done—but there's something about its very intentionality that has my heart thudding inside my rib cage. I place a knee on one of the lower sections. It looks like they're adjustable, and they've been widened, presumably to give Adam as much access as he wants to my pussy. The thought of being tied down and spread open for him like this has my core pulsing.

Once I have both knees on, I hinge forward, lowering myself down onto its padded top. The leather smells old and rich, and its cold smoothness is heaven against my poor, taut nipples. It must be, what, a hundred years old? I wonder how many women have been bent over and cuffed and defiled on this thing. The stories it could tell.

I lay my forearms down on the front two sections and rest my forehead on the horseshoe-shaped front part of the main section—it's not unlike the head rests you find on massage tables. Those kinky Victorians, or whoever made this, definitely knew what they were doing. This thing was ergonomic before it became a corporate buzzword. It's perfectly designed to take my weight, to support me in this weird, prone, exposed position. The leather is slippery, but I suppose once the restraints are on, I'll feel completely secure.

Good Lord. I really like this.

'I cannot begin to tell you,' Adam says, crouching behind me to fasten the big leather restraint around my right ankle, 'how fucking delectable you look right now, sweetheart. Your holes are so enticing. They're *right there.* The things I could do to this beautiful body of yours.'

'You can do them all,' I tell him, which is probably reckless, but I'm past caring. I want him to do all the things.

Sure enough, he tuts. 'Brave words from a girl who's about to be totally fucking captive.'

He makes swift work of my other three restraints. 'Test them for me,' he orders, and I do, flexing my feet and attempting to pull my hands through the wrist cuffs. They all hold firm, and I have a fleeting feeling of claustrophobia —or maybe it's just straightforward panic at being trussed up like this.

'Good,' he says. There's the sound of the cupboard behind me being pulled open and some tinkering noises, and then Adam's in front of me again, crouching down to eye level, those pale blue eyes positively blazing with intensity, with the promise of the acts he intends to perform on me. 'I've got some props. The blindfold, but also a carrot and a stick, if you like.'

The *carrot* is a girthy-looking vibrator, or dildo, maybe? I'm never sure of the difference. Holy shit. It's black and dick-like, with mean veins running over its surface and a hooked part that I assume works on the clit, while the *stick* is some sort of wide leather paddle, again black. Adam slaps it against his palm, and I can see that it has some give in it.

'They both look like sticks to me,' I mutter, because come on. What was that *this is nothing we haven't done before* spiel? This guy is moving the goalposts at a dizzying rate.

He raises his two dark eyebrows. 'Do you have a word you'd like to say?'

I glare mutinously at him. No way am I giving him the satisfaction. 'No.'

He smiles. 'Good girl. You can always say it if you need it. But no bitching and moaning. The paddle is just a cleaner way to spank you, and I promise you'll be fucking gagging for this piece of silicon once I start.' He moves his mouth to my ear, his warm breath and ominous words sending a shower of goosebumps over my neck. 'It's just the warm-up act while you wait for the real thing.'

With that promise, he wraps the blindfold around my head, tying it at the back, and my visual world goes black as sensation steps up to take its place. Adam's footsteps slap against the polished concrete floor as he walks around to my rear. I imagine what he's seeing, and I almost blush.

My limbs, restrained in leather cuffs.

My bottom, bared for him except for the black suspender straps bisecting both cheeks.

My most private parts on full display.

It all feels so shameful, but in a really good way, a way that has desire roiling in my stomach and beating out a tattoo between my legs. My breathing sounds louder to me, thanks to the blindfold pulled tightly over my ears. The smooth leather beneath my body isn't quite padded enough to be comfortable, and that discomfort lends an edge that isn't quite humiliation but probably isn't far off.

Oddest of all, I'm feeling as though I want to lean into that feeling of... vulnerability, I suppose. Of exposure. Of putting my entire helpless, aroused self in Adam's seriously capable hands. Of being shown off and torn open and spanked and prodded and played with and fucked, and...

My breath is coming quicker. This is a fantasy I absolutely didn't know I had, but as it plays out around me, real and vibrant, I can feel how badly I want to give myself over to it. I want Adam to know he can push me tonight, that he can listen to his judgement when it comes to what I'd like. He knows me better than I know myself in bed, it seems.

'You can open the curtains,' I burst out.

'Seriously?' His voice sounds curt with all that unleashed desire.

'Yeah. I want people to see what you do to me.' I pause. 'I want them to see how completely I trust you.' My voice sounds strangled.

'You're a beautiful, beautiful woman,' he says, dropping a kiss on my shoulder blade. 'And your trust is my most prized possession. You won't regret it.' I hear him move to the viewing window and tug the curtains, their old-fashioned brass hooks rattling as they drag across the pole.

'Mic on?'

'Sure,' I reply carelessly. 'Why not?'

Tonight represents so many firsts for me it's not funny, but who cares? I'm in a city where no one knows who I am, far away from my place of work.

Let them look.

Let them listen.

The bench is angled away from the window at forty-five degrees, which means anyone watching or passing should be able to see my pussy, assuming Adam doesn't block their view the whole time. But what matters is that I'm blind-folded *and* the window is a mirror on this side. It's not like he or I will know if people are watching or not. The fact that they *may* be watching Adam do what he wants with me, shatter me to pieces so skilfully and put me back together like I know he will, adds enough of a frisson for me.

I wait, and the first sensation comes.

A breeze between my legs.

63

NATALIE

He's fanning me, I think. A cool breeze wafts over the aching, throbbing heat of my clit as I register the sound of something soft batting the air. It's wonderful and awful in equal measure.

'Such a beautiful sight, your cunt,' he says. 'I can see how swollen it is already, sweetheart. Imagine how much it'll be begging for my cock in a few minutes.'

I let out a throaty little sound that has him throwing something on the bed with a soft thud and then hooking his thumbs under my suspender straps before letting them ping against my skin. It smarts, but I know the paddle will be way worse.

He gropes my cheeks, taking handfuls of my flesh and kneading like I'm his property and he's checking me out. That feeling intensifies as he runs a proprietary finger down between them, prodding at my entrance before swiping over my clit. It's the most fleeting touch, but I swear my soul sings at the feel of it.

'More of that later, if you're a good girl for me,' he

promises. 'Now, let's start with five on each side, shall we? If you manage those, I'll reward you. Safe word?'

'Organza,' I croak.

'Very good. Don't forget to count.'

I lie here in this strange, supported all-fours position, waiting for the first strike. Time is suspended, my heart racing, my entire body braced with the most curious combination of fear and need. There's silence, then a rush of air and a resounding slap on my right cheek that's so sudden and oddly, cleanly, painful that I let out an involuntary cry. It feels like an overreaction, but I can't help it.

'God, that's a beautiful sound,' Adam muses, then: 'Count.'

'One,' I say feebly, clenching my fists in their restraints.

'Good girl.'

The first strike on the other cheek is equally intrusive and stinging. My eyes prick with instant, violated tears while my legs struggle ineffectually to move.

Adam waits.

'Two,' I say belatedly as the stinging sensation morphs into a warm, glowing halo.

He rewards me with the briefest touch of his finger, which slides inside me effortlessly before he pulls it out.

'Just as I thought,' he says triumphantly. 'My sweet, perfect little toy is fucking gagging for this.'

He sounds every bit as smug as he was that first time he got me in a private room at Alchemy. Then, I wanted to slap him and shame myself. Now, I just want him to take pity on my poor pussy and fuck me.

We work through the first ten spanks, five on each side, and I remember to count.

'You're doing so well,' he tells me fondly. 'Are you feeling okay?'

'Yes,' I reply. It's true. I'm growing more and more lost inside this dark, wonderful prison.

'Good,' he says. I hear his footsteps travel away from me, then there's the squelch of something wet, followed by a buzzing noise. Uh-oh. I know what that is. While I was immensely grateful for my rose vibrator before I met Mr Your-Orgasms-Are-My-Job, I'm undoubtedly the sole female employee of Alchemy who has never fucked herself with eight inches of silicon. I can't help but brace as Adam's foot-steps—and the buzzing vibrator—come closer.

'I told you I'd reward you,' he says. What I'm not expecting is for his hand to squeeze under one side of my torso and tweak the nearest nipple. It's painfully hard and so extraordinarily good that I whimper.

He withdraws his hand, but a moment later the tip of the vibrator is buzzing hard against my clit, and *hooooooly fuck*. I practically come on the spot, but then it's gone.

'Count,' he orders, and the paddle hits me again. If anything, the clean, sharp sting it delivers intensifies the throbbing in my clit.

'One,' I bleat.

The vibrator is back, tracing a lazy, lubed-up, mesmerising path from my clit to my entrance.

'Get that arse in the air, high as you can,' he orders me, and I strain to obey him, arching my back as much as I can in this position to lift my bottom away from the bench. I'm a needy, greedy thing, writhing like this against that buzzing tip, attempting to push against it. If anyone is watching, they'll see just how much I want to be fucked in any way possible, and the thought of it has hot, intoxicating shame coursing over me.

'Nice,' he hisses. Without warning, he pushes the beast in hard, and I let out a strangled gasp at the welcome intrusion, because I'll take it, I'll take every inch of it until Adam sees fit to give me the real thing.

He's still feeding it into me when he hits me with the third spank of this round, and the blow makes me jolt against the vibrator. Holy crap. Holy crap. I will *not* last till ten without coming. I let out a cry because this is all so perfect that I want to die.

'Count!' he shouts at me in a deeper, sterner voice than I've ever heard him use on me.

'Three,' I say. 'Oh God, three, I—'

He rams the vibrator in a couple of inches further before administering the fourth spank of the paddle. Beneath my blindfold, I screw my eyes shut and press my lips together before breathing out the word *four.*

'Greedy girl,' he croons. 'Jesus Christ, so fucking greedy. Anyone walking past is going to see that greedy little cunt taking a rubber cock while I pink up this luscious little arse even more. You've got me so hard, sweetheart. I'm going to fuck you so, so hard as soon as you've come.'

On the fifth strike, he pushes the vibrator in a little further. Jesus, it's big, and it's so obviously a foreign object that my pussy is torn between feeling violated and dancing the Can Can.

On the sixth, it bottoms out, and I experience a whole new level of mind-bending pleasure as the clit part of it hits home. It's vibrating inside me, massaging my walls as it rubs at my clit in the craziest way, and I definitely will *not* survive this.

Then he starts to fuck me with it, using deep, rolling thrusts, my clit reaping the rewards each time it bottoms out in me. I shudder and shake and whimper through the last four counts, which come further and further apart until I've cried out *ten* at which point I hear the paddle hit the floor with a clatter.

And then? Then he just fucking holds the vibrator there, its extension a relentless, constant assault on my clit as its girth continues to shudder inside me and my burning bottom glows with its halo of heat and some strange, profound pleasure. It's so *much*, so completely overwhelming, that I'm powerless to resist it.

I don't.

I can't.

I allow the deluge to consume me with a barrage of waves so strong they obliterate my consciousness. I'm sucked under, pummelled with a pleasure so great it has me reeling. The fact of my being restrained like this, unable to move through the sensation overload, simply adds to the intensity.

When I climax, it's with full-body convulsions, my eyes squeezed tightly shut behind their blindfold and Adam's name on my lips, over and over and over. I'm turned inside out and upside down; I'm reborn. The clean completeness of this feeling is nothing I've ever, ever felt before.

As the pleasure crests and begins to ebb, the vibration is too much, and I flinch slightly. He flicks the device off immediately and pulls it gently out of my body. It lands on the bed, and then his hands are smoothing down my back, over my stinging, happy bottom.

'God, you did so fucking well,' he whispers hoarsely, dropping a kiss to one sore cheek and then the other. 'I will remember this sight when I'm on my deathbed.'

I giggle. 'So good,' I agree with a slur. I can barely form words.

'I have to fuck you now,' he says, his voice growing

firmer, that edge that gets me off hardening his words audibly. 'If you can handle more.'

My clit may have taken a pounding, but my pussy is bereft. 'I want the real thing now,' I murmur, and he lets out a pained laugh.

'Jesus Christ. Where did I find you?' He's tugging at clothes as he speaks. I hear the unmistakable rasp of his zip before the beautiful wool of his trousers brushes my inner thighs. What kind of tableau must we make? Me, blindfolded and basically naked, restrained on a spanking bench while the most beautiful man in the world, dressed in a tuxedo that probably cost five figures, attempts to take me from behind.

All I know is, I'd love to see it.

But then Adam's dragging his hot, blunt crown through my wet, swollen flesh, and I almost forget to breathe, because battery power has nothing on this.

He pushes in, wide and hard and insistent, grunting as he does, and I'm reminded that Adam Wright, esquire, is an animal beneath that fine tailoring. I squirm, using what little leverage I have to push back against him, to take him in more quickly.

'Of all the women at Alchemy, I fell for the demure, hot-as-fuck little receptionist,' he grits out, 'and just fucking look at you now. You should see your cunt taking my cock. It's truly incredible.'

I moan and roll my forehead against the bench's uncomfortably hard head support. 'You're welcome.'

He chuckles darkly. 'Christ above. Hang on tight.'

It's lucky I have no leeway on this contraption, because he pushes all the way in, then, and really lets me have it, his drives a manifestation of the extreme pent-up frustration this man clearly has, because each rolling, perfect thrust has my muscle memory activating and my already-sated vagina getting ideas.

The dildo had nothing on this. Adam Wright is the king of fucking, and all I can do is lie here like this and let him unleash total havoc on my body. It's as if the force of his desire, his desperation, is infectious. It's so arousing to have him pump me like this, as though I'm the answer to every puzzle, every problem he's ever encountered, like if he can just fuck me hard enough, bottom out deep enough inside my body, we'll both emerge on the other side whole and new and awe-filled.

He's shunting the breath out of my lungs, filling me with nothing but him. My muscles quicken impossibly, miraculously, that beautiful ache coming out of nowhere. He's painting galaxies of need from a body that five minutes ago was sated beyond belief, spinning me higher, taking me with him as he weaves his magic.

As the flutters inside me grow stronger, sharper, more defined, more urgent, he fucks me and fucks me. I wrap my fingers around the curved ends of the arm supports and hang on for dear life as the man behind me, inside me, obliterates my sanity and turns me inside out for the second time tonight.

With my movements compromised, my only outlet for this extraordinary chemical reaction inside me is my voice. I'm screaming, I realise. I'm actually *screaming* his name, over and over and over, like a sacred mantra that's my only tether to sanity. In return, his intoxicatingly low, male noises of effort and ecstasy grow louder, less contained.

'Fuuuck, sweetheart,' he groans as my body convulses around him. 'Fuck! Fuck!' With that exhortation, he grows wonderfully rigid before spilling himself deep inside me with violent jerks, his fingers white-knuckling my hip bones.

As his shudders subside, he releases my hips and, sliding his hands up my back, he folds forward. I turn my head to the side, and he lays his face next to mine. His heart is hammering against my shoulder blade, his shirt crisp against my skin, his face hot against mine.

He kisses my temple so sweetly. 'Give me just a sec,' he whispers, and then he's sliding out of me and getting to his feet. I hear the clinking of the curtain hooks being dragged across the window, and then he kneels before me again and pulls the knot on my blindfold loose. I raise my head with difficulty and blink at him.

I'm not sure there has never been a more tender, proud, adoring look on a man's face than the one I see on Adam's in this moment. I'm not sure his beautiful pale blue eyes could contain more emotion. I'm not sure I could feel more looking at any human on the planet than I do here in this room, after what we've just done.

He strokes my face. 'Let's get you out of these so I can carry you to the shower, and soap you up nice and gently, and tell you all the reasons why you're the most incredible woman I've ever met,' he whispers. 'Then I want to dry you off, and lie you down, and rub some cream on that gorgeous bottom of yours, and tell you all over again. How does that sound?'

That all sounds truly excellent.

64

NATALIE

Christmas cheer looks like a fleet of men and women in black cargo pants and long-sleeved black t-shirts standing on Adam's front porch with all manner of festive goodies. The team from the decorating company has turned up bright and early on a Saturday morning to transform his palatial home into a winter wonderland, and I can't wait. It's already the second Saturday in December, which in my eyes means at least a week lost when we could have been enjoying the decorations.

I'm going to make him keep them up for weeks and weeks after Christmas.

When Adam handed me his iPad on his jet last week and gave me carte blanche, let's just say I took him at his word. I rapidly upgraded his pathetic gesture of 'a tree in the hallway' to a full festive programme including, but not limited to, a colour scheme for each area of the ground floor, scent design by room, and intricate projection mapping across the mansion's facade.

I'm so excited!

While I'm here to make sure everything goes smoothly and that the team is clear on how to execute on their brief, I'm also in danger of getting in the way. I take tea and coffee orders and relay these to Toby, who's on duty today, and then proceed to spend a couple of hours floating around the house as I watch the magic come to life.

It's a huge brief, but the decoration company has sent a big team, so they make fast work of it. I sit on my beloved grass-green *chaise longue* in the hallway, hugging my mug of tea to my chest—the mug is Hermès, naturally—while four people light and dress the crazy twelve-foot tree that's taken the place of the flower-bearing table in the centre of the space and another three assemble a garland on the sweeping bannister that incorporates holly, ivy, eucalyptus and feathery fronds of fir.

Finally, they weave in white fairy lights and white and silver baubles, in keeping with the theme we've chosen for the entrance hall. By the time they've finished dressing the tree in the same colours and have added impeccably wrapped white and silver fake gifts underneath, the space looks incredible: truly magical and outrageously festive.

We—*I*—opted for cool colours in the drawing room where I first sat and fumed as Dr Dyson examined me. In keeping with the grey tones of the furnishings and linen walls, the tree in there and the garland on the mantelpiece are both decked out in dusky pink and pewter tones, while the ornaments have an old-world feel.

But the favourite is my beloved library. I mean, it's Adam's library, obviously. It's just that it's beloved of *me*. The bookshelves' eau de nil and dull gold accents were too dreamy not to exploit, so I gave the design team a simple, one-word brief: *Ladurée.* As an ode to the luxury French *macaron* brand, they've used sugared-almond pastels in here, bedecking every piece of greenery with duck-egg blue and pale pink velvet ribbons and pastel decorations. They've even found some baubles shaped like *macarons*.

If I thought Adam's home was beautiful before, as a canvas for Christmas it makes me want to sink to my knees in sheer delight. Now I just need to track down the master of the house and drag him around his new festive wonderland.

I finally locate him in his basement gym. It's incredible down here—he has a gym, a lap pool, full-on hammam with infrared sauna, steam room and experience showers (the citronella mist one is my favourite) and his beloved ice bath. He escaped a couple of hours ago to work on some secret project for his company, ostensibly to get out of the decorators' way but really, I suspect, to give me free rein as I oversaw the project.

Boy, am I glad I tracked him down.

I slump against the door frame, arms folded, as I take in what feels like my own private viewing of *Magic Mike*. Adam is doing pull ups on some contraption with a high bar—I have no idea what the name for it is, and I don't care, because my boyfriend is wearing nothing but a pair of black athletic shorts and footwear, and holy fucking shit.

The sheen of sweat on him. The muscles. The way his damp hair is raked back off his face. Jesus Christ. I watch as he pulls himself up again. Every single muscle in his body ripples. Those shoulders of his are fucking *huge*. Veins pop along his biceps and forearms. His glorious pecs contract. He's bloody ridiculous. There's something so obscenely *male* about this show he's putting on: the effort, the grunts as he hoists himself up and lowers himself as slowly as possible.

I realise I'm a cliché, but seeing him like this makes me want to go full cavewoman and scream *mine!*

He grins at me with effort. 'See something you like?' he huffs out.

'Hell, yes.' I stroll towards him, eyeing up the damp trail of dark hair disappearing into his shorts.

'How are the decorations looking?'

'What decorations?' I deadpan, stopping in front of him as he lowers himself, inch by trembling inch.

He grunts out a laugh that quickly turns more anguished as I smooth my palm down the slickness of his abs.

'Careful,' he warns as he pulls himself up again. I keep my hand where it is and smirk, pleased with myself, as his body brushes upwards against it so I'm basically palming his cock. Mmm. I gaze up at him through my eyelashes. He hasn't taken his eyes off me, either. It's evident just what an impressive feat this is, in terms of self-discipline as much as physical strength.

Not that that's any surprise. Adam Wright is a man who will pour blood, sweat and tears into getting what he wants, and that's as much of a turn-on for me as is the fine physical specimen he makes.

I keep my hand where it is, pressing against him. I swear, he fills out slightly against me in return.

'How many reps do you have left?' I ask innocently, batting my eyelashes.

I squeeze.

'Fuck,' he grits out. 'I'm done.' He lets himself drop to the ground, and I take a step back on instinct. I don't want a tonne of hard, muscular man landing on my socked toes. But before I can react further, he's hooking an arm around me and hauling me against his soaking wet body. His breath is ragged, his tone ominous, as he continues, 'And you're going to get it.'

My hands go to his deliciously slick shoulders. 'Oh yeah?'

'Yep.' He spins me around and, with a hand clamped around the back of my neck, frogmarches me towards the island in the centre of the gym. It's more of a decorative depository than anything else, crafted from a gorgeous chunk of matte black marble. The niches in its sides house dozens of rolled-up towels—even though Adam's the only person I know who works out in here—and on its smooth surface stand a big white bowl of oranges and a jug of iced cucumber water for his lordship.

We come to stand in front of it, my hips touching its smooth edge, and his hand bears down on the back of my neck. 'Bend over, sweetheart.' The way he says the endearment sounds more foreboding than affectionate, and I absolutely love it.

'Here?' I protest feebly. 'What if someone comes in?'

'I'd like to see them fucking try. *Now.*'

I'm not sure there's anything better than a man treating you like his plaything in the bedroom (or gym, for that matter) and a princess everywhere else. In the past week or more, his behaviour has intensified on both fronts. I feel like the early signs of Winky's thaw have given both of us the confidence to lean into this relationship, to invest in it, just as my, ahem, 'positive' reaction to him getting rougher and more stern with me in bed has ignited something in him that he's been needing to unleash.

And Adam Wright unleashing himself on me is all I want. So if he's seeing and acting on all these shameless green lights I've been flashing at him, then I couldn't be happier.

But back to the rapidly hardening dick that's grinding into the cleft between my arse cheeks. This house is so wonderfully cosy that I'm in just a yoga vest and pants with a loose, cloud-like cashmere sweater that's fallen off one shoulder. Now one hand is digging into my hip as the other strokes down my neck and between my shoulder blades.

'Be a very good girl,' he croons, his dick flexing against me, 'and I'll let you come quickly.'

The unspoken threat if I'm *not* a very good girl hangs in the air between us, thick as treacle.

Hmm. Decisions, decisions.

I'm bent at a right angle, my arms cactused either side of my head on the smooth marble, my cheek pressed to its surface. I can feel the stone's coolness at my front and my boyfriend's wet heat at my back. When he seems happy that I won't move, he strokes my hair before hooking his fingers into both sides of my waistband.

'Let's take a look at what you've got for me,' he says, and I groan. Why oh why is the act of being bent over by this guy so he can peel my yoga pants and thong off and look his fill so fucking much of a turn on?

65

ADAM

It's her breathy little groan that spurs me on—that sign that she needs this as badly as I do. This astonishing woman, so strong and beautiful, so magnificent, has given me carte blanche to run rampant over her body, and I'm damn well going to give thanks for every moment while also pushing her to her limits.

Because, God knows, she's responded so perfectly to every push so far.

I take enormous pleasure in peeling her leggings and thong slowly, slowly down and revealing the creamy white skin of her arse for my viewing pleasure. 'Very nice,' I murmur, smoothing a hand over it. My breathing is still ragged from those fucking pull-ups, and my leg muscles scream as I squat for a better look at the line of pretty holes between her cheeks.

'I'm going to be in a whole world of pain tomorrow because someone interrupted me before I got a chance to stretch out,' I muse idly, straightening up so I can bend over her. 'What do you say to that?'

She gives a little giggle. 'Poor baby.'

'I think it's only fair that we're *both* sore tomorrow, don't you?'

I slap her right cheek hard without warning at the same time that the first and index fingers of my left hand push hard inside her, and the little cry she makes as she bucks is fucking glorious.

'Don't you?' I repeat as I twist my fingers inside her body and massage her pinked-up flesh.

'Um—yes,' she manages, clawing ineffectually at the marble surface of the island.

'Quite right.' I withdraw my fingers and rush to free my now fully hard cock, shoving my shorts down till they're bunched at my ankles. 'Let's get you sore in the best way possible, sweetheart. Hmm?'

As she pants out her *yes please*, I take my cock in my fist and drag it down from her entrance to her clit and back up again. Her slickness is heavenly torture against my poor, sensitised crown.

'Tell me if it hurts against the marble,' I say, and then I'm pushing in. Yeah, she's wet, but I haven't exactly warmed her up to take me, and it's fucking tight. Dear God above, the sight of my beautiful Nat, bent over for me and taking my dick inch by slow, friction-filled inch, is an almost religious experience, and the disbelief hits me in a wave of emotion right alongside the sensory pleasure of driving, driving, until I'm bottoming out inside her.

'Fuck me, sweetheart, you are such a good girl right now,' I groan. I'm going to take her hard and fast and then drag her into the enormous shower next door and soap up every perfect inch of her skin. 'Do you want it rough?'

'You know I do,' she moans. 'I want to feel your balls slapping against my thighs as you fuck me.'

Sweet Jesus.

One of the hundreds of miraculous things about growing close to this woman has been the discovery that she comes seriously hard and, it seems, relatively easily, from penetration. I'd go down on her for hours and hours without complaint—tasting her is still an extraordinary privilege—but being able to orgasm in sync with her is pretty fucking special.

My workout has endorphins coursing through my veins. Nat showed up for her coy little fangirl routine at the best possible time. I feel strong, powerful, and my power is something I no longer shrink from. It's something I relish, something I channel.

Especially right now.

Standing up straight behind her, I pull out slowly... and then I ram the fuck home.

'Oh my *God.*' Her voice is guttural. Primal.

'Okay?' I'm worried her hips will bruise against the marble as I ram into her over and over.

'More than okay.'

She really, really is such a good girl. I'll let her come fast and hard. God knows, we both need it. I keep hold of her hip with one hand and use the other to push up her gauzy sweater so I can admire the delicate hills and valleys of her spine as I let her have it with thrust after thrust. It's so fucking deep at this angle, and the slap of my balls as they meet her thighs each time is second only to that clean rasp when my hand meets her arse.

My beautiful, classy girlfriend likes it rough, and I wouldn't be fulfilling my obligations as a boyfriend if I didn't give her what she needs. Her cries and my grunts ramp up as I continue my onslaught. Her eyelashes flicker against her cheek as she takes my pounding. She's a vision.

'Did you come in here hoping to get fucked?' I ask her gruffly.

'Obviously,' she says in a breathy voice.

I grit my teeth together in an attempt to control myself. My little minx was upstairs, in her own version of festive heaven, but she decided to wander down and see if she could persuade me to give her a good seeing to.

Holy fuck.

'I need to get a spanking bench for this place,' I decide aloud. Fuck Alchemy. I want to be able to do to Nat what I did in New York whenever I please, in the privacy of my own home. 'Would you like that?' I'm so close to blowing I can barely get the words out.

'Buy me one for Christmas,' she manages, and I grit out an anguished laugh.

'Too. Fucking. Right.' I stretch the words out, thrusting with each one, and her internal muscles begin to flutter around me, teasing my dick in the most tortuous way.

'God, sweetheart, give it to me.' I take great pride in dragging out of her and slamming home as hard as I can.

'Ahhh!' she cries.

'Yes. *Yes.* Take it.' I'm mumbling through clenched teeth as I thrust, my forehead beaded with even more sweat, my well-worked abs screaming as I fuck her nice and hard and evenly.

She's scrambling harder at the marble, her lips working, eyes squeezed tightly shut in ecstasy as her orgasm builds. She's a slave to her own needs in this perfect moment. I wind her—and myself—higher. 'Jesus Christ, sweetheart, feel how much this greedy cunt loves my cock,' I grit out.

That does it. She screams and proceeds to shatter around me, beneath me, her body draped so beautifully over this block of marble that it's almost as if it's an altar and she's the most exquisite sacrificial lamb.

My sacrificial lamb. She's surrendered to me, body and soul, and it's an offering so awe-inspiring that it has me following her over the edge of consciousness into a void that's nothing but white-hot pleasure.

'Okay,' I tell her. 'I'm ready.'

She grins up at me from her place next to me. Toby and I have carried a little two-seater sofa out into the front garden, Toby having hastily wrapped the French oak legs in cling film to avoid the cold, damp grass damaging the wood. We'll have to find a more permanent solution for the next few weeks, though. I suspect this will become one of Natalie's favourite nighttime routines.

'All right.' She aims the remote control at a box nestled to the left of the porch and gasps as the music starts up. I steady the non-alcoholic hot toddy Toby concocted for us on my knee with one hand and wrap the other arm more tightly around her.

Beyond the front door, the house is transformed with the most elegant of touches, thanks to my girlfriend's artistic eye. The trees, the fresh greenery, are lush and fragrant, the decorations complementing my interior scheme and artwork to perfection.

It's as if she's waved a magic wand and brought Christmas inside my home for the first time.

To the solemn strains of *Once in Royal David's City,* the light projection begins. It was by far the most expensive line item on the decoration company's invoice, but I suspect, from the size of the smile on Nat's face, that it'll be worth every penny. They've custom-designed the projection for the exact proportions of my home's facade, and it looks like they've delivered the wow factor.

I've turned all the exterior lights off and shut the curtains so the front of the house lies in relative darkness, excepting the lights from the street. Now, in front of us, blue-white figures that look like angels rise from the ground and appear to scale the front of the house, frolicking on the central section above the porch before breaking off and taking flight against the perfect backdrop of the plain white stuccoed walls.

It's glorious, honestly. I fucking love this stuff. The light show tells the story of the birth of Christ, and I see the holy family on their donkeys, birds soaring through the air around them, before the North Star appears over the left-hand wing in a blaze of glory. When the Three Wise Men make their appearance, the angels return, and it begins to snow in a sparkling, animated flurry that covers the breadth of the house.

Beside me, Nat oohs and ahhs, curling into me with a girlish pleasure that brings me, in turn, the most simple kind of joy. This is how contentment feels, I realise. There are moments where the quickening of one's pulse is all one wants to feel—case in point, our little rendezvous in the gym earlier. But there are also moments like this, quiet and innocent and perfect, where my soul feels healed and my mind clear.

I could sit here all night.

We watch the ten-minute cycle all the way through three times. Once we come inside, the few members of staff who work weekends will come out and watch for themselves. Toby has mulled wine simmering on the stove for them. I turn my body so I can gaze down at my girlfriend, who's stretching in my arms. It's cold even with a thick blanket over us.

'Thank you so much,' she says, throwing her arms around my neck. 'That was *amazing*. Can we do it every night?'

I laugh. 'Absolutely. And thank *you* for organising it. Genius idea.'

'You'll have to do that every year,' she says. 'Promise?'

I frown inwardly at her use of *you*, because I'm extremely clear on one thing: that this will be her project, next year and every year.

She'll soon see.

'Nice try,' I say lightly. 'You're stuck with this job now.'

She smiles a little shyly, her eyes searching my face as if attempting to make sure I mean what she thinks I mean. Her hand comes up to my face and she scratches my beard gently with her fingernails. I lean into her touch like a cat—I love it when she does that.

'I'm so lucky,' she says.

I blink. 'I'm the lucky one.'

'Nooo. I have a boyfriend who'll bend me over in the gym and rail the living daylights out of me and then snuggle with me in front of the actual *light projection* he's bought for me. You're a keeper, I'm telling you.'

I'm pretty sure my laugh carries the length of this entire street.

66

ADAM

All I have to do is get through the next hour or two.

That's what I tell myself as I step out of my car in front of Nat's parents' semi-detached house. If I can get through this, then my reward will be bundling my girlfriend into my car and driving back to London so that we can wake up together on Christmas morning.

I think longingly of my home, so beautifully festive in a way I didn't know I craved, the turkey sitting in its massive pan of brine on the hob. I think of the gifts I've wrapped and laid under the tree in the library, Nat's favourite room. I think of waking up entwined with my girlfriend, of fucking her slowly and deeply and tenderly before wrapping her up in a fluffy robe and taking her downstairs for a cup of her favourite tea and some gift-giving. I think of the long, peaceful morning we'll have together before Dad and Quinn turn up for a late lunch.

I sigh and take the hamper I've bought for Noel and Adelaide out of the boot before approaching the front door, with its pretty pine-cone-stuffed wreath, as if I'm walking to my own execution.

There's no blindsiding happening here, I remind myself. Stephen is fully aware that I've been invited to join the Bennett family for Christmas Eve drinks. This is all pre-planned. I apparently have his permission, if not his outright blessing, to attend. After all, this is the only family time Nat will get this Christmas, given she's chosen to forgo lunch here tomorrow in favour of spending the day with me.

Twenty years.

Two decades of guilt and shame and anger and what-ifs, of incarceration and self-recrimination, of repentance and rehabilitation. Of making fortunes and battling ghosts. And, most recently, of falling in love and finding forgiveness. The sheer weight of it all swirls tangibly around me, through me, drying out my mouth and tightening my throat and flipping my stomach as I ring Noel and Adelaide's doorbell.

I'm praying hard that Nat answers the door when that very slab of wood swings open and I find myself face to face with a man I haven't seen since he appeared at my trial to give evidence, his face heavily bandaged.

My first thought is that I don't recognise him at all. I wouldn't have been able to pick him out of a line up. I simply didn't know him well enough at school. I didn't give him enough of my attention—until I did.

My second is that he looks as though he's seen a ghost. The Ghost of Christmas Past, if we're to get literary about it. I may not recognise him, but I know exactly how he feels.

My third thought is that his eye looks weird. It's fine, but it's not okay. It's not acceptable. And that whopping great glass golfball sitting in his eye socket is my doing.

Good God.

My fourth, as I stand there like a muppet, is that I have no clue at all what to say to him. None at all. Introducing myself to the man whose life I wrecked feels like the worst kind of disingenuity, because of course he's all too aware of who I am. I gape at him, opening my mouth and hoping something inspired will come out.

And then he speaks.

'Hi, Adam.'

I swallow. 'Hi, Stephen.' Hastily, I shift the hamper to my left arm and stick out my right hand. He gapes at it.

Please don't leave me hanging on Christmas Eve mate, even though you have every reason in the world to do it and I deserve exactly that.

He holds his hand out and shakes mine. It's a firm hand-shake, I think. A committed one. It's not fearful; it doesn't seem unwillingly given.

'Merry Christmas,' I say as we shake.

He nods curtly, as if embarrassed, and jerks his head to the left. 'Come on through.'

As I follow him through the narrow hallway with its jaunty festoons of Christmas cards tacked to hanging ribbons, I find I'm shaking as if I've just braved a bungee jump. The fading adrenalin has me feeling weak and oddly weepy, too.

I've done it.

I've shaken Stephen Bennett by the hand.

He may not have given me the warmest welcome, but he was civil. Far more civil than our past warrants.

My reward for jumping off this metaphorical cliff reveals itself before we've cleared the hallway. My girlfriend comes out of a doorway at a trot, her arms full of a lovely baby girl who appears to be dressed as Mrs Claus. Nat's a vision in a belted sweater dress and the thigh-high, chocolate brown stiletto boots I insisted (for my own nefarious reasons) on purchasing for her in Stuart Weitzman when we were stateside.

I break out a genuine smile, because she's a total knockout.

'Hi,' she says breathlessly, pulling me into a group hug with the baby and kissing me on the lips. 'Sorry—I was trying to give this one her bottle or I would have got the door.'

'Hey, sweetheart,' I say. 'You look beautiful. And this must be Chloe, right?'

'Mrs Claus to you,' Stephen says stiffly, and I recognise and appreciate the gesture of his awkward little joke.

'Hi, Mrs Claus.' I tickle her under her chin before pulling my hand away, conscious that, while Stephen may be making uneasy peace with the idea of me dating his little sister, he may not be ready for me to lay a finger on his beautiful baby daughter. Even if she's beaming at me with all the judgement-free, drooly joy of a true innocent as Nat hands her back to her brother.

I know enough about what Nat's early years looked like. I know what she lost in material comforts. This house may not be a mansion in the Royal Borough of Kensington and Chelsea, but the Bennetts now have a decent-sized home. What's more, the warmth here is palpable before I'm even in the living room. There's no faking a vibe like this.

'There he is!' Adelaide approaches as we enter what looks to be the main living room, her arms outstretched and a smile so genuine at the sight of me that I could weep. She's wearing a long red dress and looks as elegant as always.

Behind her, the room is aglow with what looks like a real fire. A plump tree stands in the corner, decorated with the multi-coloured jumble of decorations that families tend to accumulate over years and decades.

'We're so happy to see you, sweetie,' she says as she hugs me around the hamper. 'Merry Christmas.'

'Merry Christmas,' I say, a little more hoarsely than I'd like. This is an emotional overload: being invited into the Bennett's home on such a special occasion; seeing Stephen; having to look Noel in the eye. So Adelaide's generous, effusive greeting feels like a gift. 'This is for you and Noel,' I say, glancing over her shoulder at her husband, who's hovering behind her.

'Oh heavens,' she says, taking it from me. 'How lovely. Fortnum's! My favourite.'

'Adam.' Nat's dad steps around his wife, holding out his hand. 'It's good to have you here, son. Merry Christmas.'

'Merry Christmas, Noel.' I can scarcely get the words out, and when I do, my voice cracks. Dear God. These people are so... there's no animosity. Awkwardness, yes, but no sign of hostility or even conflict. They seem genuinely at peace with my being here.

I have no idea what kind of conversations Adelaide has had to have with Noel and Stephen to bring them around to the idea of my being in Nat's life, let alone stepping foot in their family home. All I know is that the woman's warmth, her compassion, is a gift, and I can only conclude it's infectious.

'Thank you so much for welcoming me into your home,' I tell Noel and Adelaide now as she offloads the hamper onto him. 'It means the world to me.'

She lays a kindly hand on my arm. 'Of course, dear. We wouldn't have it any other way. Now, I'm sure you could use a stiff drink after walking into the lion's den.'

I laugh awkwardly, because it's an apt metaphor. 'Not at all. And I'm driving this one back later'—I gesture at Nat, who has her hand on my bicep, a show of support that grounds me—'so I'll stay off the booze, if that's okay.'

'I've made virgin mojitos,' Nat says with a grin, and that gets a real laugh from me.

'How festive.'

'Right? A bit random, but they're really good. Want one?'

'Sounds great, sweetheart,' I tell her, turning so I can drop a kiss on the top of her head. I can feel every eye in the place on me as I do.

A woman with curly auburn hair comes through from what I assume is the kitchen, holding an extremely full glass of white wine. This must be Stephen's wife, Anna.

'Anna, this is Adam,' Nat tells her.

No context needed. *This is Adam: the reason your husband only has one eye.*

Anna looks me up and down, but it's more like she's getting the measure of me than judging me.

'Adam. Hi. Merry Christmas.' She shakes my hand briskly. Not only is she very attractive, but she has an instantly likeable face—one that suggests she's smart and kind.

Somehow, seeing Anna and Chloe in the flesh, obtaining real, first-hand proof that Stephen is happy and thriving and loved, feels even more like closure than having him shake my hand.

Stephen approaches his wife and hands the baby to her. Chloe makes grabby hands as she goes, latching instantly on to one of Anna's dangly gold earrings, and Stephen laughs and tuts.

I watch as he lovingly disentangles his daughter's chubby little fingers from his wife's earring.

For the first time in twenty years, I'm starting to understand that the scars from the terrible, terrible injuries I inflicted on him have healed more than I could ever have hoped.

I'm not just talking about prosthetic eyeballs.
I'm talking about his *life*.

67

NATALIE

C hoosing a gift for a billionaire is quite the daunting task.

Choosing a Christmas gift for the billionaire you've fallen in love with is even more daunting, especially when you've technically only been together for a few weeks. Firstly, I can't compete with his spending power. Secondly, I want to find gifts that tell him how I feel about him and how grateful I am for all the care and attention he's lavished upon me while not appearing to be a total psycho.

See what I mean?

Daunting.

But as I sit on the sofa in the library, sipping a deliciously festive flavour of Mariage Frères tea, *Esprit de Noël*, I know that being here with Adam on this day is far more important than whatever I've put under that macaron-laden tree for him.

I can't begin to compensate for the memories he's lost forever, but I hope I can help him to make some new ones.

'Right,' I say, setting down my china teacup and scooting over to the tree. 'Me first.'

We're both in fluffy white robes and slippers. Adam has already given me my first two Christmas presents—two excellent orgasms—but in that robe he looks more unwrappable than any gift.

'Absolutely not,' he says. 'Anyway, you've already given me the best present I could have asked for.'

I smirk. 'Well, you gave me two.'

He leans over and takes my hand. 'I'm not talking about that, sweetheart. I'm talking about the fact that your family opened their doors to me and your brother shook me by the hand—on Christmas Eve, of all nights. Do you have any idea how impossible that moment has seemed up until a couple of weeks ago? There's nothing you could give me that can match that.'

I nod, my eyes misty. Last night, Dad took me aside in the kitchen and told me that Adam seemed like a *genuinely decent bloke*, and Stephen suggested Adam and I go for tacos with him and Anna in the new year. Seeing the men of my family accepting my boyfriend for the person he is today was a profoundly moving experience for me, so I can't imagine how emotional it's been for him.

I lean forward so I can brush his lips lightly with mine. 'I get that, but I got you some little things anyway. Just bits and pieces.'

'Okay,' he whispers against my mouth. 'Thank you.'

He seems genuinely delighted with my gifts. There was a vintage-style photo booth at the New York party, and I had our strip of photos framed. In all of them, I'm kissing him on the cheek. I also bought him some fancy shaving foam from a tiny organic producer in Wales and a daily kimchi shot subscription. It'll be delivered weekly to his office (the guy is as into fermented foods as he is into pulses).

Finally, I couldn't resist the personalised workout t-shirt

I found online. Across its dark grey surface is written MR (W)RIGHT in huge white letters. It makes me giggle every time I think about it.

'Tell me how you feel about me without telling me how you feel about me,' he says, holding it to his chest.

I grin. 'It reminded me more of how you feel about yourself.'

He jumps on me then, and it's a few minutes before he's wiping my kiss-swollen mouth and telling me to take a seat back on the sofa. He pulls a pile of beautifully wrapped presents out from under the tree. It's naughty of him to have bought me anything. I told him no more presents after the insane shopping spree he insisted on in New York.

Still, here we are. He picks them up and comes to sit beside me, his smile more tentative than expectant. He hands me the first one, and I tear it open.

Holy motherfucking shit. It's a Goyard tote. Their iconic Saint Louis, no less, in the royal blue colourway that I've often thought I'd give a kidney for, if my kidneys were that valuable. It's so beautiful it makes me want to cry.

'Oh my God!' I say. 'Honey, it's amazing! I love it so much.'

'You can change the colour if it's not right,' he says quickly. 'All I know is I've never seen a tote bag more desperately in need of replacement.'

I giggle. 'No, no, it's perfect! It's the one I would have chosen—absolutely. Thank you so much.'

He kisses me tenderly before placing a small box in my lap. It's square and flat. Jewellery, maybe? I open the paper with a quizzical look at him, but the box itself is plain black card and gives me no answers. When I take off the lid, a set of keys and an alarm fob lie nestled in black tissue, locked to a Goyard keyring that matches my new bag.

My mind is racing, and I look up at him again. His face is very serious, but very soft, and I reach up to stroke his beard, almost without thinking.

'I don't want you feeling like a visitor here,' he says haltingly. 'I know how I feel about you, and I know how badly I want a future with you. I want you living here with me—if that's what you want, too.'

I search his face, my heart thumping. This is beyond insane. Adam has spent tens of millions of pounds restoring and furnishing this house, creating the most beautiful home for himself. I can't just waltz in here and take up residence, for Pete's sake! I mean, I know I'm here every night, but it feels different. I'm his guest, which is how it should be.

'Say something, please,' he urges me.

I drop my hand from his face and stare at him in shock. 'It's not a matter of wanting to. It's—this place is crazy! It's like a beautiful luxury hotel. I can't just come and live with you and not pay my way! You bought all this. You've worked so hard for every penny.' I pause and look down at the shiny keys with their pretty keyring. I can feel myself deflating. 'I'd feel like a gold-digger.'

His laugh is disbelieving, but it's also tender. Compassionate. He tips my chin up with the softest touch, so I'm looking into his blue eyes again. I press my lips together, because I feel really teary, for some reason.

'Sweetheart,' he says, his voice so low. 'If you think, after all we've been through, that there's some kind of imbalance here, that you're not "paying your way" in this relationship, then you are fucking delusional. You've given me so much more than I could ever give you. Besides, I'm hopelessly, ridiculously, in love with you.'

My mouth falls open, but he presses on. 'I think I have been, probably, since you had your hypo and I basically kidnapped you. I love you, Nat. You are the strongest, most resilient, most passionate woman I've ever met, and the only reason this is a set of keys and not a diamond ring is because I don't want to send you running for the hills just yet.

'And I've enjoyed this place far more in the past month than I've ever been able to enjoy it before. Seeing *you* fall in love with my home has been incredible to witness.' He leans his forehead against mine. 'I just want you here with me, sweetheart. I want to come home to you every night. That's all there is to it, really.'

I close my eyes and breathe him in. For a man who's been so badly hurt in the past, I've never met someone so generous with his heart. I've never felt so astonishingly well cared for, and I've never in turn wanted to care for another human being like I do for Adam.

I never thought that being loved would feel like such a precious gift.

Opening my eyes, I pull back enough that he can see my face. 'I love you, too.'

His face softens with relief. 'Do you?'

'Yeah.' I nod vehemently. 'As soon as I saw you clearly for who you really were, I fell hard. How could I not? You have the most beautiful heart I've ever known.' I wrap my arms tightly around his neck and gaze at his dear, dear face. 'If you want me here, then I'd love to live here. I love you.'

'I'm very glad to hear it,' he says softly.

I'm pretty sure that's what he said when I told him that day in my office that I didn't hate him anymore, right before we kissed. There's a whole world of emotion swirling beneath this man's skin. That I'm the one he shows it to is the biggest privilege of my life.

He grins as he disentangles himself from my embrace and hands me another package: big, flat, rectangular. 'Keep what you just said to me in mind when you see this,' he pleads. 'This one's definitely a gamble. Just know that it comes from a place of love *and* of supreme confidence in your abilities.'

I frown, bewildered, as I tear open the paper. It feels like a big book.

It is a big book, in landscape orientation, bound in beautiful lavender leather.

Embossed on the front is the following:

Gossamer
A Wright Holdings Company?

68

NATALIE

This can't be what I think it is, surely? I look up at him, but he shakes his head smilingly.

'Take a look inside.'

I do as he says, opening the heavy cover to see that it's divided into sections:

The Pitch

The Numbers

Wright Holdings

I turn to the first section. If the house keys had my heart thudding, now it's beating wildly beneath my skin. This looks like Adam's pitch to acquire—or take a stake in— Gossamer, and my head is spinning with possibilities.

'Just keep an open mind, that's all I ask,' Adam says, squeezing my hand. 'I'm suggesting a minority stake to allow you to avail of all the opportunities I believe are out there for you, nothing more. It would still be your brand.'

The first page is a montage of beautiful products with the logos of Adam's luxury goods brands superimposed on each product. Vega's there, obviously, as are Elysian, Obsidian and Whitechapel Leathers. Front and centre is a

Gossamer campaign shot from last summer's collection. Below the montage is a single line:

Demi-couture brand Gossamer aligns well with the rest of Wright's high-end luxury portfolio.

'I think it looks good there,' he murmurs next to me as I stare at the montage. He's right. Whoever's put this together has a good eye. The Gossamer dress is palest pink, and the other brand shots are also heavy on pink, blush and cream. Not only is the overall effect cohesive, but Gossamer pulls its weight in the montage.

'It does,' I whisper, brushing the glossy paper with my fingertips.

I flick on.

This first section is a suggestion of the doors that being a Wright brand could open for me by way of their expertise, connections and cash flow, and it's glorious. More than glorious, actually—it's like looking at some insane version of my brand on steroids. Adam has reached inside my brain and reproduced my most ambitious, outlandish fantasies for Gossamer.

There's a mockup of a trunk show in a fancy hotel attended by elegant women. There's one of a concession in Selfridges, the Gossamer space chic and feminine with thick white carpet and chunky brass fittings. And, best of all, in a section entitled *Product Extensions & Licensing,* he's got someone to generate an image of a beautiful bedroom furnished in various versions of Gossamer's wisteria print, from the wallpaper to the curtains and cushions.

I clap a hand to my mouth. 'Oh my God. How the hell did you do this?'

'A very clever associate did it,' he admits. 'She did a great job. But it looks good, doesn't it?'

Yes. It looks *really* good.

Especially the next double-page spread. On the left is Omar Vega's studio, with the caption *Access to our ultra-modern studio space in central London,* and on the left, a behind-the-scenes shot of his latest Kensington Palace location shoot. The caption? *Wright invests heavily in industry-leading photographers for its brands' seasonal campaign shoots.* I grin at Adam, my brain whirring with all the magic I could weave for Gossamer if I had this kind of backing.

In the PR section, his clever associate has once again worked her magic, dressing some of the world's most beautiful women in Gossamer. I have no idea how she did it, but the images show Jennifer Lawrence wearing us on the red carpet in Cannes and Emma Watson at what looks like the Met Gala.

'We work with Emma Forrester PR globally,' Adam tells me, 'and with Halo PR in Hollywood. You don't need me to tell you the access they could get you.'

Holy shit. Both of those names are the absolute dog's bollocks when it comes to fashion PR. The doors they could open. Their retainer is probably thousands and thousands of pounds per month. I let out a little groan that tells him how close to orgasm I am from this PR talk, and he laughs.

'It gets a little less exciting from here,' he says, turning the page for me. I can feel the boyish excitement coming off him, and I grin at him before glancing down.

The next page is entitled *Centralised Functions & Streamlined Operations.* Not the sexiest title for sure, but as I take a look, I begin to smile.

'You're proposing taking my book-keeping and HR off my hands and you don't think that's exciting?' I ask him, and he laughs again.

'Fair point.'

I sigh. 'Honey. I feel like I'm in a dream—it's like you're

waving your magic wand and giving me everything good I could ever have wanted in my life.'

He brushes his lips over my temple. 'That's precisely my aim. Take a look at the numbers, why don't you? Remember, this is your baby. You've built a beautiful brand. I really, really believe in it, and I believe in you as a business leader. But if you're going to give away equity, it needs to be worth your while.'

Nervously, I turn to the next section. Adam is proposing taking a thirty percent stake for now, at a valuation of...

Holy *crap*. I jerk my head up to look at him and then glance back down. Numbers aren't my forte, but that's a *lot* of zeros.

'Is this—' I begin, and he nods.

'Yep.'

'Surely that's not right. What about our debt?'

'You've got a few credit cards, sweetheart,' he says, 'but it's honestly not a big part of your enterprise value.'

I don't know a lot about valuing companies, but I know that valuations are usually based on some multiple of sales or profit, and the multiples Adam's using makes me wonder if he's smoking crack.

'How can you justify paying that for us?' I ask him. 'We're still so small.'

He laughs. 'You're supposed to be trying to negotiate me up, not down.'

'I know, but...' I trail off. 'I don't want to be a charity case,' I say in a small voice.

He puts his hands on my shoulders and turns me to face him. I let my hands fall, defeated, onto the book in my lap.

'Listen to me. I've told you a million times, the size of your opportunity and your current financial circumstances are two very different things. That valuation there is based on your brand value and the potential for growth. You've been capacity constrained up until now. We could plug you into the Wright infrastructure and quadruple your sales in the first couple of months.

You get a collaboration going with Elysium; we pitch hard to the big soft furnishing brands for a licensing agreement; we get you some PR, and boom. Given your size, the growth could be very fast and still be very manageable.' He slides his hands up my shoulders so they're cradling my jaw. 'I am *not* acting with my heart here. Your brand equity is incredible. We just need to light a fire under all that latent potential and watch you take the world by storm.'

'Do you mean that?' I ask, furiously blinking away the moisture in my eyes.

'Yes, I do. I mean every word. You seem to think I'm some gracious benefactor, when really, I want to get my grubby mitts on your beautiful brand. I'm itching to dial it up and see what we can achieve—*together.*'

'Okay,' I whisper, as much to convince myself I understand as to convince him.

'You should take a good look at the numbers,' he tells me. 'Get some advice. Talk to your dad, Gen, whoever else you tend to bounce decisions off. The next few pages have a full breakdown of how that capital could be allocated, but I will say this. The people who run my brands don't do it for the good of their health. They compensate themselves properly. There's a suggested salary for you, and hopefully it reflects the fact that you're both the CEO and Creative Director.' He nods. 'Take a look.'

I leaf through with shaky hands, because a salary, as he knows well, has been an indulgence too far for months and months now. I squint as I attempt to decipher the financial tables in front of me—reading complex financial statements on sight is not my forte.

'Here.' He turns over a new page, and there it is, spelt out for me.

Holy fucking *shit*.

I gape at him. He has a stern look on his face.

'It's what you deserve, Nat. Nothing less. And that's just a starting point. As the brand grows in scale, this should, too.' I open my mouth to speak, but he shakes his head. 'Just know that if we were to hire an external candidate for both of these positions, we'd be looking at more than this.'

'I know you're right,' I murmur. 'It's just a lot to get my head around. Could the brand really afford this?'

'It has to. And I'm confident it can. We'll be stripping cost out in other ways, remember? Once we take out some of the operational functions, we'll actually free up quite a bit of cash. But my CEOs don't work for free, nor do my Creative Directors.' He jabs the page with his finger. 'Talent gets rewarded. That's really important.'

I nod, looking back down at the number he's proposing. My head is spinning. It's just so *much*. With every page of this book, he's removing stress from my life. Adding value and pleasure and opportunity like I can't even imagine.

'I know how it feels to undervalue yourself,' he whispers now. 'Believe me, I've been there. I know it's been a tough few years for you, but you've done the hard work to get this far. You've built an incredible brand, and it's time to have some fun. Please trust me when I say you are absolutely everything I look for in a leader when I consider investing in a brand.'

I nod again. Jesus, I've lost the power of speech. I'm going to need to lie on a sofa for a full day and allow myself to daydream about all these gifts he's throwing my way. The future was bright when I woke up, but this dazzling vista he's painting for me in both my personal and professional lives is stealing the breath from my lungs. On one of the shortest, darkest days of the year, everything feels vibrant. Blinding.

'There's one more thing,' he says. 'I'll never tell you what to do, but when I came up with that salary number, I hoped it would give you the financial freedom to give up Alchemy. As your investor, I'd like to know you were free to focus on growing Gossamer.' He hesitates. 'And as the man who's hopelessly in love with you, I'd like to free up your time and energy. I know we're both pretty work-focused, but at the very least, maybe we can work together in the evenings before we crash in front of *Ted Lasso.*'

I smile. I appreciate that he hasn't brought up my type 1, but it's there between the lines of what he's saying. Alchemy has been a lot of fun, but God knows those late nights take their toll. It's been a means to paying my personal bills and supporting Gossamer, but the cash injection and six-figure salary Adam's suggesting put paid to both those headaches.

'That makes sense,' I admit. 'I feel like I've been hanging on by a thread, to be honest.'

'Of course you have. It's bloody exhausting, doing what you do. Also, think of it like this. My goal is to give you choices and freedom. I'd love to know that all the work you're doing aligns with your purpose and brings you joy. If not—delegate it. You're a CEO, Nat. *Own it.* Focus on what you're the best at, and outsource all the other shit.'

'Say that again,' I murmur, shutting the book and laying it carefully down on the coffee table. I clamber up so I can straddle him, slinging my arms around his neck and nuzzling the skin just under his ear.

He wraps his arms around me and laughs. One hand

slides down my back to cup my bum through my robe. 'You're a *fucking* CEO. Own it, and start acting like it.'

'Or what?'

'Or I'll put you over my knee until you do.'

There he is, ladies and gentlemen.

My boyfriend.

My new investor.

My partner in love and business.

My best friend and my greatest cheerleader...

... and a kinky bastard to boot.

EPILOGUE - NATALIE

I'm wearing *the* dress. You know, the wisteria-print one with the chunky gold hardware on the shoulders. The one I've lusted over since Evan put the sample together.

I'm standing in the most beautiful ballroom at London's Corinthia hotel. On every table, huge silver bowls overflow with vintage pink and white roses as the crystal chandeliers cast their dancing light overhead.

I'm surrounded by beautiful people. Famous people. Even Omar fucking Vega is here.

Everyone is seeking me out. Everyone is complimenting me on Gossamer's new collection. Women who regularly grace the pages of *Vogue* are wearing our dresses.

It sounds like a dream. (Or a psychotic episode.)

It's not.

It's really happening.

This is the event that will officially launch Gossamer as a Wright Holdings brand to the great and good of the fashion industry while at the same time celebrating our new Spring/Summer collection.

My parents are here, of course. Stephen and Anna have just turned up. Winky and Adam had a frank—and highly emotional—catchup over a few beers in the new year, when Adam got his chance to apologise, face to face, man to man, and my brother finally got the closure he needed and deserved. I think it must have been a little deflating for him to know that there wasn't any real villain in his story, after all, but he insists it's better this way, that all that pent-up anger has really just disappeared.

Winky's insane new prosthetic, otherwise known in the family as the Sci Fi Eye, has already saved the evening when I had a total blank on a familiar-looking blonde woman headed towards us. Turns out she was the editor of *Vogue Germany*. That face recognition technology is as useful as it is creepy. The prosthetic is bloody amazing looking, too. You'd really never know half of my brother's vision is digitally generated.

Anyway, he and Adam are getting along as well as I could have hoped my brother would get on with any man I brought home, and he even entrusted us with Chloe for the day last month when he and Anna went to a foodie festival. Adam's basement swimming pool was a *big* hit with the little water baby.

When Winky and Anna came for a tour, we kept the other basement room, with its newly arrived spanking bench, firmly locked.

I've horrified myself by how easily I've acclimatised to being lady of the manor. It's shocking, really. And, given we got the Wright investment in Gossamer closed by the end of January, I've had two months of evenings with my boyfriend in his—our—palatial home. I'd like to say we've been rewatching *Ted Lasso* like he proposed, but usually we sit side by side at the kitchen island, glued to our laptops while Adam and Kamyl force-feed me pulses.

I'd like to say I miss Alchemy, but we're in there most weeks. Saturday's visit proved to be my introduction to the wonderful world of spreader bars.

Let's just say I'm a convert.

Speaking of Alchemy, the entire crew is here tonight. Even Belle and Rafe, who welcomed their beautiful little baby daughter into the world as Adam and I were flying home from New York, have come out to support me. I'm chatting with Omar Vega—who's bitchy as hell but actually hilarious when he likes you—when Gen approaches.

'Who the fuck is that?' Omar asks, his jaw practically on the floor. Given the crazily tight timeline between the deal closing and the launch of the new collection, we had to save the key pieces for the A-list celebrities who are in attendance—like Oscar-winning actor Elle Hart, who's wafting around looking pregnant and stunning in one of our more ethereal gowns. Gen, therefore, is wearing oyster-coloured Valentino Haute Couture tonight.

'My ex-boss,' I inform him out of the corner of my mouth. 'Genevieve Wolff. She runs Alchemy. Married to Anton Wolff.'

'Ahh.' He lets out a low, appreciative whistle. 'It all makes sense. Look at that couture, darling. Look at those *curves.* I need to dress that woman.'

'Get back in your crappy little demi-couture box,' I tell him, but my tone is fond. Evan and I have begrudgingly back-tracked on our hatred of Vega. I'd hate to be the poor soul trying to manage him, but he's been incredibly generous with his time and advice since I came on board.

'Your ass must make men weep, darling,' he proclaims as Gen sashays over.

She shoots him a vaguely surprised look before arching her brow. 'It certainly does,' she tells him.

He puts a hand to his heart and swoons dramatically. 'I think I'm in love.' With that, he takes his leave.

'You look incredible,' Gen tells me now, pulling me into a firm hug. 'I'm so fucking proud, I can't even tell you.' She releases me. 'Your boyfriend's an embarrassment, though. He just wept openly when someone complimented him on your collection. Let's hope he can pull it together for his speech.'

I laugh. 'Oh my God. He's been a mess all day.'

'I love nothing more than seeing men championing their women,' she says, 'but he's the real deal. I'm surprised he doesn't have pompoms with him tonight.'

I put my hand to my heart. The way Adam has been there for me, day and night, over the past quarter is like nothing I could have imagined. He may be spending thousands on all these PR agencies for me, but I swear none of them have shouted Gossamer's name—or mine—more loudly at any opportunity than he has.

'He's incredible,' I agree.

'He is. He's also completely and utterly blown away by you, both emotionally and professionally. Just as he should be. How's it going over at Wright?'

'It's amazing,' I confess. 'I always had it in my mind that if it wasn't hard, I wasn't doing it right, you know? Like I had to slog my guts out for every pound I made. But over there it's effortless. Don't get me wrong--I'm working my arse off. But it's this strange new dynamic where I work hard and then good stuff happens. The work has a purpose, and it pays dividends. That's one hell of a novelty.'

'That's precisely what it should be like,' she says with a huge smile. 'Also, if his team is anywhere near as smart and talented as him, hopefully there's an amplifying effect. They can take the magic you're creating and blow it up far more quickly than you could ever do on your own.'

'Exactly.' I take a sip of my sparkling elderflower drink. 'These billionaires are so... fearless. They're such big-picture thinkers. They're not afraid of risk or big numbers or failing. It's really inspiring. I'm learning so much.'

'I bet you are,' she says. 'Uh oh—speak of the devil.'

I look over to find my man approaching. He's in a Tom Ford smoking jacket tonight, and he looks positively edible. He definitely looks a little teary-eyed, but his smile is so wide it could crack open his face. He comes around behind me so he can wrap his arms around my waist and bury his face in my neck.

'The woman of the hour,' he murmurs against my skin. 'Are you having fun?'

'I feel like I'm in a dream,' I tell him and Gen, and he hugs me tighter.

'I was just talking to Phoebe Dynevor,' he says. 'She wants an intro, and she said she'd like to put her stylist in touch with you, too.'

I stiffen in his arms. 'Oh my *God*. Seriously? I'm the biggest Bridgerton fan ever.'

'No one would ever dispute that,' he says drily. 'You've got to give your speech in a minute—I'll introduce you two after that. Okay?'

'Okay,' I say, turning my face so I can nuzzle against him. When I glance back up, it's Gen's turn to look weepy.

'Not you, too,' I say laughingly.

'I'm sorry.' She dabs carefully under her eye with her knuckle. 'It's just—when I think about what you two were like when you first met. Jesus, it was awful. And look at how revoltingly loved-up you are now.'

I giggle. 'It was pretty rough. I'm sorry you got stuck in the middle.'

'That meeting I had to host—it was like mediating bloody Cold War talks. I'm not sure I've ever felt so uncomfortable in my life.'

'Luckily Nat found a way to break the ice that evening,' Adam deadpans, and I slap the hand that's on my stomach.

'That's so rude! I still can't believe you let him kidnap me,' I tell Gen.

'Yeah, well, looks like your Stockholm Syndrome is still alive and well,' she says, looking thoroughly unapologetic.

'It really is,' I tell her with a grin. 'And what do you know? My beast turned out to be a total prince.'

Adam releases me. 'Let's get you up on that stage before my ego balloons completely.'

'Knock 'em dead, love,' Gen tells me, pressing a kiss to my cheek.

Adam leads me over to the stage, his hand clasping mine tightly. I climb up and survey the beautiful room full of chic, dazzling people. Everyone here has given up their evening to toast my brand, and I'm humbled. I'm gobsmacked, really.

'Thank you for being here tonight,' he begins smoothly. I notice everyone in the room has quieted. They're all looking at Adam, and who can blame them? His presence is blinding.

He starts to speak. 'This evening, we're celebrating the newest addition to the Wright Holdings luxury portfolio, demi-couture brand Gossamer. While their clothes encompass the very best of sustainable, timeless British style, it's the creative brain behind the brand, Natalie Bennett, who we're really celebrating.

'Natalie is the most passionate, brave, resilient business leader I've had the good fortune to meet. I have the even greater fortune of calling her my girlfriend, but that's a story for another evening. It's her extraordinary vision and commitment to producing clothes that won't cost the earth that will really shake things up at Wright. I know that, whatever she learns from us, we'll learn more from her. She's the very best human being I know, and I can't wait to sit in the wings and watch as she takes her beautiful brand stratospheric. Please put your hands together for Natalie Bennett!'

When he turns towards me, the light of love and pride in his eyes takes my breath away far more than the thunder of applause and the roar of cheers. He brushes my cheek with his lips and whispers, 'Knock 'em dead, sweetheart,' before standing aside.

I smile at my love, and I step up to the mic.

THE END

Get your swoony **bonus epilogue** here and enjoy Adam as a family man (WARNING: may activate ovaries)
https://BookHip.com/LNGHCBJ

This is not the end for the Alchemy family!
Preorder **Always Alchemy** here:
https://mybook.to/always_alchemy

Ready for **Athena and Gabe**? 🔥🔥🔥
Preorder Audacity here:
https://geni.us/audacity_seraph

AUTHOR'S NOTE

Hello!

I thought I was writing a book about forgiveness and redemption, and I suppose I was. But really, Nat and Adam's story for me is about the life-altering magic that occurs when you find your person.

Adam leads a lonely life. Nat may have a loving family behind her, but really, her daily struggles are lonely, too. She internalises so many of her worries and responsibilities. I wanted her to find that kindred spirit, that champion, that life partner, where the sparks fly just as much in the office as they do in the bedroom.

I wanted them both to experience how quickly everything can change when someone has your back. When they devote their lives to being your own personal fairy godmother (or godfather).

Caregiving was really the most important dynamic at work here. Adam starts taking care of Nat from the moment she hypos all over him, and he never stops. Like a lot of alpha males, he can give it but he can't take it, and it was important to me to show him how it felt to be taken care of by someone simply because they wanted to.

The type 1 diabetes rep was super critical for me, too. This is such a shitty, debilitating illness. The sufferer runs to stand still every single day of their life, and it makes those who have it immensely vulnerable (poor little Ellen Wright being a tragic example). For a driven, independent character like Nat, who has an ultra Type A personality and whose anthem is undoubtedly *I Can Do It With A Broken Heart,* type 1 is a hell of a curse.

(But, like in all good fairytales, the heroine never lets the curse define her. Hell, no.)

I did a lot of projecting in this book! For eight years prior to the pandemic, I ran a small British fashion brand with my best friend. It was creatively intoxicating, but boy, was it hard work. The cash flow profile for fashion brands is bloody horrific. We were sub-scale (like Nat). We haemor-rhaged cash (like Nat).

Unlike Nat, we didn't make it. Folding the brand was the most traumatic thing I've ever done. (Spoiler alert: I'm so glad everything went the way it did! Creating worlds on paper is a million times easier and more fun!) All of Nat's joy, her heartbreak, her worries, her imposter syndrome... yep. I've been there.

Thinking about it, she may just be the character most like myself that I've written to date... (though a good chunk of me is Belle, too).

One last thing. I tried really hard to make Adam a dick. I felt like he should be way less well adjusted than he was, but it didn't happen. He kept showing up being a rock fucking solid guy, and there was nothing I could do about it. Besides, it was a lot of fun to watch Nat realise how very wrong she was about him!

So there we have it. Six books, six couples (or five and a throuple), and Alchemy is almost done. When I adopted a pen name to write the steamy, virgin romance of my heart, I never thought it would come this far in a mere eighteen months!

THANK YOU for reading. Thank you for falling in love with the Alchemy team and coming back for more, time and time again. *Always Alchemy* is up next, and boy, do I have some treats for you! Beyond that, the *Seraph* series kicks off in early 2025 with Athena and Gabriel's book (the spice factor will be SKY high in that one), and the fun I had writing the Alchemy NY launch party makes me think we might see a US spin-off for Alchemy once I'm done with those naughty Seraph executive assistants.

Let's see what the future holds...

All my love
    Elodie xx

ACKNOWLEDGMENTS

Writing can be a lonely job, especially as an indie author, so I'm beyond grateful for the wonderful community that surrounds me.

Firstly, a massive thank you to my friend Susie Tate, who is not only a best-selling author (go read *Daydreamer* - it's amazing!) but also a GP (MD for the US folks). She explained type 1 diabetes to me over and over and over and also read through Nat's hypo chapter for me, and I'm so grateful. It's such a big responsibility to represent a chronic illness, especially when you have no personal experience of it. I hope I represented it accurately. Any inaccuracies are mine alone.

A massive thank you to my beta readers, Jennifer, Stephanie and Krystal, for reading so quickly and diligently, dropping everything when I sent them new chapters, suffering through being drip-fed the group, and basically acting like fluffers with their praise. I love you guys!

Thank you also to my fantastic ARC team, who've been so enthusiastic about this book. I absolutely adore releasing my book babies to you guys, and you always blow me away with your kindness and the commitment you show to the ARC process. I'll never take it for granted.

A perennial thank you is due to my Nerds (my Facebook reader group). You are my favourite corner of the internet and I'm proud to call many of you friends. Thank you for showing up for me every day.

I love my IG followers / readers / supporters too - IG is my guilty pleasure! Thanks to everyone who shares and shouts about my books (especially Tierney - I love you!).

The best thing about being a romance author is befriending other romance authors! Seriously, it's great! I adore my romance girlies. Thank you for all your kindness and support. This is such a helpful community - it's very special.

Finally, thank you to Becca Same and the Better Faster Academy coaches. You've saved my sanity and shown me a path to success that (hopefully) avoids burnout. I appreciate you!

ALSO BY ELODIE HART

All my books can be read as standalone.

ALCHEMY

Unfurl

Undulate

Unveil

Untether

Unstitch

Unbind

Always Alchemy

SERAPH

Audacity

By my real name, Sara Madderson:

LOVE IN LONDON

Parents and Teachers

A Fair Affair

A Very London Christmas (coming to audio for Christmas 2024)

Falling Stars

Wilder at Heart

~

SORREL FARM

Food for Thought

Heaven on Earth

Make Me Sweat (related material)

A Manny for Christmas

~

STANDALONE

The Rest is History (also in audio)

Made in the USA
Coppell, TX
24 September 2024

37635110R00263